Pecking Order

Also by Chris Simms

Outside the White Lines

Pecking Order

Chris Simms

arrow books

Published by Arrow Books in 2005

1 3 5 7 9 10 8 6 4 2

First published in the United Kingdom in 2004 by Hutchinson

Arrow
The Random House Group Limited
20 Vauxhall Bridge Road, London SW1V 2SA

Random House Australia (Pty) Limited
20 Alfred Street, Milsons Point, Sydney
New South Wales 2061, Australia

Random House New Zealand Limited
18 Poland Road, Glenfield
Auckland 10, New Zealand

Random House (Pty) Limited
Endulini, 5a Jubilee Road
Parktown 2193, South Africa

The Random House Group Limited Reg. No. 954009

www.randomhouse.co.uk

A CIP catalogue record for this book is available from the British Library

Papers used by Random House are natural, recyclable products made from wood grown in sustainable forests. The manufacturing processes conform to the environmental regulations of the country of origin

Typeset by SX Composing DTP, Rayleigh, Essex
Printed and bound in Great Britain by
Bookmarque Ltd, Croydon, Surrey

ISBN 0 09 944684 7

All my thanks to Chops

for putting up with the man in the attic

As the door opens and you
hear above the electric fan a kind of
one-word wail, I am the one
who sounds loudest in my head

Edwin Brock, *Song of the Battery Hen*

1

With a sound like two twigs snapping, the chicken's legs broke in his hand. The bird transformed from a hanging bundle of limp feathers to a screeching mess and his fingers instantly uncurled. It dropped fifteen feet to the sand covered ground where it began flapping round in tight circles like a clockwork toy gone wrong.

'Grab 'em when I lift 'em upwards!' shouted the man in shit-splattered overalls, standing on a narrow ledge on the lorry's side. 'If you don't,' he carried on with a note of triumph, 'they swing back and that happens.' He nodded towards the ground but his eyes remained locked on the younger worker.

'Yeah, sorry,' the teenager replied, disgustedly peeling silver scales of chicken skin from the palms of his hands.

Despite his heavy build, the man clambered nimbly along the stack of cages welded to the lorry's rear until he was directly above the stricken bird. With its ruined legs splayed uselessly off to one side it continued its futile revolutions, the repeated cries from its open beak merging into something that resembled a scream.

He dropped from the side of the vehicle and landed with both boots on the bird's outstretched head and neck. A thick squirt of blood shot out from under one heel and all movement immediately stopped. The only thing to disturb the silence that followed was a pigeon cooing gently from amongst a copse of beech trees nearby. The man stepped back, revealing a pulp of bone mashed into the loose sand. Then, relishing the appalled attention of the audience watching from the shed above, he swung back a stubby leg and booted the carcass high into the air. A handful of reddish coloured feathers detached themselves, one catching in the current of air blowing from the extractor fan mounted on the shed's side. The feather tumbled away, up into the clear blue sky.

With arms that seemed a little too long for his body, he climbed back up the wall of cages, each one bristling with beady eyes, jagged beaks and shivering combs.

'It's simple – keep 'em hanging upside down and they don't move,' said the man, reaching into another cage and dragging two squawking birds out by the legs. Once their heads were hanging downwards in the open air they immediately went still and he lifted their passive forms to the open door. This time the youth successfully grabbed the legs, and before they could start swinging back, he whipped them inside the shed.

'You'll be doing four in each hand by lunch – now out the way,' said the man perched on the lorry's ledge, another brace of birds already dangling from his arm. Though no one said anything, something about the over enthusiastic way the older man gave out directions reminded everyone of the playground. A school boy, prematurely invested with authority by his teacher.

The youth got off his knees and, with a bird in each hand, turned around. Immediately in front of him inside the shed was a tier of empty cages, six high. It stretched away in both directions, the dimness inside making it impossible to see right to either end. The walkway he was standing on was made of rippled concrete and barely wider than his shoulders.

Coating it was a mishmash of shell fragments, feathers and dried yolk. Awkwardly he had to struggle round the person next to him, banging one of the chickens against the wall. Once past he set off into the shed's depths.

Away from the fresh air at the open door the temperature suddenly picked up and the sharp smell of ammonia dramatically increased. His way was lit by a string of naked bulbs dangling at ten metre intervals from a black cable running just above his head. A thick sandy coloured dust clung to everything. Even the top of the cable was covered in it like powdery snow on a telephone line. The bulbs themselves were almost completely obscured – only the bottom third of each was exposed, and the yellowish light they gave out made him squint. In the gloom above the residue had formed into web-like loops which curled from the roof, the occasional strand brushing the top of his head. It seemed like a living thing, a kind of airborne mould that made the very air thick and heavy. He imagined that, if he stood still long enough, the spores would settle on him, and eventually he too would become wrapped in its cloying shroud.

To his right the small conveyor belts running along in front of each cage clanked and whined, the moving surface transporting pellets to scores of cages that would soon be stuffed full of birds. Set into the ceiling above him was the occasional fan, blades lazily revolving. Their motion served only to circulate the warm air, carrying the dust into every crevice and on to every available surface.

He walked to the first gap in the steep row of cages, turned right and then immediately left into one of the central aisles. In the gloom ahead of him a dark form crouched. As he walked up to the person he had to step over a lump on the ground. Looking down he saw the tips of feathers and was shocked to realise it was a dead bird. From the layer of powder almost engulfing it he guessed it had been lying there for quite some time. Now in front of the person, he held the two birds out.

'Cheers,' said the woman emotionlessly, taking them from him and shoving them upside down into the open doorway of the nearest cage. The birds began clucking in protest, and one started flapping its wings. 'Get in,' she said aggressively through clenched teeth, forcing them with the flat of her hand. Inside what was little more than a hamster's cage, two other birds were already jostling for a firm footing on the wire mesh floor. He watched as one wing fluttered at the side of the door. With a final shove she forced them inside, breaking several feathers in the process. Swinging the wire door shut she announced, 'Home sweet home.'

2

Out in the bright sunlight the rusty coloured feather rose upward through the air, carried on the light breeze blowing between the two elongated buildings. It drifted along for a while and then gradually began to lose height. Finally it settled on the ground, just in front of a weathered pair of brogues. The leather creaked slightly as a thin, angular hand picked it up.

'Who,' said the man, gently rolling the shaft of the feather between a skeletal finger and thumb, 'is the man giving instructions?'

'That's Rubble,' replied the farm owner. 'I don't need guard dogs or anything with Rubble living here. He's my walking, talking Rottweiler.' He spoke a little too fast, trying to impress.

'Where did he get a name like that?' other hand running through a wiry beard that was shot through with flecks of grey.

'Oh, it's short for Roy Bull. Rubble just seems to fit him better somehow.'

'And he lives here, on the farm?'

'Yeah, in a caravan at the bottom of the lane down there.' He pointed to the copse of beech trees, where an occasional glimpse of white showed between the gently shifting leaves. 'He's just a child really – in terms of IQ. But he certainly likes killing things – chickens, foxes, rats, mink. Even cats, some villagers believe. And if I hadn't pulled him off the animal liberation woman last year, he'd have probably done her too.'

'Animal liberation?'

'Oh God yeah – they're a bloody menace. It's their fault we've got the mink problem around here – after they broke open the fur farm down the valley. They used the track last year to get on to the farm and firebomb one of my lorries. Rubble got the woman though, and they haven't visited again. Even so, I now have security cameras on the driveway at the main entrance and at the top end of the sheds. They're connected to a monitor in Rubble's caravan, he keeps an eye on it and patrols the place at night, hoping some of them try and come back.'

'A useful employee to have.'

'Yup – security guard, chicken culler, carcass disposer. All the really grim stuff no one else wants to do. Saves me a fortune – not that he knows it.' The man laughed harshly and extended a hand towards some steps. 'Come on, I'll show you how we produce 40,000 eggs every day.'

They climbed the metal stairway and the farm owner opened the door at the top. Immediately in front of them was another door, on the floor before it a tray holding a large foam doormat. The farm owner pointed at a thick plastic poster on the wall that read, *Anti-contamination procedures in operation*. He looked down at the tray. 'That's soaked in disinfectant. If salmonella or coccidiosis got in here it would sweep through the shed like wildfire.' They both stepped on to the mat and then went through the next door. The visitor was instantly struck by the combination of heat, smell and noise. Sounds of machinery and below that, a continual low rumble. He was reminded of being on holiday; alighting from the coolness of an aircraft and stepping into the unfamiliar temperatures and scents of a foreign land. In front of him was a row of four very narrow chipboard doors.

Along the end wall were stacks of cardboard egg trays, each one large enough to hold several dozen eggs. Propped against the wall next to them was a short handled shovel, the blade caked in a clay-like substance. Looking down at the layer of broken shells littering the floor the visitor realised that, as with most factories, the sheer volume of what was produced inside meant it became a worthless commodity to the employees.

'I call this area the foyer,' said the farm owner. 'Each of these doors leads to an aisle, I'll warn you now, they're very narrow. Shall we go through for the main performance?' He pulled a handkerchief from his pocket and raised it to his face.

'After you,' said the visitor, holding one hand before

him. The farmer opened one of the central doors and stepped through. Stooping down and taking a deep breath, the visitor followed. Behind the sound of the clanking conveyor belts at his side he could hear the massed brood of thousands and thousands of chickens. He looked at the cages rearing above his head on either side. Inside the cages nearest him, the birds tried to shrink away from the bars, but the presence of their cage-mates behind only allowed them to retreat a couple of centimetres. The low guttural sound coming from the backs of their throats became more agitated, and the visitor was reminded of the disapproving tones of old women gossiping.

The cages were stacked with an incredible density. Barely an inch was wasted between each tier and the bottom cages stopped about a half a foot above the concrete floor. Aware of the dust-covered bulb hanging just inches above his head, the visitor stepped forwards and the birds in the next cage shied away. Sensing their discomfort he felt obliged to move away from them too – but that just took him closer to other cages. Space was something the sheds had not been designed to offer.

With his handkerchief covering his nose and mouth, the farm owner raised his voice so he could be heard above the din. Pointing to the front of the cages he said, 'This conveyor belt carries the food pellets. They're shaped like grain so the birds can easily peck at them.' He pointed to a shallow trough below it. 'When they lay an egg, it rolls over the wire, out the gap and into here. There aren't many eggs now because the collectors come round mid morning.'

'How much food do the birds eat?'

'All they want. The conveyor belts turn at regular intervals. They never get fat, and if you underfeed them egg production goes down. In practice it's about one hundred grams per bird, per day. Those bulk bins at the end of each shed? They hold a couple of tons of pellets – enough to keep the birds going for a few weeks.'

The visitor peered into the cage at eye level before him. The chickens inside certainly didn't look fat: in fact they seemed the opposite. But perhaps that was due to their lack of feathers. Skinny exposed necks, pink and scabby backs partially covered by feathers that had been stripped of almost all their filaments. The spines that were left behind brought images to his mind of the narrow tree stumps jutting out of the ground in the desolated battlefields of World War One. He noticed most of their feet were gnarled and twisted, the claws overgrown and yellow.

'Why are their feet like that?' he asked.

'Standing on the wire mesh,' said the farm owner matter of factly. 'It's a problem you can't avoid. If they don't stand on wire where would all the shit go?' He pointed to the manure deflector that formed a sloping roof over the cage immediately below. The visitor saw it was covered in a good inch of thick, gritty droppings.

It was the same stuff coating the shovel in the foyer. If it got any higher the stinking layer would start poking through the cage floor of the birds above. 'Remind me to tell Rubble to shift that lot,' said the owner.

Bending down, the visitor looked along the tier and saw every deflector was similarly covered. He straightened up and, by standing on tiptoes, was just able to see into the bottom of the uppermost row of cages. Three birds were standing, one was lying motionless at the back. The visitor said, 'I think there's a dead bird in this cage.'

'Probably,' said the owner. He kicked a foot at the lowest tier of cages, causing the animals inside to scrabble back. Then he found a foothold and raised himself up to see inside. 'Brittle bones,' he declared. 'Some birds develop the disease. Something to do with not being able to move. Their legs become paralysed, the other birds push it to the back and it starves to death.'

'And who . . .' said the visitor, pointing vaguely upwards.

'Rubble clears them out, when he remembers. Let's carry on, I can feel my chest seizing up.'

They walked down the aisle, the visitor privately astounded by the merciless system. As they passed one cage the farm owner stopped and pointed to the birds inside. Each one had a short, blunted beak. 'Rubble's trimmed them. Must have been pecking each other.'

'How does he do that?' asked the visitor.

'A pair of what looks like gardening secateurs. He heats the blade up and nips off the last third.'

'And that's legal?'

'MAFF officially approved it in1997. Although we normally only bother with it when they start trying to eat each other.'

'Cannibalism?' said the visitor, half laughing at what he thought was a joke.

'Yeah. Because they get all the food they need, it rarely happens when they're in the cages. But down there,' he pointed to his feet, 'it's different.'

The visitor was confused, 'Down where?'

'The slurry pit. You climbed up stairs to get in here remember?'

The visitor had stopped and was trying to look between the closely packed cages into the darkness below.

'You'll not see much from here. Come on, I'll show you,' said the owner, plucking a couple of eggs from the nearest trough. Soon they reached a crossroads where a walkway cut across their aisle. At the point where the tiers of cages ended a shoulder width gap allowed them to see into the pit.

'It's cleared out once a year and sold off for garden fertiliser. This one's almost full. When it's empty the drop is about twenty feet. Now it's what? About six.'

The visitor looked down at the uneven floor of droppings and feathers below.

'Chickens,' he searched for the right word '. . . exist down there?'

'Sometimes a cage door pops open. Quite a few scratch out a living in the pit. Here, watch.'

He cracked one of the eggs on the edge of a cage and threw it into the part of the pit best illuminated by the weak light above. A group of creatures raced out of the shadows and fell upon the egg. At first the visitor couldn't understand their strange appearance; all he could see was bulky brown bodies interspersed with spikes. They looked like hedgehogs. But these animals moved quickly on two legs, and now he could see the outstretched necks and rapidly dipping heads. He realised their bodies were encased with manure, just the ends of ruined feathers poking out.

The farm owner laughed grimly, 'Hedgekens we call them. Half hedgehog, half chicken.' He lobbed the other egg in and their attention immediately turned to it. Like vultures at a kill, more were emerging from all around. They formed a heaving throng around the remains, desperate for food.

'And they'll eat each other?'

'Oh yeah. When one goes down, they'll try it. Right that's enough of this air for me, you can ask me anything else outside.' They walked back to the chipboard doors and out into the foyer. The farm owner lowered the handkerchief and brushed at the shoulders of his jacket with it. 'The dust in there. It makes my chest go all tight in no time.'

'Where does it all come from?'

'The bloody birds. Bits of their feathers. They preen and peck and that stuff floats off into the air.'

'So what else happens in there?' asked the visitor.

'What do you mean?'

'Apart from feeding what else . . .' in actually asking the question the visitor was suddenly aware of how stupid it sounded, '. . . what else happens?'

The owner was frowning. 'Nothing. They stand there and lay eggs.'

The visitor was beginning to comprehend how barren their environment was. It astonished him that, despite everything, nature still worked to make the animals produce an egg with such regularity.

'The birds in there,' said the visitor, nodding at the chipboard doors. 'They looked a lot less healthy than the ones being loaded into the other shed.'

'Those ones outside are straight from the breeders. They're about seventeen weeks old and due to start laying any day. So far they've been raised in big open-floored sheds. They've got about a year before their productivity starts to drop away. The ones in this shed have been going for about six months. We'll cull them in another six and get a fresh load in. Dead ones go for processing into pies, pet food, that sort of stuff.'

'What an incredible system. The efficiency levels are

staggering. And tell me, does Rubble cull the entire shed?'

'He would if he could,' said the farm owner smiling. 'No, we try to change the contents of a shed over in two days. First day we cull the old birds.' The farm owner twisted his cupped hands in opposite directions to imitate snapping a neck. 'Rubble and a few people from the village do it. They load the carcasses onto lorries and next day the fresh birds arrive. Each lorry carries a few thousand chickens, each shed holds 20,000 birds. They'll be loading up that other shed all day.'

The two men walked back down the steps and along the side of the shed. The lorry had now gone to fetch another load of birds and the space between the two buildings was deserted. From the outside, the windowless exteriors could allow them to pass for any number of modern industrial buildings found throughout the country. Only a light build-up of feathers and dust on the protective grills of the extractor fans mounted on the structure's two-hundred-metre-long walls gave any clue as to the unnatural purposes the building was being used for.

When they reached the spot where the lorry had been parked, the visitor's step slowed. Looking down at the congealed blood and scattering of feathers in the sand he said quietly, 'I didn't know that chickens could scream.'

The farmer looked nonplussed. 'Any animal can

scream if you hurt it enough. You should hear the noise a hare makes when the hounds get hold of it. Sounds just like a little girl. Even frogs can scream. Did you never, you know, play around with frogs when you were a lad?'

'No I didn't,' the man said thoughtfully, still staring at the ground.

The farmer looked his visitor up and down, taking in the smooth suit and soft hands. 'Come on then, let's get a coffee,' he said, leading the way.

They reached the office building at the end of the two sheds and the visitor looked up at the bulk bins towering above him. They had the appearance of two upside down bottles, permanently held in position by their metal frames. As if feeding a monstrous infant whose appetite could never be sated. The visitor looked back down and said, 'Funny. A farm with no farm house.'

'Eh?' replied the owner. 'No – but it's not your average farm is it? It's really a food factory – the chickens are just part of my machinery. Let's go up to my office and we can talk business.'

They went through another door, up some carpeted stairs and entered a large room. Immediately to their side was a group of humming monitors. The owner casually waved a hand at them as he walked past, 'Ambient temperature, air ventilation, water allocation, food rations . . . I can control everything from up here.

In fact I prefer to keep out of the sheds as much as possible.'

Shelves ran along one wall, with boxes untidily strewn on the ground before them. The visitor paused to read the words on a couple of egg cartons, 'Country fresh?'

'Country fresh, fresh laid, farm fresh, country laid, you can call them anything you bloody want so long as it doesn't involve the words barn or free range. Those are just two samples you're holding there, but we supply all the major supermarkets. They deliver the boxes and cartons ready branded and we fill them up. Simple.'

At the end of the room was a wide desk with a computer and rack of files. Screwed into the exposed breeze blocks of the wall behind was an enormous whiteboard with a graph depicting bird numbers and egg production by month.

Next to it was a poster with beautiful photographs of various breeds of chicken. The top of the poster read, 'British Breeds of Poultry. Produced by Fancy Fowl Publications Limited. In association with Fred Hams.'

Eric examined the different images. A Speckled Sussex Female stood with its head up, black plumage peppered with dots of white. A Gold Pencilled Hamburgh Male, with long black feathers stretching along to a magnificent tail that was almost peacock-like in proportions. A marmalade coloured Buff Orpington

Female, shaped like a tea cosy, head barely discernable from its body. A Duckwing OEG Female, sinewy white body on two muscular, widely spaced legs. The man remembered the chicken darting agilely around the yard in a *Rocky* film, Sylvester Stallone unable to get any where near it. All the birds had proud, upright postures, feathers almost glowing with vitality. The visitor thought of the bedraggled, harried, miserable specimens trapped in the sheds and said, 'Do you have different breeds of chicken in the other shed then?'

The owner glanced round to see what he was looking at. 'Oh that,' he said dismissively. 'The wife got me that a couple of years ago. Said my office was too clinical. She doesn't understand the realities of the industry, bless her. No, we only use Rhode Island Reds. Most productive chicken there is. It'll lay an egg a day, week in, week out. In fact it'd probably use its dying breath to squeeze one more out. How do you take your coffee?' He asked politely.

'Just black,' his guest replied.

The owner passed him a cup and a small teacake wrapped in silver foil. The farmer quickly tore his open, shoved the entire thing in his mouth and then threw the wrapping on the floor. Awkwardly the visitor unwrapped his and took a small bite. Unsure what to do with the foil, he popped it in his pocket.

The farm owner had moved towards the window overlooking the canteen below. 'I prefer to take my breaks up here at this time of year. It allows me to get in some quality bird watching of my own.' He laughed his abrasive laugh and pointed down at the tables. 'Don't worry, it's mirrored on their side. They can't see us.'

In fact they were visible to those below, but only as two ghostly shadows.

'We get some right little crackers coming in here for their summer jobs I can tell you. Look at the jellies on that one. Hey,' he pretended to address the girl below directly, 'do you like chicken love? Because you can suck my cock – that's fowl!'

He barked up into his visitor's face, who raised a finger to wipe the fleck of spittle he'd felt land on his eyebrow.

'Ah, it tickles me that joke. I get quite a few summer workers, students mostly. A lot of girls to work in the egg packing room directly below us. Less clumsy than cack-handed lads.'

'How many full-time staff members do you have then?'

'Just Rubble – the system means that, more or less, we just leave the birds to it. Apart from him I've got a few part-timers, who come in to collect the eggs. Let's see . . .' he raised a hand and his outstretched finger tapped the air. 'One, two, three, four on that side table. Four in the packing room. Another three not on today. So altogether a nice round dozen including Rubble.'

They looked down at the top of Rubble's head. His hair was roughly shorn to a length that allowed you to see the bony angles of his skull. It seemed to sink directly onto a pair of sharply sloping shoulders with no neck in between. The other staff appeared to have coagulated away from him and into their own little groups: part time employees, a few female students together, a mix of young lads playing cards and watched by a girl who kept tossing back her hair. But Rubble sat alone, reading some kind of comic.

'He seems an interesting character,' commented the visitor.

'Rubble? That's one way of describing him.'

'Isn't he a bit old to be reading comics?'

'Oh, he doesn't read them. Just flicks through looking at the pictures.'

'You mean he's illiterate?'

'More or less. He tried to get into the army a few times. It was his dream. But the application forms defeated him. He just about understands his pay slip, but I have to give him cash since he doesn't even have a bank account.'

'Unusual for this day and age.'

'You're telling me. I think he has a savings account at the post office in the village. He goes every Tuesday morning just before nine o'clock to get his precious comics.'

'And you say that caravan is his permanent home?'

'That's right. No radio, no TV – apart from the security monitor. Hasn't a clue about life beyond the farm. Sometimes the students ask him stuff – who's Prime Minister? Which team won the Premiership? He hasn't a clue.'

The visitor shook his head, 'There's nowt as queer as folk.'

'Aye,' agreed the farm owner before continuing, 'So you think your management trainees could learn some things from how I run this place?'

The suited man turned to address the farm owner. 'Absolutely – the efficiency levels you've achieved here could teach the industrial chiefs of tomorrow some valuable lessons in people management. As you know, the business world is a competitive place. Every employee has to pull his weight. And I believe the way you've married technology with production here is most interesting. It certainly provides some fascinating pointers.'

The farm owner had been nodding enthusiastically, but not really taking the speech in.

'So what about numbers?'

'Well the amount of seminars I run varies. But on average I'd look to bring around sixteen management trainees here, say four times a year.'

'And how much do other companies charge for this sort of thing?'

'Well I pay the Bournville factory in Birmingham £20

per person and McVities in Manchester £18, to name just two.'

'OK,' said the farmer, walking over to his desk and picking up a calculator. 'How about, with free tea and coffee in the canteen, £15 a head for an afternoon workshop here?'

The visitor considered this for a moment. 'That equates to around £1000 each year. It shouldn't be a problem.'

The farm owner beamed, 'Great – I'll hold that quote for a month.'

He handed his guest a business card and waited for one to be offered back, but his visitor just said, 'Well, I won't take up any more of your time.'

'Do you have a business card I could take?' asked the owner, a little tentatively.

The man made an act of patting the breast pocket of his jacket. 'Do you know, I'm always doing this. I've left them at my office. Can I send you one in the post?'

The farm owner raised his eyebrows and said, 'How about a compliments slip or something like that?'

The visitor felt his neck grow a shade hotter. 'Well normally I've got a stack of company brochures in the car – but it's just been valeted, so everything's in my office.'

Suddenly the roles of the questioner and questioned were being reversed, and it was the visitor's turn to feel interrogated.

'I have to be careful,' said the farm owner, his eyes narrowing. 'For all I know you could be from the animal liberation – and I've just shown you round my business.'

'Hardly,' the taller man casually laughed, trying to sound relaxed. 'You've no worries on that count, I can assure you.' But he knew the situation had slipped irrevocably.

Sure enough, the farm owner's next comment confirmed his fears, 'Well, if you could send me written confirmation of our agreement along with a brochure or some other proof of your management consultancy, I would appreciate it. Then we can arrange dates for the first workshop.'

'No problem, and thanks for the tour.'

They shook hands and the owner showed him back down the stairs and outside to his car. The visitor climbed into the black BMW and started the engine, trying to look entirely at ease in the unfamiliar vehicle.

'I look forward to hearing from you,' said the owner. The visitor put the car into gear, praying he didn't stall it. The engine responded instantly to the light pressure of his foot, and the vehicle surged up the slope. The driveway climbed sharply, then curved to the left around a screen of pine trees. In seconds the sheds were invisible, sunk into the ground and hidden by the evergreen branches. Only the tops of the bulk bins showed above the trees.

A mixture of emotions washed over him. First, to his annoyance, was the feeling of pleasure that driving the car gave him. The cool, comfortable leather supporting his thin frame, the imperceptible sense of power beneath his hands and feet. He had to remind himself of the type of people who actually drove these vehicles; the pushy capitalist pigs, hogging the roads as if their choice of car made them superior to other drivers. He tossed the business card contemptuously onto the passenger seat, hooked a thin finger behind the knot of his tie and pulled it away from his throat.

The driveway reached the narrow country lane where a discreet sign read, *Embleton Farm. Private Property*. He reached the head of the drive but, before turning the car right towards the motorway, he hesitated.

How stupid to have believed that he could pull off such an outrageous plan. Desperation had pushed him unprepared into the attempt. In retrospect it seemed inevitable he would fail – having no business card to exchange was the type of elementary mistake someone unfamiliar with the business world was bound to make. He banged the heel of his hand angrily on the dashboard; the last chance of prolonging his university career had probably just escaped him.

Without a farm to take his students round, setting up a module on the ethics of modern-day food production would be impossible. His course options would remain focused solely on care of the elderly and, next term, the numbers of students in his lectures would, no doubt, drop again. This, he was painfully aware, left his department ever more vulnerable to closure when the expected budget cuts came.

He sat staring miserably into space, trying to imagine life if he lost his job as a lecturer. He found it impossible; after all, he'd devoted himself to it for almost twenty years. Now the department he'd so carefully built from nothing was slipping from his grasp. Unless, unless . . .

The idea, fully formed and complete, popped unbidden into his head, like a demon appearing in a dream. His immediate reaction was one of incredulity at how he could have thought such a thing. A bitter laugh nearly escaped his lips. But the idea refused to go away. Stubbornly it squatted there, naked, obscene and motionless. Inviting him to examine it from every angle. Hardly wanting to, his mind's eye began doing so; and he saw that it could just work. Telling himself that he wasn't actually taking the idea seriously, Eric spun the wheel anti-clockwise and turned left towards the village.

3

He glimpsed the occasional massive country house sat far back off the road, and wondered which was the farm owner's. Not the one, he guessed, with a tray of apples and honesty box at the top of the drive; a small handwritten placard inviting passersby to leave money for whatever fruit they took. Soon he reached an idyllic village green, having to slow down as a line of ducks waddled across the road, making their way to the pond in the middle of the grass. An elderly couple was sitting on a bench watching a group of children kicking a football around. Nestled around the edge of the green were two pubs, a restaurant, tearooms and a butcher's. Directly opposite him was the village shop and post office with a traditional red phone box at its corner. He parked, climbed out and walked up the stone ramp towards the shop's entrance. Just before he reached it, the door opened with a jingling of a bell and an electric wheelchair bumped out. He had to step aside as the machine, driven by a sour-faced old woman, trundled past.

'See you soon, Miss Strines,' said the man holding open the door and staring with a pained smile at her rapidly receding back. There was no reply as the wheelchair set off along the pavement. The man's eyes then shifted to the tall, thin stranger standing at the side of the ramp, 'Afternoon,' he said warmly, and waved him inside. The shopkeeper returned behind the post office counter and the visitor looked about. Lining the entire far wall were the newspapers, magazines and comics.

Before walking over to them he paused to examine the revolving stand of cards by the door. All were very traditional, embossed with balloons, shining with silver streamers or tastefully decorated with watercolours of landscapes. All possible family permutations and events seemed to be covered. 'A lovely baby girl!' 'I'm three.' 'Happy 18th Birthday.' 'Congratulations on your wedding.' 'To my darling daughter.' 'For a very special Grandson.' 'My deepest regrets for your loss.' All of life's stages, crammed into a few wire shelves.

He moved to the displays of produce in the middle of the room. Tiny jars of coffee, small boxes of teabags, packs of twelve Weetabix, half pint cartons of longlife milk. Everything was aimed at people just popping out for one or two emergency items. He noted that the prices reflected this.

He sauntered over and picked up a copy of the *Guardian*. Whilst pretending to scan the headlines he checked the children's section of the shelves, quickly identifying the small selection of war comics he'd been told Rubble favoured. Glancing to his right he saw that the shopkeeper had gone out the back. A part of him asked himself what on earth he thought he was doing as his hand slipped a few comics inside the newspaper. Covering any trace of his tracks right from the very start. He went over to the till and while waiting for the owner to reappear, examined the plastic pots grouped on the counter. They contained an assortment of the kind of sweets that only ever seemed to be sold in little village shops. Two pence chews, single boiled sweets, traffic light lollipops. The owner reappeared.

'Just the paper, thanks,' said the visitor, holding out the correct amount of money.

'That's lovely,' replied the man, dropping the coins into the open till.

He drove back into the city, and returned the BMW to the car hire garage. At the side of the forecourt he unchained his ancient three-speed Raleigh from the railings. Then he put the rolled up newspaper into the large satchel buckled on to a frame above the rear mudguard and cycled home.

He lived on a quiet cul-de-sac, each of the houses detached and with generous lawns at the front. He parked his bike in the narrow side alley separating his house from the next and walked round to the rear, noticing fresh cat faeces in the flower-bed at the side of his patio as he did so. Shaking his head, he unlocked the back door. The inside of his house was plain, the hall frugally decorated with a few faded prints of Lowry paintings. An autographed photo of Arthur Scargill in a simple frame. He entered a small study, three walls lined from skirting board to ceiling with row upon row of books. They seemed to lean inwards, making the room seem even smaller than it was.

The last wall was left free for a straight-backed chair and simple desk with a computer in its middle. In the far corner stood the room's only truly indulgent item; a plinth with a bust of Karl Marx mounted on it. He stepped over to the desk and placed the newspaper on it. Then he climbed the stairs, thin legs easily taking them two at a time. A vase of flowers sat on the landing window-sill half way up, their plastic petals covered with a fine layer of dust. He went into the spare bedroom and removed his shoes. Next he quickly checked the pockets of his suit. He removed a handful of change and placed it on the bed, found the crumpled teacake wrapper and dropped it on to the window-sill. Then he took off the jacket, trousers and shirt. Standing in just a baggy pair of Y-fronts and old grey socks, he re-hung the shirt on a wooden hanger. Once it was positioned correctly, he fed the trousers through the hanger's lower rung and carefully placed the suit jacket over the shirt. Lastly he rolled up the tie and placed it in the suit's breast pocket, thinking that the next time the ensemble would reappear would probably be for a funeral. He returned it all to a flimsy looking wardrobe that rocked slightly as he closed the door. The suit was the only item in it.

Laid out on the bed were a featureless pair of grey trousers, pale blue shirt, brown woollen jumper and an old tweed jacket. He got dressed, pocketed his change and put his shoes back on.

Once in his study he removed the comics from the folded pages of the paper. In the shop he wasn't quite sure if he'd correctly identified the smaller format publications. But now, with time to look at them properly, he saw that his suspicions were right. *Commando* war stories, 'For action and adventure'. He looked at the titles, *Death Before Dishonour*, *Battle In The Clouds*. He didn't think this particular type of comic still existed; he could remember discussing them as a student, complaining about their xenophobic nature. Japanese and Germans demonised throughout.

He opened the uppermost one and looked at the simple pen and ink illustrations, read once again the outmoded, formal language used by the characters. 'Harry couldn't stand servicemen who let the side down', 'Nobby and his men weren't about to give up without a stout fight.' He reached a battle scene and could hardly believe his eyes as he read the narrative, 'What the blazes?' 'Watch out old boy, they're sneaking up behind you.' 'A quick burst from Sid's Hurricane and the Zero disintegrated.' 'Aiieeee!' 'Death to British pigs!' 'Banzai!' 'Aaaagh!' 'Eat lead tojo!' He turned to the last page, 'It was tough, but they made it back to their own lines and a hero's welcome. "You'll all get gongs for this!" said their station commander, shaking each of their hands in turn'. The End.

Eric picked up one of the larger comics. *2000 AD, in orbit every Tuesday*. He opened it up and studied the highly-produced, full-colour images. A policeman with the name tag of 'Dredd' emptied his pistol into a futuristic looking car. Bdam, Bdam, Bdam, Bdam, Bdam! 'Drokk that was close' he said to himself, swerving his motorbike to avoid a hoverbus, the car full of dead criminals crunching into it. The violence was far more graphic, explosions of blood flew from gaping gunshot wounds.

He picked up the last one. *Karn Age*. More picture stories involving detailed depictions of violence and death. Some in which justice was meted out by representatives of the law. Others where retribution was dealt by supernatural, sinister figures. At the back of the publication he carefully read the mass of adverts for muscle building supplements, premium-rate telephone lines, spy equipment, air guns, replica weapons and male enhancement surgery. Then he shook out the mass of loose inserts – scratch cards that guaranteed a win, garish entry forms for exotic holiday prize-draws and other pieces of junk.

Discarding the two larger publications, he opened up the *Commando* comics once again, their complete lack of advertising suiting his purposes far better. He began to flick through them, underlining with a red pen key words and phrases.

4

She knocked again, louder this time. A mumbled reply and muffled movement from beyond the door. 'Come on boys, time you two were up!' she called, opening the door so that light from the landing flooded the dim room. Spiky hair contracted back under a duvet like a sea anemone reacting to the shadow of a gull.

She walked briskly over to the window and pulled the curtains back. The last vestiges of darkness were eradicated and in the second bed on the other side of the room came the sounds of a yawn being stifled.

'It might be the start of your school holidays, but you're not wasting the entire day in bed.' She gently shook the bump in the bed to her left and the spiky hair re-emerged from under the covers, 'Come on Toby.'

Squinting eyes looked up at her, 'Oh mum, you're worse than matron. At least she gives us a lie-in on Sunday mornings.'

'Morning Oliver, did you sleep well?' she asked the other boy who was now propped up on his elbow.

'Yes, fine thank you Mrs Wicks.' Voice clear and well-spoken.

'Good, I've got bacon and eggs cooking downstairs.

You can eat it in your pyjamas. And no dallying, I want to be at the Safari Park before lunch.'

She headed back down the stairs to the kitchen and the two boys slowly emerged from their beds. 'You'll want slippers on, the flagstones in the kitchen are freezing,' said Toby.

Once they'd retrieved them from their trunks they padded down the stairs, name tags visible on the back of their pyjama collars. As they entered the massive kitchen Oliver took in the heavy wooden beams spanning the ceiling. Mrs Wicks was standing at a red Aga set into a huge open hearth at the other end of the room. 'Wicked – my mum really wants one of those cookers, but dad won't let her.'

Mrs Wicks turned round smiling, 'You should tell him you'll save a fortune in heating bills.'

'My mum tried that one already. But apparently it would be too much trouble fitting it into our house.'

'Oh, where exactly do you live Oliver?'

'Holland Park, west London.'

'How lovely,' she said, lifting the copper frying pan from the metal plate. 'Well, sit down, it's ready.'

The two boys took their places at the oak table. Already laid out were two place mats. Oliver noted the gold rims on the plates and glasses, the fake ivory handles on the cutlery. But Toby's mum was too close for him to take the piss.

Toby had already poured himself a glass of orange

juice. He took a mouthful then grunted to his friend, holding the jug out.

'How many eggs Oliver? They're free range, laid this morning.'

Oliver checked how many were in the pan before answering, 'Oh, two please. Are they from your farm?'

Mrs Wicks smiled, 'Not the big farm over the road. We have a coop in the grounds here, near the trout lake. It's too far to walk over to the main farm every morning.'

Oliver nodded as she slid two eggs on to his plate and deposited the other two on her son's. After lowering the lid on the Aga's hob, she placed the frying pan to the side and sat down on a stool by the wooden work surface. Picking up a cup of coffee she began tapping on its side with a bright pink fingernail. 'So Oliver, how are you enjoying it at Cranbourne?'

'It's great. Even though I'm in the same house as my brother Charles.'

'Isn't that good?'

'No,' Oliver scowled. 'He's a monitor and makes me clean his shoes.'

'That's not very brotherly. I didn't realise that sort of thing went on. Do you have to clean anyone's shoes Toby?'

Her son looked up from his plate, 'No.'

'Oh good.'

Oliver piped up again, 'When my father was at

Cranbourne there was a proper fagging system. He was beaten by the monitors if he didn't clean their normal shoes, cricket shoes and rugby boots.'

'How awful,' replied Mrs Wicks.

'Didn't Mr Wicks go to Cranbourne? He could tell you about it.'

Once again, Mrs Wicks smiled. 'No, Alan didn't.' She walked towards the trough-sized sink. 'In fact, Toby's the first in our family to go there, aren't you Tubby?'

Oliver widened his eyes and looked at the other boy, 'Tubby?' he mouthed silently, an open-mouthed smile spreading over his face.

'Mum!' complained Toby through a mouthful of food. 'Don't call me that.'

Mrs Wicks turned around and Oliver quickly lowered his head to hide his mocking grin.

'Sorry darling. I meant Toby. Now, once you two are dressed can you pop the bags of shopping over to Rubble's? They're in the pantry by the tumble dryer. Then come straight back – I want to set off by eleven-thirty.'

Toby nodded and flashed an upright thumb at his friend, 'OK mum, will do.'

Their feet crunched on the gravel as they walked past the gleaming pair of Range Rovers and up the drive. Water splashed from a female nude, the droplets cascading into the raised pool. 'Nice tits hey?' said Toby nodding at the statue.

Oliver stepped on to the grass for a closer look. Then, seeing the mottled orange shapes in the water said, 'Cool! Koi carp, and they're monsters!'

'Yeah,' replied Toby, swapping the bag of shopping to his other hand. 'Dad had to put the net over the water last summer. Herons took three in one day. Dad said the birds cost him six hundred quid, nearly got Rubble over to shoot them.'

'So your farm, where this Rubble lives, it's just on the other side of the road?'

'Uh huh,' replied Toby, 'over there.' He pointed to his left.

'And who is this Rubble?'

Toby smiled. 'He's a right mong. The village idiot. Dad employs him on the farm – he lives in a caravan at the bottom of a field.'

'How come your mum does his shopping?'

'Don't know – she always has. Probably because he's too thick to do it on his own. Honestly, you've never met anyone like Rubble. He's a caveman. Just wait.'

Oliver frowned, puzzling over the information. After a while they reached the track just before the farm's main driveway. 'He lives down here,' said Toby setting off along the narrow lane. A few minutes later they caught sight of the caravan through the trees, a pigeon cooing softly somewhere above them. Toby peered between the trunks and saw smoke curling up from behind a six-foot-high fence. 'He'll be over at the incinerator, come on.' He picked his way between the beech trees, and as they approached the fence both boys could hear the scraping of metal and a toneless humming coming from behind it.

Allowing a sing-song tone into his voice, as if he were summoning a dog, Toby called out, 'Rubble! It's me, I've got your foo-ood!'

Thick fingers curled over the top of the fence, black hair bristling over the knuckles. The flesh whitened as the fingers took the weight of the person on the other side and Rubble raised his face slowly over the fence top. Stuck in the stubble on his head was a downy feather. 'Toby!' grinned Rubble, chin resting on the wood. Suddenly he frowned. 'Who's this?' he asked, looking at the other boy.

'Oliver, a friend from school,' replied Toby. Beside him the other boy tried to smile.

Suddenly Rubble's head and hands vanished and a second later he walked round the side of the fence, a shovel in his hand, scrap-like feathers plastered his overalls. 'Burning chickens,' he said, throwing a glance back over his shoulder.

'Yeah, thought so,' answered Toby, putting his bag of shopping down. Oliver nervously placed his next to it. 'So, how's things? Are you busy?'

'Busy,' said Rubble nodding. 'Always busy on Sunday. Not many staff in see?' He suddenly addressed Oliver directly, 'Rubble does all the hard work. Dead chickens – they need burning. Your holidays is it?'

Toby said, 'Yeah, just started. Olly's staying for the weekend. We're off to Chester Safari Park in a bit.'

'See the monkeys? Oooh, oooh, oooh!' shouted Rubble, jumping from one foot to the other and scratching an armpit. Oliver couldn't believe someone with Rubble's features would imitate an ape. Had he really no idea of his own appearance?

Toby laughed out loud, encouraging the older man to ridicule himself, 'Hey Rubble, how about giving us a go with your gun?' He looked up at the trees around them. 'Have a crack at that pigeon I can hear?'

Rubble glanced up at the trees, quickly spotting the fat grey bird in the branches above. 'Yeah!' he exclaimed enthusiastically, throwing the shovel down. He bounded off through the long grass, weaving between the trees and heading for the caravan beyond them.

'See what I mean?' said Toby. 'He's a total retard.'

'Yeah,' Oliver cautiously agreed.

'But check out his air rifle – it's the business.'

'And that's where he lives?' said Oliver, looking uncertainly towards the caravan Rubble was approaching.

'Yup. His mum and dad used to own the farmhouse we live in. When they got too old to run the farm dad bought it off them and Rubble moved into the caravan.'

'You chucked him out of his own house?' hissed Oliver incredulously.

Toby looked a little guilty. 'No. He loves it in that caravan. Dad had it rigged-up with electricity, gas and all that. It's got a proper flushing toilet.'

Oliver frowned, smiling but shaking his head at the same time. 'So how did your dad afford to buy the farm?'

'He's got another business besides the farm,' replied Toby proudly. 'Owns a centre for processing old cars, fridges, cookers, that sort of stuff.'

'You mean recycling?' asked Oliver, sounding impressed.

'Yeah, that's it. Recycling. When he bought this farm it was nothing. Dad said it wasn't making any money. He turned it into a specialist farm for chickens. He had the sheds built and everything.' Toby looked back towards the caravan. 'Here he comes.'

Rubble was jogging back over to them, air rifle in one hand. 'He's a big 'un. Who'll pot him?'

'Olly, you have a go,' said Toby.

Before Oliver could reply, Rubble thrust the gun into his hands. 'Break the barrel over your knee,' said Rubble, mimicking the required action. Carefully Oliver levered the barrel open, slowly bending the weapon into a V shape.

Rubble held out a pellet, 'In the barrel.'

Oliver held the pointed piece of metal between a forefinger and thumb. 'Where?'

'There,' answered Rubble impatiently, pointing a blackened fingertip at the thin chamber, as if it was the most obvious thing in the world. Reluctantly, Olly slid the pellet in.

'Close it,' said Rubble, gesturing with his hands to right the gun. It clicked together and Oliver held it away from his body, uncertain what to do.

Toby and Rubble regarded him for a second before Rubble pointed up at the tree, 'Kill it!'

Oliver looked at Toby who grinned at him and said. 'Just line it up in the sights and squeeze the trigger. It's simple.'

Hesitantly, Oliver raised the weapon, still holding it away from his body. Suddenly Rubble's rough grip was upon him, invading his body space. The butt of the weapon was jerked against his shoulder, his other hand was squeezed against the rifle's stock. He could sense Rubble's frightening strength, feel his hot breath on his neck. ''s better. Now aim.'

He looked into the sights, but could only see a wavery mass of green. Imperfections on the leaves showed up as if he was studying them under a lens in biology. He opened his other eye to see where the bird was, then directed the sights until its grey plumage filled his vision. He could see the bird's throat puff out as it continued to gently coo. Subtly he shifted the cross hairs to beyond the animal and squeezed the trigger. A sharp retort and he shut his eyes.

'Aaaaaah, missed!' crowed Toby, as if it had been a penalty kick. 'My turn.'

Quickly he cracked open the gun, took the pellet from Rubble's upturned palm and loaded the weapon. To his disappointment Oliver realised the pigeon was still sitting there, now with its head to one side looking down at them. Toby dropped to one knee and took aim. The gun went off again and this time the bird jumped backwards off the branch. It dropped through the air, one wing loosely flapping back and forth.

'Shot! Shot!' exclaimed Rubble delightedly jumping up and down. He slapped Toby eagerly on the back.

'Ow! Get off will you?' said Toby, almost falling over. He stood back up, scowling at Rubble.

The older man was looking at Oliver while jabbing a thumb towards Toby, 'Sharp shooter he is!'

Oliver managed a smile, but he felt sick. His mum was treasurer of West London's League Against Cruel Sports, and he knew he could never tell her about this.

Rubble and Toby had set off to the base of the tree and he followed along behind. 'Chest shot, right in his heart,' said Rubble, picking up the lifeless bird by its feet to get a better look.

'Cheers Rubble,' said Toby, glancing at his friend for approval. Oliver kept his eyes on the bird, wishing he was at home.

Toby looked at his watch, 'Shit, it's eleven-thirty-five, come on Olly. See you later Rubble.' He handed the gun back and they set off towards the lane.

'Bye bye,' said Rubble, waving at them with the hand holding the bird. It jerked back and forth, drips of blood speckling his overalls.

5

Seeking a more comfortable position on the wire mesh floor, the four birds shifted uneasily from foot to foot. The sudden change from the large open-floored building where they had lived up until their transfer to the lorry had disoriented and confused them. The journey was a source of terror; vibrations from the vehicle, lurching movement, air rushing through the narrow cages. Now they found themselves in another cramped space, the ceiling just centimetres above their heads. New sights, sounds and smells frightened them; the sharp tang of ammonia, the whining clank of the conveyor belt, the fine dust that hung in the hot air. For the first few hours none of the birds moved other than to hesitantly correct ruffled feathers with their beaks. Through the gaps in the bars that surrounded them they could see shadowy shapes of other birds also huddled in cages that stretched off in every direction.

6

Eventually the lift doors parted and Clare Silver stepped out into the dull corridor. On either side of her was a set of double doors and, after a moment's deliberation, she pushed open the ones to her left. The grey linoleum floor tiles stretched away down the length of the corridor. Doors off it led to various silent meeting and study rooms, but she strode straight past them. Next came two doors marked with lecturer's names. Both had lists of students below them alerting the people concerned about overdue end of term assignments. Clare didn't need to look and see if her name featured.

With a purposeful spring in her step, she walked to the last door on the right, which was wedged open with a doorstop. *Student Coffee Room* read the battered notice, almost entirely covered with strips of faintly orange Sellotape. As usual the place was deserted, empty padded blue PVC seats lining the walls. Only faint depressions on two of them and a pair of discarded vending machine cups on the low table in the centre of the room gave any indication that someone had been here since the cleaners had last visited. Socialist Worker posters and notices from various charities about impending famines or human right's abuses were dotted around the walls.

She slipped the ethnic patterned canvas bag off her shoulder, lifted the flap and took out a roll of paper. Then she scanned the wall for an out-of-date poster. Seeing one for a hunt saboteurs meeting for the previous month, she carefully removed it and pinned-up her own notice.

'Protest March. Next Saturday. Meet outside the Union building at noon. Route: across campus, along Williams Street to the Chancellor's house. Don't let them get away with it!'

Once it was pinned-up she stepped back to survey the bold lettering. With exasperation she raked her hand back through her spiky cropped hair and muttered the word, "Bollocks."

She'd forgotten to say what the protest was about. Bending down she took a thick blue marker from her bag, and with some difficulty, drew over the 't' and '!' at the end of the last line with a very misshapen 'n' and 'c'. Then she added the letters 'r e a s i n g' and wrote after that, 'rents on student housing by 6%.'

She looked at the poster. Bugger, it would have to do. She removed the other poster from her bag, made the same adjustment and rolled it back up. After sliding it into the canvas bag once again, she stepped out into the corridor and saw a gaunt man unlocking one of the office doors. Clare looked at the way he stooped, head bowed, knees slightly bent, one hand resting on the door handle, the other fiddling with the lock, long shoes stretching across the floor tiles. She was reminded of a long thin pound sign.

'Professor Maudsley!' she called down the corridor enthusiastically.

The man turned to her and nodded. 'Ms Silver.'

She walked up to him, keeping the smile on her face. 'Any news on the module you were talking about the other day? The one on the ethics of farming?'

He kept his hand on the door handle and, with a little irritation evident in his voice, said, 'No, I've dropped the idea.' Avoiding any mention of the battery farm, he continued, 'I've made some inquiries and it seems it will be impossible to arrange. The last thing these places want is groups of students writing essays on their despicable methods of farming.'

'But I thought you were going to arrange it under the pretence of a management consultancy course?' she said with disappointment.

He turned back to face the door, 'No – couldn't do it. The University said there'd be legal problems there,' he lied. 'So I'm afraid it's shelved.' As he spoke she couldn't help looking at the thick foamy saliva gathered at the corners of his mouth. His breath had the same stale odour her Grandma's used to. 'Now Clare, I really must get on with this marking. Thanks for your interest anyway.' As he picked up the leather satchel the buckles where it had been strapped to the back of his bike clinked slightly. 'By the way – I got your note enquiring about research positions in my department. We're discussing budgets at the moment, so I'll let you know if there'll be any positions to apply for as soon as I can,' he stepped into his office and quickly shut the door. The resulting movement of air pushed a single feather across the tiles to her feet. The lock clicked and Clare stared down at the frail object. She picked it up and, admiring its rusty colouring, pushed it into the front of her chunky knitted cardigan as if it was a brooch. Then she walked back up the corridor, out of the department, past the shiny lift and pushed straight through the next set of double doors.

The smell of fresh coffee and faint sound of a radio playing immediately greeted her. The grey linoleum of the corridor outside had been replaced with a brighter Mexican style pattern. A light terracotta paint covered the walls along with posters of art exhibitions and cinema films. Thelma and Louise defiantly stared at her, Annie Louisa Swynnerton's painting of Joan of Arc. Police posters about domestic violence. As she headed towards the open door at the end of the corridor the sound of voices became clearer. Looking inside she saw about a dozen people sat around. Some chatted in pairs whilst a more general discussion seemed to be taking place at the far end of the room.

'God, sometimes it's like passing through an airlock

coming from Eric's side into here,' she announced to no one in particular, slumping in the nearest seat.

'You mean like leaving the Siberian steppes for civilization?' said a ginger-haired man in a baggy knitted jumper and corduroys. The other people listening nodded in sympathy.

'Rumour has it they're slashing the department's budget next year. And if a bit has to go, who's do you think it will be? Eric Maudsley's frozen wasteland or Patricia Du Rey's hotbed of research? Especially if Patricia wins this big research grant off the Economic and Social Policy Research Council. Then it's simply a question of money.'

'Don't be tight on the old man, Julian. He's been here donkey's years, poor bloke. It was him who set up the Social Studies Department long before Patricia showed up on the scene.'

This from a serious looking student, tamping down a roll-up with a matchstick.

'True Adele,' said Julian, back-pedalling. 'Don't get me wrong – I respect his subject area. The elderly are a hugely undervalued resource in modern society and their care needs serious investment by the government. But look at it. How many people chose his courses this year? About six? Eric's style of lecturing – the whole way he runs the department in fact – it's so out-of-date. Where does he think he is? 1960s communist Russia?'

'Actually he was thinking of setting up a new

module. The ethics of modern-day farming – he mentioned it to me the other week,' said Clare, keen to deflate Julian in front of everyone.

'Who, Maudsley?' he replied. 'No chance. He's too set in his ways to change now. Anyway, why were you asking, not after a research position in his department too?'

A few people looked towards Clare for her reaction.

'Yeah come on Clare,' said a young girl, leaning forwards with both hands wrapped around a mug of coffee, the word 'Fairtrade' circling the rim. 'We know you've as good as got a place in Patricia's department for next year. But what if Professor Maudsley offered you one too? Which way would you be turning as you come out of the lift? Left or right?'

'Shiiiit,' said Clare, with an American accent. 'That sure would be a hard choice.'

They all burst out laughing as she reached into her bag and unrolled the poster. 'Anyone fancy coming along on the demo this Saturday? They're trying to up the rents on university accommodation by six per cent next year. They know student debt is bad enough as it is.'

'You won't even be a student next year,' said Julian. 'Your graduation ceremony is in a couple of weeks, in case you'd forgotten.'

'Yeah, but it's the principle of it. If you ask me, it's just another step on the slippery slope to elitist higher education.'

'Yeah – I'm up for it Clare,' said Adele licking the end of her roll-up and putting it in her mouth.

'Nice one, Adele,' Clare smiled. 'Anyone else?'

A few people made vague promises to try, if they could find the time. One or two pleaded too much work on. Clare pinned-up the poster and put her bag back over her shoulder. 'Well, hopefully see some of you there. Anyway I'd better go – I've got an adult literacy lesson in half an hour.'

'Your spelling's not that bad is it?' The room fell silent and Julian realised he'd been a little too hasty in his attempt at a joke.

'I think,' said Adele with an admonishing tone, 'that you'll find Clare is taking, not attending, the class.' She turned away from the red-faced Julian. 'Where is it Clare?' she asked respectfully.

'On the west side of town. It's just a small set-up – we're working with refugees. Iraqi women mainly.'

The comment earned her some approving nods and a couple of raised thumbs. Clare turned to go and as she did so the feather fell from her cardigan. It drifted slowly to the floor, noticed only by Julian. He waited until he heard the double doors swing shut at the end of the corridor, then surreptitiously picked it up and slipped it into his glasses case.

Gradually conversations came to an end and the coffee-room emptied until, by the time the beams of sunlight shining between the slats of the blinds were horizontal, only Julian and a couple of second year students remained.

'Haven't you got homes to go to?' he asked, gathering dirty cups from the table and placing them by the filter machine.

The girls looked up from the file both had been pretending to examine. Feigning surprise, one said, 'Gosh, are we the last here?'

Julian looked slowly around the empty room and said, 'Just us.'

'Well, since we've got you on our own, could we ask a little favour?' said the other, leaving her lips just slightly open. Both stared up at Julian coquettishly and he felt a hopeful tightening in his groin.

'Yes?' he asked quietly.

The first one began toying with a strand of hair. 'Well, you know that end of term essay on matriarchal societies in Polynesia?'

Julian raised his eyebrows. 'You mean the one that is due in tomorrow?'

'Yes, well we were just wondering if we could have an extension of the deadline?'

Julian crossed his arms and theatrically began to tap one foot. 'And how long might we need?'

The other student said in the wheedling voice of a little girl, 'Two weeks?'

Julian allowed a few seconds to pass before saying in

a fake admonishing tone, 'Ten days. And not a word to anyone.'

Immediately the girls jumped to their feet and grabbed their bags, a triumphant look flashing between them.

'Thanks Julian, I wish all our lecturers were as nice as you,' said one as they started for the doorway.

As they went past him he remarked in a teacherly tone, 'Now, go on. Be off with the both of you!' Glancing down he just managed to resist the urge to pat both of them on their tight little bums.

7

As soon as the bus rounded the corner at the end of the road, the old woman stepped out to the curb and raised a stiff arm. An indicator began to blink and the vehicle slowed to a stop. The rear doors folded open and a couple of passengers climbed off. A moment later the front doors parted with a pneumatic sigh and the old woman grasped the handrail and stepped on board. Only when she was at the driver's booth did she start fumbling in her bag for her pass. Clare climbed on to the lowest step, change ready in her hand.

'Now where did I put it? It was in my hand just now. I don't understand,' announced the old woman.

As the driver dipped his head and rubbed his temples, she peered into her bag, strap wrapped tightly around her shoulder. Inside the waiting passengers began to fidget and look at each other.

'Come on Grandma, we want to get to the cinema!' someone shouted from the back.

The comment caused a ripple of laughter and the flustered woman glanced nervously towards the rows of impatient faces.

The driver looked round her at Clare. 'You want to pay chuck?' he asked, indicating with his head for her to step round the elderly lady. Clare glanced down as she lifted her foot onto the top step. By her feet lay a bus pass, a photo of a squinting woman in a hairnet looking up at her. Quickly Clare bent down, picked it up and held it over the woman's shoulder, 'You must have dropped it.'

'Oh, thank you dear,' said the woman, showing it to the driver.

Sarcastic applause broke out from the crowded seats.

Clare dropped her change into the driver's tray and as the bus finally lurched away, she made her way up the tightly curling steps to the upper deck. At the top she handed her way towards some empty seats at the back. Knees slightly flexed, legs wide apart to counter the roll of the floor, she swung out each arm to grasp one vertical pole after another and felt like an orang-utan trying to walk.

Her bus ended its run in the city centre and she walked across the station, past a couple of twenty-four-hour places churning out pies, kebabs and chips. Avoiding the greasy scraps dotting the pavement, she turned onto one of the main streets cutting through the heart of the city. As usual she took in the mass of luminous signs stretching all the way to the giant KFC at the other end of the road. It was early evening and only a few gaggles of office staff enjoying after-work drinks filled the pavement. After fifty metres she turned down a narrower side street, the drain pipes and pillar-facades of the Victorian buildings stretching high above her head. Chains had been looped across the small gaps at the rear of the buildings to prevent people from dumping their cars in spaces beyond the authority of the parking meters which, like sentinels, stood motionless at regular intervals along the street's entire length. Ahead of her two heavy female forms waddled up some steps and pushed their way through a door, one struggling with walking sticks.

A few seconds later she reached the door herself. It was painted with a thick skin of blue gloss that was chipped away in places to reveal layers of various coloured paints beneath. She climbed the steps and raised a hand to the panel of names. Her finger stopped at one marked 'Nolan Services' and she pressed. A moment later the lock buzzed and she stepped into the small foyer. A seventies style plastic chandelier hung in the air above her head. As she climbed the fake black marble steps a security guard slowly said, 'Evening Clare. Doing a night shift too?'

She looked at his shaven head and thick glasses, but before she could reply one of the huge women waiting by the lift interrupted. 'Andy,' she puffed aggressively, still breathless from climbing the six steps up from the front door. 'Don't tell us this fucking lift's broken again.'

He raised his head off his folded arms and said, 'Not sure, there's no note left by the day officer.'

'Well, the light's not even come on to say it's on the way down,' she replied.

'I don't sodding believe this,' said the other, leaning on her walking sticks and looking at Clare as if she could help. 'Three flights to get up. That's all I need at the start of my shift. Pissing hell.'

Now the two women looked at each other with desperation as the enormity of the task ahead began to sink in. One began stabbing at the lift button again and Clare saw her chance to escape, 'Listen, I'll go up ahead and make some brews. They'll be ready for when you get up there.'

'Ah, cheers Clare.'

She began to quickly jog up the steps, and on the next flight up heard a wheezing voice below her say, 'Tell that useless prick of a landlord I'll sue him if he doesn't get that lift mended properly.' A walking stick clattered against the metal carpet grip.

As Clare climbed upwards she imagined the reaction if anyone in her department knew what she was really doing that night. True, some of the women she was working with could do with a lesson in English – but they certainly weren't refugees. She thought of Jayne and Vanessa puffing up the first flight of stairs below. Past-it prostitutes who had taken to working on chat lines because they couldn't attract any punters face-to-face. She thought about how she could try and explain herself to a fellow student, 'No you misheard me, Adele. I didn't say "Iraqi destitutes", I said "Irate prostitutes". She started to giggle at her little rhyme then stopped herself, shocked that she could find her duplicity amusing.

At the third floor she entered the code into the door and went inside. In front of her was a maze of red felt partition walls arranged into small cubicles. From each one came the whisper of a voice; combined, the sound made a low pulsing murmur. She walked quietly along the top of the room and straight into the kitchen.

'Alright Clare,' mouthed a woman with thick blonde curls springing artificially from her head. She dragged hard on her cigarette and, as soon as the door had shut properly, said in a more normal voice, 'Doing a night shift then?'

'Just 'til midnight,' Clare replied, dropping thirty pence into a tin and taking three cups out of the cupboard. 'How about you, Anne?'

'I'm done in two hours, thank Christ. Got to pick the kids up from their nan's.'

'The lift's gone you know,' said Clare.

'Yeah, it's been out all day. Engineers can't come before Monday.'

'God – don't tell Vanessa and Jayne, they're struggling up the stairs now. Should be here in a few minutes.'

'Poor loves, it's bloody ridiculous that lift. Those brews for them?'

'Yeah.'

'You're a good one Clare. Though heaven knows why

you don't earn some real money up here. Get on the chat lines with us. You'll double your earnings.' She grinned impishly at the younger girl whilst pulling at a pendant hanging from an earlobe. Smoke from the cigarette held between her fingers curled up into her perm.

Clare tried her hardest not to, but felt herself blush. 'No – I'm all right with the fortune telling. Besides, I make pretty good money myself.'

'You're probably right – and I certainly couldn't do your speeches. Not quick enough with the right words.'

'I bet you could,' Clare replied. 'It's not that much different. I just get my material from the horoscopes in women's mags, splice a few together and bingo – brand new horoscopes for the week.'

'See? That's what I mean – "splice". You're educated Clare, you know all the words, can think on your feet. Me? I can just talk filthy.' She laughed a dirty laugh and stubbed her cigarette out in the massive glass ashtray.

Clare was looking at an A3 size piece of paper on the wall. It was an enlargement of an advertisement for the classified section of a men's magazine.

The headline read, 'Girl Next Door.' Next, her eye was drawn to a large red star, inside it were the words, 'Local calls, lower costs.' Beneath, the copy bounced cheerfully along, 'We've got dozens of stunners desperate to talk dirty with you. And because these horny babes are from your region, call charges are lower. So pick your nearest city and get dialling now!'

Forming a border around the ad were the usual shots of models holding phones to the sides of their heads, mostly while lying in bed. Some were laughing, some looked sultry, whilst others held finger tips provocatively to their lips.

Only six cities were listed and right next to the number for Manchester was a girl with the orange glow of a tanning salon. Black corkscrew curls cascaded over one shoulder, brown eyes open-wide and, where her hair was swept back to allow the handset to nestle gently against her ear, a large brass earring was visible. Something about her expression suggested an air of mystery. At the bottom of the ad was the line, 'More cities coming soon! Horoscopes and tarot readings also available.'

The base of the ad was taken up by a panel of microscopic small print that gave details of call charges and conditions.

'What do you think?' said Anne. 'It's Nolan's latest little plan. He reckons there's a market for chatting to girls from your local area. Same accent, same sense of humour. He's trying to cash in on all this stuff in the news about call centres being moved to India and places like that.'

Clare was scrutinising the small print, 'But it's still a premium-rate number. How can it be a lower call rate?'

'It isn't really. He's got chat rooms in other cities to

come in on it. All calls are routed through the exchange here, but he's pursuaded the other operators to cut charges by a few pence. That way the caller reckons he's getting value for money too. According to Brian, Nolan thinks it's going to make him a million.'

Clare thought for a few seconds, 'I suppose there could be something in it.'

'Anyway, how's the course going? You finish soon don't you?'

'All right thanks. And yeah – graduation is in a few days. If I've passed.'

'Oh don't give me that, Clare,' said Anne, wagging her finger. 'You're a bright one. You'll get a top grade and then you can kiss this game goodbye. Get yourself a proper job somewhere.'

'I'll have to do something – got enough debts to pay off, that's for sure.'

'Well good luck to you. I'd better get back on the phones, talking about debts.'

At that moment Vanessa and Jayne pushed through the door, both of their faces covered with a damp sheen. 'Fuck,' gasped Vanessa. 'Can I pinch a fag off you, Anne?'

'Yeah, sure,' she took a Berkeleys from her pack on the counter. 'Jayne?' she said, holding one out to the other woman.

'Cheers.' Jayne stretched out a hand, the fleshy underside of her arm swaying back and forth.

'There's your brews girls,' said Clare. 'I'd better clock on.'

'Thanks love,' they both replied. Clare and Anne left the two women leaning against the kitchen wall. In the main room Clare walked over to the supervisor's perspex-walled office.

He beckoned her inside. 'Hiya, you OK love?' he asked cheerfully.

'Yeah fine, cheers Brian.'

'Good. How late are you wanting to stay?' He was looking at the switchboard console before him. 'You've got a few hours to make up from last week.'

''Til midnight then, if that's OK.'

'Fine love – take cubicle 16. I'm signing you on at,' he glanced at his watch, 'Oooh – let's call it 6:00 P.M.' He held a clipboard out to her.

'Cheers Brian,' she replied, signing her name in the space next to her clocking on time. As she picked her way between the cubicles the voice inside each one became momentarily audible above the general hum – allowing her to hear snatches of sentences as she walked along.

'. . . go on, go on, tell me more . . . I want you to take them off, then I want you to . . . look a bit like Cameron Diaz . . . that's good, slowly, slowly . . . it's silk, and it's sliding off my shoulders . . . oh God, you're making me hot . . .'

She reached cubicle sixteen and placed her bag on

the bare desk. Then she shrugged off her cardigan and hung it on the back of the battered and slightly wobbly office chair. A price label was still stuck to the black plastic on the rear of the backrest. Thin biro read '£18 – front roller broken.'

From her bag she fished out clippings from various newspapers and magazines, a pack of tarot cards, a pack of normal playing cards, a book entitled, 'All you need to know about star signs' and a copy of *Animal Farm*.

She put on the headphones with their mouthpiece, then pressed the button on the console to let Brian know she was ready. A couple of seconds later the tiny display screen on her phone changed to 'Live' and the noise in the headset altered pitch as the line opened. Clare turned to the bookmarked page in her copy of *Animal Farm* and leaned back, waiting for her first call.

8

The sun had slipped to within an inch of the distant hills and from the top of the bulk bin by the southernmost shed, a solitary blackbird sang defiantly up at the rapidly darkening sky. Submerged in the inky shadows pooled under the beech trees, lay Rubble.

Completely oblivious to the cloud of midges jangling silently in the air above his head, he studied the bird's silhouette through the SMK 6 × 40 telescopic sights mounted on top of his Beeman FH500 air rifle. As he did so his fingertip caressed the trigger of his weapon. The movement was so delicate he could feel the reverberation as each ridge of skin brushed over a microscopic imperfection in the metal.

Then, in the hazy borders outside the tight circle his vision had been reduced to, a lithe shape twisted. The movement shared no harmony with the swaying shadows cast by the trees above him, so the barrel of the gun lowered. Eventually the shape moved forward again. In the fading light its legs were barely visible and it seemed to flow over the ground with an impossible fluidity. Every now and again a head reared up, excited by the sheer intensity of the scent given off by the prey massed in the building above it. A mink.

Silently it crept along the base of the shed, probing for the slightest gap to slip through, as pitiless a hunter as the person now bringing the crosshairs to bear over its flat skull.

The rifle cracked and his view was momentarily lost as the weapon kicked in his hands.

The blackbird cut away through the air, twittering a cry of alarm. He brought the sights back to the exact spot and there, twitching at the edge of his view, were the animal's hind legs. He shifted the gun to the side so that the prone form filled the circle. The animal shuddered briefly and then lay still.

Rubble rose from the long grass, unhitching the G10 Repeater air pistol from the holster at his hip. Though he was certain he'd got in a perfect head shot, he'd also known these animals to suddenly recover their senses from a mere nick and flee, depriving him of the satisfaction of a kill. He jogged towards the body and was still several metres away when he saw for certain no *coup de grace* would be necessary. He favoured Bisley Pest Control pellets because of their hollow points that flattened out on impact like dum-dum bullets. The exit wound above its jaw was the size of a ten pence piece. He re-holstered the pistol, propped the rifle against the shed and picked up the mink by its tail. The thin carcass hung straight down like a plumb line, blood dripping from the nose and mouth. He walked to the end of the shed then up the stairs to the rear door, holding the corpse out over the railings to stop the blood dripping on the metal steps. At the top he cupped his spare hand to catch the drips then turned and pushed backwards through the door. Once inside he used his elbow to push down the handle of the inner door.

Quickly he crossed the narrow foyer and shouldered his way into one of the centre aisles. He seemed oblivious to the wave of heat and noise as he entered the main part of the shed. Though it was almost dark outside, the grubby yellow light-bulbs in the window-less building wouldn't go off for another hour. Then, at three in the morning they would come back on. In this way mid-summer nights were permanently main-tained. The birds would respond by producing an egg and, because the lights came on so early, most birds would have laid before the collectors came round in the morning.

Nonchalantly he ambled to the small crossroads where the two men had stood earlier. In the gap between the cages he held the animal out over the edge and shook off the blood that had puddled in his palm. Then he rubbed his hand up and down the animal's back until the remainder of the viscous liquid had been transferred to its soft fur. Next he slid the hunting knife free of the leather sheath on his belt and drew the blade across the root of the tail. The mink dropped silently into the abyss, landing with a soft thud on the deep pile of droppings below. Immediately the bulky forms of the hedgekens raced from the edges and crowded round the corpse. The ones at the mink's head quickly pecked out its eyes, whilst the others jabbed futilely at the thick pelt.

'Have to wait for him to ripen,' he called down to the ravenous birds and a few cocked a beady eye up at the familiar sound of his voice. He slipped the knife back in its sheath and, with the mink's tail still in his other hand, left the building. Outside dusk had fallen. He retrieved his rifle from the side of the shed and walked back to his caravan, imagining that, above him, the beech trees were whispering their appreciation of his skills.

As he neared the caravan he began picking his way between wooden stacking crates, half full sacks of gravel and empty plastic chemicals barrels. Chicken feathers lay scattered in the thick grass like litter. The side of his house was decorated with a mass of animals' tails. Spindly, hairless ones of rats, furry sausage-shapes of mink, ferrets and stoats and the bushy brushes of at least twenty foxes. He unlocked the door and slid his rifle into the sling mounted just inside. Then he took a sharp tack from the jar sitting on the workbench to the side of the door and pressed its point into the vertebrae at the severed end of the tail. Picking up the hammer lying next to the jar, he held the tail up to the side of his home and, with one sharp blow, drove the tack through the gristle and into the plastic surface beyond.

The caravan creaked and rocked slightly on its brick foundations as he stepped inside. Immediately to the right was the thin white door of his tiny bedroom, in front of him a similar door to the bathroom and toilet. The rest of the caravan was open-plan, consisting of a kitchen area with work surface, sink and two gas rings. Beyond that was a small sitting room complete with a table that could fold down to form the base of a double bed if necessary. Rubble had never lowered it since no one had ever visited him in his caravan, much less stayed the night.

He unbuckled his belt and hung it up, the weight of the air pistol and hunting knife making the canvas fold tightly over the coat peg. Then he undid the laces of his boots and placed them side-by-side on the doormat. Still in his filthy overalls he crouched before the miniature fridge and took out the chicken he'd plucked earlier. He dropped it into a greasy saucepan and put it in the sink, pumping a handle up and down until the tap began coughing out spouts of water. Once the bird was submerged he put the saucepan on a gas ring, lit it with an almost empty bic lighter, then moved to the sofa.

The caravan had obviously been built in the 1970s – the pattern on the cushions was of interlocking purple squares on a brown background. Both the carpet and curtains were similar, but with random red lines racing across their surface. Though the caravan had been motionless for years, the narrow shelves lining the walls were all fronted by a thin mock-brass rail to stop objects falling off. Now the barrier just served to hem in dozens and dozens of comics and magazines, many of which drooped forwards, such was the weight of the other copies pressing from behind.

Sitting at the table, he reached for the copies he'd purchased earlier that week, *Death Before Dishonour*, *Battle In The Clouds* and a larger size one titled *Karn Age*. He'd looked through them twice already, just able to follow the simplistic text and brief speech bubbles. Tonight was the night he copied out any new regimental badges or operational maps from their pages. The cupboard door next to the table opened with a ping and he took out the sketchbook Mr Williams in the post office had ordered specially for him. On the shelf below was a tin box full of pens and pencils which he placed on the table. The first comic had a badge in the top right hand corner of the cover itself, so Rubble positioned his sketch pad as close to it as possible. Then, surprisingly quickly, he produced, in freehand, a near exact copy of it on the blank page – even transcribing word for word the regimental motto written in a swirling Latin text below the crest. Once it was complete he flicked through the rest of the publication, copying down more badges and a map of Singapore that appeared inside. He carried out the same exercise with the other comic, faultlessly rendering a street map of war torn Stalingrad on to the page. By now the chicken had been bubbling away in the saucepan for some time, so he created a space on the table and went over to the gas ring. A quick glance into the boiling water was sufficient – he'd been eating chicken long enough to judge when it was cooked. He took it off the heat and stabbed a fork into its breast, lifted the dripping lump from the water and dropped it on to a plate. Tomato ketchup was then liberally applied around the edges and he sat back down at the table.

Grasping both of its legs, he bent them back and twisted, the cooked meat giving way with a fleshy tear. A slightly harder yank pulled the legs out of the thigh sockets. He put one drumstick to the side, rolled the other in the red sauce, then bit into the muscle. Before he'd swallowed the first chunk he turned the leg in his mouth and took another bite, repeating the process until his cheeks bulged. The drumstick had now lost most of its bulk, but still he rotated it between his lips, gnawing away at it as if it was an apple core. Only once he'd removed every scrap, including the tendons and gristle at the top of the leg, did he put the bone down. Then he sat back and slowly began to chew.

Rubble only ever used his fingers for eating chicken. It was far easier to strip the carcass down to bone that way – knives and forks seemed crude and ineffectual in comparison. Soon he had moved on to the body itself, ripping the fibrous meat from the breast bone, digging a stubby finger into the spinal area and gouging out the lumps of marrow hidden there. Quickly the bird was reduced to a dislocated pile of bones.

Licking his lips, he wiped his fingers down the legs of his overalls, got up, threw the remains out of the window and dropped the plate into the sink. Sitting at the table again he turned his attention to the back pages of *Karn Age*. Most of the adverts were lost on him, but one, with the women's faces lining its perimeter, caught his eye. Or more accurately, the face of one particular girl attracted him. He stared at her thick black curls and deeply tanned skin, wondering what strange and distant place she came from.

Leaning closer to look at the picture, he studied her huge circular earring and fingernails that curved and stretched like talons. The darkness of her eyes, with their long lashes, fixed him from the page. Slowly his eye struggled over the words in the ad until eventually he located the one he recognised: 'horoscopes'.

He'd given up calling these numbers over a year ago. What they told him would happen never did – he was still working on the farm and he neither looked for nor wanted any other future. Unless, of course, the army were to change its mind about letting him in. But after the number of times he'd applied, it was obvious that it was never going to happen. He stared into her mysterious eyes and something about the way she looked at him hinted she might be different to the others. Perhaps it was worth another try.

He went to the cupboard above the sink and removed the biscuit tin of change. Carefully he took out almost all the fifty and twenty pence pieces inside and pocketed them. Then, after checking through the views of the security cameras showing on the monitor, he set off for the village green, comic in his hand.

Quarter of an hour later he was standing inside the phone box with the advert looking up at him. He inserted several fifty pence pieces into the slot and dialled the number next to the face of the girl that so intrigued him. A pre-recorded voice welcomed him to Manchester's 'Girl Next Door' line, then told him that his call would only be charged at £1.17 a minute, almost ten pence cheaper than most premium-rate lines. The voice asked him to press '5' if he wanted to proceed with the call. Next he was asked to press '1' if he wanted an intimate chat with a horny babe from right up his street or '2' if he wanted to have his horoscope or tarot cards read. Rubble pressed '2'. A voice then told him that, if he knew the extension number of the particular astrologer he wished to speak with, please press it now. When he did nothing the voice said he would soon be connected to an expert in the art of horoscope readings and the noise of wind chimes clinking in a ghostly breeze started up. After about a minute the music faded and a voice that was strangely accented said, 'Hello caller. My name is Sylvie Claro, would you like a horoscope or a tarot reading?'

'I want you to read my fortune,' replied Rubble with unnecessary force, trying to hide his shyness.

'OK, my child,' replied the voice. 'First I would like to know the year of your birth.'

'Is it your picture in *Karn Age*?' Rubble suddenly blurted.

'Sorry my precious?'

'The advert in *Karn Age*. Is that a picture of you?'

The voice faltered, 'Describe to me the lady in the advert.'

Rubble started awkwardly, 'You've got long dark curly hair. Um – and your finger nails are very long.' He dried up, unable to describe how beautiful he found her face.

'And my eyes,' the voice whispered seductively, 'what colour are my eyes?'

'Brown. Very big and brown,' he said in a small voice.

'Yes, that is me.'

'And your name is Sylvie?'

'That is my name. Now my child, what year were you born?'

Rubble frowned. He'd been asked this question on previous calls and couldn't answer it then. 'It's on the sixth of March.'

'*Gracias* – and the year?'

'Dunno.'

'You do not know the year in which you came into this world?'

'Nuh,' Rubble grunted quietly.

'OK, let me see,' the voice paused and he could hear vague sounds of paper being moved. 'It shouldn't be a problem – it will just take me a few moments longer to draw up your horoscope. Do you have grey hair?'

'No.'

'But you are not a youth?'

'No – Mr Wicks told me I was over twenty-one, but that was a few summers ago.'

'Stay with me. To see which stars were ascendant in that period, I must look at my charts. Please wait, they are up in my observatory.'

Clare took off the headset, walked slowly to the supervisor's office and popped her head through the door, 'Keep my line open will you Brian? I've got a punter on – I'm just off to look up his charts.' She winked and headed across to the kitchen. Inside were a couple of women she'd chatted a bit with before. She dropped ten pence into the tin and as she filled her cup from the kettle and said, 'Hey girls, I've got a right one on at the moment. First he thinks I'm the actual woman from that advert.' She pointed at the poster on the wall. 'Second he's ringing a horoscope line and he doesn't even know which year he was born in! I've told him I'm up in my observatory looking up his charts.'

'What – he's on your line at the moment?' one asked incredulously.

'Yup – he's buying everything I tell him,' replied Clare.

From the doorway an accusatory voice hissed, 'You're a disgrace to the astrologer's art.'

They all turned round to look at the purple-haired woman who had silently entered the room. Her round form was sheathed in a long black smock, over the front of which hung an enormous pentagram on a silver chain.

She held up a hand and pointed at Clare with a ring covered finger, 'I hear you filling up those callers with rubbish. Speaking about things of which you have no knowledge. Take note: you are flirting with dark forces by doing it.'

Embarrassed, Clare looked down at her mug of tea.

One of the other women butted in, 'Well I am sorry, Gypsy bloody Lee, we can't all be members of the British Astrological Society.'

The woman let out a snort, then turned back to Clare, 'I've read your tarot cards young girl. You're heading into mortal danger.'

She turned on her heel and marched back out of the door.

Clare looked at the other two woman. Seeing her shocked expression, one said, 'I wouldn't worry about any of her predictions. If she was any good how come she didn't foresee that they were going to kick her off Mystic Meg's "Live Line" in the *Sun*?' Both older women began cackling.

'Is that where she used to work?' asked Clare.

'Yeah, they caught her giving out her mobile number to callers. That's why she now works in a dump like this. Though she thinks she's above us, the snobby bitch.'

Suddenly the other woman said, 'Jesus, you'll be clocking up big time on that caller. The most I've ever kept one on for was nine minutes fifty-five. Just missed the ten minute bonus.'

'Nearly ten minutes? Most of mine have shot their bolt after about three!' said the other woman.

'Bloody hell – has my Ian been ringing you again?'

All three burst out laughing. 'Right,' said Clare. 'I'd better get back before he gives up on me.'

'Go for it girl!' said the older one as she left the kitchen once again.

Back in her cubicle she slipped her headset back on, 'Hello my child?'

'Yeah?' replied Rubble.

'I have studied my charts and the heavens look very promising for you over the next few weeks. As a Piscean the Zodiac's most energetic and forceful planet, Mars, is about to link with your star sign. This signals new horizons for you. The influence of idealistic Neptune is also growing, so if there are any ambitions inside you that you have long dreamed about, now is the perfect time to take action and go for them. What area do you work in my child?'

'I work on a farm. Have done all my life.'

Clare thought about the recent events in the farming industry. 'Well, perhaps . . .' she hesitated, 'perhaps changes will come from outside your present job.' Falling back on a fail-safe avenue, she said, 'How are your finances?'

'Finances?'

'Money. Could you do with more money?'

'Not really – I don't spend much.'

Suddenly the pips sounded. 'Hang on,' said Rubble, pressing his last two twenty pence pieces into the slot.

'You are on a pay phone?'

'Yeah – that's my last coins.'

'OK, then I must hurry. The future will smile on you. If not through your job, it will be another opportunity.'

'Could it be the army?' Rubble interrupted.

'Maybe.'

'I've tried to get into the army before.'

'Yes, maybe that is what I see . . .' The pips sounded once more. 'If you would like to speak with me again, call my extension. Three zero four. I am here most nights each week, ask for Syl–' The line went dead and Clare looked at the read out on her console. Twelve minutes eighteen seconds. She punched the air and shouted a silent 'Yes!' at the ceiling.

In the call-box a moth crawled up the window, its wings a blur on its back. Rubble stood staring at her face in the faint light. 'Sylvie, three zero four' he whispered over and over again. Then he pushed his way out of the booth and lumbered off into the darkness.

9

Eric sat in uneasy silence and tried to quell the feeling that he was a schoolboy, called before the headmaster. With hands folded in his lap he listened to the rapid tap-tap-tap of the secretary at her keyboard. Every couple of seconds she would strike the space bar with her thumb and the small thud it made gave her typing the semblance of some sort of erratic rhythm. Looking down at him from the surrounding wood panel walls were oil paintings of previous chancellors. Each one had their academic gown draped over their shoulders, the various coloured collars denoting which subject they had graduated in. He noted with interest how the style of portrait altered over the decades – chancellors from the pre-World War One period stared at him with an icy sobriety, the background of the painting a meticulous study of book shelves. Later pictures were looser in style with sweeping brushstrokes, successive painters seeming determined to beat the preceeding artist for some original touch; a hazy, impressionistic swirl of colour here, a blurred background of moving students there. One even faded away at the edges, leaving pencil markings exposed to view. He wondered how much of the University's money had been squandered on these self-indulgent shows of vanity.

There was a knock at the outer door, it opened immediately and Patricia let herself into the thickly carpeted room. Even in her heels she couldn't have measured much more than five feet. But that didn't prevent her making an impression whenever she walked through a door. It was all in her body language: confidence blended with just a touch of urgency. A demeanour that instantly caused most people to treat her with deference. But not Eric. He had seen this manner many times before – company bosses or politicians in the news, men in red coats mounting horses or grey suited types getting into the first class carriage of trains. He even observed it beginning to flourish amongst the student rugby teams as they gathered outside the union buildings. It stemmed merely from class: the imperceptible link between money, power and privilege. He despised it.

She nodded to Eric. 'Are you early, or am I late?' she asked with a breathless smile. A maroon cashmere scarf was wrapped round her neck, the ends hanging over an expensive looking coffee-coloured trouser suit.

'You're right on time,' he replied.

'Oh, thank God for that. It was a nightmare parking. Six of the spaces are taken up by skips full of rubbish from some department.'

Eric had chained his bike next to them ten minutes

before. 'They're refurbishing the biology labs – that's what all the mess is about.'

'They've finished lectures already? We're teaching the wrong subject Eric,' said Patricia. She had crossed the room and was about to sit down beside him when the chancellor opened the door to his office. Patricia's attention instantly turned to the man and she swept past the seated Eric. 'Chancellor Atkins, how are you?' she strode up to him, one hand outstretched.

'Patricia, good to see you.' As they shook hands he looked round Patricia's shoulder. 'Eric? Please, come through the both of you.' He spoke with the gentle, sonorous air of someone who has spent a lifetime wrapped safely in higher study. A lecturer, a priest, perhaps a hospital consultant.

Eric lifted himself from the low leather armchair, both knees cracking loudly as he did so. He passed through the trail of perfume left by Patricia and shook hands with the other man. As they all entered the inner office the chancellor casually said to his secretary, 'Could we possibly have a tray of coffee please Lesley?' It wasn't a question.

Once inside, the chancellor directed them towards four armchairs in one corner of the room. 'Now this is strictly an informal meeting, but one necessitated by that infamous University grapevine.'

They each took a seat, the chancellor on one side of the coffee table, his visitors side-by-side on the other.

On his cue everyone crossed their legs and with an exaggerated sigh the chancellor began, 'There's nothing quite so chaotic as the last weeks of the summer term, don't you think? I find it quite amazing to consider that, in just a short while, the students will have evaporated and we can all have time to hear ourselves think once again.' He smiled, holding one finger up. 'And continue our research uninterrupted. I for one am looking forward to a couple of weeks excavating a Beaker village just discovered on Dartmoor.'

His two visitors nodded as the door opened and Lesley came in with a tray of coffee. After pouring everyone a cup, she retreated from the room.

'Now,' continued the chancellor, methodically stirring. He lifted out the spoon, touched it against the rim of his cup so a single drip was transferred to the china, then placed it on his saucer with a quiet clink. 'As you know, the way the Social Studies Department has evolved is highly unusual. Eric, you established it long before my time. In fact, counting the early years when you lectured part-time whilst still employed as a social worker, I think you must be one of the University's longest serving members of staff by now. All your hard work has led to a strong department that, over the years, has produced dozens of well-qualified graduates. Those who have gone on to a career in social work have done so with a thorough knowledge of the pertinent issues in caring for the elderly.

'Patricia, you joined the University just five years ago to establish and head up a Women's Policy Unit. In that time you have made a dramatic impact on both the Social Studies Department and the University as a whole. Thanks to your research, awareness of women's issues has risen immeasurably. I gather that four police forces now follow your recommended procedures in handling cases involving domestic violence?'

She nodded.

'What we have though is, in effect, two separate departments within one. As you'll be aware, our Government grant has been cut again, and so I'm forced to examine ways in which we can streamline our resources. Now you're by no means the only departmental heads I'll be seeing over the next few days, but I have to start somewhere. Unfortunately I have been somewhat pre-empted in this by certain rumours; and that's largely the reason why I've called you both in today.

'Within the Social Studies Department there is a certain duplication of roles – amongst the support staff, researchers and lecturers themselves. This is, as I'm sure you're aware in the current funding climate, not economically viable. To avoid rambling on, I'm afraid to say it's unlikely we can afford to continue running the department in its present form. What I'm being forced to do is merge your departments into one. This, unfortunately, necessitates a reduction in staff levels.'

Now he stared down at his coffee cup.

'The next cycle of voluntary redundancies comes about in a year's time, and I sincerely hope we can make all the necessary rationalisations as part of it.'

The weight of his skull seemed to have magnified because, with what seemed quite an effort, he looked up and stared at a point just above their heads.

'And now we come to the dilemma facing me. I have two excellent heads of department, but room for only one.'

An awful stifling silence. With an almost plaintive note in his voice the chancellor carried on, 'Would either of you consider taking voluntary redundancy in the next cycle?'

Eric and Patricia made no reply.

The chancellor looked back down, 'No, I thought not. Well, as unpleasant a duty as it is, I'm going to have to ask you both to submit proposals outlining plans for your half of the department over the next three years. Anticipated research grants coming in, student numbers expected per course and the like. Full details will be given to you in writing, I just wanted to speak to you both in person first.' He wasn't used to the oppressive atmosphere now filling his office. Finding that it was beginning to unnerve him, he lifted his voice and said, 'For instance, Patricia, I understand you've put in a proposal for a major research project from the Economic and Social Policy Research Council?'

Patricia leaned forward and placed her cup and saucer on the table. Then, in a brisk, businesslike tone, she began, 'Yes, by strange coincidence it's a three year project looking at the Europe-wide disparities in sentences handed out to women who kill their husbands after suffering sustained domestic violence. Funding has been agreed at £125,000 *per annum*, including assistance from the EU Commission into Social Affairs – the Dutch, Swedish and Italian Governments have expressed an interest in the eventual findings. We're actually due to hear if we've been awarded the project in the next few days. I've been meaning to see you about it, but with the end of term we're all so busy . . .'

'Go on,' nodded the chancellor encouragingly.

'Well, if we do win the project I'll actually need to take on a couple of researchers who will be required to assist in some lecturing duties too. One of my tutees has already expressed an interest in any position. She's in line for a first, takes an active role in student affairs and is, I believe, an ideal candidate. Salaries for a basic grade researcher-stroke-lecturer could be comfortably covered by funds from the ESPRC grant, quite apart from what we could also apply for from the Higher Education Funding Council for England.'

'Excellent,' beamed the chancellor. 'Well all that will need to go into your proposal. And Eric, you mentioned to me the other day that you're looking at some issues not related to care of the elderly. Was it something about the ethics of modern-day food production? It sounded most interesting.'

Eric coughed uncomfortably, glanced at the chancellor then, looking down at his coffee cup, hesitantly began to speak. 'Um, it was a consideration, yes. But early investigations have been problematic. You see, the last thing these places want is any publicity.' Making up an example to illustrate his point, he said, 'I wrote to a meat processing plant just the other day inquiring about taking groups of students around – it supplies most of the major fast-food outlets in the region with their burgers. My request was flatly refused. What goes on in these places does so very much behind closed doors.'

'That's a shame. So have you anything else in the pipeline?'

Eric desperately searched his mind for something to say. 'Yes – there's some debate in palliative care circles about government funding for hospices. It could be an interesting research project.'

'Is this in response to a project on which the ESPRC is currently calling for proposals?' asked the chancellor.

'No,' replied Eric. 'I would apply for a single research grant. Perhaps myself and another colleague.'

'But no firm financial figures yet?'

'No, but obviously my early career as a social worker is a big bonus and palliative care was as much an issue then as it is today. In fact nowadays it's even more relevant, with the ever increasing size of the elderly population.'

The suggestion was greeted with a strained silence and the chancellor struggled for something to say, 'As an archaeologist you'll have to forgive my ignorance, but palliative care is . . .?'

'Care of the dying,' Eric replied matter of factly. 'Terminal illnesses – cancer and so forth.'

'Good,' said the chancellor. 'Good.' As if repeating the word would make his utterance of it any more genuine. 'Well, Lesley will be sending you both the proposal forms in the next few days. So if you could find some time in the coming weeks to complete and return them.'

As he put his coffee cup on the tray he noticed the copy of the *New Statesman* on the table. 'Oh, Patricia,' he said, picking it up. 'I loved your piece on the undermining of senior female officers within the police. "Witch Hunt", a very provocative title. And always good to see the University receiving mention in such high-profile publications.'

As they all got up, Patricia replied, 'Thank you chancellor. An edited form of the article will be appearing in the *Observer* next Sunday too.'

'Very good,' he said, then turned his attention to Eric who was standing silently to one side like a butler. 'Thank you both very much for coming in, and sorry to have to finish your summer terms on such a note.'

After shaking his hand at the door, Eric and Patricia continued across the lobby area and out into the hallway. Once on the steps outside Patricia breathed deeply, 'So the rumour becomes reality. I suppose I shouldn't be shocked.'

Eric just nodded grimly.

'Well,' she hesitated, hoping they were going in separate directions. 'I'm parked over there. Whereabouts are you . . .'

'That way too,' he answered.

They walked along in silence. Now officially in competition with each other conversation didn't seem appropriate. Yet at the same time, civility demanded it. Patricia eventually said, 'Have you any plans for a summer holiday?'

'Maybe a few days away. Some walking in the Lake District probably.'

'Have you got relatives there then?' Patricia asked, trying to string the conversation out.

'No, my parents lived in a colliery village called Burton Oak, near St Helens. Thatcher decimated it and put him out of a job. After the pit closed, my father crumbled away with it. Some people just aren't suited for a forced retirement,' Eric said.

Even though they were both left of centre in their political opinions, Patricia knew that, in Eric's opinion, her moderate views made her little more than a Tory in disguise. Keeping away from where he was steering the conversation, she asked, 'And your mother?'

'She went within months of him,' he replied emotionlessly.

'I'm sorry.'

By now they were approaching the skips Patricia had mentioned earlier. Parked with two wheels on the grass verge was a silver BMW. 'Michel is back from Brussels for a couple of days – so I've borrowed his car.' The vehicle pipped as she pressed the remote unlock. Eric noticed the ruts gouged by the thick tyres in the carefully tended grass.

'My bike's just over there,' he said, pointing to the old green Raleigh chained to the thin trunk of a nearby tree.

'Right, well – I'll see you in the department soon,' Patricia said, getting in the car.

'Yes,' Eric replied, fiddling with his keys.

He unchained the bike and turned it round. Patricia meanwhile had reversed the car back onto the tarmac. She put it into first gear, waved briefly and pulled away. Eric pushed down on a pedal, moving straight into the cloud of her exhaust fumes.

As he cycled home, he reflected on the coming process; he'd seen it applied countless times to other permanent lecturers over the years. Their specialist area of research comes to be regarded as outmoded, unfashionable or just plain irrelevant. Forced to employ the lecturer until their sixty-fifth birthday, the University then seeks a voluntary redundancy. Failing that comes a sideways move into an administrative role.

But worse, far worse, was the thought of Patricia being made head of department and assuming full control of the budget. The prospect made him seethe. All that he'd built up over the years would be dismantled piece-by-piece. First she would cut the money for any of his research programmes, diverting the funds towards her own. Then the finances for his modules would shrink. Lastly, because of his reduced presence in the department, his lecture and tutorial rooms would be taken over. Slowly all his efforts would be reduced to nothing. And he would have to watch it all from some back office, while creating the very timetables that would instigate the process. He could not, would not, let it happen.

Turning his head he spat into the road, trying to remove the bad-egg taste her exhaust fumes had left in his mouth. Wiping his lips with one hand he turned his attention to the next step of his plan.

10

Eric knocked on the door marked, John Milner BA (Hons)MSc(Psych). Receiving no answer, he continued down the corridor, looking into each laboratory as he went. In the third room he spotted his colleague and pushed opened the door. A man with thin greying hair and a short beard looked up from the table on which he was arranging piles of essays.

'Professor Maudsley, to what do I owe this pleasure? I haven't seen you in the Psychology department for many a month.' His voice carried a faint North American accent.

'Hello John. I'm just here to ask a favour actually.'

The man sat on the edge of the table and held out his hands, 'Fire away.'

'I need to borrow any basic psychology tests you might have – Rorschach cards and the like. Do you have any bits and pieces like that?'

'Plenty – though I can't give you an actual set of Rorschach cards. We try and keep those secret. They depend on the element of surprise you see. But I've got similar cards along with standard cognitive assessment tests used by larger companies assessing potential employees. I think I've even got a psychiatric test for assessing criminal tendencies. What's it for?'

'Oh, a young cousin of mine is staging a play. One of the scenes involves a psychiatrist's appointment, so they wanted to look at some tests and get a feel for the type of questions asked.'

'Sounds interesting. All that stuff should be in here.' He unlocked a wall cupboard and pulled out a few folders and what looked like a pack of oversized playing cards. 'Here's the imitation Rorschach test, always a favourite amongst first year students. You know how it works?'

'Vaguely.'

'It's absurdly simple. Too much so in the opinion of many modern-day psychiatrists. Each card has a blot on it, created by dripping ink on to the middle of a page and then folding it over. The result is all sorts of weird and wonderful symmetrical patterns. You simply ask what the shape reminds your subject of. One man's butterfly is another man's double-faced demon. Of course analysing the results is a whole different ball game.'

'That's OK, it's just the test itself, not the analysis of it that features in the play,' replied Eric.

'Right. Well this folder has a test favoured by many American companies for recruiting senior personnel in the late 1990s. And here's the criminal assessment one – the two are surprisingly similar.' They laughed at his joke. 'As I say – it's all in the analysis of the answers.'

'That's great John, can I borrow them for a few days?'

'Have them for the summer if you want – my last lecture was on Thursday. I've just got to mark this lot now,' he said, patting the nearest pile of scripts.

Eric left the department and returned to his office. Once in his seat he powered up the computer and clicked onto the desktop publishing programme. From his briefcase he took out the two Commando comics and wrote out all the words he'd underlined.

'Confidential. Spy. Agents. Need-to-know basis. Search and destroy. For your eyes only. Mission. Objectives. Operatives. Undercover. Project Alpha. Secret. Call sign. Code.'

He tinkered around with the various words, combining them in different ways, crossing some out, adding others in. Eventually he was happy. On his computer he selected an A5 size field and inside the box typed, 'Top Secret Government Project. Agents Wanted. Call–' then he picked up one of the two pay-as-you-go phones he'd bought earlier with cash and typed its number on to the base of his advert.

Next he selected some pale blue A5 divider cards from a packet in his top drawer and inserted one into his printer. After typing in 1 for 'Number of copies required' he pressed 'Print' and the machine began to click and whir. Once the process was complete he clicked the 'Close' icon on his screen. An inner window asked if he wanted to save his work and he selected 'No'. The page of text vanished from his screen. He carefully picked the ad off the printer, gathered it up with the war comics and sheet of paper he'd been doodling on and slipped everything into his bag.

11

By now the sudden noise the conveyor belt made as it started to revolve was less alarming to the birds: it seemed it wasn't the prelude to some sort of attack. None of them had fed yet and no eggs had been produced. Their hunger and thirst were mounting, forcing them to explore their tiny home. The bird in the corner brushed against the red nozzle poking through the bars and a fat drop of water welled out of the tip. It fell on to the bird's back and rolled down the richly coloured feathers. The animal felt its progress and cocked its head to regard the glistening piece of plastic. A tentative peck released a second large drip and the bird gratefully drank it. Squashed alongside, another bird saw the water and the first jostle occurred as the two sought to drink. In the other rear corner a slightly smaller hen awkwardly tried to turn itself around. When it had been shoved into the cage its left leg had been bent back, the thigh muscle was severely torn and the bone fractured. It slumped against the bars, a low guttural sound of distress rising from its throat. At the front of the cage the largest bird warily extended its head between the bars. The conveyor belt rattled along just below its beak, carrying scores of pellets on an endless loop. From their smell, the bird knew the small objects were food, but it was a type it hadn't experienced before and it was reluctant to try. It withdrew its head back into the cage, neck feathers catching painfully on the bars. But the pangs of hunger were too strong and eventually its head appeared out of the front of the cage once again. A beady eye regarded the moving pellets and, unable to resist, the chicken abruptly ducked its head and pecked one.

12

As he pulled up near the village post office he was surprised to see a group of three old ladies already waiting outside the locked door. He'd assumed he would be the first customer of the day. Sitting in his car, he watched as they chatted animatedly with each other. All wore ankle length navy rain coats and two had plastic scarves on their heads, despite the clear sky.

He undid his seat belt and checked yet again that the postcard size advertisement was safely in his jacket pocket. Glancing in his rearview mirror he saw the old lady in the motorised wheelchair he'd encountered a couple of days before. She rolled up the ramp and Eric noted with interest how the three women only wished her the briefest of good mornings. She sat hunched in the seat, one claw perched on the arm controls.

Inside the shop a shadow moved behind the windows. It glided up to the door and paused there as bolts were slid back. Then the sign flipped from *Closed* to *Open* and the door swung outwards.

'Hello ladies! And how are we on this beautiful morning?'

Eric could hear his chirpy tone through the car window.

'Fine thank you Mr Williams,' the three women crowed back in a disjointed chorus.

Once they had all teetered inside he climbed out of his car and crossed the quiet road. He stood at the newspaper shelves assessing the situation. Once again, only the elderly shopkeeper was working behind the glass screen of the post office counter. Busily he was stamping booklets, the old ladies gathered before him.

Quickly Eric squatted down and drew the piece of thin card from his pocket. Then he picked up the uppermost *Commando* war comic, slid the piece of paper inside the back cover, returned it to the shelf and picked an *Independent*.

Quietly he walked over to the shop counter and waited. The owner called out to him from behind the screened off section, 'I'll be with you in two ticks!'

Eric smiled. 'No hurry,' he replied.

As the man counted out the three old ladies' pensions Eric listened to the conversation rattle about between them.

'Did you have the ham Elsie? I had the ham. It was nice.'

'Yes, I had the ham. But Beth had the cheese.'

'Did you Beth? Was the cheese nice?'

'I didn't much care for it actually Dot. It was that rubbery foreign sort, from Switzerland or wherever.'

'Oooh I know.' She leaned closer to her companions and whispered, 'Sticks to your plate. That sort?'

Elsie nodded in silent agreement, but Beth said, 'I'm sorry?'

Elsie and Dot glanced with some embarrassment at Eric, and Dot opened her mouth slightly and pointed inside. 'Sticks,' she silently said, then pursed her lips and looked off to the side.

'Oh yes, it stuck to my plate,' replied Beth loudly.

'Well the ham was nice,' Elsie intervened. 'Thin sliced it was.'

'Yes – I prefer thin sliced,' replied Dot.

'I'll try it next Monday. Unless they have turkey, I prefer turkey to everything.'

Eric listened to their conversation with revulsion – its triviality horrified him. A lifetime of experience and wisdom, reduced to this. The type of sandwich served at their local OAP night. Memories came flooding back of his years spent working in inner city care homes. Despite the differences in the financial well-being of his former patients and the elderly ladies stood next to him, their physical state had all slid to the same level. Money couldn't change that. From the corner of his eye he looked at the way one of them stood, weight shifting uncomfortably from one arthritic hip to the other. The curved upper spine of another, forcing the head into an endless contemplation of her feet.

He'd observed this process of decline too often over the years. If he was honest with himself, he had been only too glad to get out of caring for the elderly in a hands-on way. Studying them from an academic distance was far more appealing. Developing a disdain for those you care for was, he knew, a relatively common process amongst the employees of nursing homes. Daily exposure to it had certainly extinguished long ago the sympathy he'd first felt. Gradually, as he himself had aged, those feelings had been replaced with unease. Then discomfort and fear. And finally resentment. Resentment for the fact that he was becoming one of them.

He thought back to how his own parents had died, glad that the end was relatively quick for them both. Not that it mitigated the circumstances of their deaths. When the coal strike was finally broken in 1984 his dad had returned to work, ready to get on with earning a wage. The village colliery was one of Britain's most productive and there was plenty of work to catch up on. But within weeks the killer blow came – the Tory government closed it for 'economic reasons'. Eric, only just qualified as a lecturer, had driven home unable to believe it. But it was true: the colliery gates were padlocked shut. Hundreds of men's livelihoods were destroyed and the heart was ripped out of the village. After that Eric returned home as often as he could, and with each visit the colliery buildings had sagged a little more. His dad's health mirrored their decline. In his late-fifties, he didn't stand a chance of getting another job. A lifetime spent down the pit suddenly took its toll

– his back and knees went and he could hardly get out of bed. Then his fingers seized up so he couldn't garden or even feed himself without difficulty. A year later he was dead.

Eric peered down at the backs of his own hands, noting the liver spots gathering at his knuckles, the bluish ropey veins meandering beneath his increasingly papery skin.

Old age was slowly infecting him. He knew how quickly his mind would also deteriorate if it was deprived of the daily exercise provided by his job. His career was the only thing that set him apart from the women standing next to him – and now it was being torn from him and handed over to someone who he despised.

'Just the paper sir?' The voice snapped him out of his reverie and he looked up at the wrinkled face of the smiling shopkeeper. He looked around – the three old ladies had gone and the minutes had slipped by. It was almost 8:55. He needed to hurry.

'Yes. Thank you,' he quickly answered, holding out a one pound coin. As the owner picked change from the open till, a bitter voice spoke from near his elbow.

'I was before that gentleman.'

He looked down into the crumpled face of the old woman as her lower jaw trembled and shook.

'I know Miss Strines,' said the shopkeeper, handing

Eric his change. 'But he's only getting a paper – and your disability benefit takes a lot longer to sort out.'

'Shouldn't matter – and you know it,' she croaked indignantly.

Eric pocketed the coins, mumbled an apology and swiftly left the shop. He glanced across the green, and to his relief, saw no one approaching. Once back inside his car he unfolded the newspaper and, using it as a screen, began reading the front page.

The cover headline immediately caught his attention. 'Drug giants to merge.' The story outlined how two multi-nationals were combining their operations to achieve increased levels of efficiency. Share prices in both had leapt. A spokesperson was quoted as saying how cutting roles duplicated across both operations would save millions. Eric's eyes flicked down to the spokesperson's inevitable concluding comment, the one describing how both companies were confident that no compulsory redundancies would be necessary.

A bulky form moving to the right dragged his gaze from the page. Rubble was walking up the ramp into the shop, tapping a key from a large bunch against the iron hand rail as he went. He pulled open the door and disappeared inside. Eric waited. Moments later the door was pushed open again and Rubble stepped back out, a plastic bag of comics hanging from his hand.

Directly behind him was the old woman in her wheelchair. Rubble held the door open until she was half way out, then he deliberately let go. It swung back, banging loudly on the foot plate of the wheelchair.

Instantly the old woman began to curse. 'You're a bloody thug, Roy Bull. Always was and always will be!'

Like an overgrown kid, he skipped down the slope laughing.

'You need punishing you do – you murderous bloody oaf!' she squawked.

The shopkeeper appeared and pushed the door open so her wheelchair could roll forwards once again. By now Rubble was at the base of the ramp, where he turned round, 'You're not my teacher now, Miss Strines!' he shouted back. 'Can't boss me round no more!'

She jabbed a thin finger in his direction, 'I know you killed my cat,' she spat, turning in her seat and speaking over her shoulder at the shop keeper. 'Evil he is,' she said. 'The nastiest, stupidest piece of work I ever had to teach.'

Eric saw the last comment made Rubble blink several times. He shoved two sausage-like fingers up at her, 'Fuck off!'

'Now Roy . . .' the shop keeper began, but Rubble was lurching across the grass back to his domain, his bag of comics bouncing and jerking as he ran.

13

'Yes?' Contained in the voice was an unmistakable note of irritation. Clare turned the knob and opened the door so she could peer around it without actually stepping into the office.

'Morning Professor Maudsley, I wondered if you had a couple of minutes?'

His pen was poised motionless in the air above the essay on his desk, and the sharp, mechanical, movement of his head as he looked up reminded Clare of an insect.

'Er,' he glanced at the clock on the wall but, unable to think of a plausible way to reject her request, said, 'OK – if it really will be a couple of minutes.'

'It will, thanks,' replied Clare, entering the room. As she shut the door behind her, Eric quickly reached down and closed the leather satchel lying at his feet.

In the phone box Rubble placed the card on the black metal shelf. Once again he looked over the words, 'Top Secret Government Project. Agents Required'. He licked his lips.

Clare sat in the chair opposite the Professor. It seemed

too abrupt to launch into the real reason she had disturbed him. Aware of the need not to waste his time she said, 'Have you seen my posters about the demo this Saturday? We're lobbying the chancellor over the six per cent increase in rent for university accommodation.'

Until his meeting with the chancellor a few days before, the Professor would have gladly participated in such a march. At the least it was a good opportunity for handing out Socialist Worker leaflets. But now the thought of a noisy protest on the chancellor's very doorstep made him choose his words more carefully, 'I did.'

Clare looked a little surprised at his cool response. 'Will you be around for it? It always helps to have the weight of a senior lecturer on our side.'

'When is it due to start?'

'Midday outside the union building. We'll protest there for a while and get the petition going. Then, once we've swelled our ranks with as many members of the university community as possible, we'll march down Williams Street. I've informed the police of our plans – they've approved them as long as we've passed along it within fifteen minutes. Then we'll turn into the east entrance of the campus and march along Mandela Avenue to the chancellor's house itself.'

Eric tapped a finger on the desk. 'I can certainly come for the first half of the march. But I have an appointment elsewhere at one, so I'll break off as you pass through the east entrance.'

'That's great, thank you,' replied Clare enthusiastically. 'It's outrageous what they're doing. Some of those flats aren't fit for, aren't fit for . . .' She searched her mind for a social group more deserving of such a home. Homeless mothers? Asylum seekers? Ex-prisoners? It was impossible to name anyone without being discriminatory. A glance at the watching Professor confirmed that she had strayed onto what could be politically incorrect ground. 'Aren't fit for keeping dogs in' she concluded with relief. 'I'm in Melbourne Road – those flats by the main railway line to Sheffield? Although by the railway line is a generous description. More like on it. The tracks are so close, every time a train passes the windows nearly fall out of their frames. And they want to up the rent for next year's students by almost £1.50 a week? Unbelievable.'

'I sympathise with your plight Clare. Now . . . is there anything else?' he asked, suppressing the urge to glance down at his satchel.

Rubble rechecked the telephone number on the card. Then he reached into his pocket and took out a palmful of twenty pence pieces.

'Um, yes. There was one other thing.'

Eric raised his eyebrows to invite the question.

'You know we spoke the other day about my note inquiring into research positions?'

'Yes Clare.' Before she could reply he carried on impatiently, 'And I'm sure you're aware that funding for all universities is being squeezed by our Labour Government.' He placed heavy irony on the word labour. 'I'm really unsure about the possibility of any new research positions for the next academic year. I can only repeat to you what I said the other day: your inquiry has been noted and I'll contact you immediately if any positions become available.'

Unable to resist the urge, he actually placed a hand on the satchel and pulled it against the legs of his chair.

In the phone box Rubble, with the card held close to his face, began pressing the buttons on the telephone.

'Yes, I appreciate that,' said Clare. 'I just wanted to check with you that my inquiry will be treated confidentially. That was all.'

The room was silent as Eric digested the implications of her comment. Etiquette dictated that he couldn't ask why she wanted her application kept secret. 'Of course. That's standard practice for these matters.'

Clare smiled a little awkwardly, 'Thank you Professor. I only asked because. . .'

A shrill succession of notes rang out and Clare

automatically reached for the mobile in her canvas bag – before realising the ring tone wasn't hers. She looked questioningly at the Professor; he'd stated emphatically on many occasions that he would never own such an intrusive and unsociable item. She'd always suspected the real reason was an inability to shake off in his mind their old connotations of Thatcherite yuppiness.

The phone sounded again.

'You must leave,' said Eric, voice urgent to the point of panic. His long legs carried him to the door in an instant and he pulled it open. 'It's a very sensitive call, sorry to be so abrupt.'

'No problem, thanks for your time,' replied Clare, having to lean back slightly to get past his overbearing frame. The door was shut firmly in her face. She heard the phone once more as she walked slowly down the corridor, puzzling over his strange behaviour.

14

Eric sat at his desk. He paused a second to run over his speech and then fished the phone out of his satchel. With the careful movements of a novice, he pressed the green button and held the mobile up to his ear.

'Room 101,' he said curtly.

The voice that came down the line was thick and awkward. 'I'm ringing about the advert for the project. The secret one.'

'Before we proceed, I must inform you that the work requires you to sign the Official Secrets Act. Are you prepared to do that?'

There was a second's silence and then Rubble said, 'You want me to sign the Official Secrets Act?'

'If you are selected to work on this project, yes.'

'Yes!' he said with childish pleasure. 'I'll sign it . . . if you want me to.'

'Good. Are you a British citizen?'

'Yes.'

'Are you able-bodied?'

'Able what?'

'Are you physically fit? Not handicapped in anyway?'

'No.'

'Have you been, or are you, a member of any

subversive group as outlawed by the Government's Anti-terrorism Bill, 2002?'

'I'm not a member of anything.'

'OK. Now, for the selection process you will be interviewed in your home. This is in order to conduct a psychological test. What is your address?'

'Well,' replied Rubble. 'I live in a caravan just outside Breystone.' He began speaking from memory, having studied the old road map in his caravan countless times. 'It's on the B5085, near Wilmslow.'

'Yes – we've traced the phone box you're calling from already.'

Rubble looked around him. 'You know I'm in the phone box on the village green?'

'That's correct.'

'Well,' he peered around. The only person he could see was an old woman feeding the ducks. 'I live in a caravan. It's . . .' He'd never had to give directions to his home before, and now he struggled to begin. 'You go from the village green past the duck pond.'

The voice interrupted him. 'This caravan. Is it the one on Embleton farm?'

'Yes! That's where I work, how did you know . . .?'

'We have satellite tracking. Is the caravan located on a lane? Behind a small copse of . . . are they silver birches?'

Rubble had crouched down in the phone box and was craning his head back to look up at the sky, 'They're beech trees. You can see them at the moment?'

'Of course. Now, I can send an agent to interview you the day after tomorrow. 9.00 P.M.?'

Still looking up at the sky, Rubble replied, 'Yes, 9.00 P.M. Thank you . . . sir.'

'And the last thing. Do not – I repeat – do not, leave the advert with this number on in the phone box. Keep any adverts you have with you in your caravan until the agent arrives. You must not show them to anyone and you must not tell anyone about this conversation. Is that clear?'

'Right, OK,' said Rubble, hurriedly stuffing it into the front pocket of his overalls. 'It's a secret.'

'The day after tomorrow, at 9 then.' Before Rubble could reply the line clicked and the ring tone returned to his ear.

Tingling with excitement he replaced the phone on its cradle and pushed the door open. Checking no one was watching he saluted quickly up at the sky and then set off proudly towards the farm.

Eric returned the phone to his satchel and sat back in his chair. Nervously he tapped a finger on the desk, eyes darting uncertainly round the room. After a few minutes he decided that he would go to the farm and interview Rubble purely as a sociological experiment; just to see how much a mind, wholly ignorant of the outside world, could be moulded into believing what was acceptable and justified.

15

'Gold Blend all right?' said Zoe, holding up the jar.

'You're paying, darling,' replied Clare smiling. 'I'm just as happy with the own brand stuff.'

The girl made a retching noise in the back of her throat and placed the jar in the shopping trolley. 'You bloody students, I'd rather drink soot.'

They sauntered along the aisle, bored by the whole affair. 'What else do we need?' asked Zoe, restlessly eyeing the shelves of tea bags.

'You forgot the shopping list, you dozy cow,' Clare replied light-heartedly.

'Yeah, yeah, I think we're all right for brews. Sugar?' she asked, pointing at the pallet of paper wrapped brickettes at the end of the aisle.

'No, there's a spare one under the sink.'

'Right, that's it then. Let's get out of here.'

Further down, the thin figure of a man flashed across their aisle. 'Shit! That was Maudsley.' Clare glanced into the shopping trolley. She grabbed the jar of coffee and handed it back to her friend. 'Swap that for a jar of Fair Trade!'

'You what?' asked Zoe with surprise.

'I'm not risking Maudsley finding me buying Nestlé products. No way.'

Her friend started laughing. Then she held her hand over her head and started revolving her fore-finger round and round. 'Whooo! Whooo! Attention, thought police! Attention, thought police!'

'Oh Jesus,' said Clare. 'Look, just keep clear until we're out of here will you? I don't need you taking the piss.'

Zoe replied in a mock-German accent, 'Ya, ya, I vill be vaiting for you at ze checkout.'

She walked away chuckling and shaking her head.

Round the corner Eric was standing with his back to her by the freezer section.

'Oh hi Professor, getting in a few essentials?' said Clare brightly.

The man turned around, 'Evening Clare. Yes, just a few bits and bobs.' He opened the lid of the freezer cabinet, picked out a couple of vegetarian pizzas and began examining the labels on the side of the box.

From the next one Clare lifted out a sack of Quorn and placed it on the top of her shopping. 'See you around then,' she smiled, noting him glance at the items in her trolley.

She caught up with her friend at the checkout. Conspiratorially Zoe showed her the top of a Gold Blend jar in her shopping bag. 'It's OK, I bought it whilst you were flashing him your oh-so-innocent smile.'

After they'd packed their food into bags Clare said, 'I'll let you do the honours then, while I carry this lot to your car.'

Zoe her cash card handed to the woman behind the till; as she waited for it to be approved Clare set off for the exit.

From the shop's depths Eric waited until he saw his student heading out through the doors. Then he made his way back to the freezer section, swopped his vegetarian pizzas for meat feasts and made his way to the tills himself.

Like an automaton he began placing all his items on the motionless conveyor belt. The woman in front of him collected her receipt and the expanse of black rubber began moving forwards, carrying his purchases towards the cashier.

'Oh hello Mr Maudsley,' he looked up at the middle-aged woman. When his face registered no recognition she said, 'It's Edith's daughter – Rosemary?'

She tapped the name tag on her tunic, 'Rosemary Jennings – you used to look after my mum. Before you started lecturing full-time. I'm sorry,' she checked herself, 'it's Professor Maudsley now isn't it?'

Finally the information connected in Eric's head. 'Oh don't worry about that. Sorry I didn't recognise you straight away, it's just that I haven't seen you working here before.'

'I only started a few days ago. My other supermarket

closed down and they were looking for staff here.'

'I see,' said Eric. 'And Edith – how is she nowadays?'

He could instantly see that it was a struggle to maintain her smile. 'Not so bad, I suppose. She's still in that council flat. The same one you used to visit her in. Five Pilkington Court?'

'Yes, I remember,' replied Eric.

'I'm trying to get her a full-time place in a nursing home – but it's just so hard finding her a bed, even with her angina getting worse and worse. Her doctor had to increase her medication again only the other day. The health visitor calls in once or twice a week – often to put her on a nutrition drip. It's very difficult getting her to eat anything. And I see her whenever I can. But it's hard finding time, you know, with the kids to look after and working as well . . .'

'How is her mobility nowadays?' he asked, removing his reusable shopping bag from his pocket.

She stopped passing bar-codes across the red beam. 'Oh, she's been in a wheelchair for some time now. She can just about get out of it and into her bed. And the toilet – they've put special bars in so she can still go on her own. But after having a fall a few months ago and spending the night on the living room floor, she prefers to sleep in the chair with a blanket. Not that the health visitor approves.'

Eric could picture it only too clearly. The loss of motivation. Personal hygiene slipping. Small accidents in the night and a faint smell permeating the flat. Suddenly the woman's shoulders sagged and the breath left her with a sad sigh. He kept his eyes on the woman as she glanced behind him to check no other customer was in earshot. Obviously needing to confide in someone, she said, 'To tell you the truth, it's really getting to me. Last week she announced that she'd had enough, said that . . . you know . . . that . . .' she glanced around once more and whispered, '. . . that she wanted to die.' Her eyes filled with tears. 'I mean, if she were a pet dog no vet would agree to keep her going. I sometimes think that, if she was up to it, I'd fly her over to that place in Switzerland, the one where you can just drink that barbiturate stuff and go to sleep . . . forever.'

With a jerky movement she wiped the tears from her eyes, 'I'm sorry. I should never have unburdened myself on you like that. It's just that I haven't got anyone to talk to.' She shrugged her shoulders and looked up at him in embarrassment.

'Not at all,' said Eric. 'Are there no other family members who could help? Don't you have a brother?'

'Andrew? He emigrated to New Zealand a few years ago. Edith's never really been able to take it in. She still points to his photos and asks when he'll visit. She was so proud when he graduated. I haven't the heart to tell her he lives on the other side of the world.'

'I can see why,' murmured Eric. 'Have you tried Saint Cuthbert's? They always seem very accommodating, especially if she is having trouble moving about.'

'Haven't you heard? The council are closing it down. Can't afford to run it.' Eric hadn't heard, but it hardly surprised him. 'Anyway, don't let me keep you,' she continued. 'I'm sure you're busy enough as it is.' She pressed a button on the till, 'Thirty pounds, eleven please.'

Eric handed her the cash and, as he placed the last item in his bag, said, 'Well, I hope she finds somewhere soon. And pass on my regards when you see her.'

'Thanks, I will. In fact I'm popping round in a couple of hours once I'm finished here,' she replied, waiting for the till to finish spitting out his receipt. She handed the bit of paper over and he said goodbye, heading for the basement car park.

But instead of going home, Eric drove to a more run down part of the city. He parked on the main road outside a row of fast-food takeaway places, got out and locked the vehicle. Shoes silently connecting with the pavement, he then glided down a side street choked with parked cars. The front doors of the terraced houses opened directly on to the pavement, no room for a front garden or even railings. As he strode quietly along he concentrated on the sounds seeping through the houses' front windows. A football match was obviously on; he could follow the muffled commentary from one front room to the next. In the windows with thinner curtains the flickering glow shone through clearly. The end of the road opened on to a T-junction, terraces stretching away on both sides. A section of houses had been bulldozed opposite and the gap filled with a small complex of little bungalows. Now, after years of neglect, the properties had grown shabby – paint peeled from wooden window frames, the mortar between bricks crumbled. The sign on the grass verge read, 'Pilkington Court'.

The Professor strode straight across the grass, and followed the right hand path between the first few buildings. Quickly he homed in on the corner house, slowing down as he neared it. Seeing no one approaching, he veered off sharply down the narrow alley at its side. Despite the high wooden fencing separating the alley from the street, he kept his head low. At the corner he paused, glancing at the overgrown patch of back garden lit faintly by the yellowish light coming from the kitchen windows. Various sized pots were arranged around the patio and along the rear wall of the house. He remembered when each one was home to a thriving variety of herb: now some sort of creeping weed had throttled them all. Carefully he stepped into the garden. Once beyond the patch of light spilling across the grass, he turned around and looked through the rear windows. The kitchen was empty. He directed his gaze to the next room, and there he saw the old woman, slumped in her wheelchair, mouth slightly open, hands resting high on her chest, a necklace of thick wooden beads about her neck. She was sitting at a right angle to him, facing the opposite wall. He could see the television wasn't on and he strained to hear the sound of a radio or other music. Then one of her hands slipped a fraction and he realised she must be fast asleep. Silently he moved closer, noticing the bed in the corner of the room with the metal frame for her drip looming next to it. Like some minimalist design of coat stand, it looked totally out of place next to the knitted cushion covers, embroidered bedspread and lace mats on the table. As did the aluminium bedpan sitting on her bedside table. Now, with face right by the window, he could hear that there wasn't even a radio on; she had been sitting there in silence. Just waiting to die.

Crouching down by the back door, he checked that the spare key was still under the third pot on the left. Then he moved soundlessly back down the alley and returned to his car.

As his headlights swept across his front lawn they lit up his neighbour's cat, crouched malevolently over a tiny black form, eyes momentarily flashing silver. The animal stared balefully at him for an instant longer, then darted back into its own garden. He climbed out of the car, removed his shopping from the back seat and went to examine whatever the cat had abandoned.

The shrew lay on its side, comically long snout poking between the blades of grass, a jet black eyeball almost jumping from its head. The animal's sides rose and fell with an impossible speed – the movement more of a flicker than a breath. Bending down he looked more closely at the creature. As a sociologist, his main concern was with the welfare of vulnerable humans in society. He didn't actively hate animals: but he didn't feel any affection for them either. The plight of the tiny creature before him only interested him because, if it died, it became an item of litter that he would have to clear up. He looked for any signs of injury. But this was the cruel irony; the cat hadn't been interested in actually eating its prey. Just torturing it to death. Tentatively he extended a forefinger and attempted to roll the rodent back on to its front, hoping it might scamper away. The gentle prod finally proved too much and its sides abruptly stopped moving, as if a switch had been turned off. He watched as the bright black eye slowly lost its lustre. Pursing his lips in annoyance, he picked it up by its hairless tail, walked over to his dustbin and dropped it inside.

The microwave whirred as his pizza revolved slowly around inside. Over the years his house had gradually accumulated more and more machines of convenience. In his early career he would religiously visit the laundry, aware of the wastefulness of running a washing machine in a single person household, proud to live in a home with as few luxuries as that of his childhood. But gradually the effort just seemed too much. After the washing machine, he had indulged in a dishwasher, then a microwave. Standing by the machine, he studied the television guide from the *Observer*. Spotting that *Blade Runner* was about to start his eyebrows raised and he nodded a couple of times to himself.

From a social scientist's perspective, Eric loved the film for its vision of what an unbridled devotion to capitalism would lead to. After first seeing it, he had even considered offering a course that analysed the film. It was only the disdainful reaction he was sure this would provoke from the University's 'natural scientists' that prevented him from actually doing so. But that didn't stop him, in idle moments, from planning the outline of lectures that took a grim delight in describing a world that had been slowly compressed into a claustrophobic dystopia. A writhing mass of dirty streets where all industry was privatised, where there was no such thing as society, where nature had been eradicated and animals existed solely in artificial forms. And where the only landmarks to rise above the urban skyline were the strongholds of big business such as the Tyrell Corporation's monstrous headquarters.

Eric pictured himself before rows and rows of rapt students, describing how, unless socialist principles prevailed, executives would soon be gazing down at the streets from the upper floors of these strongholds, market forces reducing the flow of people below them to mere consumer units. Indeed, when viewed from such a distance, Eric asserted, ordinary man would appear as little more than a speck and of no more consequence than an ant. What, he asked his imaginary audience, was the Government's role in this future society? Pared down to the bare minimum, the state served no purpose other than maintaining law and order – so the corporations could continue wielding their pernicious control over everyone's lives.

Smiling, he placed a glass of water on his dinner tray. Then something occurred to him and he walked quickly through to his study. Mixed in with the publications on the bottom shelf of his bookcase were a number of video tapes; mostly *Cutting Edge* documentaries or episodes of *Panorama* concerned with injustices within the British system of social care. Next to a large yellow coloured paperback titled, *Mining Memories: An illustrated Record of Coal Mining in St Helens* was a video tape with a particularly old report on how the Conservative policy of Care in the Community was turning pensioners with mental problems out on to the streets. He carried it through to his front room, inserted it into his video recorder and turned the television on. As *Blade Runner* started and the haunting strains of Vangelis' sound track began to fill the room he pressed 'Record' and went to fetch his pizza.

16

By now their surroundings and daily routine were familiar. All four birds were fully accustomed to the conveyor belt's sudden noise; now it only represented an opportunity to feed. The large forms of the people in white clothes that occasionally passed still caused stress, but they soon disappeared and hardly ever made any noise. However the birds were far from comfortable. Their natural urges to scratch at the ground and bathe in dust were reasserting themselves but only the hard grid of bars was beneath their feet. The metal dug into the fleshy pads, a continual source of discomfort. The first bird to exhibit nesting behaviour was the largest. Instinctively it sought a dark and secluded corner. There wasn't one. Eventually the egg dropped on to the sloping mesh floor and rolled into the collecting tray at the front of the cage. Often during their nineteen-hour-days the birds wanted to sleep. The cages had no perches and so their roosting instinct was thwarted too. Frustration levels were beginning to rise. The injured hen was now in considerable pain. The other birds frequently tried to flap their wings, but the confines of the cage didn't allow this. Often their attempts knocked the injured bird over and it was finding it increasingly hard to regain its feet. The width of the cage only allowed three birds to stand at the front with their heads through the bars to feed. To provide relief from the unpleasant feelings the low ceiling created, the three healthy birds preferred to remain there even when they weren't eating. The position had the advantage of allowing them to stretch and shake their necks, behaviour chickens in open surroundings indulge in all the time. Behind them the smallest bird had yet to eat.

17

Zoe took off the polythene gloves and dropped them into a plastic bag, careful to avoid touching any of the henna covering them. 'There, leave that on for half an hour and you're done.'

Keeping her head bent over the edge of the bath, Clare fiddled with the elasticated edge of the plastic cap covering her head. 'Are you sure all my hair's tucked under?'

'Certain. And you can open your eyes too, there's no dye on your face.'

Clare straightened up and removed the towel draped round her shoulders. 'Thanks mate. Right, I'll just wash the bath out before it stains.' She picked up the shower head connected to the hot and cold taps by twin umbilical cords.

'You weren't bullshitting me in the supermarket? It really is that right on?' asked Zoe, now sitting on the sofa and using the end of a matchstick to prod stray strands of tobacco back into the end of an enormous roll-up.

'God, yeah. It's a bloody minefield doing that course,' replied Clare, spraying warm water on the dots of red flecking the sides of the bath. 'I hardly dared open my mouth when I started. One wrong step and people would turn on you like a pack of hyenas. But what got me – still gets me – is the sense of righteousness in their voices when they hauled you up. It's as if, by nailing you, they're demonstrating their own PC credentials to everyone else.'

'You mean they don't really believe it themselves?'

'Absolutely. I don't think half of them really believe what they say. It's just what's expected – and if you're a student, it's the sure way to a decent class of degree.'

'That's sick.'

'Yup,' she though for a moment and then said. 'There's probably a few students who are really genuine. But you don't hear them spouting off all the time. Amongst the lecturers there's Patricia Du Rey. I've got a lot of respect for her. And at least what she's teaching is relevant and interesting.'

'What about that Professor from the supermarket?' asked Zoe.

Clare sat down next to her, 'Maudsley? I think his heart is in the right place. I mean, he lives by what he teaches. Cycles into University to save the planet, only accepts essays on recycled paper, doesn't waste a single paper clip.'

'Then again, he could just be tight.'

'True. And his courses are grim as anything. Care of the elderly. Looking after the dying and all that.'

'Oh don't, it's too depressing.'

'Mmmm. Anyway, most of the department . . .' enthusiasm suddenly flooded her voice. 'Take this little dick-head called Julian. I mean, Julian. Who'd call their kid that if they weren't absolutely loaded?'

Zoe's shoulders started to shake and Clare, seeing her friend trying to suppress a laugh, said, 'What?'

'I love it when you get on one,' answered Zoe. 'Remember that time? We must have been eight or nine? You lobbed that cooking apple into the pond where those old men were fishing? We were laughing so much we couldn't even get back on our bikes to cycle away!'

Zoe began to giggle as she recounted the story. Clare kept quiet, even though she had heard it countless times.

'That guy came charging across the grass in his wellies, grabbed us by the scruff of our necks and then marched us back to the pond to make us apologise to all the other fishermen.'

'Oh don't,' said Clare, cheeks now red and head lowered.

'And you suddenly burst into tears then turned on him and let rip about fishing being cruel and how nasty they all were to be sitting there trying to catch the poor little fish with their nasty hooks.'

Zoe was laughing openly now, while Clare held a hand over her eyes, as if to screen the memories from her sight, 'Yeah, well it is cruel. I don't care what they say about fish not feeling pain.'

Zoe carried on, 'I'll never forget the look on his face. He was so shocked by your rant he just let go of us and crawled back into his little green tent.'

Clare sighed deeply, 'Anyway, if I could carry on now?'

Zoe sat back, grinning as she twisted the top of the roll-up closed.

Clare smiled back, 'Julian is especially vigilant about correct comments being adhered to. But what really gets me about him is this: he does it all as a sad way of trying to chat up girls on the course. Only, because he's a lecturer, he doesn't dare actually ask anyone out. So he just "nices" his way around them, doing his, "I'm such a sweet, considerate guy, please fancy me," act.' Her voice adopted a pained earnestness as she imitated him, 'I really empathise with women's issues, you know that don't you Zoe?' She placed her hand on her friend's knee and gave her a sickly smile.

Giggling, Zoe shook her leg free, lit the joint, inhaled deeply and said, 'He "nices" around them, you said. Does that mean he doesn't "nice" around you?'

Clare thought for a moment. 'Not so far anyway. And there's only a few more days to go.'

'Do I detect a little disappointment?' Zoe replied, beginning to laugh. 'That Julian isn't all "nice" with you? That Julian doesn't try to . . .'

Clare cut her short, 'Oh please, I'd rather shag . . . I'd rather shag Maudsley.'

'Eeeurrrr – the living corpse from the supermarket?'

'Yeah, any day.'

They chuckled for a while, then Clare tapped impatiently on the sofa.

'What?' said Zoe, looking at the flutter of her friend's fingers. Clare quickly checked the plastic cap on her head and said resignedly, 'I'm just as bad – in my own way.'

'What do you mean?'

'The chat lines I work on for a start. In the department I tell them that I'm doing adult literacy courses for Iraqi refugees. In reality I fleece poor sad people out of their hard-earned cash. And this crap demo I'm organising. It's all a load of horse shit. I mean, a £5 a month rent increase? Big fucking deal. It's still peanuts compared to what any private flat would cost me. I'm only organising it so I appear the model student to get this bloody research position.'

'You do what you have to do Clare,' Zoe replied, her voice much firmer. 'I've told you that before. Believe me, if you can get a nice cushy position in a big university, grab it. At least you're safe once you're in.'

'Yeah, you say that. But look at Maudsley. They're making budget cuts and it looks like they're going to bin him end of next year.'

'But he's old, isn't he? He's due to retire soon anyway. You get your foot in the door and then you can apply at other universities, colleges, sixth form places, all that.

It'll beat the shit out of any position in the private sector, I can tell you.'

She held the joint out to Clare, but she waved it away. Zoe shrugged and took another drag, 'You know what the bastards did to me. A piss-poor salary and then, eleven months into the job, they bin me – because they know if I reached a year with them, I'd actually have some rights. As it was I got a thank you Miss Webster, here's a month's pay and your P45. Now fuck off.' Her voice was quivering slightly as she said, 'I tell you – they'll shit all over you.' Biting her lower lip, she stared angrily at a fly buzzing against the glass of the living room window. 'That bloody thing has been pissing me off all evening.' She reached for the recruitment section of the local paper on the table in front of her and began to roll it up.

'Don't kill it,' said Clare, jumping to her feet and opening the window a few inches.

The insect continued battling against the impenetrable surface, unaware its way to freedom was inches away.

'Go on, shoo. Get out!' said Clare, nose wrinkling with disgust, pushing delicately at it with the back of one forefinger. Suddenly it flew to the side and disappeared through the gap. Shuddering, Clare closed the window and returned to her seat.

'Anyway, Zoe, you've got a year's experience now, haven't you?' said Clare gently. 'Your foot's in the door.'

'Ha! And there's also the next wave of eager young Graphic Design graduates just entering the market too. All of them sussed on the latest editions of Quark, Photoshop and Illustrator, all of them desperate to work for what I started on. You know what really gets me? When I landed that job, I probably bumped out someone just like me. Used is what I feel like.'

Clare picked up the recruitment section of the local paper and smoothed it back out. It was folded over at the media part, various jobs circled. 'So how's the job hunt going?'

'Not too bad,' answered Zoe with a sigh. 'I've got a few to call back on Monday. Hopefully to arrange an interview.'

'That's excellent,' said Clare. 'They won't be able to resist you – you'll see.'

Zoe smiled, eyes averted, 'Yeah well – fingers crossed.' She reached for the telly guide, dropping ash on the floor.

Clare put the recruitment section back on the table, picked up their plates and carried them through to the kitchen. She turned on the taps and, as she stood waiting for the sink to fill, she heard the TV go on. The sounds of a chanting crowd filled the tiny flat for a second before the channel switched.

'Excellent! *Blade Runner* – have you seen it?' Her friend called through from the sofa.

'Yeah – about five times,' she called back, wiping a cloth over the plates.

'It's a class film,' Zoe informed her anyway. 'Ridley Scott at his best. And the music . . . who did it? Someone quite famous . . .'

The rumbling sound outside suddenly increased in volume, higher metallic notes now mixing with the engine's deeper roar. As the train sped past, every window began a minute rattling in the warped wooden frames and Clare actually felt the air shift against her face. And then it was gone and instantly forgotten.

'. . . do you know what I mean?' concluded Zoe from the other room.

'You what? I missed all that,' replied Clare, leaving the kitchen.

Zoe was excitedly jabbing the last third of the joint towards the screen. The marijuana had heightened her convictions, creating a certainty that her insight was genuine. 'It illustrates my point perfectly. I mean who are the only sorted people in the film? Apart from the ones at the top of the big corporations, it's the few lucky enough to be working for the state of course. The cops and that. The old police boss, Bryant, even says to Harrison Ford that if you're not a cop, you're a little person. Everyone else is just scratching out an existence down on the miserable litter-strewn, rain-sodden streets.'

'Yeah, but Zoe, half the Social Studies Department is

probably closing soon. That Professor Maudsley will probably be on the scrap heap in another year.'

'Maybe,' said Zoe, struggling to make this information fit her theory. 'But with a nice index-linked pension and a fat payout too, no doubt. Name me a private company who is expanding their pension schemes.'

'I don't know.'

'I'll tell you then. None. They're all closing them to new employees as fast as possible. Too much of a drag on their profits. And that shit-heap place I wasted a year at didn't even have one. I'm telling you – there's a lot of people in this country heading towards a poverty-stricken old age. No one I know is saving for their pension, and they say the state one will be non-existent by the time we retire. Get yourself into that Patricia's department and hang on like grim death.'

'OK, OK, I hear you. In fact, I'm covering my arse and applying for any positions in Maudsley's department too. Just in case.'

'Good on you, go for it. Either department will do.'

'Cheers. Anyway, I'm going to wash this stuff out of my hair and go to bed. Can you turn the sound down a bit?'

'Sure. I should crash soon too,' she stood up, stubbed the end of the joint out in the ashtray and went over to the sleeping bag folded up in the corner of the room. As she unfurled it on the sofa she said, 'On second thoughts, I might have a little number while the film finishes.'

'Fine,' said Clare from inside the bathroom. 'Just don't light it up once you're lying down. You'll burn both of us to death one of these nights.'

'Don't worry, I won't.'

When her friend re-emerged from the bathroom a few minutes later with a towel wrapped round her head like a giant turban, Zoe said, 'Clare?'

'Yeah?'

'Cheers for letting me crash here. I'll sort myself out soon, you know that?'

Clare reached over the back of the sofa and put her hands on her friend's shoulders. 'No rush, sweetie. I'll see you in the morning.'

18

Slowly the slug re-extended its tentacles, the flesh seeming to grow from its head like the tentative shoots of a plant. Eric blew on it and the twin points instantly retracted again. He was wondering how long this game would last when he heard the familiar rasping sound. His gaze shifted from the gelatinous creature on his windowsill to the wooden shed at the bottom of his garden. An instant later the front half of his neighbour's cat appeared over the edge of the shed roof. Out of sight, the claws on its rear legs continued to scrabble on the far side of the wooden structure as the animal struggled to transfer the majority of its weight on to the flat roof. And then it was on, standing upright and proudly surveying its domain: Eric's garden.

Happy with what it saw, it sat down and began licking at a front paw. Then, bending its head slightly to the side, it began rubbing the end of its foot over and around one ear. It repeated the process with the other paw, then languidly got to its feet and moved across the roof. Carefully it leaned over the edge, extended its claws and walked its front feet in a series of little steps down the front of the shed. Firmly anchored by its hind legs, the animal stretched its torso as far as it would go, then dropped gracefully on to the grass. Without pausing, it padded along the narrow path it had worn across his lawn, stopping at the base of the bird table for a brief sniff. Then it turned around, lifted its tail, backed its haunches up against the varnished surface and sprayed the pole with urine.

Satisfied, it carried on across the remainder of his lawn to the back patio. Normally it then cut diagonally across the concrete slabs to the corner of Eric's house before heading down the side alley and continuing its patrol somewhere else. But today it stopped as an unfamiliar scent passed across its nostrils. Cautiously it moved towards the house, disappearing from Eric's sight below his windowsill.

With infinite care, Eric leaned slowly forward in his seat so he could see the animal directly below. Its attention was totally absorbed by the tin of sardines he'd placed at the base of the wall earlier that morning. Warily, the cat lowered its head towards the object in a series of inquisitive nods. The end of its tail began to twitch with excitement as it reached one paw outwards. But Eric had been careful to only partly uncurl the lid – the gap wasn't quite big enough for it to extract a fish. Slightly puzzled, the cat sank on to its stomach and extended its nose towards the maddening smell.

In the bedroom above it, Eric slowly lifted the broken paving slab off his lap and held it out of the window. Once he'd lined it up with the back end of the animal below, he released his grip. Even before the loud crack and agonised yowl, he was on his feet and running to the top of his stairs. He grabbed the blanket he'd folded over the top of the banister earlier and raced downwards, through the ground floor of his home and out of the French windows.

The paving slab had broken into three pieces, a chalky mark on the patio where it had struck. Next to it the tin of sardines lay on its side in a slowly expanding pool of brine, and about five feet beyond that was the cat. Desperately it was trying to use its front legs to claw itself away, its smashed rear legs dragging uselessly along behind. Eric's long legs closed the gap in two strides and, lips pursed tight with revulsion, he threw the blanket over the stricken animal. Then he gathered it up and, holding it at arm's length, ran back into the house. Quickly he walked through the kitchen, using his elbow to open the door into his garage. Once inside, he knelt down and placed the weakly struggling bundle between his knees. Grabbing his heavy duty gardening gloves off the shelf to his side, he put them on and, afraid of what he might see, folded back the blanket to reveal the cat's head. Its lips instantly curled back and it hissed up at him. The animal's defiance angered him and he grabbed it by the back of the neck and reached for its collar. It snapped at his hand, fangs sinking harmlessly into the thick rubber, and he carried on regardless. Once the buckle was undone he threw the collar to the side, re-wrapped the animal and stuffed it into the plastic storage container ready in his car boot. He snapped the lid on, closed the boot, dropped the gloves back on the shelf, opened his garage door and drove out on to his drive.

After locking up he set off for the University, parking by the skips outside the biology department. Jumping from the car, he walked round to the rear, opened up the boot and extracted the bundle. To his relief, the lump inside struggled briefly as he lifted it out. Then he jogged into the biology department. Negotiating his way through the building materials strewn along the corridor, he headed straight to the end door marked, 'K. Howard. Laboratory Assistant'. Aware of the sounds of hammering and sawing coming from the labs he'd just passed, he urgently rapped on the frosted glass.

A hazy form appeared and the door was unlocked to reveal a woman with glasses, probably in her late-thirties. Frowning, she looked down at the blanket held in Eric's arms.

'Hello, I'm Professor Maudsley from the Social Studies Department!' he exclaimed breathlessly, the sharp smell of sawdust and urine catching in his nose. 'I've just run over a poor cat; I don't know what to do. It's horribly injured. You were the closest place I could think of.'

'Oh God, you'd better bring it in,' she said, stepping

aside and waving him into a room piled with boxes and crates. Swiftly tying up her wavy mane of hair, she went to the side of the room, calling back over her shoulder, 'I'm having to pack everything up – they're gutting the place for refurbishment.' As she cleared a space on a work surface, Eric looked at the shelves of cages. Inside the highest ones he could see gerbils and hamsters – excited by all the commotion outside they scampered manically around on their wheels. Confined in the larger cages beneath were half a dozen rabbits. All were asleep except one – who regarded him through the bars with pink, suspicious eyes. In a glass container on the floor near Eric, locusts swarmed over the wire mesh separating them from a warm light bulb.

'OK, bring it over here and let's have a look,' said the assistant, snapping on a pair of latex gloves.

'It just ran out from between two parked cars. I feel awful,' said Eric, as he carefully lowered the blanket down. Keeping his grip on the animal inside he added, 'Careful, it went for me when I picked it up.'

Taking one corner between thumb and forefinger, the assistant gingerly pulled apart the blanket's folds. Standing on tiptoes to keep her face as far away as possible, she peered in. Her features relaxed and she said, 'Oh Jesus, you needn't worry about it jumping out at us.'

Eric loosened his grip and she opened out the

blanket. During the car journey it had both vomited and soiled itself – a mixture of diarrhoea and blood plastered its shattered back legs.

'Oh no. Oh no. Can it feel anything? It must be in agony. Oh my God,' Eric ran a hand despairingly through his beard.

The cat lay on its side, tongue lolling, its breath coming in little gasps. Similar, Eric thought with satisfaction, to the shrew it had tortured to death a few nights before.

'The best thing I can do is put it out of its misery. Now where the bloody hell is the Euthanol? I only packed it up this morning.' She looked around and then settled on a large cardboard box at the end of the counter. 'I hope it's in here – everything's in a complete muddle.' Lifting up the flaps of the box she said, 'Ah yes – thank God,' and she fished out a bottle of clear liquid. Then she unlocked the wall-cupboard in front of her and took a thin syringe and hypodermic needle out from the large box inside. She put both items in the front pocket of her tunic and then carefully lifted the animal up, blanket and all. 'I'll put it to sleep next door – don't worry, it won't feel a thing.'

'Oh, thank you,' said Eric, his lower lip trembling slightly.

As soon as the side door shut he stepped over to the cardboard box and opened it. Inside was a haphazard variety of miniature racks – some full, others half empty with bottles. Spotting several more of the type she held up, he quickly grabbed two and put one in each jacket pocket. Then he opened up the cupboard, snatched a handful of syringes and needles and shoved them into the inside pocket of his jacket. Almost as an afterthought he pulled several pairs of latex gloves from the dispenser on the work surface and rammed them into his trouser pockets.

Nervously he stepped back to where he'd been standing before and looked around. On the shelf in front of him was a dank aquarium, half full of water. A label on the front read 'Xenopus Toad'. He leaned forward and peered through the greenish glass. On the other side the amphibian hung motionless in the water, limbs splayed wide, bug-like eyes dead in its head. With childish curiosity Eric placed a finger at the exact point where it's stubby snout was pressed against the glass. The animal didn't move. Then, tensing the tip of his forefinger against his thumb, he flicked the hard surface. The toad exploded backwards, powerful hind legs scrabbling in the gravel. It shot across its tiny home with a single kick, and struggled to burrow its head into the far corner, stones snick-snicking under the water. Unnerved, Eric stepped back, glancing towards the side door.

On the work surface stood a row of microscopes, each one shrouded in a protective plastic cover. Beneath the semi-opaque sheeting twin viewfinders strained upwards, like the bulging stalk-eyes of suffocating insects. Eric realised all the animals were here on a kind of death row – waiting for the dissecting blade. Then his view of the apparatus was lost as the assistant opened the side room door.

She stepped back out, Eric's blanket folded neatly over one arm. 'There – it's not suffering anymore.'

'Thank you,' said Eric, then sorrowfully added, 'I just couldn't stop my car in time.'

She smiled sympathetically, 'Don't feel guilty – it's just one of those things. By the way, it didn't have any collar on, so best I just put it in the incinerator, don't you think?'

Eric nodded, 'I suppose so.' She stepped towards him, holding out the blanket, but Eric said, 'Would you mind burning that too? I couldn't bear to ever sit on it again.'

'Of course,' she replied gently.

'Right,' said Eric taking a deep breath, 'I'd better be on my way. Thanks again.' As he stepped towards the door he saw her looking down at his jacket. Then she pointed towards his side and said, 'Er – excuse me?'

Eric's heart lurched, and he heard blood rushing through his ears. 'Yes?' he said, fearfully meeting her gaze.

She held a finger towards his pocket and said, 'What's that?'

Eric looked slowly down as she added, 'There's something on your sleeve.'

He bent his right arm and held his elbow up. The remains of the slug were smeared across the tweed. 'I wonder how that got there?' he said. 'Thanks for pointing it out – I've got some tissues in my car.'

Back in his study he went on to the internet and typed in the words 'Euthanol'. The search brought up a variety of sites, many in foreign languages. He scrolled down, clicking on a promising looking government entry. The site was titled, 'Medicines (Veterinary Drugs, Prescription Only) Order 2001.' It gave very general notes on drug classification by the Veterinary Medicines Directorate, but nothing on dosages.

He returned to the search results and clicked on a report titled, 'Too slow to win.' It was a review of a *Kenyon Confronts* investigation that exposed the widespread killing of greyhounds that were no longer at their peak for racing. The preferred poison was a barbiturate called Euthanol.

Eric picked up the bottle of the almost colourless solution and examined the label. The manufacturer was called 'Remial'. He typed that in and clicked on 'search' again. The company's web site came top of the list. He clicked on it and then, once the site came up, selected a box titled, 'Veterinary Professionals'. He was taken through to an inner screen where he selected

'Information on Products'. But his way was barred by a field asking for his username and password.

He logged off and examined the bottle, wondering how much would be required.

19

As he passed the driveway to Embleton Farm he slowed the car right down – creeping along another fifty metres or so until he saw the narrow track on his left. A ditch just to the side of the road prevented him from pulling up on the grass verge, so he turned into the mouth of the track itself, parking a short way down. Immediately he killed his headlights, gathered his satchel off the passenger seat next to him and began walking down the path. After a couple of minutes he could just make out a glow from a window floating in the darkness ahead. Then, slowly, the dull white of the caravan surrounding it became visible.

He paused under the gently shifting branches of the beech trees, shoes crackling on the shell casings scattered on the ground around him. Once again he ran through everything in his head. Suddenly a shiver ran through him and he took a long breath inwards. Something inside him said that he had reached the point of no return; if he carried on now he couldn't go back. There was still time, he told himself, to just turn around and walk away; no one would ever know. As he stood there deciding what to do he was aware of a small ticking noise in the tree above him. Something hollow bounced on the track beside him. A beechnut shell, he thought, from a squirrel feeding above. Then a small object glanced off his head and it suddenly occurred to him that it was night: and squirrels weren't nocturnal. He tilted his head backwards and, as he squinted at the shadowy leaves above, something large and dark detached itself and dropped towards him.

Involuntarily he stepped back, eyes wide with fear and confusion. Rubble landed barely a foot in front of him, sank instantly on to his haunches and extended a set of knuckles to the ground to steady himself. A grinning voice said, 'Roy Bull, reporting for duty, sir.'

Eric stared in astonishment at the black form bunched in the gloom before him, blinked several times and cleared his throat. 'You caught me by surprise.'

'Thanks,' replied Rubble, straightening up. The top of his head came to just below Eric's chin, and the taller man wondered what to do. Should they shake hands? Deciding that, instead, a show of authority was needed, he gave a business-like cough as if indicating to a room of students that he required silence. Then he looked over Rubble's head towards the caravan and said coldly, 'Shall we proceed with the interview?'

Rubble stepped backwards, 'Was that wrong? It was wrong. I only wanted to show you my stealth skills.' He sounded dismayed, as if the pathway to his rejection had already been embarked upon.

'No – I'm impressed. And surprised, that's all,' replied Eric.

'Oh right,' said Rubble. The balance tipped in his favour once more, he cheerfully set off towards his home. Eric regarded the broad sloping shoulders and thick, bullet head, sensing the hope in the spring of his stride. He followed in silence.

As they reached the caravan he looked at the mass of shapes that seemed to be swarming up the white plastic wall. 'What are those?' he asked.

Rubble didn't even look at them. 'Tails. From the vermin that come on the farm. I shoot 'em with this,' he pulled open the door and pointed at the air rifle mounted in its sling on the wall. Not waiting for his visitor, he stepped up into the caravan.

Eric quickly glanced at the darkness all around, then followed him in. Immediately he realised the ceiling was a fraction too low for him – he could feel a strand of hair on the top of his head brushing against it. Keeping his head slightly bowed he looked around from under his bushy eyebrows. The monitor in the corner filled the caravan with a weak, bluish light. He tried not to react to the smell of mildew that had closed in around him. Having decided not to risk taking the initiative, Rubble looked expectantly at him, waiting for his instructions.

'Right, let's sit down,' said Eric, pointing to the soft seats on either side of the fold down table. Rubble immediately obeyed and Eric slid on to the cushioned seat opposite, its waxy nylon surface making it feel damp.

'Before we go any further, you're required to sign the Official Secrets Act. Nothing that is discussed in this interview can ever be repeated to anyone else. Do you understand?'

Rubble nodded solemnly, watching as Eric opened a leather satchel and extracted a plastic A4 sleeve. Inside was a single sheet of paper. Earlier in the day Eric had doctored a standard Departmental Confidentiality form used for clinical research and other projects. He'd deleted all reference to the University and replaced it with the words, 'Her Majesty's Government'. He removed the lid of his Parker pen and pushed the sheet across the table, 'Would you like to read it first?'

With his hands nervously clutching his knees under the table, Rubble leaned forward and looked at the form. The text was crammed on to the page, the language onerous and long-winded. He couldn't even begin to understand it – but he was able to make out the University crest at the top of the page. Automatically he committed it to memory. 'It's OK,' he whispered.

'Good – please sign here then.' Eric put a cross in the box at the bottom and handed the pen to Rubble. In an awkward, childish hand he slowly wrote, 'Roy Bull.'

'Thank you,' replied Eric, whisking the form away. 'I needn't impress on you the importance of honouring the Official Secrets Act. Now, do you have the advertisement you used for calling Room 101?'

Rubble quickly reached for the card hidden under his sketch pad and handed it to Eric. It was swiftly returned to the satchel. Eric suspected the rest of the charade was hardly necessary, but he decided to carry it out anyway, 'What is your occupation?'

Rubble didn't reply and Eric, noticing his frown, rephrased the question, 'What do you do for a job?'

Rubble didn't hesitate, 'Work on the farm over there,' he nodded to the wall. 'In charge of the chickens.'

'And how do you look after them?' Eric asked, steering the conversation towards the answers he wanted.

'Don't look after them. I just . . . keep check on 'em.'

'So if one's ill, you call a vet?'

Rubble almost laughed. 'A vet? No, I'll wring its neck and throw it out. Can't keep ill ones. Might be catching. Egg production could go down.'

'And what about if it's old?'

'Same thing. "If it's not laying, it's not living," says Mr Wicks. It's me kills them.'

'I understand,' said Eric, taking the ink blot cards and a clipboard out of his bag. 'Could we have some more light please?'

Rubble flicked a switch by his side and two wall mounted lamps came on, little tassels swaying under the fake velvet shades.

'Right. I'm going to turn over these cards and show you the shapes on the other side. This isn't a test where your answers are right or wrong. I just want you to tell me what you see on the other side in one or two words. Is that clear?'

Rubble shifted uncomfortably in his seat. 'OK'.

Eric propped the clipboard on one knee so Rubble couldn't see what he wrote. Then, with pen ready, he flipped over the first card and glanced up at Rubble, eyebrows raised.

Rubble looked at the card, at Eric, at the card again. Frowning, he said, 'It's a big drip of ink.'

Keeping his voice neutral Eric replied, 'Yes, that's correct. But what does it look like?'

'Look like?' repeated Rubble, picking at his lower lip.

'A ship, a fish, a . . .' Eric looked at the spiky shaped lump, 'an alien?'

'Yeah!' Rubble agreed. 'A space monster.'

'Good,' Eric turned over the next card.

Rubble peered at the long jagged smear. 'The fire coming out of a US M2-2 flame thrower.'

Eric wrote 'aeiou' on the paper, 'Next.'

A squat shape, with a bulbous top and splayed bottom. 'A shell for a German Leichter mortar.'

The pronounciation was awful, but somehow the knowledge was there. Eric wrote out a line of exclamation marks. 'Next.'

A blurred horseshoe shape, edges blurred. 'The Sudetland.'

Shocked, Eric looked up, 'I'm sorry. Did you mean the Sudetenland?'

'Yes,' replied Rubble. 'Sudetenland,' emphasis on the syllable he'd missed out. He sat back, awaiting the next card.

A round shape, with slightly irregular edges. 'A Mills Bomb, number 36.'

Eric looked at him questioningly.

'A British hand grenade,' Rubble explained. 'But that one's had its pin removed.'

They continued onwards and every answer Rubble gave had a military slant to it. After they reached the final one Eric said, 'That's excellent,' packing the cards away. Earlier at his house, Eric had examined the two tests his colleague in the psychology department had lent him. But he'd decided the questions were too specific and detailed for his purposes. He folded the top sheet from the clipboard in half and placed it in his bag. Underneath was a list of questions based on those from his recent video recording of *Blade Runner*.

'Right, I'm now going to ask you a series of imaginary questions. Just relax and answer them in your own time.'

Rubble nodded nervously.

'It's your birthday. You receive a gift. It's a calf skin wallet. Do you accept it?'

'Someone buys me a present?' Rubble asked, sounding surprised. 'Yeah, I would.'

'You've got a young son. He shows you his collection of butterflies, along with the jam jar he suffocates them in. How does it make you feel?'

'OK.'

'You're watching television. Suddenly you notice there's a wasp crawling up your arm. What do you do?'

'Kill it.'

'You're in a restaurant. People are eating boiled dog. Do you have any?'

'If they give me some.'

'You are in a desert. You look down and see a tortoise lying on its back, belly baking in the hot sun. What do you do?'

'Take it with me.'

'Why?'

'If I'm in a desert, I might need to eat it later.'

When he reached the final question on his list – the one asking how the subject felt about his mother, the one which prompted the replicant in *Blade Runner* to blast out the stomach of his interrogator from under the table, Eric found himself hesitating. He looked into Rubble's emotionless eyes, and just said, 'Very good, that concludes the test.'

Rubble stared down at the table, resignation like a blanket round his shoulders.

'It's rare that I interview a candidate with a

psychological profile as perfect as yours,' Eric announced.

Rubble looked up, registered Eric's smile, but his own expression didn't change. Eric saw that he didn't understand. 'You've passed. Well done.' He held a hand out across the formica. Rubble looked at it for an instant.

'I passed?' he asked incredulously. 'I have?'

'Absolutely, you're now an agent for Her Majesty's Government.'

He grabbed Eric's hand with both of his and simply squeezed. After a couple of seconds one of Eric's knuckles cracked. 'Congratulations,' said Eric, pulling his fingers from Rubble's thankful grip. Then, just to satisfy his own curiosity, he continued, 'Last thing – and this is very much a formality. We conduct interviews in the applicant's home so we can gain a more thorough insight into their personality. Can I look around yours?'

Rubble stared at him nonplussed. 'You want to look around in here?'

'Yes,' said Eric getting up.

'Well, I don't have much.' Rubble began pointing, 'Here's the sitting room. Kitchen. Over there's the bog. And shower.'

'These comics. Your collection?' said Eric, twirling a finger round, noting the slight pain in his knuckle.

'Yeah, been buying them for years,' he said proudly.

Eric removed a magazine from the shelf. *Great Battles of the 20th Century*. The top right hand corner of the cover was taken up by a yellow flash loudly proclaiming, 'First issue, half price!'

Eric opened it up and saw a detailed diagram of El Alamein. 'One of the ink blot cards reminded you of the Sudetenland. How did you know that?' he casually asked.

'Mr Williams in the post office,' said Rubble, getting up too. 'He lets me ask him things about what's in the magazines. Explains bits to me.'

'I see,' said Eric, putting the magazine back. 'And this book?' Eric nodded at the child's sketch pad on the corner of the table.

'Maps. From my comics,' Rubble opened it, revealing an intricate rendition of a city centre. It was labelled 'Berlin. May, 1945.'

Eric went over to the fridge. 'What sort of food do you like?'

'Don't mind,' replied Rubble, getting up too. Eric could see he was getting flustered again. He opened the small white door and peered inside. Two chickens. Milk, cheese, eggs, yoghurt. Some carrots, partially covered in mud.

'Mrs Wicks brings me a bag of stuff once a week. Buys it from my wages. And I'm allowed all the chickens I want off the farm.' As he spoke Eric was opening cupboard doors, slowly approaching the other end of the room. He saw Rubble's eyes flick nervously towards his bedroom door.

'And is this your bedroom?'

Rubble stepped defensively towards the door, but didn't dare refuse the inspection, 'Yes.'

Eric turned the plastic handle and pushed the thin door open. A salty smell, one he recognised from his own sheets. He flicked the light switch on, but did not step inside. A dishevelled single bed, blankets bunched at the bottom, sheets stained half way up. A yellowish pillow pushed up against the headboard. Taped to the wall above it was a large pencil sketch of the head and shoulders of a Romany-looking woman. Long black, curly hair, a large round earring, big brown eyes. He turned to the far end of the room. More tails.

'What sort of animal are they from?' asked Eric.

'Cats,' whispered Rubble, shame filling his voice.

Eric turned and looked questioningly at the shorter man.

'Some of the villagers thought I'd killed their cats. You know – when they come to the farm hunting. Trying to kill chickens. Miss Strines reported me, and Constable Jardine questioned me about it. But she didn't look in here. I said I hadn't.' His arms hung at his sides. 'Have I failed?' he asked miserably.

Eric looked at the forlorn collection of appendages and allowed himself a brief smile. As he pulled the door closed he said, 'Not at all. Your answers to the police questions show initiative. Well done.' He pointed Rubble back towards the table and, as they stepped towards it, he regarded the back of the younger man's skull. Here was a brain all but untouched by the educational system, a mind at the opposite end of the learning spectrum to his. Yet, for all their differences, he felt a stirring of affection for him. He reached out and gave him a fatherly pat on the back.

20

Once he'd read the opening paragraph he turned straight to the conclusion and read that. It seemed to answer the questions posed at the start of the essay. He quickly skimmed through the pages in between, occasionally dropping red ticks on to the text where he spotted dates or significant names. Quickly he reached the final page again, casually wrote a 'B' at the end and tossed it on to the pile of other marked scripts on the floor by his desk. He turned to his computer and jiggled the mouse so the screen returned to life. He entered the grade on to a spread sheet, leant back in his chair and sighed. Then, tensing the ball of one foot against the floor, Julian spun himself through one hundred and eighty degrees and looked out across the dark campus. Rising above the trees on the other side of the park was a hall of residence.

A multitude of windows glowed, various coloured curtains giving it the look of a strange mosaic. Once again he found himself wondering whether to bring a pair of binoculars into his office, after all, not every pair of curtains was completely drawn.

He imagined all the students in there. In their bedrooms. Socialising, drinking, planning which pubs and clubs to spend the night in. So free and full of life.

Slowly he got up and went over to the photo on his middle bookshelf. His tutorial group from the previous year. Sat on the lawn outside the department, smiling at the camera, eyes in shadow from the sun directly above. His eyes lingered over one particular female student. Alice. He seemed so close to succeeding with her. Had given her plenty of undeserved 'A' grades, encouraged her to apply for a research position in the department. He looked at her sitting there, delighted with her 2:1. Days away from graduating. Days away from when it would have been safe to make his move. But then she vanished – lured down to London by a graduate training position with some multinational.

Eyes narrowed with regret, he slid his hand round the back of the photo frame. From the shadow behind he pulled out the feather he'd retrieved from the coffee-room floor a few days before. He held it before his face and ran a nail down the stiff edge, listening to the filaments rasp. And he thought about Clare. Considered her.

21

They sat facing each other, the satchel on the table between them. Rubble still couldn't relax. He fidgeted and scratched, uncomfortably looking around.

'Is there something else you want to tell me?' the Professor gently asked.

Rubble shrugged his shoulders. 'Just can't believe it. All this – me working as a Government agent.'

'Well, it's for real – you can believe it all.'

'But I've been turned down by the army. Lots of times. I never thought I'd work on secret stuff.'

Eric smiled condescendingly at his mention of the army. 'You can't compare the army and its personnel to the type of people we employ. Oh no.' He wagged a finger. 'This work is far, far more sensitive. It calls for a very . . . particular sort of person. And your psychological profile and experience on this battery farm are both ideal.'

Rubble's crooked smile reappeared and he put his thick forearms on the table.

'Now,' Eric carried on, 'you're familiar with euthanasia?'

Rubble's forehead bunched up and he struggled with the first vowel, 'Youth. . .'

'Anasia,' Eric quickly finished the word for him. 'You know how there's so many old people around? Your village is probably full of them.'

Rubble's face was still registering blank and Eric, sensing the need for an actual example, said, 'That Miss Strines you mentioned. The one who said you'd killed her cat. How old is she?'

Rubble looked as if he was smelling sour milk. 'Really old.'

'There you go. Now, many of these old people have had enough of living. They don't want to struggle on any longer. They just want a nice peaceful death, in their own bed. And the Government can't afford to look after them all either. It costs us a lot of money, and they're not really much use any more. They don't actually do anything – not even work.' He paused, wary of loading on too much information too quickly. 'Everything clear so far?'

Rubble was thinking. Tentatively he raised a finger, as if in class, 'Like the chickens?'

Eric breathed a sigh of relief. This was the association he was looking to create. 'How do you mean?' he asked encouragingly.

'The chickens are no good either after a while. They get old and stop laying.'

'And then what happens?'

'I kill 'em.'

Eric placed his palms together with a soft pat. A

single, faint clap. 'That's exactly what this project is all about. Any old people who've had enough just contact us on a special phone number. We agree a night to visit. Then they take a sleeping tablet before they go to bed and we arrive later on, let ourselves quietly into their house and put them to sleep. They never feel a thing. No pain, no suffering. After that we call the undertakers and they have a nice funeral, just as if they'd died normally. No one else, not even their family, needs to know that we helped them to sleep. It's all a big secret.'

Rubble nodded his understanding.

'OK.' From the bag in front of him Eric took out the other pay-as-you-go mobile he'd bought. Earlier that day he'd charged it up, but hadn't added any credit to it. Next he took out a charger. 'This is the phone I'll contact you on. You don't need to know its number. All you do is keep it plugged in and out of sight. Now where are your plug sockets?'

Rubble pointed to the wall by the small cupboard next to him. 'Perfect, we'll plug it in there and put the phone in the cupboard, out of sight. When I call you it will be in the evening for a job taking place later that night. Happy?'

'Yeah!' said Rubble enthusiastically, looking at the phone on the table.

'When the phone rings you press this button to answer it and this button to end the call. Now show me. Which button to answer?'

Rubble pointed at the green button.

'And which button to end the call?'

His finger pointed to the red button.

'Excellent', Eric continued. 'Now, you're to continue with your job as normal – do everything you usually do. The jobs I'll call you about are just an occasional extra. Payment is in cash at the end of the month. £75 per person you put to sleep, OK?'

Rubble nodded again and then said, 'I'd do it for free.'

'I'm sorry?'

'Serving my country. I'd do it for free.'

'Very commendable, thank you,' Eric replied. 'Your role is as an injector. I'm the co-ordinator for this area, most nights I drive two or three agents like yourself to different jobs. The entire project is top secret, and conducted on a need-to-know basis. I am known as Agent Orange. You will be Agent White. Any equipment I give you is to be returned after each job. You are to keep nothing. Understood?'

Rubble nodded once again.

'For every job I'll pick you up from here and drop you off at the address, or near it. When I drop you off I'll let you know where the subject has left the backdoor key, so you can get into their house. You go inside, administer the injection, lock the door again and wait for me at your rendezvous point. Once I pick you up, you return everything to me and I'll drive you back here. All clear, Agent White?'

Rubble replied, 'Yes sir, Agent Orange.'

'Good. Now this,' Eric removed a syringe and hypodermic needle from the bag, 'is what you'll put the subjects to sleep with. For real jobs I'll give you a syringe with the correct dose already loaded up. But now I need to train you.' Eric looked to the fridge. 'Could you bring me one of those chickens?'

Eagerly Rubble got to his feet and did as he was ordered. As he placed the dead bird on the table Eric noticed the grime under his fingernails and ingrained in the wrinkled skin of his knuckles. 'You'll also need to wash your hands thoroughly.'

Looking slightly sheepish, Rubble went over to the sink and poured some washing-up liquid on to a scouring pad. Then he began scrubbing away at his hands as if he was removing rust from an engine part.

Eric pulled open the paperbacked plastic wrapper and removed the syringe. Then he did the same with the needle, pulling off the protective cap and fitting the thin length of metal mounted in its lime green plastic base to the tip of the syringe. 'OK, the medicine we use is almost clear, so sterile water is perfect for training purposes,' said Eric taking out a small bottle of mineral water from his bag and removed the cap. Next he lowered the needle towards the neck of the bottle. Like a mosquito's proboscis, the metal tip entered the liquid and Eric drew two millilitres into the barrel. He held it to the light, flicked the plastic side to dislodge any air bubbles to the top, then gently squeezed the plunger until a single bright bead welled up from the needle's tip. Rubble watched in silent fascination. 'Now, we don't want to cause any pain. So you need to follow this part very carefully.'

Eric cast his mind back to his days as a social worker, and the many home visits where he watched as the district nurse trained a newly qualified student. 'First we'll practice inserting the needle. The key to a successful injection is puncturing the flesh with confidence.' He held up the needle so they could examine the tip. 'You see how the end of the needle is cut away at an angle to form a sharp point?'

Squinting at the tip, Rubble nodded.

'That's called a chamfered edge. What you do is approach the arm at about this angle,' he held the needle at about 45 degrees to the chicken's thigh, 'and push the very tip in with a firm action like this.'

He smoothly inserted the needle about one centimetre into the skin.

'You see how I didn't slide it in too slowly, but I didn't stab it either? Now, you try.'

Rubble held the syringe like it was made of gossamer.

'OK,' said Eric, 'now bring the tip of the needle towards the skin and press it in.'

Eric was surprised at the younger man's deftness of touch. Despite his thick, gnarled fingers, he inserted the needle at precisely the right angle and to exactly the right depth.

'Excellent. Now slowly push some water in. That's right, good. Did you feel how you had to push to get the needle through the outer skin?'

Rubble nodded.

'That's just how it feels when you enter the vein on someone's arm. Veins are made up of three layers, so you have to press fairly hard to get the needle through. But once you've punctured it, the needle moves around more easily, so you know you're in.'

Rubble practised a few more times, then Eric rolled up his sleeve.

'OK, you're ready to practise on me. He exchanged the needle for a clean one and refilled the barrel with water. Then he laid his right forearm on the table, underside up. He pointed to the crook of his elbow. 'There's a good vein – easy to see, plump and straight. Run your finger over it. Can you feel it under the skin?'

Slowly Rubble placed a finger on the bluish line and nodded.

'Right, keep your finger there to stop the vein moving about and, with your other hand, insert the needle.'

His face intense with concentration, Rubble brought the needle up against Eric's skin and, a little too firmly, punctured the surface. He didn't stop pressing quite quickly enough and Eric felt the needle pass through the other side of the vein and enter the tissue beyond. A sharp pain shot down into his fingertips and Eric winced. Rubble looked up and, seeing the pain in Eric's face, pulled the needle straight back out. Blood immediately welled up out of the tiny puncture and began spreading out beneath the flesh in the form of a livid, purple haematoma.

'Not to worry,' said Eric through gritted teeth, pulling a handkerchief from his pocket and dabbing at the wound. 'Let's try the other arm.'

They located the same vein on his left arm and this time Rubble completed the injection perfectly. 'Great. Now, you can tell if you're in properly by pulling the plunger out a tiny bit and seeing if any blood enters the barrel.'

Rubble pulled at the 't' shaped top of the plunger and a wisp of red was dragged up into the water, where it slowly lost its shape and definition inside the syringe. 'There you are, that's perfect. Now push in a couple millilitres of water.'

Gently, Rubble pushed the plunger in and Eric felt a coldness entering his forearm. 'OK, that's enough. Now you can pull the needle out.'

The metal tip reemerged from Eric's arm, followed by a tiny dot of blood.

'Well done, you're a natural,' said Eric encouragingly.

Once the man had gone Rubble stood in the centre of his living room and took several deep breaths. He looked with wonder at the wire for the mobile phone leading unobtrusively into his cupboard. Crouching down, he opened the door and lifted up the handset, testing its weight in his hand, turning it over, smelling the new plastic. Everything was for real, he was actually a Government agent. 'Hello, Agent White,' he said quietly into the mouthpiece.

Suddenly he remembered something. Quickly he sat down at the table and pulled his sketchpad and pens towards him. Then, selecting a new page, he drew from memory – and with almost perfect accuracy – the crest that had been at the top of the Official Secrets Act he'd signed earlier. Once it was finished he examined the image of the pair of wings on the star-studded shield, puzzling over the Latin inscription curling on the banner below it, *Per doctrinam ad astra.*

22

Clare sat smoking a roll-up in the Entertainment Officer's study, nervously looking down on to the flag-stoned concourse leading up to the Union building's main doors. Students hurried in and out of the entrance below, laughing, slapping backs, hugging books – the end of term had given everyone a lift.

Eventually Clare said, 'There's a few people gathering – that crowd over there. Must be at least fifteen lads.'

The Entertainment Officer craned his head back to look out of the window. 'That's Castle Halls football team. They always meet there for twelve o'clock on a Saturday.'

'Oh,' said Clare, suddenly nervous again. Then, to her relief, she spotted three or four people off her course sit down on one of the wooden benches lining the walkway.

Standing up, she jammed the roll-up out in the ashtray on his desk. 'There's some people I know, wish me luck.'

'Yeah, go for it,' he said without enthusiasm, looking back down at his *NME*.

Clare picked up the clipboard and half a dozen

placards she'd made the previous night and jogged lightly down the stone staircase.

'Excuse me, excuse me,' she called out, manoeuvering her way through the throng of people in the foyer.

As she squeezed past a couple of girls they spotted what she was carrying, 'Rent march?' one said, pointing at the signs under Clare's arm.

'Yeah! We're meeting up outside,' said Clare, carrying on through the doors, anxious that the others might give up and leave before she could get to them. She made her way over to the group on the bench. 'Hi there, it's a good day for it!' she exclaimed cheerily, propping the placards up at the edge of the bench so people could clearly read the bold message of *No rent increase!*

Her fellow marchers nodded and agreed. One bloke got up to examine how she'd attached the cardboard squares to the lengths of dowelling. Clare recognised him from a previous march against proposals to extend a nearby stretch of motorway. 'Good work, Clare. Is that trenching tape?' he asked, running a finger over the lengths of black sticky plastic securing the signs.

'Um, I don't know Simon. It's just what the man in the ironmongers recommended,' replied Clare, wrong-footed by the question.

The two girls from the Union foyer joined them, and a couple more drifted over from the opposite side of the concourse.

'Hi, thanks for coming,' Clare addressed each one in turn, clutching the clipboard to her chest. 'OK, it's a quarter-to-twelve. Let's put our names down now and it'll get the ball rolling. Er, has anyone got a pen?'

Simon quickly produced one from a pocket of his German Army issue coat. The clipboard was passed round and each person added their name to the printed grid. 'Great, now let's try and get as many people to sign the petition as possible. Then we set off at midday.' The group looked at her uncertainly and Clare realised with dismay that she would have to initiate the proceedings. She picked up one of the placards and holding it by her side, called out to the passing flow of people, 'Help stop the rent increases! Sign our petition now!'

Most suddenly appeared to be deaf, hurrying past with heads down. One or two looked questioningly at her, eyes flicking over the sign, before carrying on regardless. Praying some of the others would join in, she tried again, 'Don't let them rip you off! Stop the rent increases!' She felt herself beginning to flush. From next to her Simon whispered, 'How much will the rent increase actually be?'

Clare looked at him, 'Oh – nearly ten quid,' she exaggerated.

'Save yourself a tenner! Stop the rent increases!' he shouted aggressively.

The mention of money caused a few people to slow

their steps. A couple stopped further down the concourse to watch.

Seeing the effect this latest cry had, the two girls from the foyer joined in, 'Save yourself a tenner! Stop the rent increases!'

More people slowed and someone said, 'Ten quid? Is that how much it will be?'

Clare tried to answer that it would probably be nearer five a month, but Simon cut in savagely, 'Ten fucking quid. A week. It's a piss take!'

'Ten quid?' said the person to his mate. 'Fucking outrageous!' He turned to Clare, 'Here, I'll sign.' He grabbed the clipboard and held up one knee for a platform. She saw with relief that the heading she'd typed out the previous night simply read, 'I oppose the scandalous rent increase in University accommodation.' There was no mention of money. After scrawling his name and address, he handed the clipboard to his mate who did the same. 'Cheers guys,' said Clare, 'we're marching at twelve.'

All of a sudden they looked uncomfortable. 'Ah, we've got some stuff to sort out . . .' one said edging away. Simon shouted above their excuse, 'Save a tenner! Sign now!'

More people stopped to add their signatures and Clare thankfully took a step back. From her left a voice said, 'Looks like you're on a roll.'

She looked down and saw Patricia Du Rey smiling up

at her, a silk scarf around her neck, expensive handbag over one shoulder. However often she saw Patricia, it never failed to amaze Clare how tiny her tutor was.

'Pat! Hi – are you joining us then?'

She shook her head regretfully, 'I've got to get to the airport, Michel is flying in from Brussels at 12:45 and I only have him for the weekend.'

'Ah, that's nice,' replied Clare.

'But I'll gladly sign,' she took a gold pen from her bag and Clare retrieved the clipboard from Simon. 'Thanks for your support,' she said.

'My pleasure Clare. It's good to see some students still taking an active involvement in issues.'

As she added her name to the petition Clare noticed her newly painted lilac coloured nails. 'That's a beautiful shade of polish,' she said.

Patricia held up one hand. 'Do you think so? Thanks. I've just had them done in that new place by Tesco Metro.' She lowered her voice so only Clare could hear, 'If you go in this week, they'll do your toenails for free.' She winked at Clare, then waved goodbye to the group, heels clicking on the slabs of stone as she walked away.

After another ten minutes passed they had collected seven or eight sheets of signatures. But no extra people for the march. Clare looked at her watch. 'OK everyone, we only have police clearance to be on Williams Street until 12:30. We'd better get going.'

They were just gathering together when a couple of

lads from the football team sauntered over. 'What is it? Ten pound rent increase?' asked one with a broad estuary accent, lower lip hanging down.

'Yes,' replied Clare eagerly, holding out a clipboard. 'Do you want to sign?'

'Ten quid?' He looked down at his brand new trainers, then pulled a wadge of notes from his pocket. Voice full of derision, he said, 'That's fucking peanuts.' He waved the money in front of her face. 'If you're finding it hard to afford your place, you can always spend a few nights at mine, like.' A slow lick of his lips.

Catcalls sounded from the rest of the team behind. Clare lowered the clipboard and held up a finger. 'In your dreams you loser.'

Both lads started laughing and began stalking back to their mates. A few steps away the one with the new trainers turned round and said, 'You're probably a lesbian anyway.'

Clare was about to shout something back when Eric stepped between them, satchel under his arm. 'Is this student using sexually abusive language against you?' he asked sharply, peering questioningly at Clare. She looked beyond the professor's pointing finger at the crestfallen footballer, the rest of his team dissolving away behind him. Discriminatory language of a sexual, religious or racial nature broke Union Rules; all she had to say was yes and he'd get an official warning from the University. Probably a decent fine too.

'It's all right. I've got more important things to do than waste time with him.'

Eric replied, 'Oh, it's no waste of time. I'll happily deal with it.' He turned to the footballer. 'Your Student Union card please.'

The student weighed up the option of running for it, but Simon had stepped behind him and was waiting within grabbing distance. Reluctantly he pulled out his wallet and produced his Union card. Eric noted his name down. 'I'll refer this to the Union Executive. You will, no doubt, be contacted soon.'

The young man walked quickly away, catching up with his mates as they loitered at the corner of the Union building.

'Thanks Professor,' said Clare, setting off down the main concourse. At the top of steps leading down on to Williams Street she stopped, noticing the two police cars parked half on the pavement below. She turned to her fellow marchers, 'Excellent, the police are already here. Who wants a whistle? I've only got three.'

As they headed down the steps and on to the pavement a policeman got out of his patrol car, 'Is this it?' he asked flatly, looking at the small group before him. 'Nine of you?'

Clare tried to sound positive. 'Absolutely! Can we get going?'

The policeman took a deep sigh and bent down to the driver's window of the first car. 'You might as well head off. No point in using two patrol cars for this.'

'Right, Sarge,' answered the driver. The car slipped into the traffic and disappeared.

Shaking his head very slightly the police sergeant walked to the car behind and said to the driver, 'OK, I'll lead them on foot, you follow in the car behind. They're only going a few hundred yards.'

The driver nodded wearily and the blue lights on top of the patrol car began to silently flash. The car slowly edged into the road, blocking the traffic behind.

'Go on then,' said the sergeant, holding out both hands to the empty road in front. Clare held up her placard, inhaled deeply, and was just about to shout out her slogan when a voice robbed the breath from her lungs.

'Spare any change?' a slurred voice said.

She looked down and saw a man sat with his back against the litter-bin by the bottom step. She recognised him from the small park area on the campus; usually he sat on a bench, maroon beret on his head, waving a bottle of cider around.

'Sorry mate.' A reflex reaction, accompanied by an explanatory pat of an empty pocket. Slightly embarrassed the rest of the group looked anywhere but at the man. Clare raised her placard again and stepped into the road.

'What do we want?' she screamed.

The chorus sounded behind her, 'No rent increases!'

'When do we want it?'

'Now!'

Someone began blowing a whistle and the gaggle set off down the road, attracting the occasional beep from motorists passing in the opposite direction. Shoppers stopped to watch the tiny procession, quizzical expressions on their faces. Occasional smirks. Shadowing them on the pavement was Eric. He'd undone the flap of his satchel and was thrusting Socialist Worker leaflets into the hands of anyone who would take them. After five minutes Clare's voice was growing hoarse. She turned around and, seeing Simon directly behind her, said, 'Fancy taking over for a bit?'

'Cheers!' he answered eagerly, and spun around. As he walked backwards he began clapping his hands, 'No ifs, no buts, no rent subsidy cuts!'

The group seemed relieved at having something else to shout about and joined in the chorus with renewed enthusiasm. Clare lifted the whistle hanging around her neck and began blowing quick blasts in time to Simon's clapping.

A short while later and they reached the east entrance to the University campus. The smell of food from a Louisiana Fried Chicken take-away hung in the air around them. They gathered on the pavement and the driver of the police car pulled up beside them so his colleague could climb back in.

As Clare thanked them Eric handed out two leaflets

to a couple of young men in suits coming out of the take-away joint. One, cheeks bulging with chicken burger, accepted Eric's leaflet and looked at the headlines of 'Blair-faced liar! Government reneges on another key promise! Smash the capitalist liars!'

The police car quickly accelerated away, allowing the backlog of traffic to finally speed up. Someone pressed a car horn. Another joined in and the students turned to the road, a couple holding up thumbs to say thank you for the support. But the driver, with his hand hanging out of the window, had curled his fingers and thumb into a circle. Slowly he began shuffling his hand up and down, a look of contempt on his face.

A mini cab driver had wound down his window, and as he passed the huddled group, he shouted in a heavy local accent, 'I've just missed my fare you bunch of pricks!'

Clare looked uncertainly at her fellow protesters. 'I think we'd better get back on campus.'

As she went to try and lead them away the suited man asked Eric very politely, 'Are you a student or a lecturer then?'

Eric nodded, 'A lecturer.'

'Then what the fuck,' he went on, voice suddenly hostile, 'are you handing this shit out for? What are you paid, around thirty grand?'

Behind them the traffic was speeding up. Someone yelled, 'Fucking student twats!' as they went past.

Eric calmly said, 'It's hardly relevant what I earn.'

'It is in my opinion,' answered the man. 'There you are, claiming a nice big salary off the Government – the capitalist Government – that pays your wages from my fucking taxes.'

'But it needn't be this way,' said Eric, face reddening. 'The system could be so much better.'

'I'm happy enough mate,' said the man, holding up the burger. 'I'm free, I'm full and I'm off to get pissed. My only complaint about this system is parasites like you.'

Eric looked at the reconstituted chicken meat hanging from the bread, grease staining the disposable napkin it was wrapped in. He didn't know where to start.

At that moment an empty coke can was thrown from a car. It bounced off a placard and clattered to the pavement. 'Wankers!' someone shouted. The man took a massive bite out of his burger as he and his friend began to walk away.

'Um, let's get through the gates,' said Clare uneasily, and they all moved quickly towards the entrance. 'Professor, are you coming with us?' asked Clare, trying to give Eric a dignified way out.

Eric stood rooted to the spot. 'No,' he answered softly. 'No, don't mind me. I must be elsewhere.' Without saying goodbye he strode off back in the direction they had just come.

23

Eric walked angrily along the campus perimeter. A short distance behind him, the University grounds opened into a small area of parkland, on the other side of which were a few halls of residence.

During the day it was the domain of students and drunks, often both. At night the atmosphere changed, despite the globe-shaped lamps lighting the pathways. A series of rapes a few years before and regular reports of students being jumped by local lads ensured most people skirted round the park once it was dark.

Deciding he needed to sit down for a while, Eric slipped through the next gap in the fence and, looking for a bench, set off along a footpath that lead between the rhododendron bushes. Soon he heard some slurred mumbling and as he entered a small clearing, he saw the beggar he'd noticed during the march, slumped on a bench. A three litre bottle of cider was clutched between his knees. Empty cans of Tennent's Super lay at his feet. Despite the warm weather he wore a threadbare blazer, woollen jumper and grey trousers, shiny at the knees.

Eric hesitated, wondering whether to turn back or stick to his side of the clearing and creep past. But the man's head lolled round and he said, ''ternoon to you, sir.' A hand went up to his temple and he flicked a feeble salute.

Eric realised he knew him. When he was a social worker the man's wife had been one of his cases. She had developed senile dementia and it was Eric's responsibility to arrange home help and, eventually, a permanent bed for her in a care home. Her husband's inability to assist in anyway had infuriated him.

The man was ex-armed forces, a paratrooper, if his memory served him correctly. That in itself was enough to provoke Eric's disdain, but the husband also seemed incapable (or unwilling as Eric suspected) of cooking or cleaning. Meals-on-wheels ended up providing for them both. All the man wanted to do was drink.

After his wife died he went further downhill, frequently turning up at the soup caravan Eric used to work in as a volunteer during the evenings. As the junkies descended from their shooting gallery on the top of a nearby multi-storey car park, he would come lurching down the road. Barely able to spoon the food into his own mouth, he was frequently sick on the kerb.

'Mr Aldy, how are you?'

The man fought to get himself upright, squinting hard and trying to make out who he was talking to. 'It's Eric, from the soup run.'

The old man's eyes narrowed even further as he grinned. Four teeth left in his head, lips curling inwards over bare gums. 'G' bless you, Eric. Have a seat, here.' He went to pat the bench by his side but missed. He began keeling over and Eric had to move fast to push him back upright.

'How are you Bert? Having a celebration?'

The man's chin had sunk on to his chest and he was staring at the ground beyond his splayed feet. ''bration, indeed.' He suddenly realised he was still holding a bottle of cider. 'Drink?' He struggled upright and lifted the bottle from his lap. It swayed in front of Eric.

'No thanks Bert,' said Eric, guiding it back between the grey flannel knees. 'And how are you keeping?'

The rumble came from far back in the his throat, 'Ooooooh not so bad, 'kyou.'

Eric searched the ground around the bench.

'Where's your beret Bert?' he asked loudly.

'Uh?'

'Your beret, from the paratroopers.'

'Kids. Kids have taken it. Taken the lot. Jus' my clothes lef' now. 'roken the door in. Can't even lock it.'

After Bert's wife had died, Eric arranged for him to be moved to a smaller council flat. It had been burgled repeatedly. First the electrical goods. Then other small items, including his medals. Next time the furniture and kitchenware. And now, it seemed, anything that could be worth a few pounds.

The man's eyes had closed and his breathing had begun to deepen. Eric looked at the folds beneath his chin, hanging over his collar, top button done up. He couldn't stop himself asking, 'Still in the same flat Bert?'

The old man didn't reply.

Eric leaned a little closer, 'Still in 50 Wood Road?'

''ty woo droad,' he mumbled.

'That's still your present address?'

'Mmmmm.'

Unsure if that was a yes or a no, Eric asked, 'Is that where you live now Bert?'

In reply the man let out a pig-like snore.

Frustrated, Eric got quietly to his feet, leaving the man to his drunken slumber.

24

'It was absolutely, ab-so-lute-ly, hideous,' sobbed Clare, writhing on her back, a cushion over her face.

In the armchair next to her, tears were coursing down Zoe's cheeks. 'Nine? Only nine of you?' She burst into a fresh fit of laughter. 'Oh my God. What did the policeman say again? Go on, tell me.'

She could hear Clare's muffled shouts of 'No, no, no!' coming from beneath the cushion, so she leaned forwards and dragged it off her friend's face. 'Tell me!'

Clare got a grip on herself, sat upright and took a deep breath. 'He said,' voice barely under control, 'is that it?'

They both fell back in their seats and began howling at the ceiling once again.

'Nightmare,' said Zoe, reaching for the half-burned joint in the ashtray. She sparked it up again and took a long drag. From the sofa Clare put on a local accent and said, 'I've missed my fare you pricks!'

Zoe started spluttering, the smoke erupting from her nose and mouth in a series of little clouds. 'Bitch!' she gasped, flinging the joint at her friend and doubling over in a coughing fit.

Clare quickly fished it out of her lap and took a

couple of drags herself. She rolled her eyes up and said, 'It must be top three for my most cringeworthy experiences ever. It's up there with the apple in the fishpond outburst.'

'God it sounds it,' said Zoe, wiping the tears from her eyes. 'And half the people only signed because they though it was a £10 a week increase. That's hilarious.'

Clare looked around the flat, suddenly serious. 'I know. Can you believe how cheap this place is? I felt such a fucking fraud.' She handed the joint back to her friend.

'Don't think that. You did what you've got to do. If organising that march helps you get a job in the department next year, it was well worth it. And you said Patricia saw you outside the Union building beforehand?'

'Yeah, she even signed the petition.'

'There you go then – it was definitely worth it for that.'

'I suppose so,' replied Clare. 'But that was the first and last I ever organise. It was horrible. Anyway,' her voice picked up, 'how's your job hunt going?' She picked up the local paper.

'Not bad. I've got three to call back on Monday to arrange times for going in with my portfolio.'

Clare looked at her friend, conscious that she was avoiding her eyes. Appreciating that Zoe's confidence had been badly knocked, Clare thought back to when she'd failed her maths 'A' level. She believed the world had come to an end, and it was Zoe who had picked her back up. All summer they'd crammed for it together and, when she retook it, she had passed. Determined to provide the same sort of support for her friend she said, 'That's excellent. They won't be able to resist you, you'll see.'

Zoe smiled, looking steadily at the telly even though it was switched off. 'Yeah well, fingers crossed.'

'They're slow aren't they? About getting back to you with an interview date?'

Zoe continued looking at the telly. 'Yeah, but most of these places are run pretty haphazardly. It's just a question of the studio manager finding a free half-hour to look through your stuff.'

'Oh,' said Clare, looking at her friend's profile. She glanced back at the paper, noticing it was well over a week old.

25

The sudden buzzing made Rubble jump. He looked around him, unsure of where the sound was coming from. Then it repeated itself and he knew it was the phone in the cupboard behind him. He knelt down and opened the door. It lay on the top shelf, waiting to be answered.

Carefully, as if it was a new born chick, he lifted it out. Following the instructions he'd been given, he pressed the green 'OK' button and waited for something to happen. The tiny diode by the handset's aerial blinked twice before Rubble remembered he should place the phone to his ear.

'Hello?'

'Agent White?'

'Yes – it's me.'

'Agent Orange here. I have a job for you tonight. Are you available?'

'Yes sir!'

'Good. Be ready for a 1:45 A.M. pick-up.'

Agent Orange hung up and Rubble looked at the phone. The display read O^2 once again. He placed it back inside the cupboard and gently shut the door. Kneeling there, he drummed his fingers on his thighs while he thought. Balaclava, black jumper and hunting knife would do – he should go properly dressed he decided. For stealth and secrecy. He went into his bedroom and removed the items from the tiny wardrobe built into the corner. Glancing at the small clock by his bed he saw the digital numbers read 10:43 P.M. He turned out all the caravan's lights and, back at his table, parted the curtain slightly to look out into the blackness beyond. Everything was quiet as he sat back in his seat to wait, the side of his face lit by the softly glowing monitor.

After what seemed like half the night a pair of dipped headlights turned into the top of his track. He watched as the lights passed along behind the trunks of the beech trees before the vehicle crept round the bend in the track and stopped about twenty metres away. The lights suddenly died, but the engine kept running. Rubble gathered up his stuff and left the caravan. Outside the night was thick and heavy, the air perfectly still around him.

As he neared the car he could see Agent Orange's marble white fingers curled around the steering wheel. They seemed so smooth and thin. A hand gestured him towards the passenger door so he walked round the front of the car. In the bottom right hand corner of the windscreen, above the tax disc, was a small sticker. Rubble noted, with some surprise, that it was marked with the same crest that he'd seen at the top of the Official Secrets Act document.

He opened the door and looked in.

'Good evening Agent White. Get in please.'

He climbed inside, the car creaking slightly on its wheels as he did so. Agent Orange reached up to turn on the interior light. As he did so Rubble realised he was wearing latex gloves. That's why his hands had looked so white through the windscreen 'What are those?' Agent Orange asked, pointing to the balaclava, jumper and knife on Rubble's lap.

'For stealth,' answered Rubble, holding the items up.

Agent Orange quickly replied, 'No balaclava and no knife. You're to look like any normal person. Maybe someone walking home from their girlfriend's. The jumper is OK.'

Rubble mumbled an apology, opened the door and threw the balaclava and weapon out.

Once the door was shut Agent Orange handed him a pair of latex gloves and announced, 'Tonight's subject is an elderly woman. She lives alone in a flat and called us last week for our services. She's left her key by the backdoor under the third pot on the left. Normally she sleeps in her wheelchair, or in a bed in the sitting room. But it's a four room ground floor flat, so you shouldn't have any trouble finding her.'

Once Rubble's gloves were properly on, Eric turned the interior light off and the headlights back on. They reversed backwards, rear of the car wreathed in a soft red glow, purple foxgloves hanging from the crimson hedge. Back on the main road the car headed straight for the motorway, where its speed picked up. They drove in silence until the pooled lights of the city's edge became visible.

'Never been here before,' Rubble suddenly stated.

'To Manchester?' asked Agent Orange.

'Yeah.'

Eric pondered over this new piece of information, worried that the complicated network of streets might confuse and unsettle him. 'Are you bothered about built up areas?' he asked.

'Nope,' replied Rubble. 'Got maps for lots of them. Stalingrad, Berlin, Kosovo, Kabul.'

Shortly after they were driving down the main road he'd parked on earlier. Now it was completely deserted, the take-away shops empty. Rubble looked at the neon signs, watching them flash on and off. Up ahead a black cat ghosted across the road and both men avidly watched it right up until the moment it vanished beneath a gate. Eric turned down a side street and drove to the T junction at the end. As he swung the car slowly to the right he nodded at the cluster of bungalows opposite, 'The subject lives in number five, far right-hand corner.

As they passed the bungalow itself he added, 'That's her garden fence, go down the side alley there and round to the back door.' Eric drove to the end of the road and pulled up in an empty layby in front of some locked-up shops. Everything was black and silent. He reached under the seat and removed the syringe, then handed it with gloved fingers to Rubble. 'Remember, the key is under the third pot to the left of the door. Once you've completed the job, put the key back, return to this spot and wait for me behind those shops. I've got another agent to drop back home on the other side of town, so I'll be about twenty-five minutes.'

'Yes sir, Agent Orange,' Rubble replied. Climbing from the car, he gently pushed the door shut, imagining he was a spy dropped behind enemy lines on a mission. Hands in pockets, he loped off up the pavement as Eric pulled away to find a parking space on a nearby street.

26

As Rubble walked along the pavement blank windows looked down at him from all around. He glanced excitedly towards several, noticing the curtains drawn tightly together on the other side of the glass. Soon he was at the small complex of bungalows and he headed straight for the corner property, passing quietly down the side alley and into the back garden. The first window he came to looked into the kitchen. The blinds were only half down and he stooped forwards to peer under the lowest slat. A simple kitchen. In the middle of a small table a teapot sat safely encased in a knitted tea cosy.

He stepped carefully past the back door to the next window. His view through this one was obstructed by a drawn pair of curtains. He moved to the centre of the glass where the material didn't quite meet, stood on tiptoes and looked through the gap.

On the bedside table a night light shed its yellow glow around the room. He was just able to make out the figure of the old woman asleep in her wheelchair. She sat with closed eyes looking at the wall, hair tied back in a bun. Rubble crept up to the back door and tipped up the third pot along from the step. Underneath it a key gleamed. He picked it up, carefully inserted it into the keyhole and unlocked the door. It opened with a gentle click and Rubble slipped into the kitchen, closing the door behind him.

Silence.

He tiptoed across the lino floor, the soles of his boots making a small clicking sound as he went. Then he was on to the carpet in the hallway and confidently approaching the front room.

He walked in and began to look around. On a small chest of drawers by the door stood a collection of china figures. A young boy in a nightshirt holding aloft a candle. A shepherdess clutching a lamb to her breast. Women in 1920s dresses frozen in the middle of dance steps. On the bedside table was a cluster of pill bottles, the labels indecipherable to him. Over on the mantel-piece an assortment of silver framed photos jostled for prominence. Black and white snaps of two babies, then colour ones of a girl and boy. Both dressed in knitted cardigans, one pink, one blue. A terry towelling nappy bulky beneath the boy's shorts. A woman snuggled up to a man on a picnic blanket. The girl and boy, older now and in school uniform. Awkward smiles and knock-knees. A young man, undoubtedly the boy of a few years before, proudly brandishing a rolled up certificate, mortar board on his head.

His attention turned to the old woman, still he couldn't make out any signs of breathing. Only when he was kneeling at her feet, softly folding back the blanket draped across her lap was he able to make out the light sigh of her breath. His eyes kept returning to check her face as he turned the blanket right down, revealing two thin arms. One hand cupped the back of the other, so the underside of both forearms were exposed to his view. He removed the protective cap of the syringe and picked out a particularly plump vein just below the papery skin.

Slowly the tip of the needle punctured her flesh and entered the vein. As he began to press the plunger in, the old lady's other hand suddenly clamped over his wrist. He froze. Then, when nothing else happened, he looked fearfully up at her face.

Rheumy eyes stared down at him, a faint smile on the bloodless lips.

Confused, Rubble continued looking back at her, unsure if she was actually awake. Or if she could even see. Her lips shut, but the smile remained there, as did the gentle, encouraging pressure on his wrist. With an imperceptible shrug Rubble emptied the syringe into her arm, watching as her eyelids slowly drooped shut and her hand slid off his wrist and back onto her lap. After extracting the needle he recapped the empty syringe and returned it to his pocket. Then, still kneeling there, he gently folded the blanket back up around her.

*

At the row of shops he slipped into the dark shadows behind an industrial size wheelie bin. Crouching amongst the urine-soaked rubbish, he waited for Eric to return.

Ten minutes later he heard a vehicle pull up on the road in front. He peeped round the corner and saw Eric's car idling there. Quickly he emerged, crossed the pavement and got in.

'Mission completed?' asked Eric as he began to pull away.

'Sleeping like a baby,' said Rubble, face flushed with pride.

'Sleeping? You mean she was still breathing?' asked Eric sharply.

'I think so,' replied Rubble, less confidently.

Eric stopped the car. 'She wasn't dead?'

'I gave her the full dose – look,' Rubble took the empty syringe out of his pocket. 'I did as you said.' Voice now anxious.

'Yes, you did well,' Eric reassured him, taking the empty syringe and putting it under the seat. 'I'll just go and check.' He opened the car door, unfolded his legs and disappeared up the deserted street and down the side of the bungalow. With practised ease he unlocked the door and went straight through to the front room.

Edith sat in her wheelchair and Eric stared at her chest, searching for the faintest rise or fall. Seeing no movement he placed a finger on her cheek, the skin felt cool through the latex gloves. He knelt down and held his palm under her nose but the glove prevented him from feeling any exhalation. Reluctantly he leaned forwards and brought his face up close to hers. In the corner of the room a clock ticked. Licking his lips, he slightly parted them and waited for the sensation of moving air across their moist surface. He didn't know it, but the drug was shutting down the old woman's internal systems, sedating her to the point that her brain, gradually suffocating, was desperately sending signals for more oxygen. Suddenly her mouth opened with a loud fleshy gasp. Eric fell backwards in terror. Scrambling to his feet, he stared in shock as another grotesque noise came from her. He couldn't bear to stay there any longer, waiting to see if the woman would actually die. Horrified he left the flat, dismissing the attempt as a failure.

Once back on the motorway Rubble quietly said, 'She squeezed my hand.'

Eric looked at his passenger, 'I'm sorry?'

Rubble frowned, 'When I was doing the injection, she put her hand on mine and squeezed it.'

'Just that? She didn't say anything?'

'No.'

Eric turned the information over in his head, 'A muscle spasm I should imagine.'

Rubble didn't say that her eyes had been open. He

preferred to imagine the old lady's gesture had been one of gratitude; it felt so good when people thanked him for his work.

27

Clare sat with her elbows on the desk, her copy of *Animal Farm* before her. Three clicks sounded in her headphones, letting her know that a caller had dialled directly through to her extension. She looked at the display on her phone. Line five – Girl Next Door line. A local caller.

Quickly she shut the book and reached for her horoscope cuttings. They were just lined up in front of her when the line opened.

'Hello, Sylvie Clara speaking. Would you like a horoscope or a tarot reading?'

'Is that Sylvie?' Rubble almost shouted. For the entire day after his first mission he'd been bounding round the farm, unable to keep a smile off his face. One or two people had asked him what he was so chuffed about, but he'd replied, 'Nothing.' Desperate to tell them: to tell someone. The urge grew inside him – his dreams had come true yet he had no one to share his happiness with. He wanted to shout his achievement to the sky. Then he'd thought of Sylvie.

'It is me,' replied Clare.

'It's me Sylvie, from the other night.'

Clare remembered the thick awkward voice, but struggled to recall anymore. 'Go on my child.'

'You did my fortune. Told me I would come into money.' This prompt didn't help her; she told most of her punters that.

'And?'

'I have! £75 and he says more to come. Is it true?'

Suddenly Clare remembered the conversation. It was the man who didn't even know his own birthday. What a stroke of luck. She slowed her speech, keen to drag the seconds out. 'Ah, you wish to know if you can expect more money from this person?'

'Yeah! He says there'll be more jobs. But he didn't tell me when. It's secret work,' he couldn't resist adding.

Clare picked up on the deliberate addition to his comment. 'Secret work, you say?'

'Yeah.'

'Well, I'm finding your chart now. One moment.' She rustled paper on the desk, flicked through a magazine, pausing to read a caption below a photo of Brad Pitt. 'Ah yes, here it is. Neptune is now moving into adventurous Sagittarius. This indicates that there does seem to be the possibility of more money, but it isn't very clear. Tell me more about this secret work.'

'But I'm not allowed.' Aching to reveal everything.

'It will help me to discover if there will be more of this . . . particular work.'

He couldn't hold back any longer. 'It's for the Government – but it's secret. You won't tell?'

'Of course not my child. Everything you tell me is in confidence.'

'I put an old woman to sleep. I'm a Government agent now.'

Shit, this is a right one, thought Clare. 'You put her to sleep? How?'

'With an injection. The man taught me how to do it, once I passed the test. I'm a Government agent now,' he repeated, keen to impress her.

'A test? I do not understand,' said Clare, eyes on the timer on the telephone's display.

'I passed the test. Questions and pictures. Funny pictures. But I passed and now I'm working on this project. He said it was £75 for each one I put to sleep.'

The conversation had now begun to unsettle Clare. 'Who was this person you put to sleep?'

'Don't know. The man drove me there. It was an old woman, sat in her wheelchair she was. She'd had enough though, wanted to die.'

'And you injected her? What with?'

'Dunno. The man gives me the syringe.' The pips sounded. 'Will there be more jobs? £75 for each one he said!'

Clare hurried, 'I think so, yes. Call me if you do get more work. I don't know your name. What is your . . .'

The line went dead. Clare sat back in her seat and breathed deeply. She stared at the console, then pressed the call-wrap-up button and walked over to Brian's office.

She knocked on the glass and he glanced up from the switchboard, looking agitated. Flexing a forefinger, he beckoned her in. 'This bloody Girl Next Door thing is going off big time,' he said, head lowered again. 'The punters love it, shame the girls don't.'

'That's what I was going to . . .' Clare answered but Brian carried on, rubbing a hand over his bald head as he did so.

'We're getting some real fruitcakes crawling out of the woodwork. Trying to find out which pubs and clubs the girls drink in. Think they're really talking to nymphomaniac Cat Deeley look-a-likes.'

'That's what I wanted to mention Brian,' Clare said more forcefully. He looked up. 'I've just had one, this guy said someone had paid him for killing someone. He wanted me to tell him if there'd be more jobs.'

'What do you mean, murdered someone? Like a contract killing?'

'No. He said he was an agent on some Government project.' Clare realised this was beginning to sound surreal. 'He said he'd killed an old woman who wanted to die.'

'Sweetie,' said Brian. 'It sounds like he's got some sort of a death fantasy going.' He pressed a few buttons and looked at his screen. 'You had him on line nearly five minutes. That's not bad. Is he calling again?'

'I think he will.'

'Well, get him to talk about it more. Sounds like you could get ten minutes out of him. And don't worry Clare, euthanasia isn't legalised yet you know.' He lowered his voice, 'Though with some of the old hags working in here, it should be.' He winked and Clare couldn't help laughing. 'But seriously, if he sounds really unhinged, give him the number for the Samaritans. That's all you have to do to keep within ICSTIS regulations.'

'All right,' she said uncertainly.

Then, remembering about the slow progress of Zoe's job search, she scooped some change out of her pocket. 'Brian?' she asked, holding up a pound coin, 'have you got some twenties for the phone in the kitchen?'

Brian scowled, 'Don't bother with that sweetie. Nolan's set it so you only get about ten seconds per twenty pence. Use this one,' he nodded to the spare console on the corner of his desk. 'Press nine for an outside line.'

'Thanks,' replied Clare, smiling. She got the latest phone bill for the flat out of her bag and sat down. Once she'd slipped the earphones on, she called the enquiries line printed at the top of the bill. Soon she was connected to another office, almost identical to the one she was in. After typing in her account number a digitised voice told her someone would be with her soon. Pan-pipes playing *Greensleeves* started up, and Clare's head drooped. Eventually a customer care operator came on to the line.

'Good evening Miss Silver, how can I help you?' In the background Clare could hear the murmur of many other people as they answered similar calls.

'Hi, yeah. I'm just calling to request an itemised phone bill please.'

'For your next phone bill?'

'No, for the one you've just sent me please.'

'That's no problem, Miss Silver. It will be with you in a few days' time. Is there anything else I can help you with tonight?'

'That's it, cheers.'

'Thank you for calling Top-Tel, we're with you 24 hours a day.'

She hung up the phone and stood. Brian was busy rerouting calls, panels flashing all over the computer screen. She tapped a finger on his desk and mouthed, 'Thanks Brian.'

He held up one hand, little finger bent back, and gave her a dinky wave.

28

Rubble felt so elated that, once he was in the middle of the village green, he let his legs buckle and fell onto his back. Spread-eagled in the damp grass, he grinned up at the stars and thought how wonderful the world suddenly was.

After a while he got back up and began the walk home. But it didn't seem right just to return to his caravan as usual. No, tonight he decided to indulge in a little tree climbing. See what the villagers were up to on this special night.

He skirted round the pond, reached the other side of the green and set off down a narrow bridleway that led into the woods bordering the south side of the village. Amongst the trees the air was heavy with the rich scent of ferns. He left the bridleway, brushing through the knee-high plants, stopping for an instant as a female fox let out its grating cry from deep in the woods ahead.

Just a few metres to his right the trees abruptly stopped, cleared many years ago to make way for the back gardens of the cottages that formed the perimeter of the village. Near the garden fence of one he could hear the undergrowth being disturbed. He listened more carefully, and amongst the rustling of old leaves and twigs he could hear snorting little breaths; a hedgehog rooting around for food.

He walked on another fifty metres or so until he got to one of his favourite trees; the one from which he liked to watch the family. He swung himself up into the lower branches and looked across to the rear of the house. As usual bluish light flickered from three of the rooms; in the kitchen the mum was watching a programme showing someone else cooking in their kitchen. In the sitting room the dad's crossed legs extended from the sofa as a boxing match was fought before him. Every now and again the half curled up hand resting on the arm of the sofa twitched. Upstairs the two children were sitting on a bed watching something else.

Rubble squinted to try and make out what it was. It looked like a group of people roughly his age sitting in a large room talking. He watched for a while, but nothing appeared to be happening. Every now and again the picture would cut to a different angle, sometimes the camera so near to the people, he couldn't understand why they were unaware of it. In the kitchen, the mum turned her TV off and went upstairs, ducking her head into the children's room. Then she walked down the corridor and went into the bathroom. Rubble watched her barely distorted form on the other side of the dimpled glass as she picked a toothbrush from the pot on the windowsill and began cleaning her teeth. Back on the TV in the children's room a person had gone into the bathroom there and had started to brush her teeth too. Face inches away from the camera, just like she was using it for a mirror.

From somewhere nearby he heard a faint mechanical whirring. He looked at the gap between the family's cottage and its neighbour. On the pavement beyond the two homes he saw Miss Strines trundle past in her wheelchair. Far more entertaining. He dropped from the tree and bounded through the undergrowth, stopping three cottages along. Swiftly he climbed up into the lower branches of the nearest tree and awaited her arrival.

Soon he heard the wheelchair's approach, the whine lowering in tone as she stopped to open her garden gate. It swung inward and she manoeuvered herself on to the patio. Spying from between the leaves, Rubble watched as she slowly turned the wheelchair round and pushed the gate shut. Then she drove herself across to her back door, triggering an exterior light. The rear of the house was bathed in white as she reached across to the drainpipe running down the side of the house. From behind it she removed a key and opened the door. After returning the key to its hidden peg she went up the ramp and into the kitchen. The light inside then came on and the back door was shut.

Moments later a lamp in the sitting room clicked on. To his annoyance, the first thing she did was draw the curtains shut. He watched as a variety of moths and other insects were drawn from the trees around him to the exterior light. Lazily they circled it, their flight paths becoming ever more agitated. But before they actually started flying straight at the bulb, the light clicked off, glowing orange for a second before the darkness engulfed it. Rubble lowered himself from the branch and dropped on to the soft ground below.

Back in the caravan he drew all his curtains, then sat at his table. He went over the conversation with Sylvie in his head; she seemed so interested in his job. He dwelled on her voice, the strange way she pronounced her words. How she slowly drew out the letter 'r'. He imagined what it would sound like if she were to gently whisper his name. 'Rubble, Rubble, Rubble.'

Getting up he went into his bedroom and carefully removed the picture of her from his wall. He carried it back to his table and propped it up against the drawn curtains. Then he went to his fridge and removed the small chicken he'd plucked earlier that day. He placed it on the edge of the table, severed neck pointing towards Sylvie's image, other end towards him. The hole at its rear gaped where he'd scooped out its giblets. Keeping his eyes fixed on the picture before him, he unbuckled his overalls and let them drop around his ankles. Then he freed himself from his grey underpants and pulled the chicken toward him. Once inside he began sliding the dead bird back and forth, murmuring 'Sylvie, Sylvie, Sylvie.'

29

'Thank you, Sunai,' smiled the seated woman as the petite Thai lady filled her cup. Once she began pouring coffee for the next person the woman continued, 'OK, so we're all agreed? £500 to Respect For Animals, £500 to the Holland Park Hunt Saboteurs Society and, thanks to Rowena's vigorous lobbying, a special donation of £250 to the Labour Animal Welfare Society to help fund their research into the worrying rise in incidents of badger snaring.'

Everyone around the table nodded their assent and a middle-aged woman smiled her thanks. At the far end of the room china gently clinked as a young Thai man stacked their dirty dinner plates directly into plastic crates.

'Very good, then this meeting is officially adjourned.' Theatrically she knocked the curved underside of her silver dessert spoon against the tablecloth and a tiny dot of lychee juice was left behind on the French lace. Various women gently clapped and the few men present sat back in their chairs to ease the pressure of their stomachs against their waistbands. After a few moment's satisfied silence quiet conversations began to spring up at different points around the table. The young Thai man silently carried the crates from the room as coffee was slowly sipped. Half an hour later and the evening had come to an end. Coats had been retrieved from the cavernous area beneath the stairs and the dinner guests began filing out into the hallway.

'You must give me the number of your caterers – the chicken and coconut soup was gorgeous.'

'Was that a Barbara Hepworth in the dining room? I don't know how your Gerald does it, he has such a knack for collecting.'

'It's Poppy's birthday in two weeks. We've booked this superb place on the King's Road. Olly must come – I'll put his invitation in the post.'

The last person to leave paused in the stained glass porch to politely enquire about his hostess' son. 'How is Olly doing, Georgina? He seemed a little subdued as I arrived.'

The woman glanced up, as if she could see through the ceiling to where her son lay asleep. 'He's all right thanks, Martin. But he did have an awful experience a week or so ago.'

'Oh?'

She smiled graciously towards the road, waving at a Mercedes as it pulled away from the front of her house. Then she pushed the door almost shut and continued in a low voice, 'He spent the start of his summer holidays at a school friend's, the father of whom, I understood, owned a farm in Cheshire. It turned out to be a bloody battery farm. The family was absolutely grotesque. Olly said the mother wore a shell suit to breakfast. And the outfit she had on when I picked Olly up? Horrendous.'

The man nodded sympathetically, taking some cigarettes from his herringbone jacket and offering her one. She smiled briefly, waited for it to be lit, inhaled deeply, then carried on, smoke emphasising each hissed 's' of her next sentence. 'Olly was so quiet for the drive home. So quiet. But I eventually got it out of him. He'd had a truly horrid time. Their son had spent most of the time trying to make him kill things around the farm – aided by what can only be described as the village idiot if Olly's account of him was anything to go by. And who, I might add, the farm owner employs to kill the wretched chickens.'

'The poor lad,' interrupted her visitor, 'which village was this in?'

'The village?' answered the woman dismissively. 'Oh, some place called Breystone. Just off the M56. I didn't have to witness the battery farm, thank god, but apparently it's on the opposite side of the road. The farmer's house though? Beautiful. Eighteenth century perhaps.' She waved her cigarette. 'They've ruined it of course. You can spot it as you leave the village – they've mounted these vile horse's heads on the gateposts at the top of the drive. Fake Victorian street lamps lining the drive. Sherlock Holmes style. The obligatory fountain in front of the house, complete with coloured lights under the water and a hideous statue of a nymph reclining on a sea-dragon. A kind of ruination of Rutelli's *Fontana delle Naiadi* in, I forget which *piazza* in Rome.'

'The *Piazza della Repubblica*,' the man said.

'Of course – I should have guessed you'd know,' she answered with an admiring smile. 'Anyway, the whole place was terrible. You just don't know whose kids are getting into boarding school these days. I knew he was a farmer, obviously hoped he wasn't leader of the local hunt. But what did he turn out to be? A scrap metal merchant who abuses chickens for a sideline.'

The man shook his head. 'But Olly's over it now?'

'Yes, thanks for asking, Martin. He's going on a wind-surfing course down in St Ives next week. Hopefully that will help him completely forget the whole episode.'

She pulled open the door and tossed her cigarette butt deep into the rosemary bush in their front garden. 'Just flick yours in there, the gardener will tidy them up.'

After doing the same he said, 'Well, thanks for a lovely meal.' After lightly kissing her on the cheek, he walked off down the quiet street. Preferring not to use his mobile phone, he went round the corner and stepped into a call-box. Inside he dialled a number from memory.

'Hello' said the voice at the other end.

'It's me,' he stated flatly. 'I've just got an address for a place up in Cheshire that will very much interest our friends in Manchester.'

'Don't say anything more over the phone. Meet me at the usual place, Friday night.'

30

Eric positioned himself so he could watch her face from between the gaps in a display of biscuit tins. She looked tired, but was being cheerful enough with the person she was serving. Half-closing his eyes he thought that maybe she was a little red around hers. A good sign, he concluded.

Almost closing time in the shop, it didn't take long before he was placing his wire basket on the small metal ledge at the end of her till. He began to transfer his groceries on to the black conveyor belt, but she was preoccupied placing a wad of banknotes into a secure container under the till. Unsure as to whether he should say anything, he decided to let her notice him first. Sure enough a few seconds later he heard her say, 'Oh, evening Mr . . . Professor Maudsley.'

Eric looked up, a faint look of surprise on his face. 'Fancy that – I've picked your till again. It must be the quality of service.'

'Thank you,' Rosemary smiled, and passed a loaf of bread through the thin red beam. The machine beeped and she picked up a four-pack of baked beans. Eric placed the empty basket on top of the pile at his feet and straightened up. 'How's Edith? Any luck with finding her a bed yet?'

Keeping her head lowered she said, 'Actually, I haven't seen her for a bit. Daniel was taken ill at school and I had to go and collect him instead of visiting her the other day. Nothing serious though.'

'Oh,' said Eric.

Registering what appeared to be a look of disapproval passing for a moment over his face, Rosemary added, 'I tried to ring her. But she often doesn't hear the phone nowadays, especially if she's in the kitchen.' Suddenly she plucked a handkerchief from the top of her sleeve and sneezed into it. 'Pardon me. A customer just bought several bouquets of lilies – they set my hay fever off something rotten.'

Eric moved to the other end of the till and removed his reusable shopping bag. He had expected to be making gentle inquiries about where she had been laid to rest. Perhaps even probing as to the cause of death, confident her doctor would have signed it off as an exacerbation of her existing heart problems. Instead he found himself placing the unneeded shopping quickly into his bag.

His silence making her uneasy, Rosemary said, 'I'll try and pop round soon, though I'm on a late shift tonight and Daniel has a football tournament all of Sunday.'

Eric looked up and, as he handed her the necessary

cash, said, 'Please pass on my regards when you do see her.'

She smiled in acknowledgement, giving him his change. On the way back to his car he thought things over. There was no way he could risk returning to Edith's flat to ascertain if the dosage he'd given her was sufficient. He thought about what she weighed – it couldn't be much more than a large dog. Seven stone at most. He doubted Patricia weighed much more. But he couldn't afford to botch her injection too. What he needed to do was work out how much Euthanol was required to finish off a much larger patient. Then, if he applied the same dosage to Patricia, he was assured of success. As he was about to take the steps down into the basement car park he heard a familiar voice nearby.

'Spare some change please?'

He looked to his left and saw Bert's bulky form sitting on the pavement, hand cupped to a passerby. Quickly Eric jogged down the concrete steps, dumped his bag on the backseat, then climbed back up to street level once again. A member of staff was asking Bert to move on from the supermarket's entrance. Eric watched as he struggled to his feet, pockets jangling with small coins as he did so. The old man began a shambolic walk along the pavement, the last few shoppers steering well clear of his uncertain progress.

Eric shadowed him through the city centre, watching him pause at the tables outside a bar to gulp down the lukewarm dregs in the glasses left on one table. Other drinkers watched him with distaste and Eric heard a young man say jokingly to his mate, 'Dave, at least buy your dad a drink.'

'Piss off,' his friend laughed, reaching into his pocket and flicking a ten pence piece contemptuously at the old man. The coin bounced unnoticed off Bert's arm and rolled away across the pavement. The drinks all finished, he registered the customers as if for the first time, and began asking them for change. A glass collector barred his circuit of the tables and Bert waved him feebly away, telling him that, as a para, he had protected the freedom of little runts like him. The staff member didn't move and Bert resumed his wandering to the outskirts of the city centre.

He made his way slowly through the jumble of narrow streets behind the main railway station, walls covered with fly posters, women standing on street corners. At the end of one road was an off-licence, its windows crowded with neon coloured stars shouting out special offers and deals. Bert went inside and Eric had to stop in an empty doorway. Scrawled on the surface of the door before him were the words, 'Urinal only please.' Eric was puzzling over whether the message was sarcastic or a serious request when a voice behind him said, 'Looking for business?'

He turned around and politely shook his head at the hollow-cheeked woman, but she wasn't giving up.

'A nice slow blow job? My place is just round the corner.'

'No. Thank you,' he said awkwardly.

She shrugged her shoulders and walked back to her position on the other side of the road. Another woman had begun to make her way over to try her luck when Bert reappeared on the pavement, a three litre bottle of 'Brite-Strike' cider held in each hand. Even from fifteen metres away Eric could see the silver flash on the label proudly announcing, '8.3%'.

Bert disappeared round the corner and Eric followed. Several roads later he turned into one with a sign reading 'Wood Road'. Slowly he made his way to number 50 and Eric observed as he pushed a broken door open and made his way into the ground floor flat.

Back at his car, Eric removed the mobile from his glove compartment, turned it on and checked for a signal. He dialled the number and a few seconds later the phone in Rubble's cupboard started to ring.

31

Startled by the sudden noise, Rubble stopped stirring the chicken broth. As he stared at the cupboard, thin bones rotated slowly around in the simmering liquid, before coming to a rest at the bottom of the saucepan. Then he threw the wooden spoon into the sink and leapt across the room, landing on his haunches before the little door and yanking it open.

He picked up the handset, pressed the green button and said excitedly, 'Agent White here.'

Eric replied, 'Agent Orange here. Are you available for another job tonight?'

'Yes, sir,' Rubble immediately answered.

'Good, be ready for a 1:30 A.M. pick-up.'

Eric pressed the red button on his phone and returned it to the glove compartment. Looking at the people walking past Eric decided that he needed somewhere quieter to prepare the syringe. A glance at the dashboard clock told him he had a few hours to use up, so he started his car and set off across the city.

Fifteen minutes later he parked in a quiet courtyard behind a detached house in a far trendier area. Quickly he slipped on his rubber gloves. A small and deserted seating area was lit by an exterior light on the rear of the building. Using its glow, he sucked up twice the previous dose of Euthanol into the syringe. Then he replaced the protective cap, removed his gloves and returned the items to the small box under the driver's seat. After cracking his knuckles, he climbed from the car, locked it and walked round to the front of the building. Situated on a tree-lined street, the ground floor of the house had been converted into a two-room restaurant. Above the front entrance a sign read, 'Pulse. Vegetarian cooking for the heart and soul.'

Eric pulled open the door and entered a short hallway with stripped wood floorboards. Spanish guitar music floated around him, the aroma of freshly baked bread infusing the air. On each side of him Notice-boards were covered with assorted adverts, announce-ments and appeals.

Pausing at a section marked *Wimmins stuff*, he read a few.

'Hi, my name is Tony and I'm looking for a female travelling companion for a trip to India.'

'Fully biodegradable tampons. Now available from the Eden Worker's Co-operative. 114 Bakewell Street.'

'Gatesley Women's Refuge urgently requires donations for our work with battered sisters.'

Moving past other notices for skill-swap schemes, organic fruit and vegetable delivery companies and a variety of charity posters, he turned right into the no-smoking room. Lit only by candles, he could see a few people finishing off meals, sipping wine or drinking coffee. He crossed to the small counter in the corner. A pale skinned woman, face completely free of make-up, hair tied back in a pony tail, patted her hands on a striped apron and said, 'Hello Professor Maudsley.'

'Evening Naomi.' She had been on his course a few years ago and had helped run the restaurant ever since graduating. 'I know I'm rather late, but is there any food still being served?'

She smiled, 'I'm sure we can rustle you up something. Two seconds – I'll just check with the kitchen.' She retreated through a small door, returning less than a minute later. Pointing up to the large blackboard mounted on the wall to her left she said, 'We've got the Nutty Mushroom and Stilton Crumble, Sweet and Sour Cashew Nut Parcels and *Lentejas Gratinadas* left. Everything on the dessert section is available, apart from the Apple, Date and Cider Strudel.'

'In that case, could I have the Nutty Mushroom and Stilton Crumble followed by Pear and Almond Tart please?'

'Of course. Anything to drink?'

'Just a glass of tap water and a pot of coffee.'

'Can I recommend the Colombian? It's from a worker's co-operative we've been helping out recently. It's absolutely delicious.'

'Sounds wonderful, thank you.' Eric removed a copy of the *Guardian* from the rack in front of the counter and sat down at a table beneath the blackboard. A few minutes later Naomi appeared with a tray holding two plates, his water and coffee. She placed everything on the table, finally handing him a mismatched set of cutlery wrapped in a recycled paper napkin and tied with a piece of twine. 'Bon appetit,' she said quietly and retired behind the counter.

Eric took his time eating, slowly flicking through the paper, drinking his glass of water with infinitesimal sips. The other diners had long since departed and the only sounds were of the kitchen being cleaned by the time he reached the start of the sport section. He closed the paper and folded it in half, finished off the last of the cold coffee then removed a balsa toothpick from the small earthenware pot in the middle of the table and worked an errant fragment of nut out from between his molars. Then he got up and carried his dirty plates and cups over to the counter. 'Naomi!' he called through. 'Could I settle the bill please?'

She reappeared, wiping wet hands on her apron. 'Everything OK?' she asked.

'As delicious as usual,' replied Eric, removing ten pounds from his wallet.

'Good, that's,' she glanced down at the bill for his table. 'Eight pounds thirty please.'

He handed her the note and said, 'Please donate the change to this month's charity.'

'Thanks Professor,' she smiled, dropping the coins

into a jar. Taped to the front was a business card that read, 'Richmond's Cat Rescue Centre.'

Back in his car he put his gloves back on. The drive to Breystone took less than an hour. As he turned on to the track he dipped his lights and rolled slowly along, trying to see the glow from the windows of Rubble's caravan through the trees ahead. Suddenly a dark form dropped into the pool of light before his car and Rubble squatted there, grinning blindly at the glaring head-lamps. He hit the brakes, coming to an abrupt halt and Rubble stood up. He walked round the front of the car and opened the side door.

'Hello Agent Orange.'

'Get in Agent White,' snapped Eric, still shocked by Rubble's unexpected appearance. 'How long have you been waiting up there?'

'Don't know. An hour or two,' replied Rubble, unable to remove the lopsided smile from his face.

After handing Rubble some gloves, Eric put the car into reverse and they backed up the track and on to the road. Soon they were cruising along the motorway, Eric scrupulously keeping within the speed limit. 'Right, the subject lives in a small flat in the city centre. He mentioned to me that his door is broken, so he hasn't bothered leaving us out a key. You can just let yourself straight into the property. Now . . .' from under his seat he removed a syringe three quarters full of clear liquid, '. . . put that in the front pocket of your overalls. Good.

OK, we'll stick to the same routine as last time: I'll drive you past the property so you can see exactly which one it is. Then I'll drop you off a bit further up the road and you can walk back, head down the side of the house and enter his flat through the broken door. Once you've put him to sleep, walk back to our rendezvous point.'

'OK' nodded Rubble and, as he rubbed his hands together, the thin rubber squeaked.

After a while Eric turned off the motorway and drove carefully along deserted streets. Soon they had left the pleasant suburban areas behind and entered a run-down part of the city. Bin bags and the occasional woman stood at the top of alleyways. Broken glass, embedded along the top of back yard walls, glittered as they drove by. A burglar alarm flashed on the wall above a shop's canopy, its thin high wail disturbing the night.

Eventually they turned down Wood Road, and Eric slowed the car to a crawl. 'See that house with the gate hanging off its hinges?' Rubble nodded. 'Our subject lives in there – ground floor flat, number 50.' He let the car slide on a few yards further and parked opposite a boarded-up pub, smoke damage staining the bricks black above the ground floor windows. Eric looked back over his shoulder, 'Just head round to the side door. As I said, it's been left open for you. He usually sleeps on a mattress on the floor in the front room. Go through the kitchen and it's the first room on your right.' As Rubble went to open the door Eric tapped on his upper arm and pointed across the road. 'Once you've completed the job, wait for me round the back of that pub. After I've taken another agent to a job, I'll come back for you. I should be about twenty minutes. Good luck.'

Rubble climbed out and pushed the door shut.

Eric pulled away, drove to the end of the road and parked just round the corner. After turning his lights and engine off, he sank down as low in his seat as possible and waited.

Rubble trod carefully up the alleyway, avoiding bits of splintered wood as he approached the door. It hung partially open, the bottom panel kicked out, a hinge half-wrenched off. With the toe of one boot he pushed it open, hands held in front of him, ready for the unexpected.

A single flickering strip light struggled to illuminate the kitchen, its neighbour in the casing grey and dead. Rubble stepped inside and looked around. Apart from the empty bottles of cider lying at his feet, the room would have been almost empty. A saucepan on the cooker, remains of baked beans inside, the sauce dried out and cracked with little lines. In the sink was a single plate, the end of a fork sticking out from underneath it.

Rubble listened. He could hear faint music; the rhythmic banging of a big bass drum, a chorus of wind instruments over the top. And a slow heavy rasping. He stood still, relaxing when he realised it was a human snore. As Agent Orange had promised, his subject was sound asleep.

He walked slowly down the hallway, its thin carpet curling at the edges and bent completely back at the front door. Free newspapers clogged the mat, colourful flyers for pizza delivery places spilling from the pages. He stopped at the first door on the right and eased it open an inch at a time, all the while checking that the regularity of the snoring on the other side didn't alter. When the gap was wide enough he looked round the door. Faded blue curtains hung across the window, the yellowish walls marked with lighter coloured squares where pictures used to hang. On the floor in the corner a lamp with no shade, a bare bulb softly lighting the room. Next to it was a cheap cassette player, military band music coming from its tinny speakers. Further along the base of the wall was a mattress with a large lump of an elderly man lying across it, one arm resting on the carpet. The folds of flesh encasing his throat quivered slightly as another snore rumbled out.

Rubble examined the rest of the room. In the opposite corner was a single chair, one arm snapped off. Clothes draped over the back. A gas fire and, on the mantelpiece above it, two photos, propped against the wall. Both were crumpled and bent as if they'd been torn from their frames. He crossed the room for a closer look.

The first was of a young paratrooper, crouched on a parched runway, one hand resting on a Vickers medium machine gun. Behind him a Valletta transport plane was being loaded up. His dark glasses contrasted with the whiteness of his teeth. He glowed with health, the muscles knotted across his forearms.

Rubble looked at the next photo. The same man in the canteen of some army barracks. He was brandishing a pint at the camera and his other hand was raised with three fingers pointed up. Three what? Rubble wondered. He leaned forwards, studying the tattoo of the badge on the person's forearm. Underneath the familiar winged crest were the words, '3 Para. *Utrinque Paratus*'. He knew most of the regiment's history from Mr Williams in the post office. Now the setting in the other photo clicked. Operation Musketeer. 3 Para had parachuted into a foreign airfield and taken on the local soldiers who had seized control of a canal nearby. He looked again at the man's three raised fingers. Enemy kills perhaps? Rubble wondered who the soldier in the photo was. Probably the old man's son or younger brother, he thought.

He turned to the grey-haired figure sprawled diagonally across the mattress. Age had withered his limbs and bloated his stomach.

He wore a tatty cardigan and old trousers, legs rucked up over his ankles to reveal mismatched socks. Silently Rubble crouched down and, very gently, pushed the cardigan sleeve up the arm hanging off the edge of the mattress. To his surprise he saw the tattoo, now smeared and faded beneath the sagging skin. Its definition was almost lost but Rubble could just make out the number three and outstretched wings of the regiment's crest. He couldn't believe it was the same man. He rubbed the palm of his gloved hand up and down the back of his neck, suddenly unsure about his duty. Putting an ex-paratrooper to sleep; it didn't seem right. But then he thought of his own duty as a Government agent. He went back to the photo for another look. This wasn't the same man smiling back at him, Rubble told himself. This one was fit and honed; a fighting machine. The one on the mattress was weak and vulnerable, robbed of his strength. No use to anyone.

He took the syringe out of his pocket. Kneeling down by the sleeping man's arm he lightly slid the needle into a bluish vein in the crook of his elbow. The snoring turned into a snort and he moved his arm on to the mattress, the syringe hanging from it like a parasite. In the corner the music came to a stop. Rubble's eyes remained fixed on the man's eyelids. The tape clicked over and a trumpet struck up the next march. Rubble waited patiently for the old man's breathing to steady and then, millilitre by millilitre, emptied the Euthanol into his arm.

Even before the syringe was empty the breathing

had slowed right down, becoming too gradual for snoring. Now it was just an open throated inhalation, followed by an equally gradual release of air. Rubble put the cap of the syringe back on, returned it to his pocket and waited. Minutes later the man's throat began a wet rattling noise. Then he let out a long deep sigh, as if someone had given him news he had been waiting for a long time. Rubble felt warm fruity air wash over his eyelashes and the old man didn't breathe again.

He crossed the ex-para's hands on his chest and stood back up. Looking at his mismatched socks, Rubble stepped over to the chair and rummaged through the pile of clothes. Eventually he found one to match the one on the old man's right foot. Crouching back down, he removed the odd sock, replaced it with the correct one, straightened his ruffled trousers and left the house.

Over the road he waited in the shadows behind the pub until Agent Orange's car rolled to a stop outside the car park entrance. He hurried over to the vehicle and quickly climbed in.

'Mission successful?' asked Eric, hand on the gear stick.

'Yes sir,' Rubble answered promptly.

'You waited until the subject had stopped breathing?'

'Yes sir.'

As soon as the words were out of his mouth Eric put the car in gear and they headed off down the street.

'Well done Agent White, you've done a first-class job. That is your work completed with flying colours for tonight.'

32

'Anyone for coffee?' asked Julian, holding up the round glass jug from the percolator machine.

'What sort of beans are they again?' said Adele from the corner of the room, soles of her DM boots against the edge of the low table, a half-completed roll-up perched on her knees.

Julian picked up the foil pack, 'It's produced by a Colombian worker's co-operative. Patricia got it from Pulse, so it's bound to be a good bet.'

'Go on then,' said Adele and Julian filled up a cup and walked round the table to where she was sitting, tongue flicking along the edge of a Rizla.

'Clare could I,' he pause for no more than a heartbeat, 'tempt you?' One eyebrow raised a fraction.

Clare looked up and noticed the expression on his face. 'No, I'm caffeined out at the moment, cheers.'

Julian shrugged and handed the cup to Adele. 'Anyone else?' he asked the rest of the room and a couple of people replied 'Yes please.'

Clare resumed her conversation with Adele, keeping Julian's brown corduroys in the periphery of her vision. As he passed back in front of her seat he made an exaggerated shuffle to get round her, brushing her knees as he did so. Keeping her gaze directed at the table, Clare wondered whether the contact could have been deliberate.

Adele still hadn't lit her roll-up and was impatiently turning her mobile phone over and over in her hand. 'Anyway, as I was saying, sorry about missing the march. We had an absolute nightmare in the flat. The boiler went and the landlord's handyman wasn't answering his phone.'

Clare knew Adele rented a flat with three other girls in one of the most expensive parts of the city. When questioned once, she had explained it away with a vague mention of an unbelievably good deal. The owner, she claimed, lived overseas, and hadn't put the rent up in years. 'We had to use all our towels to try and soak up the leak – the whole kitchen was flooded by the time we got a plumber round.'

Clare wondered if Adele was aware that the burst boiler story was amongst the most clichéd of excuses for missing something.

'The march sounded great though.' Adele continued. 'How many signatures did you get?'

'I reckon well over 300,' replied Clare. 'People were mobbing us outside the Union.'

'Brilliant, that should make the bastards think again.'

'Yeah, hopefully,' answered Clare. 'So, you got any plans for after graduation?'

Adele looked scornfully at her roll-up. 'Nope.

Probably just bum around a bit. Do a bit of travelling, South America or somewhere like that. I'm certainly in no hurry to join the rat race. You?'

Clare wished she shared Adele's laid back attitude to getting that first graduate job. She said uncertainly, 'Not really. I'm sure you know I'm looking into post-graduate positions. Here or another university nearby.'

Adele nodded thoughtfully, 'Yeah, I fancy doing an MA once I've had a bit of a break. It's another way to use up a year or two isn't it?' she grinned.

From the doorway Patricia's voice sounded. 'Sorry to interrupt Clare, but could I pinch you for a moment?' She was holding up an A4 sized brown envelope. 'It's about an essay.'

Clare started to frown – all her essays from Patricia's modules had been returned to her long ago. Then she saw the fixed stare on Patricia's face and realised she must be referring to something else.

'This coffee is spot on Pat,' said Julian. 'Don't you agree guys?' he asked the rest of the room. Several students nodded their thanks as Clare edged round the table.

'I'm glad you're enjoying it,' replied Patricia as she moved away from the open door. Once outside she ushered Clare further down the corridor and into the first available room. Without bothering to turn the lights on, she shut the door, excitedly grabbed Clare's hand and whispered, 'I've had a little phone call from the ESPRC. Well, someone I know on their allocation committee. They're officially announcing it in two days' time, but, according to him, the grant is ours!'

Clare noted how Patricia used the word 'ours', and whispered back, 'That's brilliant Pat. Well done – you really deserve it with all the work you've put in.'

'Thank you. Anyway, I know this is premature, but I thought it would brighten your day.' She raised the envelope. 'In here is an application form for a position as a researcher and part-time lecturer.' Clare felt blood rush to her cheeks. 'It's a bit improper, before I've even advertised for one I know, but,' Patricia rolled her eyes, 'well, when you want the best, you have to bend the rules occasionally. Don't let anyone see you with this, but get thinking about research areas that interest you and make sure they correspond with what the research project will be about. We can even structure it so you end up with an MA.'

Feeling her eyes filling with tears, Clare said, 'Thanks Pat – I can't tell you how much it would mean if you offered me a position.'

Patricia corrected her, 'Clare, I am offering you a position.' She held out the envelope.

Clare didn't know what to say. Looking down to take it, she noticed all the polish had disappeared from Patricia's nails. Before she could stop, she found herself gushing, 'Your nail polish has gone.' Immediately she blushed at the silliness of her comment. 'I'm sorry.'

Patricia smiled, 'I chipped the polish on one. Typical isn't it? Just after you have them manicured. The easiest thing was to remove the rest of it. At least my toenails are still perfect though!' she added cheerfully.

Clare had recovered enough composure to say, 'Pat, I would so love to work in your department. Your courses have opened my eyes to so many social issues . . .'

Patricia placed a hand on Clare's forearm to interrupt her. 'You don't have to pursuade me how suitable you are,' she said smiling. 'I've already offered you a position. I thought you'd be an asset to the department ever since I was your tutor for your dissertation last year. Your enthusiasm and insight stood you apart from the other students straight away. Too many see this course as an easy ride and a ticket to cheap booze, as I'm sure you know.'

Clare lowered her eyes and, with heartfelt honesty, said, 'I wouldn't have enjoyed doing my dissertation half as much as I did without your guidance. To have someone with as many commitments as you prepared to sacrifice half her summer helping me – writing letters on my behalf, suggesting material for research, places to visit, it was . . . well, it was inspirational for me. You didn't need to do so much.'

'But Clare, that's the beauty of doing something you really enjoy. Work doesn't seem like work when the subjects you are dealing with are so interesting. As I'm sure you'll discover. Now don't tell anyone about this,' she said, placing the envelope in Clare's hand. 'And return it directly to me when you've done it.' Squeezing Clare's hand one more time, she opened the door and disappeared up the corridor.

Clare stood there for a few moments, pressing the envelope to her chest and enjoying the surge of elation flooding through her. Then she sat down at the desk behind the door and slid the application form out of the envelope. She had nearly finished glancing over it when she heard a voice, low and urgent, approaching down the corridor from the coffee room. She put the form back into the envelope just as a blurred head and shoulders passed along the other side of the frosted glass window above where she was sitting. The door was pushed open and Adele backed into the dark room, mobile phone pressed to her ear. Unaware of Clare sitting almost behind her, she continued speaking.

'Listen Mummy,' she hissed, 'it's a graduate trainee job with Nestlé. Do you realise how many people get to the second round of interviews – let alone graduates off some mickey mouse course in sociology?' She continued whispering, a home-counties accent suddenly evident in her voice, 'I bloody want this job OK?'

She paused as her mum made her reply.

'I don't care how you do it. Transfer it from your account that Daddy keeps topped up or something. Bloody well ask Daddy how to do it. I need enough for a return flight to London, I am not, repeat bloody not, travelling by crappy train. And I need a decent outfit. There's an Yves Saint Laurent in the big department store up here.'

A pause.

'Great.' Sarcasm heavy in her voice. 'No Mummy, that's fine. I'll just go in my bloody dungarees and Doc Martens. Listen just because you bought me that flat doesn't mean I want to live up here permanently. Unless you want me to get a job as a social worker or something in the north of England.'

Another pause during which time she drew angrily on the last of her cigarette, 'Yeah, yeah. Just put Daddy on, will you?'

Adele listened for a while and when she spoke again, her voice had softened. 'Thank you Daddy. When will it be in my account? Excellent. Honestly, you won't regret this. I'll get that job, you wait and see. Nestlé! You don't get much bigger than that. Love you, Daddy.'

She ended the call and began to look about for a bin to dump the end of her roll-up in. As she turned round she saw Clare sitting quietly by the door. In the dim light Adele turned white and she stood there, motionless.

Clare wasn't sure what to say. Adele, of all people, was a complete fake. Memories flooded her mind of all the times she had sat there and passed politically correct judgements on ill-considered comments made in the coffee room. Part of Clare wanted to laugh with relief; there were others on the course just as hypocritical as her. But to express any kind of sympathy would only expose herself. And she couldn't afford to do that. Instead she smiled coldly at the other student and, as she got up, said, 'More coffee Adele? Nescafé perhaps?' Then she left the room without waiting for an answer.

Hours later and Clare was still shaking her head, unable to believe Adele's act. Then she realised where she was; sitting in a call centre waiting to make money out of vulnerable people's hopes and fears. Uneasily she ran a finger along her mouthpiece, wondering how much of a better person she was. Or even if she were worse than Adele. Before she had time to decide, her line clicked three times and, clearing the thoughts from her head, she readied herself for a caller who had dialled her extension.

'Hello, this is Sylvie Claro speaking. Would you like a horoscope or a tarot reading?'

'Sylvie, it's me,' Then, as if he was her only caller, the person stupidly added, 'From the other night?'

Despite everything, she instantly recognised the voice and its childish enthusiasm. Before she could say anything, it boastfully continued, 'I put another one to sleep. The man called again and gave me another mission!'

Clare remembered with dismay the details of their

earlier conversation. 'So my child,' she hesitated. 'You say it was a success?'

'Yeah! It was an old man this time. I wasn't sure about doing him at first, ex-para he was. But that was long ago. He's turned fat and was snoring his head off like a pig, cider bottles all around him.'

Clare considered how to handle him, wondering if she should cut him off. Deciding that he'd only call someone else if he couldn't spout off at her, she said, 'So you must have a lot of money to spend.'

'The man hasn't paid me yet. But he was really pleased with me, said I'd done a first class job with flying colours. That's why I'm calling – can you see if there will be many more missions?'

Clare paused for a few moments. The whole thing was too creepy. Rather than claim to be looking up his charts to spin out the call for longer, she decided to get off the phone as soon as possible. 'Let me see. Taurus is coming into the sphere of the dynamic Mars, which indicates a very auspicious time for you. And with a full moon on the wane, I'd say that yes, you can expect a long and fruitful run with this work.'

'How soon will he call me again?'

'Oh, soon my child, soon.'

'Great!' An awkward pause. 'Well, thanks. And, um . . .'

She could tell he was building up to ask her something else. Memories of abysmal school-age fumbles appeared in her mind and she cut him off with a speedy, 'Thank you, and good night.'

Sitting back, she blew out a long sigh. Something about the way he talked worried her. He was obviously very uneducated, but occasionally words would appear in his speech which were entirely unexpected. As if he was repeating something a third, and more intelligent party, had said to him. Remembering that Brian always kept a copy of the local paper on his desk, Clare hit 'call-wrap-up' and walked over to his office. After knocking lightly on his window, she opened the door a little and said, 'Mind if I borrow your paper?'

'Course not, sweetie. Help yourself.'

She picked it up and went back to her cubicle. Once her headset was back on she re-released 'call-wrap-up' to open her line once again, then unfolded the paper and began scanning through the pages, searching for any reports of a murder of an old man. As usual there were plenty of incidents of old people being battered and robbed. She passed one story about a seventy-six-year-old woman being mugged in the street for a few pounds. Another about a fake gas inspector who'd duped his way into an eighty-three-year-old man's flat, assaulted him, tied him up and taken his life savings. But nothing on the suspicious death of an ex-soldier, or the discovery of an old woman's body either for that matter. When she reached the TV and horoscope section she knew the following pages were only full of adverts. She refolded the paper and opened her book once again.

Over the next three hours she completed fourteen more calls, two lasting for over ten minutes. Not bad for a Wednesday night. Once the clock on her console clicked midnight she pressed the 'log off' button and packed her stuff up. Passing the cubicles she could hear the quiet murmur of a voice coming from each one. At Brian's office she opened the door and put the paper back on his desk. She waved him goodnight, but he was too busy analysing the call statistics on his computer screen. Ahead of her the door opened and two more girls came in; this was peak time for the chat lines.

33

Baffled, Eric turned back to the front of the paper and scanned through the stories more slowly. But it was obvious there was nothing about an ex-soldier's death inside. He couldn't contain his surprise; it was now two days since the mission and he was sure someone would have discovered the body by now. Curiosity filled him, making him fidget in his seat. He dropped the paper into the bin, rose to his feet and stared out of the window of his office, across the twinkling lights of the city towards where the old man had lived.

Succumbing to the inquisitive urge nagging at him, he left the building and drove to the area behind the station. Once again he passed the shabby off-licence, retracing his previous route until Wood Road appeared on his left. Slowly he turned into the road, scanning ahead for any blue flashing lights. It was deserted. Slowing down a fraction he stared at the building, looking for signs of police tape at Bert's door, instead seeing the faint light still glowing from behind the thin blue curtain drawn across his front window. No one had noticed a thing.

As he pulled into his close a short while later he noticed a sheet of paper stuck to the lamp-post on the corner. He drew to a stop and wound down his window to read it.

Bold hand-written letters spelt out the word, LOST. Below it was a poorly photocopied snapshot of his neighbour's cat. Lying on what appeared to be a pile of tea towels, it smugly regarded the camera. Eric thought of all the times it had sprayed acrid urine round his garden, laid turds in his flowerbeds and abandoned the corpses of small animals on his lawn. Glancing over the few lines below the image, he spotted a phone number and mention of a reward before he eased the vehicle forward again.

Just as he was locking his garage a trembling voice said, 'Eric?'

He turned around to see his neighbour standing on her front doorstep. With slippers covering her feet, she was reluctant to step onto her drive. Eric walked to the knee-high fence separating their two front lawns.

'Mrs Fleming, is everything all right?'

'Well, not really. I don't know if you've seen any of my posters. Frank's gone missing, I haven't seen him for days. I'm worried sick he may be trapped in someone's shed. I was hoping you could just check yours for me?'

'Of course. Now I think of it, I haven't seen his little face looking at me from the top of the fence in days.'

'I know,' she frowned. 'It's horrible not knowing

where he is.' A hand went to her throat and she fiddled anxiously with her collar.

'I'll check right now. Though I haven't been in it myself for well over a week.'

'Oh, thank you, it will just help me sleep better knowing he's not in there.'

Eric walked down the narrow passageway and into his back garden. He crossed the lawn to the shed at the bottom and glanced over his shoulder. Light suddenly shone out from his neighbour's French windows as she opened the curtains. He heard the doors being slid back, so he opened his shed and poked his head into the dark interior. Just inside the door was a bag of chicken manure fertiliser and he tapped his fingers on the neck of the sack while calling with unnecessary loudness for such a small space, 'Frank!' Then, thinking about the animal's impromptu cremation, he whispered to the shadows, 'Can you hear me up in catty heaven?'

From her garden his neighbour called in a high tremulous voice, 'Franky, Franky, Franky! Come to Mummy!'

Eric waited a few moments. 'I'm sorry, Mrs Fleming. He doesn't appear to be in here.'

'No,' she agreed mournfully. 'Thanks anyway.'

'That's no problem, and I'll keep my eye out for him. Don't worry, I'm sure he'll reappear soon.'

As he walked back across the lawn to his own house

he reflected on the concern shown for a missing cat while, if events so far were anything to go by, old people could lie dead and undiscovered in houses and flats throughout the country.

34

The toilet roll made a soft drumming sound as Eric pulled a length of tissue clear. He tore it off, bunched it into a loose ball and pushed it into his trouser pocket. Back in his office he waited until ten-past-eleven; he knew from the departmental timetable that, by then, she would be well into her last tutorial of the year. Slipping out of his office he locked the door behind him, walked quickly down the corridor, went through the two sets of double doors and entered Patricia's half of the floor.

He rarely ventured in here and looked with distaste at the mass of colourful posters brightening the walls. As he passed the main tutorial room he could hear her voice inside, confident and authoritative, yet not too serious. Just as he went past the door some comment caused a swell of laughter from the many people packed inside.

At the end of the corridor he knocked on the door marked, 'Mrs P. Du Rey BA MA.' A voice on the other side said 'Come in.'

He opened it up and Lisa, Patricia's young secretary, looked up from her computer. Surprised, she said, 'Hello Professor . . . I'm afraid Pat's in the middle of a tutorial. You probably passed . . .'

'Don't worry,' said Eric with a hint of urgency in his voice, 'I just need to borrow a couple of recent Government Green Papers I know she has.'

'Oh, right . . . um, which ones?' she said, starting to get up.

'No, no, no,' said Eric, waving theatrically with his hands. 'Don't let me interrupt you. It'll be far quicker if I just pop in and get them, I know exactly where they are.'

Lisa sat back down in her seat and said a little uncertainly, 'OK then.'

Eric quickly crossed to the other door leading into Patricia's private office. On his side of the department this area was a reading room: he didn't believe in the head of the department having an office any larger than that of his co-lecturers. And to have a private secretary was unthinkable. He opened the door and, leaving it slightly ajar, went over to the bookshelf behind Patricia's desk. Scanning the shelves he waited until the sound of typing next door restarted. Then he pulled the tissue from his pocket and turned his attention to Patricia's handbag hung over the back of her leather chair. The top zip was open and Eric could immediately see her keys nestled next to a purse and small make-up bag.

With his long forefinger and thumb he teased them out from between the other items. As soon as they were clear he gripped them tightly to stop them clinking then wrapped them in a muffling layer of tissue. Then he pushed the lump to the very bottom of his pocket.

Turning round, he grabbed the nearest three Green Papers off Patricia's shelf and walked back out. 'Here they are,' he said cheerfully, holding them up and heading straight for the door. 'I'll just photocopy the bits I need. Back in half an hour or so.'

He walked quickly to his office, dropped the publications on his desk and went straight back out. Not wanting to wait for the lift's slow arrival, he ran down the stairs, unchained his bike from the railings outside and cycled as fast as he could to the small key cutter's shop by the train station. At the booth he took Patricia's keys out of his pocket and scrutinised the collection.

He'd been to Otter's Pool Lodge a few times when she had first taken her post at the University. But, when a return invitation to his house for drinks and dinner never arrived, she had stopped asking him. It didn't really bother him – he had decided the size of her country home was obscene. Then the professional coolness had settled between them, growing stronger as the months passed and their different approaches to both lecturing and politics gradually became apparent.

Now he decided the key to her back door could only be one – Otter's Pool Lodge was a converted barn in the exclusive countryside south of the city. He remembered the back door was an aged oak one, with a huge black handle and hinges.

The key he held up to the man looked like an antique, something from a Dickensian novel. Inside the booth the man raised his eyebrows and wiped his hands on the thick apron around his waist. 'Not your standard cut,' he observed, taking the key from Eric's outstretched fingers. 'It'll be six pounds.'

'That's fine – I'm in an awful hurry. My wife's about to catch the train home, and she's lost hers. Can you do it for me now?'

'Course,' said the man, turning to the machinery behind him. He set Patricia's key in some clamps and then picked a blank key from a selection hanging from the wall at his side. He placed it in the machine and began moving the handles to trace an outline around Patricia's. As he did so the cutting bit lined up against the blank key below mirrored his actions. A piercing, grating whine started up and Eric could smell metal in the air. A few minutes later the man turned back round. He placed a brand new key on the counter and took a cloth from his pocket. 'I'll just clean this old one up for you mate.'

'No!' Eric said sharply. 'It's fine. I haven't time. Please.' He held out his hand.

The man in the booth looked at him. 'Six quid then.'

'Sorry to be abrupt. Here.' Eric scrabbled in his pocket and found the necessary money. The man handed the key over. 'Thank you,' said Eric, slipping Patricia's key back onto its ring and the spare one into his jacket pocket. Then he swung a spindly leg over his bike and raced back to the department, knees pumping up and down.

After jogging back up the stairs he returned to his office and grabbed the Green Papers off his desk. Making an effort to breathe normally, he walked back through to Patricia's side of the department, noting with relief that her tutorial hadn't ended early. He knocked on her office door and went in, 'All done,' he said, smiling. 'I'll pop them back in their proper place.'

Without waiting for Lisa to answer he entered Patricia's room and returned the Green Papers to her collection. With teeth clenched, he unwrapped the keys from their tissue wrapping and wiped them down. Then, holding them in a pinch of tissue paper, he carefully reinserted them back into her handbag.

'Thanks ever so much,' he said casually, walking back past Lisa's desk, swinging the door shut and leaving a sour smell of sweat behind him.

35

Another champagne cork popped and several people whooped with delight. Bubbles welled up out of its neck and Michel held the bottle well clear of his suit, allowing the froth to drip into the plastic cup Pat was holding out below.

Crowded into her office was her entire departmental staff. In the corner Clare, there on the pretext of asking Patricia's advice about MA courses and feeling slightly embarrassed to be part of the proceedings, chatted to Patricia's secretary, Lisa.

'So Pat,' said Julian, his cupped palm full of peanuts. 'Does this mean we'll all be upgrading our computers? I've had my eye on one of those wafer thin monitors they've had in all the banks for ages.'

Several staff members indulged Julian's remark with polite laughs but, with the same thought having occurred to them, they all watched Patricia for her reaction.

With the hand holding her cup, Patricia began drunkenly wagging a finger at Julian, oblivious to the champagne spilling down the back of her hand and dripping onto the carpet.

'Now, now,' she light-heartedly admonished. 'We'll

have to see how the budget stretches after I've had my brand new I-Mac.'

They all guffawed, taking her answer as a positive sign. Michel had finished topping up everyone's cups and placed the empty bottle of Piper-Heidsieck alongside all the others lined up on the filing cabinet. 'Well everyone, I've thought of another toast! Here's to the ESPRC for their wise decision and another three happy years in the pursuit of research and,' he paused dramatically, 'recreation!'

The room cheered in agreement and plastic cups were raised to glistening lips. Once everyone had taken a gulp Patricia said, 'And I'll just like to raise a toast to Michel for kindly supplying us with all this delicious champagne.' She turned unsteadily to address her husband directly, 'Us poor academics, we're only used to celebrating with . . .'

At that moment there was a knock on the door and Eric stepped round it, a bottle of Cava in his hand. A hush instantly fell over the room, but before the silence could become too obvious Patricia loudly exclaimed, 'Eric – I'm so glad you're here. Please, come in and have some bubbly.' Subtly she nudged her husband as she stepped towards Eric.

His eyes flashed behind his glasses as he quickly took in who else was in the room. 'Thanks. Here, I've brought a little something,' he replied, handing Patricia the bottle as Michel appeared with a plastic cup and another bottle of Piper-Heidsieck.

'Your good health Eric,' he said, filling the cup and handing it over.

'And both of yours,' answered Eric, with a meaningful glance into Patricia's eyes. 'I got your email announcement earlier, but I had to get some end of term bits and pieces out of the way first.' He held up his cup, 'Congratulations!'

All three drank again, Patricia and Michel desperately trying to think of something to say as they swallowed. But Eric spared them the effort by continuing, 'So Michel, you've got a few days away from Brussels?'

'Unfortunately not. I just whipped over when I heard the news this afternoon. I'm on the last flight back tonight. There's a lot of work to be done sorting out the legal side of some new fishing quotas.'

'I see,' said Eric. 'And Pat, surely you're going with him for a few well-deserved days off?'

Patricia had never heard Eric being so affable. 'No such luck,' she said, clutching her husband's arm and smiling up at him. 'Not yet anyway.'

Michel said to Eric, 'I don't think she would be allowed on the plane, not in her current state at least.'

'Oh don't,' said Patricia. A little embarrassed, she looked up at Eric. 'I'm awful at handling my drink for the vertically challenged amongst us, alcohol gets straight into the blood. It's all to do with body weight.'

'I imagine it is,' said Eric, eyes straying to the inner crook of her elbow. 'Still, some things deserve a celebration.' And he raised his glass again, encouraging Patricia to take another sip. As she did so she swayed against her husband, and he jokingly said, 'Careful! I think it's a taxi home for you tonight dear.'

At that moment Clare and Lisa squeezed past, 'We're just nipping next door to the coffee room,' said Lisa, holding up a packet of cigarettes by way of an explanation.

'Filthy habit,' said Patricia good-naturedly. 'Not at all like drinking.'

They all smiled as the two younger women carried on past. On the other side of the room Julian noticed as they went out of the door. He patted his trouser pocket to check his cigarettes were inside.

In the coffee room Lisa and Clare slumped on to the soft seats. 'Shit. I'm quite pissed,' said Clare, sitting back.

'Not as bad as Pat. Did you see her stagger just now? She's really going for it.'

They both grinned as Lisa took out two cigarettes.

'You don't mind me scrounging?' asked Clare. 'I've got some roll-ups in my bag.'

'Don't be silly,' replied Lisa. 'Anyway, you're about to graduate – you've got to give up the rollies soon. Move on to proper fags.' She handed Clare a Marlboro Light and lit their cigarettes.

'When do you get your results? It's soon isn't it?' she asked a little more seriously.

'I was hoping you could tell me that,' said Clare with mock disappointment. 'Early next week according to the last prediction.'

'And then what are you going to do?' asked Lisa, blowing smoke up at the ceiling.

Unsure of what she might know, Clare studied Lisa's profile for a second and then said, 'It depends on my class of degree. I'd like to do an MA somewhere if I can.'

'Like here perhaps?' Lisa smiled, and leaned closer to whisper, 'Pat got me to file your application earlier. I think it will be excellent to have you in the department.'

Clare smiled, 'Cheers, I can't wait to be honest.'

'Oh, hello you two,' said Julian from the doorway, acting surprised at seeing them. 'You've had the same thought as me.'

He sat down opposite them and when Lisa didn't offer him a cigarette from her pack on the table, he lit up one of his own. 'Did I hear mention of an MA just then?' he asked, looking at Clare.

'Yes. I was just saying to Lisa, if I get the grade, I wouldn't mind doing one.'

'Well,' he said condescendingly. 'With this grant now in the bag, there's likely to be a couple of positions here next year. In fact,' he went on with a sly look, 'you seem to be the only undergraduate invited to this little soirée.'

Clare tried to hide her agitation by taking a drag on her cigarette, 'Nah, I just happened to be in seeing Pat about which universities she recommends.'

'Mmmmm, really?' said Julian, arching his eyebrows. Clare had the sudden urge to punch him in the face.

Sensing the tension, Lisa cut in. 'Anyway, it looks like this grant is,' she lowered her voice, 'the last nail in the coffin for poor old Maudsley.'

Julian glanced towards the doorway, 'Yup, I think that's true. Still, it's about time he got more opportunity to do some gardening or whatever it is retired people do.'

The two girls looked at him disapprovingly.

Seeing their expressions he said, 'Oh come, come. He's well past it. I think he secretly knows it too.' He leaned forward, monopolising the conversation. 'Try and get yourself in Pat's department Clare. I for one would look forward to . . .' he got to his feet, crotch level with their eyes, '. . . working with you.' They both had to roll their eyes upward to look at his face. 'See you in there.' He ground out his cigarette and walked back into Patricia's study.

As soon as he was out of the room they looked at each other. Lisa announced, 'I want to. . .'

'. . . puke.' Clare finished the sentence for her. 'Do you think he heard us?'

'No we were whispering.'

'God, he's vile isn't he?'

'Tell me about it,' said Lisa, raising herself up in the seat. 'He's always drifting into Pat's office with bullshit requests for staples and stuff. Strangely, the conversation always ends up with him asking what I'm up to after work. He gives me the creeps.' She shuddered as if someone had trickled icy water down the back of her neck.

They both stubbed out their cigarettes in silence and Lisa said, 'Fancy another?'

'Oh, go on then,' laughed Clare and they lit up again.

'So I wonder what Maudsley will do,' commented Lisa quietly.

'I know. Poor old bloke. He lives for his job here.'

'Yeah, even though Julian is a complete twat, he's got a point though. No one wants to do his courses. Pat's having to teach bigger and bigger classes, mark more and more essays, while he has hardly anything to do.'

A part of Clare wondered if she should come out with her next comment. But, feeling light-headed with the champagne, she threw caution to the wind. 'I did one of his courses this term.'

Outside the door Eric, on his way to the men's toilet, paused.

'It was dire. Most lectures there was me and about two others. If I'd have charged the ones who couldn't be arsed to show up for photocopying my notes, I could have made a fortune.'

Lisa giggled and Clare carried on, slightly louder,

'Don't tell anyone, but I actually asked him about research positions in his department next year. First time anyone's actually tried to jump on a sinking ship.'

The comment stung Eric and the corners of his mouth twitched downwards. As the two girls began to laugh he passed like a long silent shadow across the doorway.

'Let's get back in there before they neck all that champagne,' said Lisa.

As they reentered Patricia's office Michel was shaking hands and patting backs. 'Good to see you again Lisa. And it's Clare isn't it?'

'Yes, thank you for the champagne.'

'You won't tomorrow morning,' he laughed, turning to Patricia. 'Are you sure you're OK?'

'Go on, away with you,' Patricia flapped a hand a little too vigorously, the hair on one side of her head squashed flat where she'd been hugging him. 'Call me tomorrow – you know there's no way I'll wake up to the phone tonight.'

He winked at her, heading for the door and almost bumping into Eric as he slipped back into the room. 'See you about Eric. And make sure my wife gets home safely will you?'

'Of course Michel, good bye,' said Eric, stepping back so the other man could leave.

One of the younger lecturers was searching through the empty bottles. When he realised only Eric's Cava remained, he turned to his colleagues. 'Who fancies moving on to Gio's Wine Bar?'

Flushed with free alcohol, cash so far untouched, everyone except Patricia, Eric and Clare agreed enthusiastically.

'Right, let's do a whip. Tenners in?'

Everyone started rummaging in their pockets.

'Pat?' Lisa asked. 'The night's still young you know.'

Already more drunk than she had been in a long time, Patricia knew moving on to another venue for yet more drink was going to be impossible.

'No, you lot go and have a good time. I've had more than my limit for one night.'

'Oh come on Pat, are you sure?' someone else encouraged.

'No really,' she said, holding up both hands and sitting down on the edge of her desk.

'I should be getting off too,' said Clare, feeling like an intruder and aware she only had the bus fare home.

'Bollocks!' said Lisa, and then clamped a hand over her mouth. 'I mean, no way. You're coming with us. We can let a student off the whip can't we?' Lisa asked the room.

A chorus of 'Yes' and 'Of course' followed and Clare smiled.

'Eric?' someone said hesitantly.

He looked gravely at his questioner, 'No thank you.' His tone didn't invite any attempt to dissuade him.

As they filed from the room, everyone said their goodnights and thankyous. Soon the group had headed off down the corridor, voices suddenly growing fainter as the double doors swung shut behind them.

'Well,' said Patricia, running a hand through her hair and looking unsteadily around her at the discarded cups, bottles and bowls of nibbles. 'I'd better clear up.'

'I'll help,' Eric quickly said and began piling paper plates onto each other.

'No, really Eric.' Pat said, feeling uncomfortable now she was alone with him. 'You needn't, I'm sure you want to get off home.'

'It's fine, don't worry,' he answered.

'Thank you,' replied Patricia as she gathered up the few cups with any champagne still left in, 'I'll empty these down the loos.'

When she walked back in a couple of minutes later Eric had just finished filling two cups with Cava. Before she could object, he said, 'Actually Pat, I'm glad we've got a few minutes alone. It seems as good a time as any to tell you that I'm taking voluntary redundancy.'

Patricia stopped in her tracks. Reluctantly she took the outstretched cup. 'Oh Eric,' fighting to clear her head, 'is it because of those awful budget cuts? Surely they're not set in stone?'

Eric smiled grimly and knocked his plastic cup against Patricia's, forcing her to drink again.

'Not really. I've been feeling more and more lately

that it's all a bit much for these old bones.' He looked down at the skeletal hand holding his cup. 'The budget cuts just made my decision easier.'

He took another sip, barely allowing more than a drop into his mouth. Patricia gulped again.

'Well I think, I think it's . . .' she struggled to arrange the sentence in her head before attempting it, '. . . it's a scandal if a career as distinguished as yours is cut short by this Government's actions. And they wonder why we're suffering a brain-drain to the likes of America?'

Eric lowered his head. 'You're too kind.'

Patricia stood there, realising she could see the top of Eric's head twice. Blinking to try and clear her double vision, she placed her cup on the desk and began to gather up plates, pouring the leftovers into one bowl. Dry roasted peanuts cascaded to the floor. 'Bugger,' she crouched down, and had to put out a hand to stop herself toppling over. Quickly Eric tipped some drink from his cup in to hers.

Looking down at her, Eric was suddenly struck by a sense of her vulnerability. Knees bent, her hand scrabbling over the carpet like a hungry crab searching for food, he thought, 'Am I supposed to lose my department to you?' He focused malevolently on the swirl of hair at the crown of her head, saw the wisps of grey pushing through the dyed brown strands. Feeling his eyes boring into the top of her skull, Patricia said, 'Have you any plans for retirement?'

Eric breathed in slowly, then knelt down beside her to help scoop up the last of the peanuts. 'Not really. I may move to the Peak District, indulge my love of walking. The Derbyshire Health Authority has a very good standard of care for its pensioners, which, let's face it, is what I'll soon be.'

Uncomfortable once again with his proximity, Patricia tried to move away but her crouching position made it difficult. 'Walking. That sounds a lovely idea,' she said, struggling to her feet. 'I sometimes dream about doing more things like that myself.'

Eric looked up and wanted to scream in her face, 'Then why don't you, you stupid bitch! Leave my fucking department alone!'

As Patricia stood upright the blood rushed from her head. Seeing her beginning to lose balance, Eric quickly stood as well, grasped her by the shoulders and guided her back to the desk so she could sit on its edge once again.

'Thank you Eric,' she said, massaging her temples and breathing deeply for a few seconds. 'Now I must be getting home. I'm feeling really quite woozy. Can we talk about this tomorrow perhaps?'

Eric was collecting the empty bottles together and lining them up on a filing cabinet.

'Let me call you a taxi. Do you have any numbers?' he asked.

'Lisa's phone – she has a sticker on it.'

Eric dialled the number and ordered a cab. 'Five minutes,' he said, walking back to Patricia's desk. He picked up their cups. 'Well Pat – it's been a pleasure working with you.'

She stared at the full cup, unsure if she could hold any more alcohol down. But refusing was impossible. 'And you too,' she began drinking again.

Eric watched as she just managed to place the cup on the desk.

'That really is me . . . enough for me,' said Patricia, slurring her words.

He realised that he had pushed the voluntary drinking as far as it would go. 'What you need is some milk. Stay here.' Grabbing a clean plastic cup, he walked out of the office and into the coffee room. He opened the fridge that the coffee percolator stood on and took out a carton of milk. Filling the cup three quarters full, he removed a hip flask from his pocket and added a large splash of vodka to it.

Back in the office Patricia was sitting slackly on the edge of the desk, arms wrapped about herself, head hanging forwards.

'Here Pat, this will settle your stomach,' he held the cup just below her nose. Patricia tilted her head back, trying to focus on it. 'Oh, thanks.' A hand took it and she lifted it slowly to her lips and gulped it down.

'Well done,' said Eric, taking it off her and dropping it into the nearest bin. 'Right, let's go downstairs.' He picked up her coat, helped her into it and then hung her handbag over her shoulder. After putting the latch on her office door, he pulled it shut and guided her down the corridor. On the ground floor a metro taxi was idling outside the entrance. Eric wished the security guard good night and led Patricia to the doors. Once she was safely in the back of the taxi, it pulled away and Eric poked his head back into the reception.

'She'll sleep well tonight,' he said, smiling.

'It certainly looked that way,' agreed the security guard.

'Well, good night John.'

'Night Professor Maudsley.'

He walked round the corner to where his bike was chained up. Taking the mobile phone from his jacket, he dialled a number. 'Agent White? I have another job for you. Tonight.'

36

All three healthy birds were now laying but restrictions within the cage were creating visible signs of stress. Heat from their closely packed bodies and the ever-present dust caused them to preen more aggressively. Now they pulled at their feathers, frequently yanking them clean out of their flesh. This merely served to increase dust levels still further. Though the healthy birds were able to monopolise the front of the cage without contest from the injured bird, squabbling disagreements frequently broke out over access to the water drip. The largest bird had unchallenged access to it at all times, but the other two had yet to establish who ranked second. Occasionally a different person passed. This one was dressed in blue, not white. It behaved more erratically than the others, stopping to peer into cages, sometimes shouting, often running a key along the bars and terrifying them with the shrill noise. The feet of all four birds had become malformed. Unable to wear their claws down by scratching at anything, the talons had curled inwards. Lesions had broken out on the fleshy underpads of the largest bird's feet. The pain made its movements sharper, its head bobbed more jerkily and an aggravated clucking came almost continuously from its throat. Hunched in the back corner, the fourth bird was silent.

37

The taxi pulled up, diesel engine chugging loudly in the silent street.

'Cheers Lisa, I really owe you for tonight. It was great fun. And I'll give you the taxi fare tomorrow,' said Clare, grabbing her bag off the back seat.

'Don't be stupid. You don't owe me a penny. I'll see you in the department.'

Clare thanked the driver as she got out. Once she'd got her front door open she turned around, waved and the vehicle pulled away. Looking into the tiny hall she saw the morning post still lying on the doormat. From the other side of the living room door came the low drone of music. Shaking her head, she picked up the A4 sized envelope and went through.

Zoe was sitting in front of the gas fire, two stainless steel knives balanced on the horizontal bars, their tips inserted into the flames. On the hearth next to her was a couple of tea towels and a plastic bottle, the bottom of it cut away.

Clare took in the dirty plates, half full cups and general mess in a single glance. 'What are you up to?' she asked, frowning slightly.

Blearily, Zoe glanced over her shoulder, 'Hot knives. Fancy one?'

'No thanks. Want to know how my day went?' said Clare, collapsing on the sofa and examining the envelope.

'Yeah, course. Just hang on a sec.'

Zoe placed the neck of the plastic bottle between her teeth. Then she wrapped a tea towel around the handle of each knife and withdrew one from the flames. Carefully she placed a large lump of cannabis resin on its flat surface. A wisp of smoke curled up. Then she extracted the other knife. Holding the one with the resin stuck to it just below the cut away end of the plastic bottle, she pressed the blades together, sandwiching the resin between the two hot surfaces. Instantly the bottle filled with a thick yellow smoke and Zoe inhaled deeply. The bottle emptied and she dropped the knives back on the hearth, removed the bottle from her mouth and slumped on the carpet, back against the base of the sofa.

A series of tiny coughs sounded at the back of her throat, but she refused to open her mouth and let any of the smoke escape. The coughs increased in strength, turning into little explosive exhalations, sounding just as if she was trying to suppress the urge to laugh. Eventually she could hold it in no longer and her mouth opened with a pained 'aaaaahhh.' Barely any smoke came out and she ground both fists against her sternum, eyes tightly shut.

'Is that worth all the trouble?' asked Clare, looking dubiously at her friend.

Zoe's head lolled back and with eyes still shut, she replied hoarsely, 'Don't knock it till you've tried it.'

Clare sighed and pulled the sheets of paper from the envelope. Every telephone call was listed there, with dates, durations and costs. She looked at the table, saw the recruitment section of the paper below a dirty plate and slid it out. Then she examined the list of numbers called over the past fortnight, searching for any from the job section in front of her. It soon became apparent her friend hadn't rung a single one.

'Zoe,' Clare announced, voice serious. 'What are you doing?'

'I told you. Hot knives. They're a blast.'

'No, I mean with your job search. You haven't called a single company.'

Slowly Zoe raised up a hand and gripped her forehead just below the hairline. She turned her head to Clare, and with her hand held there like a sun visor, opened a pair of heavily bloodshot eyes. In the shadow below her fingers, she squinted at the itemised phone bill Clare was holding up.

'Oh shit,' she mumbled.

'So what's going on?'

She shut her eyes again, 'Can you turn off that lamp. It's too bright in here.'

Clare reached over and switched off the small

reading lamp by her side. Now the room was just bathed in the glow from the gas fire and a lava lamp in the corner. As Zoe went to speak a train thundered past, drowning out the noise of her first words.

Once it was past she began talking again, head bowed towards her knees. 'I couldn't face going through it all again.'

'Through what again?'

'The interviews. Trial days. Being sat down in front of a Mac and told to work out some layout with the studio manager stopping every now and again to check over your shoulder. Having everything analysed, discussed. I'm not ready for all that stress again.'

'So you decided just to take me for a ride instead? Doss here, rent free. Smoke dope all day?'

'No, I meant to ring those numbers. But I . . . didn't. I just need some time to get my head together. Then I'll start looking for work again.'

'Zoe, you don't really reckon sitting in here all day is getting your head together? You stay up every night 'til the small hours and then get up after lunch. That's what's really doing your head in. You've got to get a grip. Get back out there, get back in . . .' She stopped short of saying 'the running'. She didn't want it to sound like a race. It wasn't what Zoe needed to hear. 'Get back to using a Mac. It's what you're good at, what you trained for.'

Zoe brought her knees up to her chin and hugged her shins. 'I suppose so.'

Gently Clare added, 'I'm due to be out of this flat once term officially ends next week.'

Zoe pursed her lips, 'What if you get that job in Patricia's department? Surely you'll be able to stay on then?'

Clare felt a pang of anger. 'If I get that job they won't let me stay here. I was lucky to get this flat in the first place – it's meant for undergraduate single mums with kids. Not lecturers or researchers. Besides, if I'm earning a wage I'd prefer to pay for somewhere that's not like living at Waterloo junction.'

Zoe nodded, 'Yeah, you're right. And you're right about the job hunting. I'll get the paper tomorrow.'

Clare stood up and went into the kitchen. She searched for a clean glass, but Zoe hadn't washed up. After rinsing one out she opened the fridge, looking for some milk. The carton inside was empty. She filled the glass with water and went back into the living room. 'It's the way you lied to me Zoe. That's really pissed me off.'

Her friend didn't look round. 'I'm sorry mate. I didn't mean to. Things just sort of. . . slid.'

Clare stopped at the hearth and looked at the blackened knives lying there. 'You should lay off the gear too. It's no good for you if you're feeling bad in the first place.'

Zoe nodded meekly and Clare went into her room and shut the door. Once her light was off Zoe muttered 'Downer,' to herself. She reached over for the packet of Rizlas on the table.

38

'Evening Agent White,' Eric said tersely as Rubble got into the car beside him.

Sensing anxiety in the older man, Rubble replied a little warily, 'Evening Agent Orange.' He pulled on the pair of rubber gloves that were waiting for him.

'Tonight's operation should be very straightforward.' Eric continued briskly, his sentences clipped and tense. 'The client has supplied me with a key. She lives in quite a large house, and sleeps in the master bedroom. You'll find it at the top of the stairs. She assured me that she'll be sleeping soundly for our arrival. Don't be put off by her age. She's no spring chicken, but she's not as old as the other two you put to sleep.'

'Why does she want finishing off then?' asked Rubble.

'Some sort of disease. To do with her bones I think. They can't cure it.'

Rubble nodded, studying the plastic rear of the tax disc holder on Eric's windscreen. His eyes shifted to the parking permit just above it; he could see the faint outline of the crest showing through. 'Does the Government pay for your car and stuff like that?' he asked pointing at the corner of the windscreen.

Eric looked at where his thick finger was directed and thought he was pointing at the tax disc. 'Remember Agent White, we work on a need-to-know basis only. And you don't need to know that,' he snapped.

They set off back to the motorway, and were soon cruising at just below 70 mph. As Eric drove along he kept fidgeting in his seat and glancing across at his passenger. Rubble kept his eyes fixed on the road ahead and his mouth shut.

Eventually Eric said, 'How are you finding the work so far Agent White?'

Rubble glanced at him uncertainly, 'Enjoying it.'

'You can be honest Agent White. It's not unusual to have . . . negative emotions.'

'Negative?'

'Yes. Perhaps feelings of remorse?'

Rubble looked at him blankly.

'Guilt. You know . . . um, doubts. About taking . . . about taking another human being's life.'

Rubble shook his head.

'You never find yourself dwelling on the missions you've completed?'

Thinking he was being tested, Rubble kept his answer short, 'No.'

'What about now. Any feelings of nervousness at this moment?'

'No.'

They drove along in silence, the inside of the car

growing ever more hot and claustrophobic in Eric's mind. When they reached the turn off he had unbuttoned the top of his shirt and wound the window down a little. They slowed to a halt at a set off traffic lights leading on to a small roundabout and, even though there was no other traffic in sight, the lights stubbornly remained on red.

Irritated, Eric looked into his rearview mirror and shut his eyes. On the road behind him he saw an image of the bodies of Bert and Edith lying there. Bert's nearer the car, Edith's further up the road, almost swallowed by the darkness. Ahead he saw Patricia standing in his path. Just a simple obstacle to get past and then he would be secure. Once she was behind him, he could move forward – put more and more distance between himself and the memories of all three.

He opened his eyes and revved the engine, willing the lights to change. The red glow suffused the inside of the car, catching on the white rubber stretched over his knuckles as they gripped the steering wheel tight. The smell of exhaust fumes drifted into the vehicle and he remembered getting a mouthful from Patricia's BMW outside the biology department.

The orange light came on as he forced himself to think of his father and how retirement had destroyed him. Then both bulbs died and the one below glowed green.

There could be no going back now. He let his foot off

the clutch and moved forward, driving across the roundabout and slowly through the lanes. The countryside bordering the road was almost entirely farmland, interspersed with occasional driveways that curled away across landscaped grounds to large houses.

After a few minutes Eric changed down through the gears and rolled to a stop beside a dense row of conifers. A sign at the top of the driveway said, *Otter's Pool Lodge*. Eric focused on the small gaps between the branches, making sure the house beyond them was completely dark. 'OK, this is it.' He reached below his seat and handed Rubble a loaded syringe. Carefully he placed it in the pocket of his overalls. Next Eric handed him a large shiny new key and a small pocket torch. 'Now, proceed across the lawn and round the back of the house. Open the kitchen door and go through into the hallway. You'll see the stairs to your left. At the top a door will be straight in front of you. That's where she is. As I said before, she should be fast asleep. But if she does wake up confused you are to restrain her and give her the injection anyway. Now, I've got several other operations in the area tonight, so I won't be able to pick you up for a few hours. Once you've completed your operation, wait for me in the garden. There's not much traffic out here, so you'll know it's me when I park at this spot. Everything clear?'

'Can I climb up a tree? Wait for you up in the branches?'

'Yes, that's a good idea. Wait for me up a tree, it's a very safe place to hide.'

Rubble got out of the car and gently closed the door. Eric put the car into first gear and, keeping his revs right down, slowly eased away. At the next turning he doubled back to the city, heading for the all-night garage near his house. He pulled up to the side of the pumps, dropped his rubber gloves into a bin full of them from the forecourt's dispenser and walked over to the window hatch. Taking in the notice telling him he was on CCTV, he ordered a pint of milk and a box of paracetamol. The young man inside picked a small bottle of pills off the shelf behind him then set off round the counter to get the milk from an open-fronted fridge. Craning his neck to see the image on the screen by the till, Eric realised the tall thin man staring at a window was himself. It reminded him of the footage he'd seen on Crimestoppers when the presenter asks for help in identifying a particular suspect. Fearfully, he wondered if what he was looking at would ever end up on national television as part of a documentary.

The attendant returned, asking for payment before he pushed the items through. Eric drove back to his house and, once in his kitchen, knocked back a couple of pills with a gulp of water straight from the tap. Then he made himself a cup of cocoa, sat down at the table and tried to concentrate on that day's *Guardian*.

*

The back of Patricia's house was covered in a thick layer of ivy and Rubble had some trouble finding the small oak door. The key turned smoothly in the lock and it swung open with a slight creak. In the corner of the kitchen a fridge-freezer juddered to life as the thermostat triggered the cold air mechanism inside. Next to it the green numbers of an oven clock glowed. Rubble looked at the kitchen table and the bag thrown on to it. A bunch of keys lay carelessly splayed on the wooden surface. Testing the floor with his foot, he guessed it was solid wood, and he walked carefully across it into the hall. To his left stairs stretched upwards, lit by moonlight shining in from a round shaped window set deeply into the thick wall. He climbed up them, a massive beam in the ceiling not far above his head. He stopped outside the half open bedroom door and listened. In the gloom he could see a double bed, ruffled down one side. A thin strip of light shone from under a door in the corner of the room. Frowning, he crept across the deep pile carpet to the bed and, once he was standing by it, saw that it was empty. A dark, wet patch was visible across the pillow and sheet. Puzzled, he noticed a large cooking pot on the carpet next to the bedside table.

Slowly he turned his head and looked at the glow coming from beneath the door on the opposite side of the room. Silently he walked round the bed, careful to avoid the high-heeled shoes on the floor, one toppled over on its side. At the door he bowed his head and brought his ear to within millimetres of the wood.

On the other side a tap dripped.

Rubble reached out and slowly turned the handle. The door swung partly inwards without a sound and, inch by inch, he opened it further. The first thing he could see was a towel rail on the wall just inside. As the door opened wider he could see a sink in the corner of the room and next to that a toilet. On the floor beside it was a wicker basket piled high with a jumble of toilet rolls. The next thing that came into view was a free standing shelf unit, crowded with bottles and jars.

The door was half open when he saw the partly wet nightdress crumpled on the carpet.

He edged the door open further and now he could see an empty shower unit in the opposite corner of the room. Next was the end of a bath. And in it, a pair of feet. They lay below the surface of the water, motionless.

His eyes narrowed and he looked at the lilac painted nails, waiting for movement. When nothing happened he stepped forwards and opened the door fully. As the hinges reached their limit they let out a long, high pitched creak.

He craned his neck round the door, saw a pair of submerged knees, thighs, crossed hands over a stomach, a pair of slack breasts. Finally he looked at Patricia Du Rey's face, eyes shut below the water, lips tinged blue and hair like tendrils of an aquatic plant floating about her head.

The tap continued dripping and the overflow let out a single glug as water drained into it. Rubble stepped fully into the bathroom and examined her more closely. The flesh all over her body was laced by an intricate network of wrinkles. Crouching down by the bath, he reached into the chilly water and lifted out a cold hand. Its surface was as deeply furrowed as that of a raisin. He let it fall back and looked up at her face. Trapped in the underside of each nostril was a silver sphere. He pinched her nose, squeezing out the two bubbles. They floated up a couple of inches and popped at the surface.

Back down in the kitchen his stomach rumbled and he remembered what Agent Orange had said about not picking him up for several hours. He walked over to the fridge in the corner of the room and opened the door. The shelves were stacked with strange things. A jar containing lumps of square shaped pale cheese in a thick oil. Another with green berry-like objects with small red things shoved into their hollow middles. A small bottle full of a watery brown liquid. He smelled the neck and recoiled at the sharp aroma of dead fish. The door was lined with little shelves and the top one held a row of eggs. Something he recognised. He plucked four from the rack and slipped them into the front pouch of his overalls, alongside the unused syringe.

Outside he locked the door, walked back round to the front of the house and crossed to the large cedar tree in the corner of the garden. Sitting up in its boughs he took out an egg and pressed his thumb through the brittle surface. Then he held it above his open mouth and pulled the shell apart. His mouth flooded with thick mucus. Locating the egg yolk with his tongue he punctured it, washed the mixture around his mouth and swallowed. Then he placed the empty shell back in his pocket and took out another egg.

Around three hours later he saw headlights approaching along the narrow lane. Recognising the tone of Agent Orange's engine he climbed down and was waiting by the hedge when the car pulled up.

He climbed in and Eric immediately pulled away. 'Was the operation a success?'

'She's dead, but I never killed her.'

'Pardon?' said Eric, braking hard and looking at Rubble.

'She was in the bath. Drowned.'

'You found her in the bath?'

'Yeah.'

'With her head under the water?'

'Naked she was. Sick all over her nightie. She must have been ill with that disease.'

'You're quite sure she was dead?'

'Yeah. She'd been in there a bit. The water was cold and she'd turned all wrinkly.'

Eric mused on the information. 'So you didn't inject her?'

'Nope,' Rubble fumbled in his pocket and brought out the syringe. 'Here.'

He handed it over.

Eric took it and noticed how it glistened. 'Why is it wet? Has it leaked?'

'Egg white,' explained Rubble.

Preferring not to ask for an explanation, Eric just dropped the syringe back under his seat. So that was it, he thought. Patricia had been removed. The project was over.

When they reached the caravan he took back Rubble's gloves and Patricia's key. 'Thank you Agent White, you have done very well.'

There was a note of finality in his voice and Rubble looked alarmed.

'It is policy to rest our agents every three jobs, so you will not be hearing from me again for a while.'

'I've done something wrong,' Rubble immediately said. 'Not injecting her – was that it?'

'Agent White, you have done nothing wrong. It's just regulations. Now, I really must be going,' he held out a hand and Rubble shook it uncertainly. Then he got out of the car and stood silently by as Eric reversed back up the lane.

In the grey of early dawn he turned off the motorway

and followed the signs for *Fairwind Waterpark*. Soon he had parked at the side of a small lake with a fenced off area next to it full of tarpaulin covered sailing boats, masts rising at erratic angles into the slowly lightening sky. Only when he went to get the mobile phones from the glove compartment did he realise he'd forgotten to take Rubble's back. Cursing himself, he retrieved his own, scooped up the syringe from under the seat and got out of the car.

He walked to the water's edge and, standing on the top of a concrete slipway, opened up the back of the phone, ripped the SIM card out and ground it to pieces under his heel. Then he surveyed the perfect stillness of the lake before him. Hidden in the bullrushes on the other side, a coot made its chirruping call. Raising his arm he hurled the phone far out over the water. Its slowly turning shape cut through the still air, descending on a long arc before puncturing the glass-like surface. The splash was gone in a split second but a quivering wound remained, spreading slowly outwards. Quickly now Eric pulled the plunger from the syringe, spilling the contents over his hands. He flung both halves and the key into the dense reed bed to his side then held his glistening fingers up. A strangled noise escaped him and suddenly he stumbled forwards into the shallows. He waded out beyond the concrete slipway until his feet connected with the soft bottom of the lake. Falling to his knees, he held his hands below the water, churned them around in the gritty mud, then furiously began rubbing one against the other. Ripples from his activity advanced across the lake, meeting the last of those created by the phone's splash, engulfing and then overwhelming them as they continued on their way. After several minutes Eric was finally satisfied. As he walked calmly back to his car, arms hanging limply at his sides, the drips that fell from his fingertips were tinged with yellow by the rising sun.

Getting back into his car he concluded that all he had to do now was dispose of the remaining Euthanol and syringes back at his house. Then all means of connecting him to Rubble and any of the murders had been destroyed.

39

As she stifled her sobs behind the tissue the crowded room looked on in shocked silence.

'I'm sorry,' Lisa sniffed.

Clare gritted her teeth to suppress the waves of grief that were travelling up from her chest, making her lower lip tremble. With a voice hoarse from the lump in her throat, she tightened her grip around the other girl's shoulders and said quietly, 'You don't have to carry on.'

In the corner of the coffee room someone was hastily preparing a pot of coffee. On the padded seats, Julian tapped a biro slowly against the spine of a plastic folder.

'No, I want to. Michel wanted you all to know.' Resolutely she wiped her nose and dabbed at her eyes. Taking a deep breath, she continued. 'He tried ringing her from Brussels yesterday morning. When he couldn't get an answer he rang a neighbour. She went round with a spare key for the back door and found her . . . found her . . .' the sobbing started again and she struggled to make the next words comprehensible, '. . . dead in the bath.' Again she began to cry and various students and staff reached for cigarettes. After a few minutes Lisa was able to carry on. 'Michel flew straight back. The police think she had been sick in her bed and got up to clean herself off. It looks like she ran a bath, but must have passed out or fallen asleep after she got in.' Again she began to sob, choking on the words. 'Because she's so small her feet didn't reach the other end of the bath. So she slid under the water and drowned.'

The room was silent. Eventually someone whispered to their neighbour, 'Was she really that drunk?'

Several people remembered her being unsteady on her feet, holding onto her husband for support. Lisa carried on, 'Michel told me to tell you all that no one must blame themselves for this. He said, if anything, it's his fault for bringing along so much champagne.'

Lighters clicked and matches flared as more cigarettes were lit. The room was silent except for the tap, tap, tap of Julian's biro. Eventually he said, 'I wonder where this leaves the grant from the ESPRC? I presume it was awarded to the department and not Patricia personally?'

They all glared at him in silence. Clare felt like she was sitting too close to a giant cinema screen; trying to absorb everything was making her feel dizzy and sick. Behind the mass of thoughts crazily playing out in her head was the sombre realisation that someone she admired and liked immensely was now dead. Needing to take her mind off the terrible news and all its consequences, she picked up a copy of the local paper lying on the coffee table. The right hand column of the front page was topped by the headline, 'Leading academic dies in bath tragedy'. She read the first line again. 'Patricia Du Rey, a head of department at Manchester University has been found dead in her bath.'

Unable to look again at the photo of Patricia next to the University crest, Clare started turning the pages, eyes numbly wandering over the articles inside.

Someone else murmured, 'Where's Professor Maudsley? He must have been the last person with her.'

Lisa was looking at her nails as she quietly spoke. 'John, the security guard on duty that night, said Eric put her in a taxi not long after we'd all left. Said she looked really the worse for wear.'

Clare had reached page thirteen as she flicked through the paper before a small paragraph, boxed off in the corner of the page, caught her eye. The headline read 'War vet found dead.' Her vision seemed to tunnel in as she focused on the words.

'Albert Aldy, an ex-paratrooper who was decorated for his part in the Suez Crisis, has been found dead in his flat on Wood Road this Tuesday. Concerned neighbours, bothered by an unusual smell, first alerted the authorities. According to a council spokesman, the body had lain undiscovered "for several days". Albert, or Bert as he was more fondly known, lost his wife eight years ago and is not survived by any children.

'A familiar figure around the city centre parks, usually wearing his old paratrooper's beret, Bert liked nothing more than to tell passers-by about his time in the army, especially his exploits on the rugby field when playing scrum-half for the Combined Armed Forces. The same council spokesman added that, due to cutbacks, Bert's flat has now been boarded up.'

At the very end of the piece, added almost as an afterthought, was another small paragraph.

'In a tragically similar case the body of Edith Jennings was found by a door-to-door salesman earlier this week. Unable to get an answer at her door, the representative of the double glazing company glanced through the front window only to make his grim discovery.'

Clare looked away from the page and sat gazing at the floor, then she abruptly closed the paper, shoved it into her bag and got up. The rapidity of her movements caused everyone in the room to stare. 'Can I borrow the paper?' she asked no one in particular.

'Of course,' someone answered.

'Thanks. I'm sorry, but I've got to go,' The people sitting between her and the door moved their knees to the side so she could squeeze past. As she walked quickly from the crowded room, Julian watched her departure with interest.

40

When Rubble saw the photo on the front page of the newspaper, he knew he had to have one. Handing his comics to Mr Williams, he pointed to the uppermost copy, 'And that.'

The shop owner looked surprised, 'The *Manchester Evening News*? Not like you to be following gossip from the big city Roy.'

Rubble placed a dirty fingernail by the University crest alongside the woman's face, 'I want the government badge. For my collection.'

'The University crest you mean?' answered Mr Williams. Rubble's eyebrows dropped even lower. 'Well, with the paper, that's £3.85. I'll put it on your account.' Everything was placed inside a plastic bag and Rubble set off back towards the farm.

When the six women arrived mid-morning to collect the day's eggs, he returned moodily to his caravan and sat there looking over his comics, not wanting to be near anyone. He remained there until the egg collectors had gone, then took his air rifle from its sling and walked up to the packing shed. The day's produce was piled neatly in enormous trays by the double doors, ready for collection by the various supermarkets the next day. He transferred six eggs to a smaller carton then stalked back to his caravan, hoping to come across a cat or any other intruder to shoot at.

In his kitchen he mixed the eggs up with some milk and cooked an enormous mound of scrambled egg. Placing two slices of bread on a plate, he spooned the mixture on top of it and doused it all in ketchup. Sitting at his table and shovelling it all into his mouth, he opened his comics once again. But he couldn't concentrate on the pictures. Listlessly, he turned the pages, reaching the section of advertisements at the back. Despite always checking for them, he'd never found any other pieces of paper asking for Government agents. Maybe they only recruited once in a while. He slid the comics to one side and stared again at the front page of the local paper. He got up, crouched down at his cupboard and pulled the door open. The mobile phone lay there, its little green light blinking in the shadows and miserably he wondered when it might ring again.

After staring at it for a couple of minutes, he took out his sketchpad and sat back down at the table. Opening it up he turned to the crest he'd copied down from the top of the Official Secrets Act form he'd signed. It matched the one on the front of the newspaper, even down to the letters on the ribbon below the shield. Mr Williams' words echoed in his head, 'The University crest.'

Carefully he tore round the badge and photo, then placed the piece of newspaper at the top of the next blank page in his sketch book. In a matter of minutes he sketched an image which bore an almost exact resemblance to the woman from the newspaper.

As he leaned back against the foam cushions, he remembered something. When Agent Orange had dropped him off the other night, he'd forgotten to pay him. He was now owed money for two successful operations; he didn't expect anything for the third, since she was dead in the bath already.

He didn't really care about the money; what was far more important was when Agent Orange would call on him for another operation. But Sylvie had said he was about to come into money – so when would he be paid? It was easily a good enough reason to call her again. He went to the biscuit tin of coins in his cupboard and scoured it for silver. When he'd first started ringing the chat lines, his store of change had quickly vanished and the same thing was happening now. Finding only a few twenties, he pocketed them and set off for the phone box.

After pressing all his money into the slot he dialled the number. By the time he'd got past all the messages and music, he guessed most of his money had gone. Eventually he got to the point when he could tap the number 304 in. Immediately the voice he so badly wanted to hear came on to the line, 'Hello caller, my name is Sylvie Claro, would you . . .'

'It's me,' he announced.

41

Clare's eyes widened and she reached for the paper in her bag. Almost forgetting her accent, she said, 'My child, I do not know your name.'

'Rubble.'

'I'm sorry?'

'Rubble.'

'Rubble?'

'Yeah.'

Frowning Clare said, 'I have been examining the heavens. I think I know more of your secret work, I find it very interesting. The man you put to sleep, the ex-paratrooper . . .' She looked at the page of the newspaper. 'Did he serve in the Suez Crisis?'

'Yeah, I told you he did. He was in Three Para, Operation Musketeer. Three Para killed a load of the enemy and I reckon he potted three. Probably using a Vickers machine gun.'

'And before the soldier, you successfully completed another operation didn't you?'

'Yeah,' said Rubble proudly. 'Some old woman. Sleeping in her wheelchair she was.'

Clare glanced at the newspaper report again to

recheck the facts. 'Could you see that from outside her house?'

'Yeah, through the window.'

'But how could you see into her bedroom? Did you have a ladder?'

'No, she slept in the front room. It was a bungalow. I just looked through a gap in the curtains.'

Clare was still unsure of how genuine the caller was. 'So the project you're working on,' she continued probing. 'Who is the man giving you the money?'

'That's what I'm ringing you about. When will he pay me?' Rubble said impatiently.

'He owes me for the first two – the other night's was dead already.'

'Other night's?' Clare whispered, unsure if she wanted to hear what was coming.

'She had drowned. Didn't need to inject her, I gave him back the syringe. Full.'

Clare felt information shifting in her head. Connections were being formed, but she didn't quite know what they were leading to. 'You're saying the same man picked you up last night and took you to a house to put a woman to sleep?'

'That's right.'

'So what do you mean saying that she had drowned?'

'In her bath. She'd been sick in her bed – the man said she had a disease.'

He could only be talking about Patricia, Clare

thought. Suspiciously she said, 'What did she look like? This one from the other night.'

'Little. She was very little.'

Clare realised she was staring at Patricia's photo on the front of the paper, and she was talking to a local caller. 'You're just looking at the *Manchester Evening News*.'

Rubble registered the doubt in her voice, and was keen to impress her with the truth. 'On the front of the paper? Yeah, that's her photo. But I saw her in the bath. I was meant to put her to sleep.'

Clare went silent, trying to think clearly, determined to expose him as a sick hoaxer. 'So, if you saw her in the bath, tell me about her.'

'How do you mean?'

Aware Patricia would have been naked, Clare tried to think of a distinguishing feature. 'I don't know. Tell me about her toenails.'

'They were painted.'

'What colour?'

'Purple.'

Clare's stomach lurched and a wave of nausea washed over her.

'The same colour as her fingernails?'

'Her fingernails weren't painted.'

Clare took a deep breath, 'This man, he drove you to her house, so you could, could . . .'

'Put her to sleep. Like the other two. But now he says

I'm to be rested.' He couldn't hold the question in any longer. 'When will my next job be?' he whined.

The walls of the cubicle seemed to be closing in around her. She bowed her head and closed her eyes. 'To tell you that I need to know more about this man. Describe him to me please.'

Rubble weighed up the command. As long as he didn't mention his code-name, it would be OK he concluded. 'He's very tall and thin. And he has a beard.'

'What colour is his beard?' Clare interrupted.

'Dark brown, but with bits of grey in it.'

'What else? I need more details.'

'He has big brown glasses and stares a lot.'

'Big brown glasses? You mean like the old NHS ones?'

'What?' said Rubble.

'The frames are thick and brown?'

'Yeah.'

An image of Eric appeared in Clare's head. She began biting her lower lip, her mind racing.

'And these missions, they sound really interesting. What has he employed you to do?'

'It's a secret Government project. It's all to do with youth and agers.'

'Youth and agers?'

'Yeah, that's what he said.'

Clare thought hard. The phrase obviously wasn't right. It was as if Rubble was parroting back a word he had misheard. She said the words over and over in her mind, speeding it up and softening the pronunciation. 'Rubble, do you think the man said the project was about euthanasia? Is that the word he used?'

At the other end of the line Rubble ground his knuckles against his brow. 'I don't know,' he frowned. 'Maybe. I just want you to tell me when he'll call again,' he added impatiently.

Suddenly the pips sounded.

'Have you any more money?' Clare asked urgently.

'No,' Rubble complained. 'That's it.'

Frantically Clare scrabbled in her bag, searching for something to write with. 'Rubble, where do you live?' Her fingers closed round a pencil. 'What is your number?'

'Number? I only have a code-name.'

'Telephone number! From where you're calling me.' Tip of her pencil pressed against the paper.

'Dunno,' said Rubble, staring at the meaningless writing on the noticeboard in the booth. 'When will I get the money?'

'Where do you live!'

Rubble paused, surprised by the sharpness in her voice. 'On the egg farm at . . .'

The line went dead.

'Shit!' hissed Clare and the point of her pencil snapped. Needing time to think, she hit 'call-wrap-up' and put both elbows on the table. Intertwining her fingers, she pressed them hard against her mouth, as if in fervent prayer.

The description fitted Eric perfectly. She went over all her recent dealings with him; how she had been sitting in his office when he had received a call on a mobile phone. The look of panic on his face went it began to ring. Rubble was calling the 'Girl Next Door' line, so he couldn't be that far away. Just before he was cut off, he said he worked on an egg farm. Eric had been scouting round local farms trying to arrange a new module on the ethics of modern day farming. She remembered him shutting his office door in her face; the feather that had scooted across the floor to her feet.

She looked down at her cardigan, it was the same one she'd been wearing that day. The same one she wore most days and, of course, the feather was now gone. It must have dropped off and drifted away, completely unnoticed. Now Rubble had also disappeared back into the infinity that was the phone system, the feather was her only scrap of evidence. She would have to try and find it. She remembered that, after pushing its end into the front of her cardigan, she had headed straight to the coffee room in Patricia's side of the department to pin up her other poster about the protest march there. The only possible chance of finding it was if the feather had fallen off in the coffee room; she knew the cleaners hardly ever bothered vacuuming right under the seats.

She logged off and swept all her things into the canvas shoulder bag. Quickly she got up and made her way between the box like cubicles to Brian's office.

'Hi Brian. I'm sorry, something really important has come up. I've had to log off early. Can I make up the hours on my next shift?'

Brian's face showed only concern, ''Course you can, sweetie. You go and sort out whatever it is.'

'Cheers,' said Clare, hurrying off once again.

As the cab pulled up she could see a couple of lights on in Patricia's half of the department. She strode through the foyer, waving hello to the nightwatchman and then waiting impatiently as the ancient lift slowly descended to the ground floor. Eventually the squeak of the wheels grew louder and the panel above the door chimed. As soon as the doors parted she got in and started stabbing the button for the fourth floor. With a slow and unquestioning obedience that somehow reminded her of an elderly butler, the lift closed its doors and began to laboriously climb once again. On the fourth floor she turned right, into Pat's department and walked up the corridor to the coffee room, all the while scanning the floor in the hope the feather might be lying unnoticed next to the skirting board. The coffee room itself was dark and empty, so she flicked the switch and stood in the doorway as the strip lights came to life with a series of faint plinks.

The ashtrays were half full, a few dirty cups on the tables. A copy of the *Big Issue* and yesterday's *Guardian* on the table in the top corner. Clare spotted a Rizla on the floor and her hopes were raised; perhaps with it being close so to the end of term, the cleaners hadn't been in at all.

She walked round the low coffee table to where she'd pinned up the poster for the demo. It was now partially covered by an Amnesty International notice about human rights abuses being committed against women in The Sudan.

Down on her hands and knees, she began searching under the thickly padded seats. The shadows were too dark for her to see anything. Back on her feet she picked up the small table in the corner of the room and noisily placed it on the coffee table. Then she pushed the padded chair that had been next to it into the gap created. In this way she was able to drag each of the chairs along and look between them right up to the base of the wall behind. The odd drawing pin, a paper clip; but no feather.

'Looking for something?'

The voice behind made her jump. She turned around to see Julian leaning in the doorway, an inquisitive half smile on his face.

Clare tried not to show her irritation, but the hand she raised to her cropped hair betrayed her emotion. 'Just something I may have dropped in here a few days ago. The cleaners have probably swept it away by now.' His expression was only riling her further so she turned to the seats themselves, wondering whether the cushions would come out.

'What was it?' said Julian. 'Something you'd pinned on your cardigan perhaps?' He glanced meaningfully at her chest.

Clare immediately crossed her arms. 'Yeah it was . . .'

So he knew what she was looking for. She considered whether to go along with the game or just ask him outright if he had the feather.

But Julian couldn't resist playing his trump card straight away. 'It wasn't a rather pretty rust-coloured feather by any chance?'

'It was. Have you got it?'

He pushed himself upright and, with a little flick of his eyes and turn of his head, announced, as if speaking to a careless child, 'Come with me.'

He set off to his office just down the corridor and Clare, quickly weighing up her options, could only follow. Once inside Julian went straight to the CD player in the corner of the room and pressed play. The Violent Femmes came on, urgent folksy guitar riffs filling the room. He paused and Clare could tell he was waiting for her to give his choice of music her approval. Seeing the whisky bottle and plastic cup on his desk, she hesitated in the doorway. She caught sight of a pair of binoculars in the top drawer.

'Come in, come in,' he casually instructed, crossing the small room back towards her.

She took one step inside and he pushed the door shut. 'Sit down and chill Clare, you seem stressed out.'

'Look Julian, I am pretty stressed actually. Do you have the feather or not?'

'Yeah, yeah. It's somewhere around here. But I was wanting to have a little chat with you.' He gestured towards the chair and she reluctantly sat. Perching himself on the edge of the desk, one foot almost brushing the edge of her knee, he continued, 'I'll square with you. I know Pat had all but offered you a position in the department next year. The big question is this; what will you do now?'

'What do you mean?' Clare answered coldly.

'Well, I presume any application you were about to submit will now be judged the same as all the others we receive once the position is advertised.' She noted his use of the word 'we.' 'It's going to attract a lot of interest too – with or without Patricia running the place.'

'And?'

Julian brushed at an invisible speck on his corduroys. 'I'd be more than happy to give you a . . .' he looked up into her eyes, '. . . a personal recommendation. I think working with you would be a real pleasure.'

Below the sleeves of her cardigan Clare could feel the hairs on her forearms standing on end.

'Well, if I do apply for any position and, if recommendations are an accepted part of the process, that would be great. Cheers. But at the moment Julian I really need that feather back.'

Julian made a clucking noise against the roof of his mouth. He slid off his desk and meandered over to the bookshelf. Unwilling to look round and give him the pleasure of an audience, Clare sat stiffly in the chair staring straight ahead. The whisky bottle was, she noticed, half empty.

The tip of the feather was drawn down the side of her neck and played across her ear. Immediately she leaned back, angling her head to look up. Julian twirled it back and forth between a finger and thumb, 'This what you're looking for?'

Standing up, Clare had to push the seat back to create some space between the two of them. She held out a hand, 'Thanks Julian.'

He held it up to his face and brushed it against his lips, 'Want to show me what you use it for?'

His eyes had lowered slightly and, staring at her breasts, he stepped forward to re-close the gap between them. Clare brought her knee hard up into his groin. With a breathless 'guh' he doubled over, one hand grabbing the corner of his desk, feather skittering across the surface. She snatched it up and ran straight for the door. Once it was open she risked a glance back into the room. Julian was in exactly the same position; his other hand clutched tightly between his legs.

In the corner of the room the CD carried on playing, banjo-tight vocals angrily straining as she slammed the door shut behind her.

42

Eric sat back in the armchair. Waiting in the chancellor's outer office again, this time his mood was altogether different. The rhythm the typist was tapping out on her keyboard seemed upbeat, triumphant almost. He looked at the paintings of previous chancellors crowding the walls around him and met each man's eyes in turn, defiance shining in his own. But then his eyes lighted on a portrait of a portly gentleman, cheeks and nose touched with red. The similarity to Bert was unmistakable and Eric abruptly lowered his eyes, unable to meet the old man's unblinking gaze.

The door behind the secretary opened and the chancellor quietly called out, 'Eric, sorry to keep you waiting. Yet another journalist calling for a quote. Please come in.'

On hearing the door click open Eric had instantly adjusted his expression to a worried one. He rose slowly and walked across the room.

'Some tea please, Lesley,' the chancellor whispered to the secretary, then to Eric in the hushed and sympathetic tones of an undertaker, 'How are you bearing up?' He placed a hand on Eric's upper arm and gently guided him to the chairs on the other side of the room.

'More than anything, I just feel tired,' Eric replied wearily. 'It's such a terrible shock.'

'Indeed, for us all. Quite the most awful thing. You know, I've been to Pat's place quite a few times for social functions. I've even used the very bathroom they found her . . . found her . . .' His words trailed off.

The two men sat and the chancellor carried on, 'But, as they say, life must go on and it's our duty ensure the education of our students isn't affected in a negative way by this tragedy. Firstly, I'd like you to take over the running of Patricia's half of the department.'

To hide the relief he felt certain was flooding his face, Eric looked down. 'If you're confident I can step in, then I'd be only too happy to help out.'

'Of course I am, Eric. As the remaining head of department, it's only natural you steer the ship from now on. So, if you're in agreement, I think we'll need to phase out many of the modules Patricia ran on a solo basis. I propose students due to start any of her modules for the next academic year are contacted and asked to select one of yours or one of the remaining courses being run by the other lecturers in the department.'

Eric nodded his agreement.

'As regards the ESPRC's grant, I've had our lawyers look at the contract. The money was awarded to the Social Studies Department. Nothing in the agreement stipulated that the funding was dependent on Patricia heading up the research. Therefore I think you should oversee that project too. This means you now control the entire departmental budget. I know Patricia mentioned taking on some extra staff to assist in the extra work that will be created by the research project. Again, you have final say on who they will be.

I know all this significantly increases your workload, but I believe with your leadership and some hard work over the summer, we can turn this tragedy into a triumph of resilience for the Department of Social Studies, and the University as a whole. Of course if you need me for anything, I can be easily contacted at the dig on Dartmoor.'

Back in the office Eric typed out a memo to the entire department informing them of the changes. Then he typed a separate note to Julian asking him to consider becoming deputy head of Patricia's old department, taking on responsibility for the research project. He printed it off, sealed it in an envelope and went through to what was Patricia's side of the department, eyeing with disapproval the posters lining the corridor walls. They wouldn't be up for much longer, he thought. In Patricia's office he asked Lisa to give him her file regarding the recruitment of new staff for the research project. Hesitantly Lisa handed over a thin manila folder and Eric walked down the corridor to Julian's office.

He was just placing the envelope and file in Julian's pigeon hole when he heard music coming from the other side of the door. He knocked and seconds later the volume was turned down and the door opened. When Julian saw who it was an unmistakable look of fear washed over his face, 'Yes?' he croaked.

'Julian, I was just leaving these things in your pigeon hole, but far better if we can speak in person. It's about a change of position for you.'

Julian's arm dropped from the doorframe and, limping slightly, he returned to his chair. Slightly puzzled by his strange behaviour, Eric closed the door and sat down in the chair on the other side of the desk.

'Have you received my internal memo?'

'Yes, I just received it. I don't know whether to congratulate you . . . given the circumstances.'

'Well, you may find deciding on a reaction to what I'm about to say difficult too.'

Julian considered trying to pre-empt the coming accusation, try and claim Clare had invited herself into his study and was obviously incensed when he rejected her advances.

But before he could say anything Eric continued, 'I'd like you to consider taking over the research project. Of course I'll oversee it as head of department, but I think you are the right person to become deputy head.'

Eric had never seen anyone look so lost for words.

After several stupid blinks the younger man whispered, 'Thank you.'

'Can I take that as a yes?'

'Yes. I'd be delighted to.'

'Good. Now, I've got Patricia's file about regarding new staff. Given the need to recruit researchers before the next academic year, the first thing you'll need to do is get advertisements into the *Guardian*'s educational supplement.'

He opened the file and saw an A4 sheet with draught wording for an ad. It invited applications for two positions as researchers/assistant lecturers. 'Well, it looks like Patricia has saved you one job,' said Eric, handing the sheet of paper over. Underneath it he saw, to his surprise, a departmental application form already completed. He took it out and read through Clare's application and CV. A post it note on the front, written by Patricia, read 'Other position to be filled from respondents of job ads or CVs sent in on spec.'

Eric looked at over two dozen CVs from post-graduates at universities and colleges throughout the country. Each one had a covering note requesting that, if any position were to arise in the department, could they be sent an application form immediately.

'What do you make of this?' asked Eric, handing Clare's application to Julian.

He looked over it with one hand under the table lightly cupping his tender testicles, 'With all due to respect to Patricia, that's highly unprofessional. And, I think from a Department of Employment perspective, it could be against the law.'

'Yes,' said Eric, remembering Clare's comment about joining a sinking ship. Looking at her CV, he scanned her address, stopping at the telephone number. He handed Julian the rest of the file, keeping Clare's CV back. 'I'll deal with this – so you can get on with the proper procedure for recruiting. Now, if I can leave you with that, I've got some major course restructuring to work out.'

Back in his office he immediately rang Clare's number. The phone was answered after two rings.

'Hello, Clare here.'

'Ms Silver, it's Professor Maudsley speaking.'

A pause that lasted just a fraction too long as Clare waved frantically at Zoe to turn the TV down. 'Professor Maudsley. Hello.'

'You won't be aware of this, but with Mrs Du Rey's death, I've been asked to take over the running of her department.'

'Oh,' replied Clare quietly.

He carried on in the same ominous tone. 'Part of my duties entail the overseeing of the research project into the discrepancies in sentences being handed down to battered women who kill their husbands, and in that capacity I've just been looking through a folder Mrs Du Rey had regarding applications for research positions.'

In her flat Clare rolled her eyes at Zoe. Her friend sat frozen on the edge of her seat. The table in front of them was covered with estate agent's listings of properties for rent in the city centre.

'To be frank, I'm surprised at her unprofessionalism. Apart from going against the spirit of how we like to employ people here in the Social Studies Department, it's also, I suspect, against employment law to award jobs before they have been advertised. I presume that Mrs Du Rey requested that you apply prematurely?'

'Yes,' said Clare.

'Well, I must inform you that you'll need to reapply once the positions are formally advertised in a few day's time. And you can be assured your application will receive no such favours with me. It will be judged strictly on merit alongside all the others. However, I can say that, comparing your CV to those of numerous postgraduates who have sent in applications speculatively, you fall some way behind your competitors.'

'So you won't give me the position?'

'How can I say that until I've seen all the applications?'

Clare realised he would never admit outright to her that she would be turned down.

Before she could think of anything to say, Eric announced, 'Now, I have many other matters to attend to. Goodbye.'

43

Slowly Clare replaced the receiver. 'I don't believe this. Eric's been given the whole department. He saw Pat's file for job applications for the research project. My one's sitting in it before the job's even been advertised. He just told me to forget about getting a position.'

As Zoe began to stick Rizlas together quickly, Clare stared at the feather standing upright in a small earthenware pot on the table. 'You're sure that's a feather from a Rhode Island Red?' she asked.

'Positive,' Zoe replied, unease making her rush her words. 'My gran used to keep a few in her garden. My favourite was this one called Clutterbuck. She was a right character. But one day an egg was cracked and some of the white seeped out. Chickens peck at anything shiny. Tin foil, marbles, anything. Clutterbuck pecked at the egg, got a taste for the white and that was it. After that she started pecking open any egg that was laid. Gran had to wring her neck. I was gutted.'

'Well, I seriously believe Maudsley was trying to kill Pat.'

'I know, you've told me already,' said Zoe, all her emphasis on the word 'already', as if she didn't want to hear it all again.

Acknowledging her friend's tone, Clare immediately responded. 'Yeah, and you haven't come up with any decent alternative explanations for . . .' Clare held up a hand and began counting off points with her fingers, '. . . one, totally against his beliefs, Eric gets a mobile phone just as Rubble starts getting calls from this mysterious man who fits Eric's description perfectly. Two, Eric's been sniffing round factory farms in the area and Rubble lives locally and works on a battery farm. Three, a couple of old people no one cares about die. The sort of people Eric would know all about when he was a social worker before becoming a lecturer. At exactly the time of their deaths, Rubble claims he's killed an old man and an old woman. Four, Eric was just about to lose his department to Patricia and now,' the strength suddenly left her voice, 'she's dead.'

Zoe was careful to sound sympathetic, 'OK, OK, all good points, I agree. But you're also saying some ex-soldier and an old biddy have been killed as part of a process intended for Patricia.'

Clare picked up the local paper and thrust it at Zoe. 'This ex-soldier and this old biddy, not made-up people. Real ones, killed as part of some sick euthanasia plan.' She reached over and picked up the feather between a forefinger and thumb. 'Now he's in control of the whole department and my chance of a job has just disappeared. I'm giving the feather to the police.'

Zoe instantly replied, 'You can't. What evidence have

you got? One feather – which you say blew out of his office on a draught of air. And some crank caller you only know as Rubble. And who, you think, works on a chicken farm. I admit, Rhode Island Reds are the preferred choice of chicken for battery farms. But, until this bloke calls again, you can't do anything.'

'Shit!' Clare cursed by way of a reluctant agreement. 'I can't believe this . . . this scrap, is all I've got.' She picked up a hardback book she had borrowed from the departmental library and carefully placed the feather between its pages for safekeeping. Getting to her feet, she paced backwards and forwards thinking, then tore out the report on the ex-paratrooper's death. After refolding the paper at page two, she called the number in the panel on the side of the page for the editorial desk.

'Yes, hi. Could I speak to the reporter who wrote a piece in yesterday's paper about an ex-paratrooper, Bert Aldy.'

She was put through to another phone and repeated her request to someone else. 'Oh Bert.' The person replied. 'Chris Lynham covered that one. Why do you want to know?'

'He served with my dad. I'd like to know when he'll be buried.'

'Hang on I'll ask him, he's over by the water cooler.'

Half a minute later the same voice returned to the line. 'Petersfield Garden of Rest. His ashes are in the plot reserved for council burials.'

'His ashes?' asked Clare.

'Yeah. Where there's no family to claim the body it gets cremated there. Just the vicar and someone from the council at the service. Dead sad really, pardon the pun.'

'What about the old lady, Edith Jennings?' Clare asked, sounding desperate.

'Hang on love, I'll check.'

A heavy rustling sound as a palm closed over the mouthpiece. Clare was just able to hear a muffled voice saying, 'Chris, the old bint who popped her clogs. What's happened to her? Didn't the daughter go mad after you asked when the was last time she'd seen her mum alive?'

A few moments later the hand was removed and the voice said, 'Her daughter had her cremated the day after she was discovered.' The tone of his voice shifted. 'Something you want to share with me about this love?'

'No. Thanks for your help,' Clare hung up. 'Shit – they've been cremated already. There's no evidence for the first two murders.'

Looking freaked out, Zoe lit up the joint. After taking several massive drags she offered it to Clare.

'No cheers, I need to keep my head straight. I need to think about this.' She sat back with an exasperated sigh. 'I've got to do something.'

'Yeah,' agreed Zoe. 'But accusing him could land you

in some serious shit. And it certainly will guarantee you don't get that job.'

'Zoe, I think we can safely assume my chances are screwed on that one.'

Her friend took another drag and then said, 'What about playing some mind games on Maudsley? Judge if he's guilty that way.'

'What do you mean?' asked Clare.

'Do you know where he lives?'

'Yeah – I had to drop an essay off at his house in my first year.'

'Start posting him chicken stuff. Eggs, feathers. See how he reacts to that. At the very least it'll do his head in until this Rubble character rings again.'

Finally Clare smiled.

44

It was the best Eric had felt in weeks. A fresh supply of energy coursed through his limbs and, though his thoughts occasionally strayed to the things he'd orchestrated with Rubble, he was finding it easier and easier to push those memories away – especially with all the planning he had to do now he was sole head of department. He imagined that, when the fresh demands of a new term arrived, all recent events would be a dim and distant part of his past. Humming Aaron Copland's *Fanfare for the Common Man*, he climbed out of the shower and, standing on a wicker mat lying on the lino floor, he briskly rubbed himself dry with a rough towel. Bending over, he worked a corner of the material between his toes, slack scrotum swaying between his legs as he did so. Then, straightening up, he selected the towel's opposite corner and pushed it into each ear and started making small, circular movements.

Hanging it back over the small radiator, he picked up his shaving brush and soap off the windowsill and turned the sink tap on. He held the brush momentarily under the stream of water then began rotating its end against the soap until he'd worked up a lather. Dipping one finger into the thick foam, he then scribed a circle in the misted up wall mirror, wiping his fingertip over the surface until all traces of the shaving foam had disappeared and a clear view of his face had been created.

Without his glasses on he had to bring his face close to the mirror in order to see himself clearly. Carefully, he applied the brush to the lower edge of his beard where the stubble had begun to creep down his throat, forming a bridge with the straggling mass of greying hair that sprang up from his groin, coated his torso and congregated under his arms.

Picking up the Bic razor, he brought the blade up to below his chin and scraped away the foam, creating a neat edge around his throat. Then he lightly pressed the blade over the upper part of his cheek bones, clearing away the individual hairs that had begun to emerge from the skin there.

Still humming, he removed what little foam was left on him with a musty smelling flannel, then tilted his head back and examined his nostrils. Even though he'd trimmed them only a few days before, a few straggling hairs had begun to emerge from each dark crevice, like the first tendrils of a creeping plant seeking the light. He snipped them away with the special blunt tipped scissors that sat in the pot alongside his tooth brush then walked naked into his bedroom to dress.

Downstairs in the kitchen he decided against the demands on his attention that listening to Radio Four would require. Instead he tuned the machine to Classic FM, slowly scribing a triangle in the air with one forefinger as the gentle tones of Bach's *Concerto in D Minor* filled the room.

He dropped a couple of pieces of bread into the toaster and stood by the machine, continuing to conduct the imaginary orchestra crowded into his kitchen. When the toast popped up he spread the margarine in time to the violins' and harpsichord's gentle cadences, then sat down at the table.

Chewing appreciatively, he began to compile a mental list of all the issues that needed his attention that day. In the background the softly spoken voice on the radio made several requests too many for its listeners to relax, before a fresh piece of music began. The lone trumpeter gave the piece's first few bars a military feel and, with a sudden twinge of guilt, he thought of Rubble slowly settling back into the tedium of his life on the farm, occasionally checking on the mobile phone in his cupboard. Waiting in vain for it to ring again. But Eric would never do that. Although he knew the number off by heart, he would never call again, never allow any further communication to pass between them.

In his study he packed a few items into his leather satchel, put his bicycle clips and helmet on and then opened his front door. Immediately he noticed fragments of broken eggshell littering his front step.

Frowning, he turned to the door itself and saw it was streaked with yolk and egg white. Great drips of it ran down the wooden surface, catching in the carved ridges at the bottom. Shocked, Eric stepped out on to his front lawn and turned to face the house.

More eggs had been smashed on the windowsill of his front window, viscous pools surrounding the crushed shells. Then he looked at his garage door. Yolk had been used to daub four enormous letters across the metal surface. As he registered each individual letter, he heard a door open to his right and a voice start to say, 'What a lovely morning . . . oh my god, someone's vandalised your house.'

Eric turned to Mrs Fleming, his head surging with thoughts, emotions. Possibilities.

'How disgusting,' she carried on. 'What have they used? It looks like, yes it is. It's raw egg, I can see shells on your windowsill! And look! They've spelled a word across your garage door. It spells "scum"!' All enthusiastic, as if she'd solved some great mystery.

Eric smiled without humour, 'You're right.'

'But who would do such a thing?'

Eric shook his head, tried to sound casual. 'I imagine it's just kids playing a prank. Perhaps a disgruntled student – some have just got their end of term grades. It's nothing.'

'Will you call the police?'

An odd sound came from Eric's lips and he had to

smile so she would realise it was an attempt at chuckling. 'No, no. I wouldn't bother them with something so trivial; they have far too much on their plates nowadays.'

His neighbour frowned, 'Far too much to help find my Frank. They were absolutely useless when I called in at the station. They asked me if I'd had him fitted with an identity chip. The thought of it. Inserting a microchip under my poor Frank's fur. After that they just gave me the number for this cat rescue centre called Richmond's.'

Eric was already walking back to his front door. 'Sorry I can't chat, Mrs Fleming. I'd better get this cleaned up or I'll be late for my students.'

Inside his house he immediately phoned Julian, asking him to pin a note on his door cancelling that morning's tutorial for the few first years that had opted for his module. By the time he came back out with a bucket of soapy water, cloths and a washing-up brush, his neighbour had gone back inside her own house. Methodically he cleaned away all the egg, starting with the letters, having to scrub the bristles of the brush over the egg yolk where it had begun to form a crust. As he worked his mind raced, trying to calculate what this could mean.

His immediate conclusion was that it had to be somehow connected to Rubble; the imbecile had obviously told someone. But Rubble didn't know a single thing about his real identity. So, even if Rubble had talked to someone, how had they identified him and, furthermore, traced his address? And why take this course of action and not go directly to the police?

Even though he had come out with it on the spur of the moment, the more he analysed the situation, the more his comment to Mrs Fleming seemed to make sense. It had to have been kids or a student. His thoughts turned to the footballer from the march who, thanks to his report, had been disciplined and fined by the University authorities. He was a third year history student, if he remembered the details rightly. He'd probably waited until his degree was safely awarded, then decided to get his petty revenge. His choice of eggs was just an unfortunate coincidence. Eric hoped.

45

The man walked up the steps to the pub doors where his way was barred by two bouncers, 'Three quid mate.'

The man raised his eyebrows, 'To get into a pub?'

'Late night bar and live music,' came the explanation.

'But I'm not staying late, I'm just popping in.'

The bouncer grinned at him, but didn't move.

Shaking his head, the man pulled a handful of change from his pocket and picked out three pound coins.

Inside, people jostled at the bar, trying to attract the attention of the few exhausted looking bar staff. A lot of young men in green and white striped football shirts were crowded round a massive TV screen. Celtic versus Rangers, two minutes to go. In the corner a group of seated musicians chatted happily amongst themselves as they tuned their instruments. Pints of Guinness covered the tables around them, and mounted on the wall above their heads was a violin case with the words 'Mulligan's of Dublin' painted on its side.

The man made his way through the crowded main bar and into a quieter backroom. Nailed to the walls at regular intervals was a variety of Irish memorabilia. A battered metal sign saying *Cork Ferry – 3 miles*. A mirror with the words 'Dunville's Old Irish Whiskey' painted across it. A wooden plaque announcing 'Ireland's finest, brewed in Dublin'.

Sitting behind a long table at the far wall was a panel of three men. The newcomer made his way over and nodded to each of them in turn.

'Drink?' asked the overweight one in the middle.

The man looked at the table and saw all of them were drinking lager. 'Why do you always meet here if you don't drink the black stuff?' he asked, sitting down.

They all shrugged and the man in the middle said, 'Anonymity. What are you having?'

'I can't stay, thanks anyway. My wife's booked us a table in town for 8:45.'

He lit a cigarette. In the main bar a solitary violin started up, followed by a whistle and then a drum.

'The man you want lives in Breystone – or a house just outside it going back towards the motorway. It's almost opposite the battery farm where your lady friend was nearly strangled. Look for two big gateposts with horses' heads on the top. A long driveway with those fake Victorian street lamps lining it and a large fountain of a female nude in front of the farmhouse.'

'And this guy owns the chicken farm?'

The man nodded.

'No doubt about it?'

'I'm positive.'

The fat man sitting in the middle turned to the sharp-featured man on his right who was smiling as he tapped the ash of his cigarette into a tray already brimming with butts.

For the first time he spoke, 'We've been trying to work out where this bastard lives for some time. And all the while it was just over the road from the bloody farm. You're sure of your information now? Whoever lives in that place will end up in hospital for quite some time.'

Realising he was now speaking to the senior member of the group, the newcomer said, 'Please, I don't want to know any details.' He got to his feet and the man on the right lifted his hand up. The newcomer shook it in silence, did the same with the other two men, then stubbed out his cigarette. Nodding at them all once more, he walked back out into the main bar.

46

Large patches of the birds' feathers were now completely gone. They no longer preened but picked. Disagreements between the second and third birds were more frequent – pecks were delivered to sensitive exposed flesh. During one such squabble, the largest bird was almost knocked over. Pain flared up from the lesions covering the soles of its feet and it lunged savagely at the bald neck of the offending bird. Blood was immediately drawn and the animal sought refuge in the corner of the cage occupied by the smallest bird. Weak and malnourished, leg swollen and useless, it was unable to move when the other bird pecked at it. The bleeding bird felt its scabby back being attacked again and it began shoving at the bird in the corner more desperately. The smallest bird dragged itself into the centre of the cage where it lurched to one side, protesting loudly. The heads of the other birds all cocked to one side and they regarded it in silence for a couple of seconds. Then, as if a signal had been passed between all three, they simultaneously attacked it.

47

Rubble spent the day in a subdued mood, collecting up dead chickens from the cages and piling them into a sack. When he reached the aisles' first intersection he removed a corpse from the stinking collection in his bag. Stepping to the gap between the cages, he looked into the slurry pit beneath his feet. Normally the hedgekens shadowed his movements from below in the same way ducks in a park will paddle hopefully alongside anyone wandering round the edge of their pond.

But today he could see them all crowded below a cage further down the aisle. Squawking and pecking at each other, their attention was on something above. Rubble walked down to the spot and saw a chicken with its featherless neck poking through the bars. The head lolled sleepily against the squeaking conveyor belt carrying grain. The other chickens in the cage were viciously pecking at its back and blood was dripping through the bars and into the pit below.

Rubble unclipped the cage door and dragged the semi-conscious bird out by its swollen twisted leg. After looking at the extent of damage on its back he decided against keeping it for eating: it appeared that its cage mates had already been doing that. Instead he dropped it on to the aisle. 'Extras!' he called out and kicked it under the gap below the lowermost cages. The body dropped into the pit and the hedgekens immediately fell upon it. Picking up his sack of carcasses, he headed out of the shed and down the stairs to the incinerator.

In the early hours of the morning he lay brooding in his bed, thinking about the mobile phone. Although it had been silent for under a week, it seemed far, far longer to him. Agent Orange's speech had taken him completely by surprise. There had never been any mention of resting him after just three jobs. Now, with his role as a Government agent put on hold for who knew how long, his life was unbearably empty. Just the chickens and their never ending chorus.

He got up and walked into the living room area and looked at the monitor. He flicked between the cameras but the view of each was completely devoid of life. Opening the cupboard, he sat on the floor, staring at the tiny light of the phone as it winked on and off, on and off. The way the bulb suddenly went out reminded Rubble of how the light behind Miss Strines' house had died, leaving behind a faint orange glow. He thought about how she'd unlocked the back door and replaced the key behind the drainpipe. If anyone needed putting to sleep, it was her, he decided, climbing into his overalls and pulling on his dark jumper.

In the egg-packing room he rummaged around in the boxes under the sink until he found a yellow pair of marigolds. They were nearly as good as his Government ones, he concluded, shoving them into his pockets and turning out the light. He would show Agent Orange that he didn't require any rest. He'd been selected as a Government agent and it was the only time he'd succeeded at anything. It was his duty and he would stick to it.

Once again the wind was blowing. It seemed to pick up at night as if sunlight drained it of its strength. Or darkness increased it. But amongst the trees its progress was hampered, dense leaves and branches absorbing each gust so the air inside the copse felt motionless and heavy.

As he paced cautiously between the trunks, Rubble let his fingers trail through the waist-high bracken, enjoying how the marigold gloves numbed the sensation of the fronds brushing against his fingers. He bent his head back to look at the canopy above and saw the moon shining between the leaves. He got to the tree behind Miss Strines' house and leaned against it, studying the rear of her property. Staring at the black windows.

He thought of her curled up in her bed just beyond the thin layers of glass. Gleefully he imagined her face as he stepped into her bedroom. He decided then that he wouldn't speak, wouldn't risk replying to any of her cruel comments. He knew how easily she could exert the power of the classroom over him, making him stumble over his words, trip up on his thoughts. No, he wouldn't say a thing. Just walk up to the bed and twist her skinny wrinkled neck until it snapped.

As he vaulted over her back fence it creaked loudly. His feet connected with her lawn and he lifted his hands off the top of the fence, causing a horizontal strut to spring back against a vertical post with a thud.

From the garden to his right he heard rustling; probably a foraging animal disturbed by the noise. He was halfway across the lawn when the security light mounted beneath her gutter came on with a click. The sharp light shone across the grass, partly spilling into the neighbours' gardens.

'Something's out there,' a small voice whispered.

Rubble looked to his right and saw the tent pitched on the back lawn shivering slightly as its occupants stirred. Sleeping bags rustled again as the glow of a torch shone from inside the frail structure, illuminating two forms sitting up inside.

'Daddy! Something's scaring us!'

He had just made it back into the trees when a bedroom window was pushed fully open. 'Right you two! Any more noise and you're coming back inside,' a voice announced, in a hoarse whisper. 'You wanted to sleep by the forest, you better get used to sleeping near the animals that live in it.'

The zip of the tent opened with a lazy buzz and a little head emerged, 'But we heard something running. Something big, like a monster.'

'Laurence, there are no monsters. Now do that zip back up and go to sleep.'

The head disappeared into the tent and the window closed again. Rubble waited for Miss Strines' security light to go out, then retreated back into the woods. He was filled with frustration. The missions he went on with Agent Orange always seemed to work out fine. He was determined not to return to his caravan without a result. Crossing the village green he walked quietly along a side road until he reached a large house with handrails and ramps leading up to the doors. Even though he had never entered the building, he knew a load of old people were inside; it was where his own parents had gone when they were ready to die. He crept around the side of the building, stopping at each ground floor window and gently trying to pull them open. But all were properly shut. Looking up, he saw one or two on the first floor were slightly ajar; but he couldn't get up to them without a ladder.

Angrily he walked back to his caravan, deciding that, on a warmer night and without this annoying wind, he could well have a bit more luck.

48

As Clare opened the front door, a delicate smell instantly made her mouth water. She paused for a moment before identifyng it as frying chicken. She walked into a surprisingly tidy flat to see Zoe at the cooker, stirring pieces of meat round and round in a frying pan.

'What sort of chicken is that? It smells delicious.'

'Just normal stuff from the supermarket,' answered Zoe, glancing over her shoulder with a smile.

'Then you must be using some sort of seasoning. It smells far too good.'

'My secret ingredient.' She picked a small foil wrapped cube off the work surface and held it up. Clare took it and said, 'Chicken stock?'

'That's right,' her friend replied, sounding pleased. 'Chicken stock. It's the only way to make the stuff taste of chicken. So come on – how was he acting?'

'I don't know. The bastard cancelled his tutorial. I was hanging around in the coffee room for ages. Heard footsteps and it was that creep Julian pinning up a note saying Eric was ill and his tutorial was cancelled. Thing is, he must be riled – that was his end-of-year tutorial for his first years. The note said to leave any work in his pigeon hole and it would be returned next term. That's a real cop-out.'

'Shame. It would have been useful to see his face. I bet he's shitting himself.'

'Maybe, but I need more. I've got to track down this Rubble bloke.' She pulled a notebook from her bag as Zoe tipped a bowl of sliced peppers and mushrooms into the pan. 'I went on the internet at the library this morning and got the number for the headquarters of the RSPCA down in this town called Horsham. I'm going to ring them and see if they have a list of battery farms around here.'

She went into the front room and sat down in the armchair next to the phone. 'Oh – how's the job hunt going?' she called out.

Zoe appeared in the doorway, spatula in hand. She brushed the nails of her other hand up and down her shirt front, examined them and said, 'Got an interview tomorrow.'

'Well done girl. You'll be needing to put me up soon. This flat's been booked for some convention being held on the University campus. We've got another three days and that's it.'

'No worries. I'll register with all the local estate agents this afternoon. With the end of term, there'll be loads of flats around,' answered Zoe, going back into the kitchen.

Clare picked up the phone and called the RSPCA. An

automated answer service gave her various options She waited on the line, refusing to press any buttons, until eventually a woman's voice spoke to her.

'Hello, the RSPCA. Can I help?'

'Yes, I'm trying to locate the nearest battery farms in my area for a university project. Can you supply me with any such information please?'

'To be honest, I'm not sure. Please hold the line.'

She waited for almost five minutes before the voice came back on the line, 'I can give you the number of the British Egg Industry Council. They should be able to help.'

'Oh,' said Clare with disappointment. 'I was hoping you might have a list of farms by region – I'm phoning from the Manchester area.'

'I can only give you the number for the British Egg Industry Council,' she repeated brusquely.

Clare sensed the woman was now sticking to written guidelines or perhaps the whispered commands of someone more senior, 'All right then, cheers.'

She noted down the number and thanked her, though she wasn't sure for what. Immediately she phoned the number she's been given and an elderly-sounding lady answered the phone. She sounded as if she was in her kitchen, not an office. Clare repeated her request and the woman's voice instantly hardened with suspicion.

'What sort of a project?'

Clare hadn't expected such an aggressive answer. In her haste, she hadn't prepared a detailed speech. 'Well, it's a general project really, examining the productivity of battery chickens compared to free range ones. Mortality rates, that sort of thing.'

The voice was now curt and official, 'Please send your request in writing with evidence of the university you say you're studying at. We'll then consider it.'

'But I need to make a start pretty urgently. Is there not just a standard list of farms and phone numbers you could send me?'

'You could be anyone. Because our clients have to be careful about divulging their locations, any request needs to be in writing. Do you need our address?'

'Forget it,' Clare hung up as Zoe sat down on the sofa with a plate of stir-fried noodles in each hand. She handed one to Clare.

'The bitch. You'd think I was wanting to read her diary or something.'

'Who, the RSPCA?' asked Zoe, stabbing a piece of chicken meat with her fork.

'No, they weren't interested. Just gave me the number of the British Egg Industry Council. So I rang them. You'd have more luck phoning the freemasons and asking for a full and frank divulgence of their membership.'

'So nothing then?'

'Nothing.'

'What next?'

'I don't know. If only I knew something more about how the law worked. Don't most solicitors give you the first appointment for free? I could go to one and just throw everything on the table. See what the response is.'

'What you mean a feather and a newspaper clipping?'

Clare sighed with exasperation. 'It can't end here Zoe. It just can't. People don't get away with stuff like this. Do they?'

She looked uncertainly at Zoe who was thinking about the statistics for unsolved murders and the number of people who simply vanish each year. 'No they don't,' Zoe made herself say. 'Rubble is your key to all this. He'll ring again. It's just a matter of time.'

'Yeah, you're right,' answered Clare, examining the lumps of meat interspersed with the noodles and chopped vegetables. As she ate her food she remembered reading an article in the University paper about the availability of ethnic foods in the city. Once she'd finished her meal she said, 'Cheers Zoe, that was tasty. While I'm waiting for Rubble to ring, let's make Maudsley sweat a bit more.'

'What are you planning?' asked Zoe, suddenly full of life.

'Show you later,' answered Clare, mischievously.

After dumping her plate in the sink she left the flat and caught a bus back into the city. Jumping out at the terminal, she walked the few streets to where a large cluster of shops and restaurants formed the city's Chinatown.

Selecting the largest supermarket, she climbed the steps into a cavernous room stacked to the ceiling with produce. Unlike her usual supermarket, there were no signs hanging from the ceiling telling her where different types of food were located. Everything was piled directly onto shelves that were free of glossy point-of-sale signs detailing special offers or two-for-one deals. Any notices she could see were handwritten in Chinese characters. She had no idea what they said. She walked past a twenty foot length of shelving devoted entirely to different types of noodle. Next came a section of tinned produce, exotic fruits and strange varieties of mushroom. She spotted a row of blue tins all labelled 'Mock Duck'. Looking more closely at the label she saw that it was chunks of fried gluten, one side pressed with tiny bumps to give the impression of skin. Next to them was a deeper shelf stacked with what appeared to be irregularly shaped brittle pancakes. Lifting one up she was shocked to see it was an entire duck, stamped flat and dried out.

Ahead of her was a row of open shelves overflowed with crates of fresh fruit and vegetables. Pak choi, spring onions, chillies, limes, beansprouts. Plastic wrapped packets of pale round objects. She searched for the English translation on the label and found the words 'fish balls with seaweed'. In the refrigerated section she recognised various types of seafood. Comatose crabs half-buried in crushed ice, claws bound with rubber bands. Rows of red snapper lying on their sides, cloudy dead eyes staring upwards. And then came the poultry section.

Chicken carcasses cleaved in two. Shrunk wrapped parcels of giblets. At the very end of the section she saw a crate of severed chicken feet. She remembered being in halls on her first year and the group of Chinese students who always ate their evening meal together, sometimes all of them hunched around an enormous plate of fried chicken feet. Holding the things in their fingers, nibbling and tearing at the tendons with their teeth.

She looked into the crate. The long-nailed toes were partially curled inward, like fingers on a hand when it is completely relaxed. The undersides of the feet even had little fleshy pads. Examining the severed ends she could see the cleanly shorn bone and a thin layer of flesh. She plucked a plastic bag off the shelf and gingerly picked one up. The foot was cool and dry in her hand. Quickly she dropped it in the bag, then tried to scoop up a handful. But her nails caught on their claws and a shiver went through her. Instead she used a forefinger and thumb to pick one up at a time, dropping them into the bag until it held about twenty.

She walked to the small row of tills and handed them

over to a round-faced Chinese lady. With lightening speed, she spun the bag round, knotted the neck and dropped it on a scale. 'One pound fourteen.'

Clare handed over the money, thanked her and walked back down the stairs on to the street.

49

Eric was sitting in his study reading through Patricia's proposal for the research grant when he heard the creak of his letter box and the thump of something falling on his mat. He went to the window and gazed at the back of the postman as he made his way round the close, red bag hanging from one shoulder, hair blowing in the morning wind.

Eric stepped out into the hallway and looked at the items that lay at the base of his door. With their messages of 'Our best-ever rate!' and 'Enjoy the Gold Standard', the two envelopes were obviously from credit card companies. How they got hold of his name, he didn't know; he'd never owned a credit card in his life. He dropped them straight into the small waste-paper basket in his study, then sat down to examine the plain brown jiffy bag.

It weighed a fair amount, probably the same as half a bag of sugar. He squeezed it gently with his fingers and could feel the oddly shaped contents through the layer of padding. His name and address were written in clumsy block capitals, as if the person had been holding the pen in their fist or writing with the wrong hand. As was often the case, the postmark had only partially printed – he could see the package had been posted yesterday; but not from where.

He removed a paper knife from his top drawer and, holding the package flat on his desk, slid the point beneath the envelope's flap and sliced it open. With his other hand he lifted the unopened end of the envelope up, but whatever was inside refused to budge. He lifted the end higher and shook it. Suddenly something gave way and a jumble of chickens' feet flooded on to his desk, spilling across the document. Involuntarily he pushed himself backwards, eyes wide in shock. The contents lay there, twisted and stiff and a coppery, sour smell began to fill the room.

He lifted up the envelope and tentatively looked inside. Crumpled at the bottom was a scrap of paper. He jiggled the envelope up and down, but it was stuck. Slowly he pushed his hand inside and grasped the paper with the tips of two fingers. His hand came back out, covered in scales of chicken skin. 'I know what you've done,' it read. And that single word again: 'Scum'.

Eric sat staring for a long time, his mind reluctantly accepting the fact that his plan had been compromised. This second action couldn't have been the work of any disgruntled footballer. Someone, somewhere, knew.

By using a pair of tongs from the kitchen he was able to pick up the severed feet and place them in a large bowl without too much difficulty. What took longer was removing the scales of skin. Semi-translucent, they became almost invisible on the pages of the proposal in front of him. Each one stuck stubbornly to the paper, forcing him to use the tip of his paperknife to prise them off.

Back in the kitchen he emptied the claws into the bin, placed the bowl and utensils in the sink and then scrubbed his hands. For the rest of the morning he paced round the house, trying to make sense of the situation and uncover some answers. It was useless trying to study Patricia's document; his mind was consumed by the dilemma. It ate away at his concentration like a locust on a leaf. Again and again he found himself staring out of the window at the swaying tops of the fir trees in a nearby garden. As the strength of the wind picked up and then ebbed away his mind vacillated wildly from possibility to possibility. Every avenue he went down led to the same conclusion: Rubble must have told someone. It was the only possible explanation.

By late afternoon he reluctantly left the house and walked to a public phone box several streets away. But, with the phone in his hand and finger above the button he paused again. He was loathe to make contact. The plan had appeared to work so perfectly – by breaking his rule of never speaking to Rubble again, he was linking himself to the only thing that could connect him to the murders. His shoulders and neck felt tight and a headache throbbed at the base of his skull.

Slamming the phone back down he strode angrily home, the wind swirling around his head, teasing his hair, pulling it out of place.

Back in his kitchen he held up a glass of water and watched two paracetemol as they slowly dissolved in a stream of tiny bubbles. As soon as the water touched his lips he realised how dry his mouth and throat were. It occurred to him that he hadn't eaten or drunk a thing since breakfast. Lethargically he went to his cupboard and looked at the tins inside. Though his stomach felt empty it was a hollow, tight sensation and he knew that he could only handle soup. Examining the shelves he saw to his dismay there was only one can inside: cream of chicken.

He thought of the farm-owner telling him what sort of food the dead chickens were used for and he gave up opening the tin. Instead he buttered a couple of pieces of bread and ate in silence at the kitchen table, a glass of water by his elbow, a small bone moving under his temples as he chewed.

By mid-evening he felt mentally exhausted. He realised he'd been watching a sporting event on the television. It was, he concluded, a clear indication of how preoccupied he was. Normally he would immediately switch over whenever sport came on. He flicked the TV off and wearily climbed the stairs. As was his habit, he filled the bathroom sink half full of hot water to wash his face and neck. After staring in the mirror for a while, mind still absorbed by the issue of Rubble, he walked across the landing to his bedroom, forgetting to pull the plug or even brush his teeth.

Once in bed he switched the light off and lay back. In the darkness he listened to the sounds of his house settling down for the night. The usual succession of metallic clangs from the boiler in the cupboard outside on the landing, the occasional creak from timbers in the attic, a knocking sound from the pipes running under the floorboards. As the minutes passed the noises lessened in frequency and a quietness began to assert itself.

Now, with his head rigid and tense against the pillow, smaller sounds became audible. The quiet hum of the fridge in the kitchen downstairs, a faint tick-tick as gusts of wind blew against the windows, making the glass shiver slightly in the window frames. And a faint, high-pitched noise he couldn't quite locate.

The sound had an uncomfortable quality to it, as if it carried a note of pain. It sounded again and the memory of the chicken's last screech before Rubble landed with both feet on its head forced its way back to the front of Eric's agitated mind. The harder he tried not to, the more he found himself concentrating on the noise. It was at once piercing and insubstantial; one second it seemed to be carried from far away on the night wind, the next it could have been coming from under his very bed. He turned on his side and pressed one ear against the pillow. But with every new gust of wind the sound carried into his room again. A sharp, beseeching note that suddenly ended as the wind died down. He wasn't sure how long it took for him to doze off. At one stage he lifted his head from the pillow and saw that the glowing numbers on his bedside clock read 2:17 A.M. It seemed that for the rest of the night, he slept for only a few minutes before the noise would rouse him yet again from his restless slumber.

Eventually dawn started to break and, as the light grew stronger behind his curtains, the wind dropped at last and with it the sound finally ceased. He heard Mr Robert's car start up as usual at 6:45 so he could get on the motorway just ahead of the morning rush, he listened to the sound of the Morrisons' front door opening and their dog gratefully running around, claws scratching on the paved driveway. He got up just after 7:30 and looked at the sunken eyes of a desperate man in the bathroom mirror. With a forefinger and thumb he prised his eyelids apart and examined the threadlike network of red lines stretching across the surface of each eyeball.

After splashing his face with the cold water lying in the sink, he went downstairs in his pyjamas and sat at his desk. A while later he saw that he was holding a pen in his hand. He looked at the sheet of paper on the desk before him. It was covered from top to bottom in an endless repetition of Rubble's phone number.

50

Clare gazed at the telephone console on the desk in front of her. It was now almost 11 P.M.; she'd got into the call centre early in the hope Rubble would ring. Knowing he had never called her later than 10:30 P.M., she reluctantly accepted the night was likely to be fruitless. Deciding to give it just another hour, she was about to press the 'call-wrap-up' button and go to the kitchen for a cup of tea when Brian's voice sounded in her headset.

'Hi ladies, Brian speaking. I know a lot of you are having an unpleasant time with the Girl Next Door line, so Mr Nolan's come in to talk to us about it. All incoming calls are on hold, so as soon as the last live calls are dealt with, he'll begin.'

This will be interesting, thought Clare, leaning back in her chair. After a couple of minutes Brian spoke again, 'OK, there's only two calls still going, so I'll speak to those girls myself later. Now, here's Mr Nolan.'

Clare heard some low scratching noises as the headset was adjusted, then a gruff voice said, 'They can hear me now?'

'Yes.' Brian's voice in the background.

It suddenly occurred to Clare that she had never

actually seen the owner before, so she stood up to look over the top of her partition screen. One by one almost every other woman did the same until a mass of heads bobbed up out of their small compartments. Visible through the glass panes of Brian's office was an obese giant of a man. Sweat glistened on his bald head and, with fingers covered in gold rings, he pulled a handkerchief from the breast pocket of a suit that, despite looking hideous, obviously cost a fortune. Dabbing the material to his forehead, he began speaking in an abrupt manner, 'OK, Girl Next Door is, if you don't already know, going like the frigging clappers. Since it went live the percentage of calls answered in this place has dropped to under 85 per cent. Not your fault girls, but it's unacceptable.' He looked down at Brian, who shrank back fractionally in his seat. 'What you lot will do something about though, is your exit rates. There's too many of you just cutting off callers when they start getting a bit over excited. The thing is, Girl Next Door is what you make of it. Use your brains and the sky's the limit. You've got a ready made five minutes of small talk before the punter even starts choking his chicken. Do your homework girls. Find out how the local football teams are doing. Who scored on Saturday, who's out injured, was the latest Johnny Foreigner a wise purchase? Find out about the latest trendy bars, which roads are currently being dug up if you're driving into the city centre, where the next multiplex is being built, which is the best place in town for a pizza. You've got a whole city in common with these callers – use it to your advantage.'

Clare wanted to ask about the threats of violence, callers' claims they knew where the office was. But her line was closed: this was a one-way conversation.

'Now, if you can't handle it, you're free to leave. I can fill your seat like that.' He clicked his fingers. 'There's plenty of girls trying to turn tricks out there,' he glanced at the windows, 'who would jump at the chance of earning some easy money in a nice warm office by just talking dirty to some bloke who didn't manage to pull. It's up to you.' Now his voice hardened. 'The calls are lining up so make your decisions. Sit back down or fuck off.'

He nodded at Brian who pressed a few buttons and every console in the room started to flash. One by one the girls' heads disappeared and the quiet murmur of voices started to fill the room.

In Brian's office Mr Nolan took off the headset, the underside of the plastic band shiny with sweat from the top of his skull. Hesitating at the sight of it, Brian slowly slid it on.

'Right, that seems to have sorted the stupid bitches out,' said Mr Nolan, coughing into a handkerchief. 'I'm getting out of here, those musty partition walls really set my chest off. Any of them walk out, I want to know their names, and tell them they can whistle for any wages owing.' Without another word he opened Brian's door and left the office.

In her cubicle Clare waited another five minutes then hit 'call-wrap-up' and walked over to the kitchen. Inside Mary was in the middle of an intense conversation with Jayne and Vanessa. The three women nodded quickly to Clare.

'However bad it gets up here, it's never going to be worse than working the streets down there,' continued Mary. 'Don't forget – the lower you sink, the harder it is to climb back up. And when you're touching the bottom, no one wants to let you past. Because if they do, where does that leave them? Believe me, I've been there.'

'True, but some of these callers are really getting to me,' answered Jayne, drawing so hard on a cigarette, flecks of glowing ash flew from the end.

'Tell her about the one you had earlier, Jayne,' said Vanessa.

Jayne blew out a thin stream of smoke in disgust. 'Oh God – if it wasn't for old Davis at the local nick, I'd have given up this job by now.'

Clare listened in silence, dunking a tea-bag in and out of the steaming water in her mug.

'This really sick bastard rang. Nice at first, as they usually are. Then suddenly he turned. Started whispering about razors and all sorts. I could tell he wasn't going to stop and I was about to press the "exit" button when he suddenly said, "Don't go for that button." Well you can imagine my shock. It was like he was close enough to actually see me.' All four women thought about the mass of dark windows in the empty office block facing their building. 'Then he said he knew where I was working, what I looked like. What I was doing. I don't know if he heard me scrabbling for a fag on my desk, but he said he liked the way cigarettes made my voice a bit husky. That was it, I hit "call-wrap-up", went straight through to Brian's office and got him to give me the last caller's identity for my line. 'Course, the bastard was ringing Girl Next Door, so it was a local number. I gave Sergeant Davis a call . . .'

'Who's this Sergeant Davis?' Mary interrupted.

'You never dealt with him?' asked Jayne, incredulously. 'He used to work vice around here for years. Heart of gold is what he's got. He'd look out for us – tell the nasty punters to piss off out of it, follow any non-payers and tell them not to show their faces again. We used to offer him freebies in the back of his van, but he'd never take them. Just wanted to make sure we were safe.'

'Probably had a daughter or ex-girlfriend who'd been on the game,' said Vanessa.

'Anyway,' Jayne continued. 'He's custody sergeant at Stanton Street nick nowadays, so I called him and got him to check the location of the number. Turned out to be a phone somewhere out in Culcheth. So the sicko is, thank God, bloody miles away.'

Clare had been taking all this in and said, 'So Brian can get the caller's number off his computer?'

The three women looked at Clare and Jayne said, 'Easily. That thing's got everything on it. Clare, if you get any of those callers on your horoscope line, tell us right away won't you?'

'I already have. He's not threatened me yet, but he's scary. I'm expecting him to call all the time – he's got my identity number so he just comes straight through to me.'

'And he says he knows where you are?' asked Mary.

'Well, kind of. But it's more like I want to know where he is. Just to put me at ease.'

'Right girl,' said Jayne. 'When he next rings, put your phone on "call-wrap-up" so no one else can get through and delete his identity. We'll get his number off Brian and ask Davis to find out where he's calling from.'

Clare smiled, 'Cheers you three, that would let me sleep better at night.'

51

The thin keening noise floated into his bedroom again. Bloodshot eyes snapped open in the dark. As he stared up, the sound gradually died away, its whereabouts now a maddening torment. He threw back the covers, walked to his bedroom window and lifted the corner of the curtain. Strong moonlight bathed his back garden, creating shadows behind the pale shrubs. On his lawn he could make out a line of small footprints where a cat had patrolled the damp grass. He looked up at the dark sky and watched the ghostlike form of a cloud floating silently across the heavens. The wind picked up again, and with it the noise. But this time, fully awake and standing up, he was able to discern that it was originating from somewhere on the other side of his house.

Silently he entered the spare bedroom, standing in the dark and awaiting its return. After a couple of minutes he heard a moaning under the eaves as a gust of wind gathered strength. With it came the high-pitched note. Only now he was sure it was coming from outside the front of his house. Whatever or whoever was making it, was probably standing on his front lawn.

He stepped up to the curtains and, grasping the edge

of one in each hand, flung them apart simultaneously. The square of grass was empty, the cul-de-sac beyond it deserted. Yet still the needle-like noise was there, filling the air around his head, lancing his very brain.

Wildly his eyes roved around in their sockets and suddenly the mystery was revealed. The answer was, literally, under his very nose. The lightly crumpled tea cake wrapper was sitting on the polished tiles of the windowsill before him. As the gust of wind pressed against the glass it caused a draught to seep in around the old wooden window frame that was just strong enough to push the foil wrapper fractionally forwards. The same note began to emanate from it and Eric stared malevolently at the object. It squatted on four points of foil, its upper surface peaked by two glinting horns. The wind changed direction and the wrapper slid slightly to the side, defiantly shrieking up at him again.

The fingers of Eric's hand shot out and he snatched it up. Savagely he crushed it then, raising his other hand, began rolling it around and around between his palms, compacting it into a smaller and smaller ball. As he did so, tiny creases in the metallic surface left a web of angry red lines across his skin. Eventually he held up the object that had caused him so much distress. Still it hadn't been punished enough; he would use his teeth to grind it. He shoved the object to the back of his mouth and bit down on it with his molars. Instantly the foil connected with his fillings and a jarring pain shot through his head. His mouth opened in a silent howl and, as the saliva-coated wrapper dropped on to his bare foot, tears of rage squeezed from his tightly closed eyes.

Yawning loudly, Clare opened her bedroom door and shuffled, barefoot, across the living room to the tiny hallway. The clunk of the letterbox had finally roused her from her bed and there on the mat was a single letter.

She bent down, picked it up and stepped back into the room. Drawing the curtains, she flooded the sofa with sunlight and Zoe immediately raised a hand over her eyes. Empty cans and a full ashtray littered the coffee table. In the kitchen Clare flicked the kettle on and finally spoke. 'Brew?'

'Cheers mate, beautiful,' said Zoe, sitting upright and blinking groggily at the wall.

The sound of paper ripping was audible from the kitchen and Clare appeared in the doorway. 'Lovely,' she said sarcastically. 'An official "get out of the flat" note from the housing department. We've got until midday tomorrow, then the cleaners come in and bin everything still here.'

'Great,' said Zoe, rubbing her eyes and yawning at the same time. Still sitting in her sleeping bag, she used the remote to turn the radio on, just catching the end of the 11 o'clock news on Radio One.

*

In his kitchen Eric sat hunched over a cup of tea, staring at nothing. Feelings of nausea prevented him from eating anything, yet his acute nervousness compounded the empty feeling in his stomach. The piece of paper with Rubble's number on it was still on his desk, but now, in the cold light of day, he decided against calling it. He hadn't left the house for two days, ignoring several calls from the University about whether he could attend various end of term events. He looked around the room, suddenly aware of the blank expanse of wall around him. Standing up he stared out of the window, but the row of fir trees and roof of the house beyond only added to his sense of confinement.

Acting on impulse, he poured his half finished cup of tea down the sink and opened the side door to his garage. One of the gardening gloves had slipped off the shelf and it lay on the garage floor, one forefinger pointing towards the garage door and beyond.

'So,' said Clare, looking flustered as she slipped the library books into her bag. The cans had been cleared away and the window was open. 'The green grocer's round the corner has cardboard boxes by the tills. You're alright packing up the kitchen stuff?'

Zoe looked around, "course. I'll make a start in here too. Aside from the CDs and lava lamp, what else is yours?'

'The video is mine. TV was here.'

'And what about the posters?' asked Zoe smiling.

'Yeah – pack them . . .' she noticed her friend's expression. 'They're really studenty aren't they? OK, let's leave them.'

'Thank God you said that,' said Zoe. 'If we're getting a flat together we can buy some nice prints from Ikea or somewhere. Don't worry – they'll be on me. When I get this job we're going to live in a decent place.'

'Oh God!' said Clare. 'I'd totally forgotten. The interview's at four o'clock isn't it? Don't worry about packing the flat, you get ready to wow them.'

Zoe waved her hand, 'I'm prepared Clare, don't worry about it.'

'Well, if you're sure. I'll only be a couple of hours. I've just got to return these books and clear out a few things from my locker in the department.'

'Stop flapping and just go will you? I can manage.'

'Right. See you later then.' The front door shut with a bang and Zoe let out a sigh before flopping down on to the sofa.

He took the M62 away from Manchester and towards Liverpool, coming off at the junction for St Helens. Soon he was driving along a winding country road that led him through fields of wheat, their surfaces occasionally ruffling as the light breeze shifted. He wound down the window and perched an elbow out of the car, enjoying the tickle of air going up his sleeve as he cruised along the empty road.

Looking at the countryside around him he found it strange to think that no visible indication remained of the myriad tunnels lacing the ground hundreds of feet below. When he was younger the whole area was dotted with collieries, their headgears jutting up out of the landscape, pit wheels slowly revolving. A mixture of nostalgia and regret seized him and he wasn't sure if it was the wind blowing or his emotions that made a tear spring up in the corner of his eye. Soon he passed a couple of deserted rugby pitches, their posts standing forlorn and rusting. Immediately after he entered the village where he had grown up and he slowed the car to stare at the narrow terraces of houses, all built to accommodate the families of men who toiled their lives away in a place never touched by sunlight. He passed the post office, almost unchanged, plate glass windows giving him a glimpse of the austere interior. As usual it was closed. At the next corner was a Chinese takeaway and Eric almost grinned when he imagined the reaction such a place would have caused if it had opened here when he was a lad. Turning right at the village green he noticed with interest the new play area added at one edge – bright, primary coloured tubes of metal making up a collection of slides, see-saws and climbing frames. Three young boys watched his passing from the top of a space ship, all blank faces and idly swinging legs.

And now he reached the street where his parents used to live. His chest tightened as he parked at the top of the road and started the walk to his childhood home.

Though the few cars dotted along the street were all different to the ones when he was younger, the houses themselves hadn't changed much. The passage of time had taken its toll on many, balding pebble-dash exteriors and flaking wooden windowsills common to most. Hardly able to look, he reached number forty-three and saw with a shock the overgrown front yard and boarded-up ground floor windows. Glancing reluctantly up to his old bedroom he realised the curtains were missing. An aching despair filled him and looking back down he saw the *For Sale* sign lying where it had fallen, almost hidden in the long weeds. The house was empty, deserted since the last occupants moved out, the council obviously unable to find a new tenant. Hearing footsteps to his side, he turned to see an old man approaching. Eric raised his eyebrows, ready to say 'Hello' as soon as the person looked up. Wondering whether they might recognise each other. But the person kept his eyes on the pavement, shuffling wordlessly past with mouth shut tight, a loaf of economy white bread hanging from one hand.

Memories of when the street felt like it was inhabited by one big family forced their way into his mind. Though life was hard, they were all in it together. Front doors were left open, the young and old cared for by everyone alike. Gritting his teeth to stop the tears, he walked on, heading for the colliery site, wondering whether the buildings had finally been renovated and put to some use. Reaching the end of the road he looked out across an empty space. It had been turned into park area, gritted paths leading up landscaped slopes. A notice-board stood just beyond a gate designed only to let pedestrians through. The logo at the top read, *Transforming places, changing lives*. Below that a plaque read, 'This outstanding leisure resource was opened in 1992 by Councillor Sidney Bold. Local partners: European Union, British Coal, National Power, Burton Oak Miners Welfare.' Squeezed into the space at the bottom someone had scrawled in orange pen, 'Robbie Rules. LFC.'

Eric remembered when the announcement came that, not only was the old colliery being nationalised, a power station was being built next to it too. As news shot around the village of the amount of money being invested on the government project, he had run down the road with the other children, laughing and shrieking, rolling around on the village green, unsure why all the adults were celebrating. Headgears were soon raised over the additional shafts, and a brand new main building constructed. He could still picture the functional white lettering lining its side, *National Coal Board. Burton Oak Colliery*. And behind the low building the cooling towers slowly rose up, truck after truck load of concrete arriving every day for weeks on end. By the time he was walking across the fields to secondary school in the next village, the mine was one of Britain's most productive, churning out over 700,000 tons of coal each year.

His mind moved forward to the day when he stood on this spot and watched as the crackling series of explosions collapsed the cluster of five towers, their bases blowing out and the massive structures folding in on themselves like pots of wet clay. Once again he heard the grinding screech as the cables round the pit headgears snapped tight and the metal structures slowly toppled like giant animals being dragged to the ground.

Now through the gate, he trudged up the reddish-coloured path. Examining the edges where the grass hadn't quite grown over, he saw the pieces of crushed concrete and realised he was walking on the remains of those mighty towers. He felt like he was treading on a grave. The path led him up to its crest, allowing him to look out over an area laced with paths and dotted with small hillocks, shallow lakes and copses of young trees. Birds were singing everywhere, poppies gathered in red clusters and rabbits lolloped slowly towards their holes. He stood still and heard the faint sounds of children's voices, a barking dog and a moped, or maybe a chain-saw, being carried to him from he didn't know where. The area didn't feel natural – there was a man-made quality to it that Eric imagined would never quite be shaken off.

Leaving the path he climbed the grassy slope still higher, aware of the bumps pushing through the thin turf under his feet. At the top he sat down and looked back at the little village. He thought about his reluctant return after the mine was shut down. Having to sit by the bed trying to meet his father's haunted eyes. The thought of ending up like that had plagued him all his adult life, and now it made him dizzy with fear. Flung onto the scrap heap and left to die. As if to steady himself, he thrust his hands into the grass, fingers grasping for a grip in the soil. It crumbled too easily and, looking at his nails, he suddenly realised what the unnaturally regular hillocks before him were made of – spoil tips generated by the power station. He peered between the blades of grass at his feet and realised he was sitting on the biggest one of all. Jumping up he fled down the slope, desperate to be away from the place and its atmosphere of a slaughter, covered up and greened over.

Back in his car he set off back to the city; there was nothing for him out here. The department was what he'd built his life around and whoever knew what he had done would have to do more than call him scum if they wanted to drive him from the job he clung to. He resolved to go back in to the department and try to carry on as normal; act like he'd done nothing wrong.

At the least it would force his tormentor into taking further action, and by doing that they might even reveal themselves to him.

In his house Eric buckled up his satchel with fingers that felt clumsy and weak. Another headache was coming on so he agitatedly swilled two paracetamol around in a glass, impatient to get the cycle to his department over.

Outside the department Clare stared up at the fourth floor windows.

'Cheer up. It might never happen,' said a porter, walking through the doors.

Clare smiled briefly then followed him into the foyer. 'Any staff up on the fourth floor?' she asked him.

He turned around with eyebrows raised, 'Haven't seen anyone all day,' he replied.

For once the lift was waiting at the bottom and she went straight up to the fourth floor. She stepped out of the lift and looked to her right. There was no music or even lights on in Patricia's side of the department. Clare's locker was located in Eric's side. Warily she pushed her way through the doors, walking slowly along the grey floor, glancing into empty rooms on either side. The place was even more deserted than usual, notice-boards stripped bare now the term was, to all intents and purposes, over. She tried the door to the room holding the department's modest library but, as she expected, it was locked. Instead she headed to the row of pigeon holes for the academic staff and stopped at the one marked 'Library'. Pulling the three books from her bag, she was about to place them in the small space when she saw the tip of the feather poking out of the pages of one. Scolding herself for such carelessness, she carefully took it out and then carried on to find her locker. After opening it up, she looked at the four thin folders and clear perspex pencil-case inside. They were hardly worth coming back for. Unzipping the pencil case, she slipped the feather inside where it lay on top of a few biros and a pencil. Then she gathered her possessions up in her arms and made her way back to the lift. No one had called it down so the doors opened as soon as she pressed the button. Getting in, she looked at the stainless steel walls one more time, surprised to realise she would actually miss the trundling old contraption.

At the ground floor the doors slowly parted and she stepped out into the foyer. She had almost reached the exit before she remembered her posters for the protest march were still pinned-up in the coffee rooms. Not wanting to leave any trace of herself now her hopes for a position in the department had been dashed, she turned around just as the lift set off without her.

'Oh dear, that'll cost you a five minute wait,' said the porter from behind his desk. 'Do you want a box for that stuff. I've got one here.'

'Thanks,' said Clare, walking over to him. He placed the cardboard box on the counter and she put her things inside, pencil-case on the top. Lifting it up, she stepped back over to the lift as the porter, whistling happily to himself, sauntered off down the corridor.

As Eric pedalled along the quiet tree-lined street a light breeze blew through his lank hair and he breathed deeply, trying to pursuade himself that the exercise was making him feel better. Behind a tree some thirty metres in front of him, two young boys crouched. Their eyes were fixed on the trunk of a tree on the opposite side of the road. Behind it a third boy monitored Eric's progress. As his bike drew level with their hiding places the boy brought his hand down in a chopping motion. Immediately his two playmates jumped into Eric's path. Both held their position, waiting for the other to lose his nerve. Though Eric's fingers had immediately snatched at the brakes, there was no way he could stop in time. Eric couldn't understand what they were doing, there was going to be a collision if they didn't move. With less than three metres to go one of the boys leapt back on to the grass verge, and a micro second later the other boy did the same. The third boy ran into the middle of the road shrieking, 'Chicken! Chicken! Chicken!' at the boy who had bottled it first. The winner quickly joined in the chant, pushing the loser over as he tried to get up.

Then, to all three boys' surprise, the tall cyclist simply jumped backwards off his bike. Riderless it rolled onwards, veering towards the kerb. Fear, anxiety, frustration and stress: all the emotions that had been jostling for supremacy in his head were suddenly converted to rage. Eric spun round and in three enormous strides, closed the distance between him and the two boys on the grass verge. The one lying on his back stood no chance of escape. Thin fingers grasped his collar and, as he was hauled to his feet, he found himself looking into a crazily grimacing face.

'Who told you to play that game!' he screamed.

'M . . . M . . . Mark did!' answered the boy as Eric's bike crashed on to its side further down the road.

'Who's Mark?' he shouted.

'Him. Mark Endacott,' sobbed the boy, pointing to his mates watching from a safe distance in the middle of the road.

But Eric was certain there was more to their chants of 'chicken' than a simple game. He began to shake the boy, 'Who really got you to jump out! Tell me! Tell me!'

The boy grasped Eric's jacket, trying to stop his own body from being violently thrown about, but the man was using too much force. Fabric tore and, as the boy's head whipped back and forth, his reply came out in a series of disjointed syllables, 'No . . . no . . . no . . . one . . . did.'

Abruptly he was flung to the ground, buttons spinning off onto the tarmac. Eric stepped towards the other two youngsters, arms outstretched. But with his first movement towards them, the youngsters had raced, terrified, away.

'What the hell's going on!' someone yelled from a first floor window.

Eric's head spun around and he saw a youngish looking man leaning out of a first floor window. 'Chris, are you all right?' he called down.

Openly crying, the boy was trying to crawl away, 'Mr Elliot, help! He attacked me!'

The man's head disappeared and the seriousness of the situation dawned on Eric. His long legs carried him back to his bike and, as the man came running out of his front door, Eric was pedalling furiously off down the street.

He careered around the corner and raced along the main road, eventually stopping at a public telephone box. Inside the line clicked a few times before the number started to ring. It was quickly answered.

'Is that Agent Orange?' The same awkward voice, overflowing with enthusiasm.

'Yes it is,' answered Eric, trying to regain his breath. 'Agent White, I have reason to believe you have mentioned your missions to another person.'

No reply.

Eric couldn't tell if the connection had been broken.

'Have you mentioned your work with me to anyone?'

Rubble shut his eyes and drew in a deep breath. He was just about to admit everything when Eric added impatiently, 'Someone on the farm?'

At the other end of the line Rubble opened his eyes and raised his head. He hadn't told anyone on the farm. 'No,' he answered.

'Not any of the part-time workers, or the owner?'

'No, I haven't,' he replied more confidently.

'Then someone in the village then? That man in the post office – Mr Williams?'

Rubble decided that, unless asked about talking to someone over the phone, he could deny everything. 'No,' he repeated.

'You must have told someone,' Eric insisted, resisting the urge to smash the handset against the glass. 'Someone you bumped into on the village green. Maybe someone you went to school with?'

'I never.'

From what Eric knew of Rubble's limited existence, there was no one else he could have spoken with. Fresh doubts entered his head; perhaps he hadn't said anything after all. A wave of helplessness surged through him as he racked his brains for another solution.

After a few moments silence Rubble tentatively asked, 'Do you know when my next mission will be?'

It was Eric's turn to deliver an abrupt answer, 'No.'

'Oh, because. . .' the line suddenly went dead.

After Eric had slammed the phone down, he stood there with his head bowed. A few seconds later something metallic rapped on the window.

'Are you finished in there?' a wavering voice asked from outside. Eric glowered at the little old lady as she gestured with her twenty pence towards the phone. He pushed his way out, not bothering to hold the door open for the woman as she struggled to wheel her shopping bag in before her. Back on his bike, he completed the journey to the department, barely aware of the traffic and pedestrians around him. After chaining his bike up outside, he removed his leather satchel and stepped into the foyer. Waiting at the lift doors, a cardboard box cradled in her arms, stood Clare Silver.

The door banged shut behind him and she turned around. Their eyes met, then Clare instantly looked back at the lift, her posture now rigid. As Eric walked slowly over she hugged the box closer to her chest. She couldn't believe how deranged he looked. His hair, messed up by the wind, stood out in all directions. His jacket hung open, buttons missing and ripped at the lapel. His cheekbones jutted out even more than usual and the rest of his face seemed to have withered slightly. But what shocked her most were his eyes. They made him look – she searched her mind for a second before finding the right word: hunted. He was now at her side.

'Just come to clear out my stuff,' she said.

He made no reply, completely uninterested in anything other than the thoughts which were so obviously troubling him. She stared at the metal doors, willing the ancient lift to speed up. His presence next to her was creating a tension she was certain must be palpable to both of them, she could certainly feel it down the entire left-hand side of her body. With each creak of the lift's mechanism, the urge to back away from him was growing stronger.

Next to her Eric's mind went over and over the words his tormentor was using to describe him. Scum. Scum. Scum.

Desperately she searched her mind for something to say, his stony silence unnerving her more and more. After what seemed like hours, the panel above the lift doors finally pinged. Letting her breath out in relief, Clare whispered almost to herself, ''s come.'

Next to her Eric clearly heard the word 'Scum.'

His head rotated to its side and he leaned slightly forwards like a preying mantis preparing to strike. 'I beg your pardon?'

Clare repeated herself more clearly, 'It's come. The lift.' Unable to break the intensity of his stare, she nodded at the doors in front of them as they slowly started to open on an empty lift.

Eric looked into her eyes, registered for the first time the anxiety flaring in them, then glanced at the box. Clearly visible in the perspex pencil-case on top of the files was a single red feather. Suddenly he knew. Stepping backwards he said, 'I've forgotten to lock my bike,' and walked out of the main doors.

Oblivious to what he'd seen, Clare whispered to herself, 'Thank God for that.' As soon as he was round the corner she fled down the corridor, leaving the building by its rear exit.

After standing at the side of the door for a few seconds Eric walked back into the foyer and climbed the stairs two at a time. In his office he removed a manila file and then walked rapidly to a call-box in the city centre where he dialled Rubble's number once again. As soon as the phone was answered he said, 'Agent White, have you ever mentioned your missions to a female?'

Silence again.

'Answer me, Agent White or I'll have you arrested!'

'Yes,' came the weak reply. 'But she's only a fortune-teller on a chat line. And I've only phoned her a few times.'

'And you've described me to this person?'

'Yes.'

'What exactly did you tell her?'

'That you have a beard, and that you're tall and wear glasses.'

'And what have you told her about our missions?'

'Just that I'd put the old man and woman to sleep. I told her the third one was already dead in her bath.'

'And has she tried to get more information out of you?'

Rubble thought for a moment. 'Yes, last time she wanted to know my name, where I was phoning from. But my money ran out.'

Eric opened the manila file and slid Clare's CV out. Looking at her address at the top he said, 'OK Agent White. You've committed a gross breach of discipline.' He paused for effect. 'However, you can make up for your mistake.'

'How?' asked Rubble, a pathetic note of hope in his voice.

'By undertaking a special mission for me tonight. It will be slightly different to your other ones, but if you complete it successfully, I won't report you for breaking the Official Secrets Act. I'll pick you up after midnight. And Agent White?'

'Yes sir?'

'You must have no further contact with this fortune-teller. Is that understood?'

His answer was barely audible, 'Yes sir.' A world of misery packed into both words.

Once the conversation was over Rubble walked slowly into his bedroom. With tears welling in his eyes, he removed the picture of Sylvie from his bedroom wall and ripped it into little pieces.

After Eric had hung up the phone he strode straight to

the park bordering the edge of the campus. Making his way to the clearing between the rhododendron bushes where he'd encountered Bert Aldy, he sat down on the bench and waited for a young couple to amble past, arms wrapped around each other. Once alone he stepped over to the cast-iron bin where he'd dumped the last of his syringes and Euthanol a couple of days earlier.

Looking in he saw the same bottles, cans and ice-cream wrappers that had been there before. Reaching in, he began rummaging around, but quickly it became obvious the syringes were no longer there. Salvaged by some desperate addict. He began delving about with more urgency, now dreading the possibility that the last precious bottle of Euthanol had been taken too.

The same couple reentered the clearing, both now holding choc-ices. Eric heard their footsteps but carried on anyway. They looked at the old man, head and shoulders right inside the bin, skinny backside pointing up at the sky and listened to the clink of bottles and cans as he ferreted around.

'Aaaah that's so sad,' said the woman, reaching for her purse.

'Leave him love, he'll only spend it on booze. Come on,' said the man, leading her away to look for a bench elsewhere.

Eric's hands scrabbled about, sticky with the remnants of old ice-lollies and dribbles of soft drinks.

Finally, wedged in the fold of a crushed can, he found the phial. Thankfully he stood up, wincing slightly at the ache in his lower back.

Syringes. He needed syringes. Shoving the tiny bottle in his pocket he set off for the spot by the multi-storey car park where he used to help with the soup run many years before. He shouldered open the graffiti covered door, flinching at the sharp reek of urine. Quickly he made his way up the bare concrete stairs to the roof. Some things, he concluded with a twisted smile, never change.

In a corner by a junction box that now supported several mobile phone masts, lay the detritus of heroin users. Blackened wraps of foil, numerous cigarette butts, crushed boxes of matches, empty bic lighters and several discarded syringes. He crouched down and prodded about, looking for a couple whose needles weren't too rusty. He soon found two that would suffice, one with a smear of blood crusting the inner surface of the barrel. From amongst the rest of the debris he picked two protective caps, placed them carefully over the needles and then set off back down to the street.

52

Clare surveyed the living room, looking confused. The only change since she'd left was a pile of boxes in one corner, the uppermost one full of old newspapers that had built up around the flat. Shaking her head, she dumped the box with her things from the department in the armchair and was heading straight back out of the door when she saw Zoe's post-it note stuck to the top of the TV.

'In town having my interview at Shout-About-It Design. Should be back around six. Keep your fingers crossed!'

Clare found a pen by the telephone and scrawled on the bottom of the note, 'Zoe, am at the call centre. I'll ring to see how it went. Keep your fingers crossed Rubble phones!'

Then she picked up her canvas bag, slipped out the front door and set off for the centre of town.

The afternoon and evening crawled by. She'd completed all the crosswords in her women's magazines by nine-thirty and had resorted to filling in people's eyes with red biro, giving everyone a grinning, sadistic appearance. One romantic photo story about a handsome man walking his dog in the park, and passing a woman just as her high heel snapped, was transformed into a demonic tale of evil.

'Here let me help you,' leered the man, bloody eyes glowing.

Clare was just adding a row of gore-dripping fangs to the docile labrador when the phone beeped three times.

'Good evening caller,' said Clare hopefully. 'My name is Sylvie . . .'

'It's me. Rubble.'

'Rubble!' She tried to temper the excitement in her voice. 'How good to hear your voice again. How are you my child?'

She waited anxiously for a reply and thought she could hear a slight sniffing sound. 'Rubble, are you there?'

When he spoke, his voice was low and fractured with emotion, 'I can never speak to you again.'

'I'm sorry my child?'

'The man knows I told someone about our missions.'

Clare thought of the eggs and chicken feet. She hadn't thought about the consequences for Rubble.

'I had to tell him that I'd spoken to you. He was going to throw me off the project. Then he said I could stay if I do another, special, job.'

'Another job? Where?'

'Don't know. He said it will be different from the others. But I wanted you to know you were right about everything. And I wish I could speak to you more . . .' a pause as he gathered his courage, '. . . Sylvie.' Saying her name for the first time made the lump in his throat swell suddenly. Tears sprang into his eyes for the second time that day. He knew that he couldn't say goodbye without bursting into tears. Horrified at the prospect, he slammed the receiver down and bent his head over the handset, eyes tightly shut.

'Shit!' Clare yelled, ripping her headset off and jumping up from her seat. Jayne's head appeared over a partition screen a few feet away. 'Clare, you all right?'

'It was him again,' she replied, mouth tight with frustration.

Jayne's face hardened in response, 'Right – you've hit "call-wrap-up"?'

'No!' said Clare, instantly pressing the button.

'Right – into Brian's office. And what number line are you on?'

'Twenty-six!'

Jayne marched up the narrow aisle, walking sticks thudding on the carpet, buttocks wobbling with each stride. Clare ran to catch up with her and they burst into Brian's office together. 'Brian, Clare's line, number twenty-six. We need the last caller's number.'

'Jayne,' said Brian. 'It's against ICTIS regulations to give you that.'

'Bollocks to those regulations,' she advanced towards

his desk. 'We need to know where this sick bastard is calling from.'

Craning his neck to look past her bulk, Brian asked Clare, 'Is it really important?'

Clare nodded just once.

'OK, hang on,' said Brian. He highlighted the box on his monitor for line twenty-six and maximised it. Six columns filled the screen. Extension: 26. Operator name: Clare Silver. Operator activity: Horoscopes/ Tarot readings. Activity time: 27 minutes, 46 seconds. Total number of calls: 6. Last call duration: 22 seconds.

Brian right clicked on the last call and an inner box came up. Sighing, he grabbed a pen and post-it note. Jotting the number down on it, he said, 'Remember girls, it's my job on the line giving you this.'

'Cheers Brian,' they both answered together. Jayne reached over to take the slip of paper, but Brian held it just out of her reach for a second.

'You'll be the death of me, Jayne Riley,' he whispered with a smile and then placed it in her palm.

Jayne just gave him a wink and ushered Clare out of the room. In the kitchen she took a mobile phone from her pocket. 'Tell you what,' she said to Clare. 'You brew up while I give Davis a ring.'

'OK,' said Clare, her face still tense.

Jayne retrieved the number for the front desk of Stanton Street station from her phone's memory and pressed 'OK'.

'Hello, Duty Officer Davis please.'

The teaspoon clinked as Clare nervously swirled around the tea bags in each cup.

'Jason? It's Jayne.' Clare looked up on hearing the new tone in Jayne's voice. Was this how she speaks to her punters? 'How are you my darling?'

As the policeman replied Jayne smiled at the wall, as if they were face-to-face. When she spoke again, her words were infused with a sweet warmth. 'That's good to hear. And your family?' Clare found herself wanting to drink the sound in. No wonder Jayne was the most asked for voice on the chat lines. Then her expression became more serious.

'Yeah, 'fraid so. He's really spooking one of my girls. One who really doesn't deserve this sort of shit. Can I give you his number?'

A pause, then she read it out, 'OK, we owe you for this Jason. You're a godsend my darling.'

She ended the call, and when she spoke again her voice was business-like. 'He'll ring us back in about twenty minutes,' she announced, dropping the scrap of paper in the bin. 'You feel up to taking any more calls?'

Clare shook her head. 'No. I'll just wait in here.'

'OK love, I need to clock a couple more up. My mobile's on vibrate so I'll keep it on the table in front of me. As soon as he rings I'll come back in. And don't worry, he'll be calling from miles away. You'll see.'

Once Jayne was gone Clare retrieved the scrap of

paper from the bin. After shoving a couple of twenty pence pieces in to the tiny pay phone mounted on the wall she rang the number, her forefinger hovering millimetres above the large red 'Connect' button. In Breystone the phone in the call-box started to ring, the noise carrying across the deserted village green. Down the road from it, a dark blue Volvo, crowded with five people all dressed in black, slowly approached. As the car drew level with the call-box it went over a sleeping policeman and the three men on the back seat heard their baseball bats clonk against each other in the boot.

'Well, that's the only bastard policeman in over thirty miles,' one remarked and his two companions grinned.

The man in the front passenger seat peered curiously at the red phone box, his elbow resting on the edge of the open window. As the car drove on in its search for the driveway with the horses' heads mounted on its gateposts, he said to the woman driver, 'Ever wonder who the hell phones call-boxes?'

Clare let it ring for well over three minutes before accepting that she must have missed Rubble. Cursing under her breath, she hung up, then hitched herself up onto the sideboards and sat there anxiously sipping tea.

Two cups later, Jayne hurried back through the doors, the phone trembling in her hand. 'It's Davis!'

she said, pointing at the handset and then pressing 'OK'.

'Hi Jason.' The same honeyed tones. 'Thanks for calling back so soon.'

She listened for a few seconds. 'Ah that's great. Yeah, I'll tell her now – she's right beside me.' She looked at Clare. 'He's ringing from a public call-box in some little village called Breystone. It's right out in the countryside apparently.' Suddenly she laughed. 'Jason says he's probably got bored with shagging animals and fancied talking to a human for a change. Listen Jason, we appreciate this, you know that don't you? All right, yeah. You too, bye.'

She pocketed her mobile. 'There you go Clare, nothing to worry about.'

'Thanks Jayne,' Clare smiled. 'All the same, I think I've had enough for tonight. I'm going to log off and head home.'

'OK, you do that. Take care of yourself and I'll see you soon?'

''Course,' Clare replied. Back in her cubicle she gathered up her things and waved goodbye to Brian as she passed his office. Just as she was about to walk through the exit, the tarot reader who used to work on Mystic Meg's lines stepped out of her cubicle. Their eyes met and she raised a finger in warning. Before she could speak Clare slipped through the exit and pushed it quickly shut behind her. Outside she jogged to the main road and flagged down a cab.

Her front door was barely ajar before the heady smell of hashish filled her nostrils. 'Damn,' thought Clare, remembering she'd forgotten to ring Zoe about her interview.

She shut the door behind her, wondering if the fumes signified the need for congratulations or commiserations. As soon as she stepped into the front room, she knew. Zoe was slumped on the carpet in front of the gas fire, two black tipped knives and a cut off bottle arranged on the hearth. From the stereo came the mournful sounds of Leonard Cohen.

'Zoe?' Clare called gently.

Zoe propped herself up on an elbow and half looked over her shoulder. 'All right?' she stated flatly, avoiding her friend's gaze.

'How did it go?' asked Clare, sitting down on the sofa.

Zoe continued staring into the quietly hissing gas fire. Her words were groggy, 'They'd given it to someone else before I even got there. A keen young graduate in Diesel jeans and a skateboarder's top. He was already sat on a Mac wowing them with his prowess on Photoshop.'

Clare leaned forward and placed a hand on her friend's shoulder. 'I'm sorry Zoe, but fuck them. Would you want to work for an outfit that treats prospective employees like that? They're bound to shit on their staff too.'

Zoe heaved out a great sigh. 'Don't know if I want to work for any outfit, fullstop.'

Clare frowned in sympathy, 'You'll find a place somewhere decent, believe me.'

Zoe didn't reply.

Clare decided it was time to change the subject. Lifting her voice, she said, 'Guess what? I've found out where Rubble lives – and I don't want to go out there on my own. Fancy coming for a little drive?'

'What, now?'

'Yeah. God knows what Maudsley is up to, but Rubble mentioned that he's going to be doing another job, so I've got to see him as soon as possible.'

Zoe lay back down. 'I don't think so Clare. Maybe tomorrow yeah?'

Clare pursed her lips, looking with disappointment at the apathy-filled form lying on the carpet at her feet. 'Well, can I borrow your car? I really need to see this guy.'

'Yeah,' replied Zoe unenthusiastically. 'The keys are on the hook in the kitchen.'

'Thanks. I'll see you in a bit.' She stopped in the doorway on her way back out, 'And Zoe? Go easy on the hash. Trust me, it's doing you no good.'

Zoe placed both knives between the bars of the gas fire in an act of silent defiance. 'Clare,' she announced. 'Tonight I intend to get completely off my head.'

'Whatever,' Clare replied, slamming the door shut

behind her. Just down the street was Zoe's silver Polo. She unlocked the door and set off for the motorway.

53

'So, about tonight's mission,' said Eric, easing the car into the slow lane.

Rubble sat meekly next to him, head bowed, rubber-coated hands folded in his lap. 'As I mentioned, it's not the same as your previous ones. Tonight's task is normally carried out only by agents far more senior to yourself. So, if you succeed, you are effectively promoted to the next level.'

Rubble looked hopefully up at Eric, determination setting his features in stone.

Eric continued with his speech, 'Tonight's subject is classed by the government as a subversive. Apart from being a member of the animal lib . . .' Rubble looked up sharply at the words, like a dog scenting prey. '. . . you don't need to know what she has done. Just think of her as our enemy. Now, on this mission you will not be supplied with a door key. You will get into the subject's flat through a kitchen window at the back. Earlier reconnaissance identified that the panes of glass are loose in their frames. The flat is very close to a railway track. When a train passes you are to use the noise as cover for digging out the putty holding in the window. Once you've removed a pane, undo the handle and climb in. Everything clear so far?'

Rubble nodded again, watching a single set of headlights approaching them on the other side of the crash barriers.

Eric began speaking again, 'The flat only has one bedroom, so your subject should be easy to locate. She is not – I repeat – not, very old. So be ready for a struggle. Eliminate her as you see fit – perhaps you could snap her neck like you would a chicken's.' He reached under the seat where the two full syringes lay ready. Handing one to Rubble he added, 'And to make sure she's dead, inject her too.'

As Eric concluded his speech, he glanced to his right as a silver Polo sped past them in the opposite direction, 'OK, we'll be at the subject's property in about twenty minutes.'

The group slowly trudged across the open field, making a beeline for the glowing windows of the farmhouse in the distance. Three of the men had baseball bats balanced over their shoulders, looking like a bunch of American dads making their way home from the ballpark. The woman walked alongside them, a baseball bat held in each hand. Childishly she swished the tip of each through the long grass. Behind them all came the last man, carrying a large holdall and a petrol can.

*

Eric parked a few streets away and led Rubble to a patch of waste ground, wonky football posts spanning a muddy crater at one end. The railway line lay behind a chain-link fence topped with barbed wire. After pacing alongside the barrier for a few dozen metres Eric spotted a section at the base that had been partially bent back by kids or animals.

'Agent White – make that gap larger and we'll proceed to the back of the subject's flat.'

Rubble fell to his knees and ripped the fence upwards.

'Enough,' said Eric and they both squeezed through.

Clare's flat was at the other end of the short terrace of bungalows, along the back of which ran a shoulder-high fence made up of wooden panels embedded in a concrete base. As they made their way along the grass verge between the fence and the tracks, they had to step over old mattresses and negotiate their way round broken microwaves, battered old hoovers and countless bags of rubbish that had been tipped there by the occupants of the properties beyond. Stamping down a patch of thistles directly behind Clare's flat, Eric was easily able to peer over the top of the fence and look at the kitchen window. A dull glow shone from deep within.

'OK the subject appears to be in,' stated Eric. Beside them the rails began to faintly ping and whine. It was a strange sound, like the sound of a stone bouncing over an ice-covered lake. From his pocket he removed a stubby handled screwdriver. 'Use this to dig out the putty. Hurry, a train is coming.'

Rubble snatched the screwdriver, gripped the handle in his teeth and vaulted silently over the fence. Eric watched as he bounded across the small concrete yard up to the kitchen window. He crouched there, screwdriver poised at the ready.

The noise being carried along the rails steadily increased in volume, the pings becoming louder and merging together so that, when he finally heard the train engine itself, the narrow bands of metal sounded alive. A second later the train nosed round the curve in the track, a hurtling torpedo of yellow light. Eric raised a hand to shield his face as it raced past, slack-faced drunks framed for an instant between his fingers.

The noise died away and he peeped back over the fence. Rubble squatted below the level of the window, waiting for the next train to pass. Several minutes later the rails started to sing again. Eric dropped to his knees and moments later a heavier, slower engine appeared, more guttural in its tone. Soon the diesel engine chugged by, dragging behind it an immense and thundering procession of freight carriages.

When Eric looked back over the fence, he saw Rubble removing one of the lower panes of glass and reaching inside to release the window handle. It opened outwards and he lifted himself up into the gap.

Placing a foot on the edge of the sink, Rubble climbed carefully across it and dropped out of Eric's sight into the kitchen beyond. With knees flexed and feet placed far apart on the lino floor, he remained motionless, frowning at the heavy, smoke-filled atmosphere.

Outside, the last carriages of the freight train trundled past. He stood up and moved to the kitchen door. The sitting room was lit softly by a strange lamp with moving globules of what looked to Rubble like egg yolk inside. He stared at the posters on the walls. A silhouette of a man with his fist raised upwards. There was writing underneath it, but after the 'Che', Rubble couldn't understand any of it. But he recognised the other posters easily enough. A hammer and sickle on a red background. And another poster stamped with the letters, 'CCCP'. Symbols of a hostile power.

He moved into the room and was edging towards the door in the corner when he spotted the girl lying face down on a rug in front of the gas fire. By her head blackened knives formed a cross on the hearth. Her face was turned to one side, eyes shut and saliva glistening at the corner of her slightly open mouth.

Rubble stepped round the sofa and stood over her, one foot on each side of her waist. Then, in one swift movement, he sat down on the small of her back, hooked a forearm under her throat and gripped the top of her left shoulder. With his other hand he cupped her chin, forcing her head up and to the side. Just like the diagram in his magazine on the SAS. Then he bent her body backwards, raising her up to his bowed head. Her eyes had opened wide and she reached with two feeble hands to where his forearm was crushing her windpipe.

Pressing his lips close to her ear he hissed, 'Die subv . . . subs . . .' He struggled with the unfamiliar word. 'Subservice!'

Then he wrenched his hands in opposite directions. Her neck instantly gave way with a loud click and he found himself looking into her eyes, even though her body was still facing the carpet. He dropped her lifeless form back to the floor. Then he removed the syringe from his pocket and emptied its contents into the vein in her neck.

After standing back up, he looked at the armchair beside him. A cardboard box lay there and balanced on a small stack of files inside was a pencil-case made from clear plastic. Rubble squinted at the feather inside, recognising it as the same type the chickens had on his farm. Glancing towards the kitchen door to check Agent Orange couldn't see, he unzipped the case, took the feather out and carefully placed it in the front pocket of his overalls.

As soon as his feet touched the ground on the other side of the fence, Eric grasped him by the upper arm. 'Did you kill her?' he whispered, looking desperately into Rubble's eyes.

'Yeah. Broke her neck. And stuck her in the neck with the syringe.'

Rubble thought Eric had collapsed as he suddenly crouched down, hands going up to the sides of his face.

'Are you all right sir?' he asked, wondering whether to hook his hands under the other man's armpits and haul him back to his feet.

Eric breathed deeply several times and stood up. 'I'm fine Agent White,' he said, wiping his face while weighing up the syringe in his jacket pocket with his other hand. 'Time to take you home.'

They stood behind the hen coop at the bottom of the landscaped grounds while the heavy duty zip of the holdall slowly creaked open. A full sized chicken suit was pulled out and handed to the woman. Off to the side, one of the men was carefully soaking two lengths of rag in petrol. The woman climbed into the suit and, holding the head under one arm, said, 'If this goes wrong, I've got no chance. Forget running, I can hardly walk in this.' She began raising up one of the massive foam claw feet in explanation.

Her companions were all pulling on black balaclavas. 'Don't worry about it. The only person who wont be doing any walking after tonight is the bastard in there,' said one, nodding towards the farmhouse.

54

After doing a slow circuit of the village green, Clare came to a halt by the red phone box outside the post office. She got out and walked up the stone ramp to the front door. A small sign with a *Consignia* logo said, *Closed.*

Clare began looking at the bits of paper pinned to the notice-board in the front window.

'Aquarium for sale. 20" × 18" × 12". Includes pump, gravel and stand. No fish. £30 o.n.o.'

'Baby sitter. Responsible and mature. 16 years old. £6 per hour.'

Then, at the bottom of the noticeboard she saw the words 'Egg collectors wanted.' She read on. 'Enquire at Embleton farm. Good rates of pay. Call any day between 11 and 12 o'clock.' In the corner of the piece of card was a small map, showing Embleton farm to be just down the road leading back to the motorway.

Clare got back in the Polo and drove out of the village. A minute later she passed a narrow lane and immediately after it saw a sign at the head of a tarmaced drive. *Embleton Farm. Private Property*. She parked in front of the gates and, leaving the headlights on, climbed back out. A small camera mounted on top of one of the gate posts looked down at her as she searched for a buzzer or some sort of intercom device. Nothing. The Polo's headlights shone down the driveway, illuminating a row of fir trees. Above them she could just make out the tops of two dark bottle-like shapes. Grain silos, she guessed. Flicking the headlights off, she picked a lighter from out of the glove compartment, locked the car and climbed over the metal gates. As she walked down the driveway her trainers creaked in the silent night air. Soon the road began to slope downwards, curling behind the fir trees and ending at a sort of office building with metal shutters covering the windows. Wooden palettes were stacked by a side door, and she could tell no one lived inside.

'Where's the sodding farmhouse?' she said to herself, squinting at the pair of long, low sheds before her. Pacing slowly along between them, she could hear the hum of extractor fans and every so often the sharp smell of ammonia floated past her. She came to the end of the sheds and stopped, tapping one foot impatiently against the sandy ground. To her left was a small fenced off area, to her right a copse of trees and behind them the faintest smudge of something white. A narrow path led into the trees and she stepped tentatively along it, barely able to see her feet until she emerged on the other side by a caravan. Debris littered the ground surrounding it and, as she approached, she could make out a mass of long, thin shapes adorning its side.

A man lay under each Range Rover, cutting into the fuel pipe of each vehicle and plugging the jagged hole with the soaking rag.

In the shadows on each side of the front door stood the other two men.

'Check out the number plates,' whispered one.

Both vehicles began with the numbers 1 and 3, but the digits had been positioned so close together they looked like the letter 'B'. The rest of the registrations read, 'ABY 1' and 'ABY 2'.

'Sad twat,' his mate replied.

The woman stood by the fountain, vision now drastically reduced by the two small eye holes, knees trembling inside the suit.

'Hello?' Clare called out. 'Anybody in?' No reply. Stepping closer she flicked the lighter and saw the objects were a mass of severed animal tails. A shiver went right down to her coccyx. It had to be Rubble's home. Awkwardly, she tried the little handle on the door and it swung open. 'Hello?' she called again, louder this time. When no one replied she stepped inside, immediately aware of the musty aroma. In the main part of the caravan she flicked the lighter on again and could just make out the stacks of comics and magazines straining from the shelves all around. On the table was a pile of ripped up paper. Suddenly she felt the urge to be out of there. Quickly she turned around, walked back to the door and jumped off the low step, glad to breathe in the clean night air once again.

Unsure what to do next, she walked round to the top of the caravan and spotted the narrow lane leading towards the road. Unwilling to go back inside Rubble's home, she decided to find a pen and paper in the Polo and write him a note. She began striding up the track, feeling better and better as each step took her further away from the foul lair behind her.

The gravel crunched slightly as both men, on tip-toes, ran to their mates waiting by the front door of the farmhouse. A barely visible blue glow scurried up both lengths of cloth and seconds later the fuel tank of the left-hand Range Rover exploded with a roar. A moment later the second vehicle also went up, glass from a side window flying outwards and peppering the front of the house.

Clare looked up in surprise. Above the trees a short distance away two mushroom clouds of flame slowly rolled up into the sky. A burglar alarm started up, its shrill tone further shattering the quiet night. She quickened her pace and a few metres later she could make out the road up in front. Headlights were approaching so she stood still, waiting for the vehicle to go past. Their shine grew brighter and, just as the car was about to sweep by, it slowed to a crawl.

The long burst of light flickered round the curtains, like an impossibly long flash of lightning. At the instant it suddenly doubled in strength, a sound like gravel being hurled against their windows made them all jump in their seats. The boy ran to the window, opened the curtains and stared, open-mouthed, outside.

Both vehicles were burning brightly and, lit by their fierce glow, was an enormous chicken. It started high stepping backwards and forwards, flapping its wings and jutting its head back and forth.

'It's doing . . . it's doing the funky chicken,' the boy said incredulously.

From behind him his father snarled, 'It's fucking dead more like!' He started towards the door.

'Don't go out there!' his wife cried, trying to grab him.

'Get off me woman!' he shouted, shaking himself free of her long-nailed grip, shirt tearing. She fell back on to the sofa as he ran down the corridor and threw the front door open. A baseball bat swung out from the shadows and, with a hollow tock, connected with his left kneecap.

*

Rubble twisted round in his seat to look at the silver car parked at the top of the farm's driveway. Eric began to slow down as they neared the turn off for the narrow lane. Ahead and to their right twin balls of flame slowly rose up over the trees.

'That's Mr Wicks' house,' said Rubble, undoing his seat belt. 'It's on fire. Let me out!'

Eric scrutinised the explosions as they gradually turned inwards and consumed themselves. 'Wait – we must not be seen together. I'll drop you off on your lane and you can investigate once I'm gone.'

Abruptly he spun the wheel round and turned into the top of the track.

Mr Wicks' leg buckled and he fell forward on to the top step. Instantly blows began raining down on him from all sides.

Toby stood speechless in the hallway as a balaclava clad man turned to face him, 'Your daddy's a torturer, son.'

Mrs Wicks ran screaming down the corridor, slammed the door shut and drew the heavy metal bolt across. Clasping Toby tightly to her side, she reached for the telephone.

Out on the steps the men had pinned Mr Wicks' moaning form down. One lay across his knees as another unlaced his Loakes, pulled them off and positioned his feet on the edge of the lowermost step.

Slowly the giant chicken approached, lifting its clawed feet clear of the gravel. She reached the group of men, pulled the flaps of the hold all apart and removed the sledgehammer.

The man pinning down his knees then spoke. 'I want you to think about your chickens. Think how it feels to be trapped in those cages, your feet bent back, curled in and generally fucked.'

With some effort, the woman raised the sledgehammer to shoulder height and brought the metal head down on the top of one foot, shattering the delicate bone structure inside.

His scream carried across the grounds and went far into the black countryside beyond.

The car's sudden turn into the lane took Clare by surprise and she could only stand there, lit up by Eric's headlights. Then, from the darkness beyond, came a terrible sound. It was a scream that went beyond human; the kind of noise any living thing is capable of making when subjected to unbearable pain.

Inside the car, Eric stared at Clare. 'Silver,' he hissed.

'Who is that?' asked Rubble.

'I thought you'd . . .' Eric said quietly, his voice dying away. Things had spun completely out of control. 'Another subversive. You must eliminate her!'

Suddenly the headlights of the car before her snapped on to full beam and, even before the engine revved loudly and the tyres spun on the loose track, Clare instinctively knew she was in serious trouble. She turned around and with the car lurching towards her, used its bright lights to sprint back along the lane. Hearing the vehicle gaining on her fast, she jumped across the grass verge and plunged into the copse. Halfway in she hid behind a tree. The car skidded to a halt and she heard both doors open. Then, to her horror, Eric's voice rang out, 'You must catch and kill her!'

Pushing the tree trunk away from her, she careered out the other side of the copse towards the nearest shed. Grabbing the metal rail she ran up the steps, feet clanging loudly, giving her position away.

From between the trees she could hear someone crashing through the undergrowth, quickly getting closer. As she reached the door at the top, she frantically grabbed the handle with both hands and pushed. To her relief it opened and she staggered straight into another door, something soft and spongy under her feet. Opening this one she found herself in a narrow room. Scrabbling against the wall she located a row of switches and, using her palms, turned them all on. As the strip light above her flickered into life, the whining sound of conveyor belts beginning to turn reached her. She looked desperately around: no phone. To her side was a small shovel and a pile of cardboard trays. Picking up the shovel, she tried to jam it under the handle of the door – but the shaft was just too short to create an effective wedge.

A foot landed heavily on the metal steps below. Jumping across the narrow room, she pushed open one of the middle doors. As in a nightmare, she realised she was standing at the top of a never ending aisle, no gaps, nowhere to hide. Thick, musty air. A string of yellow bulbs stretching away in front of her, perspective decreasing the distance between each one, before the gloom finally swallowed them up. She was vaguely aware of a clucking sound building in strength all around her.

The footsteps were rapidly climbing the steps outside and she began to run, cursing herself for smoking so much as her lungs wheezed in and out. Seconds later the chipboard door crashed off its hinges and behind her Rubble's frame filled the doorway.

She staggered on, but a few steps later she glanced over her shoulder and saw the heavily built man charging up the aisle, head down like an attacking bull. The distance between them was closing fast and Clare knew she wouldn't make it even half-way up the aisle before he caught her.

The Volvo pulled quickly back on to the road, mud splattered around the wheel arches. It sped back towards the village, away from the motorway and any approaching police. As the car neared the top of the driveway to the farm the man in the passenger seat nodded at the silver Polo parked there, 'Looks like Embleton Farm has got another visitor.'

'I hope they realise the caveman who nearly killed me lives there,' said the woman driver, unwelcome memories causing her to raise one hand to her throat.

'Let's stop and see if he's around,' came an adrenaline-charged voice from the back. 'We're ready for him this time.'

'No way, the police will be here soon. Besides, he was one scary bastard,' replied the woman, carrying on up the road.

Clare reached an intersection forming a small cross-roads in the aisle and stepped round the corner out of the path of his frightening charge. Leaning on the edge of the cages she shouted breathlessly, 'Rubble!'

His head snapped up and seeing her standing there, he began to slow down. Battling to control the fear in her voice, she called out again, 'It's Rubble isn't it?'

By now he had slowed to a walk. With deliberate strides he rounded the corner and turned to face her. With thick arms hanging at his sides, chest rising and falling, he took another menacing step closer. Resisting the urge to back away, Clare stood her ground and searched the eyes boring into her, hoping for a hint of uncertainty or even curiosity about how she knew his name. But she saw only hatred.

'Rubble,' Clare repeated more quietly. 'It's me – Sylvie Claro.' She tried to smile.

He took in her cropped, reddish-coloured hair, blue eyes and almost boyish features. As he bellowed the word 'Liar!' a fist swung up and slammed into her stomach. The breath was ejected from her mouth with the force of vomit and Clare's legs buckled. She fell painfully onto her knees as another blow crashed into the side of her head. Seconds went past and slowly the pinpoints of light filling her vision cleared and the high-pitched humming in her ears died away. She found Rubble sitting across her chest, knees pinning her arms to the concrete floor.

Opening her mouth, she tried to repeat that she was Sylvie Claro, but no words came out. She realised Rubble's stubby fingers were curled tightly round her throat.

'You aren't Sylvie,' Rubble murmured.

She began thrashing her head violently from side to side, 'Am, am, am, am!' she croaked frantically.

Something in her desperate insistence caused Rubble to loosen his grip a fraction. Gratefully Clare sucked in air. 'I work as a fortune-teller for a chat line,' she quickly rasped, knowing every single word had to count. 'You've been tricked. You haven't been working on any Government project. Your contact is called Eric Maudsley, he's a lecturer at the University. He used you to try and kill another lecturer, Patricia

Du Rey. The woman you found drowned in the bath.'

A tremor ran across Rubble's thick lips. In his mind's eye he pictured the front of the newspaper and the crest by the photo of the woman he'd found dead in the bath. It was the same crest as on Agent Orange's car and on the top of the Official Secrets Act form. He remembered the words of Mr Williams in the post office: 'The University crest you mean?'

'You've been calling me on the Girl Next Door line, extension number 304. I told you that you were going to come into money. Sylvie Claro is just the name I use at work.' She had read somewhere that in hostage situations it is important to make the kidnappers see you as a real person, and not just something to be bargained with or disposed of. 'My name is Clare Silver. I'm a student.'

The icy possibility that this girl was telling the truth fell heavily into the boiling anger filling his brain and it began to dawn on him that his new found role in life could all be false. The realisation spread out across his mind and his posture lost more of its rigidity.

Clare felt the pressure on her arms ease slightly as he leaned back, a worried look now on his face. She immediately wriggled one arm free, 'Let me go, please.'

Movement away to her side. In the gap under the chicken cages she could see a pair of brogues slowly approaching along the main aisle.

With authority loading each syllable, Eric issued his command, 'Kill her!'

Slowly Rubble lowered his head. He looked at the person whose words were threatening to destroy his recent happiness and made his choice.

Clare felt the tenseness return to his arms and just had time to say 'No,' before her breath was abruptly cut off. Gritting his teeth, Rubble began crushing harder. Instantly the veins across her temples snapped tight and with each heartbeat, her eyeballs felt as if they were being pressed further from their sockets. The hum of blood returned to her ears as her free hand frantically scrabbled across the concrete floor, fingertips catching on fragments of shell, chicken shit and feathers. She reached into her jeans hoping to find something to jab into his eyes. But Zoe's car keys were in her other pocket. Now the humming noise had drowned out the sound of the clanking conveyor belts around her. Fingers slid into her back pocket and with her vision rapidly dimming, she located a small laminated square. She pulled it out and bending her elbow, held up her Student Union card.

Eric reached the intersection and looked round the corner. Rubble was leaning forwards, elbows locked. All the weight of his upper body was being transferred through his ramrod straight arms and on to Clare's windpipe. He looked at her purple face, eyes rolled up into her head, tongue lolling obscenely from her mouth. Deciding she was as good as dead, he checked once more for the syringe in the breast pocket of his jacket. Then he raised the short-handled shovel above Rubble's head.

Rubble stared at the card, eyes focused not on Clare's name and photo but on the University crest in the top right hand corner. Her wrist slowly drooped and the card fell from her grip. Again his grip loosened.

The narrowness of the aisle didn't allow Eric much back swing so he bent his knees slightly to help maximise the force of the blow.

Rubble began to look uncertainly over one shoulder. In the periphery of his vision something was moving very fast. Automatically he shrugged his shoulders and bobbed his head down.

The edge of the shovel glanced off the top of his skull, taking a large flap of skin with it. The blade carried on, clanging into the front of a chicken cage, wedging itself between the bars. Inside the terrified birds tried to back away. Rubble felt a hot sheet of blood slide down the side of his head. He let go off Clare's throat and twisting his torso round, dived at Eric's ankles, grabbing both of them and pulling sharply. Eric lost his grip on the shovel and fell heavily, the back of his skull cracking on the concrete.

Blood coursing down his face and neck, Rubble started clawing his way up Eric's legs, reaching a hand up towards the older man's throat. 'You lied, you lied!' he wailed.

Trying to kick his legs free, Eric scrabbled backwards across the intersection, dragging Rubble with him. Suddenly there was no floor beneath his palms and pain shot through his spine as his upper body hung out over the pit, arms flailing wildly. Only Rubble's weight pinning his legs prevented him from tumbling over the edge. Below him the hedgekens began to gather, curiosity aroused by the commotion above.

Miserably hugging his legs, Rubble accused him again, 'You tricked me.'

'Pull me back,' pleaded Eric.

With one hand Rubble wiped the blood and tears from his eyes – and saw the full syringe lying in the aisle. Knowing it was meant for him, he picked it up, gripped the protective cap in his teeth and pulled it off.

'You tricked me, you tricked me,' he sobbed to himself, looking down at Eric's exposed shin and seeing the thick vein running across his thin calf. Expertly, he slid the needle in and began pushing the contents into Eric's bloodstream.

From below the level of the floor came a long screech of terror. Blood was now pooled around Rubble's elbows. Once the syringe was empty he rolled onto his side. With the weight removed from his legs, Eric plunged into the pit. As he hit the manure one side of him instantly sank into the acrid, feather-strewn pile of droppings. Rubble raised himself onto one elbow and leaned over the edge for a better look. As he did so the feather fell from the front pouch of his overalls. In a series of lazy circles, it drifted down to join the remains of the bird it had come from. Seeing no movement from Eric, Rubble lay back and looked up at the fan slowly turning in the gloom above him.

When such a large object landed in their pit the birds had scattered, but now they began to edge out of the shadows. Eric felt as if his bones had turned to jelly. Part of him was aware of his surroundings and he tried to lift his free arm to shoo the gathering creatures away. But another part of him felt as if it was still plummeting downwards, deeper and deeper into a softly cushioned world. And this part of him was quickly taking over, quashing the urge to ward off the approaching birds. Telling him that it was far too much bother lifting up his heavy arm. Much better just to relax and sink into the comforting layer below.

All around him heads were cocked to one side as a mass of beady eyes keenly regarded him.

He sighed deeply and his own eyes filled with water as they began to shut. But before his lids fully closed his tears twinkled for an instant in the dim light shining down from above. Several hedgekens saw something glisten and they raced forwards, provoking a general rush. As Eric's brain slipped from consciousness he was faintly aware of a pecking at his face.

*

After a couple of minutes Rubble heard a retching sound above the agitated clucking coming from the cages all around him. Ignoring his own pain, he rolled back on to his side, then raised himself on to all fours. With head pounding, he crawled back around the corner. The girl now lay in a foetal position, head in a pool of watery sick.

Scooping her easily up in his arms, he turned sideways and then carefully carried her back down the narrow aisle and out of the shed. Knees getting weaker with every step, he made his way up the farm driveway and towards the front gate. Ahead he could see two figures shining torches into a car parked on the other side of the barrier. Beyond that blue lights flashed in the grounds of Mr Wicks' house.

Seeing movement, one of the policemen directed his torch across the top of the gate, picking out the slowly approaching blood-soaked figure and the limp body of a woman cradled in his arms, 'Jesus Christ, it looks like we'll need that other ambulance after all.'

ACKNOWLEDGEMENTS

A variety of people were kind enough to help me with this book. My thanks go, in no order of preference, to –

Ruth Alty for teaching me how to administer an injection.

Hugh Coe for his insights into the politics of a university department.

Heather Pickett from Compassion in World Farming for providing me with so much information on battery farming.

Ruth Larsen MRCVS for her explanation of the veterinary drug used for putting animals to sleep.

Nick Soye for bringing me up-to-date with call-centre technology.

Chris Alexander for enlightening me on the art of tele-astrology.

Guy Rhodes for sharing his intimate knowledge of fowl husbandry.

The Cheshire businessman who unwittingly took me on a guided tour of his battery farm.

For more information about the author go to www.chrissimms.info

ALSO AVAILABLE IN ARROW

Outside the White Lines

'Here is a new crime writer who really knows his stuff – a compulsive and compelling read.'

The Killer: he strikes without warning, killing brutally with no remorse. Roaming the motorways looking for his next victim, even he doesn't know where and when his next murder will be.

The Hunter: determined to hunt the Killer down, jeopardising his own police career in the process.

The Searcher; obsessive, lonely, misunderstood, the Searcher spends his nights scouring the motorway for unwanted objects, his only contact with the outside world.

A final confrontation brings the Killer, the Hunter and the Searcher together in a chilling finale.

'Simms' fresh approach, and the way the story weaves between three viewpoints, makes this one of the most promising debuts in crime for some time. From the prologue's brutal first pages to the satisfying crunch of the final chapter, the prose is spare, lean and mean'
City Life, Manchester

'A gritty, suspense-filled first novel . . . here is a new crime writer who really knows his stuff – a compulsive and compelling read' *Publishing News*

Arrow Books
0099446839
£5.99